AT FIRST SIGHT . . .

The first time Coral set eyes on Gerard she had been half-naked. But in that instant, as their eyes met in the glass, she might just as well have been completely naked.

Why should she feel so completely overwhelmed when this young man looked at her? What was this sensation of helplessness that seemed to possess her under that steady, relentless stare?

Even now at the sound of his voice, his words only half-heard through the bedroom door, her hands shook, and her knees turned to water. What was happening to her?

It wasn't even as if she *liked* him, either. Liked him? She couldn't stand him! For one thing, he was English. . .Then again, he was not a true Christian. In some civilized countries like Spain, men of Gerard's persuasion had been put to torture for their blasphemies.

She tried to imagine him stripped and sweating as he turned upon a spit. *Stripped.* She pictured his body, and felt a sudden choking pang of emotion, an indescribable feeling she had never known before. Quickly she put the mental picture out of her thoughts. What right had he to break into her mind and heart, upsetting her in this way?

Also By
Petra Leigh

Garnet

Published By
WARNER BOOKS

A Warner Communications Company

Coral

PETRA LEIGH

WARNER BOOKS

A Warner Communications Company

WARNER BOOKS EDITION

Copyright © 1979 by Petra Leigh.
All rights reserved.

ISBN: 0-446-91088-0

This work was first published in Great Britain by
Star Books, a division of W. H. Allen & Co., Ltd.

Cover art by Walter Wyles

Warner Books, Inc., 75 Rockefeller Plaza, New York, N.Y. 10019

A Warner Communications Company

First U.S. Printing: December, 1979

10 9 8 7 6 5 4 3 2 1

Contents

PART THREE: UNITED STATES

Coral

PART ONE
IRELAND

(1)

Beginner's Luck

The first time that Gerard Mallory set eyes on the Maguire sisters, they were both half-undressed.

Old Dermot Maguire, the Irish actor-manager, had sent him ahead up the dark, narrow stairway backstage at the Wexford theatre, telling him:

"Go on with you up to the gentlemen's dressing room, and I'll join you in one moment, my dear sir . . . A trifle of business to attend to with the stage-doorkeeper, you understand."

So Gerard made his way upstairs as directed, and peered through the gloom, as best he could, for the autumn evenings were setting in early, and outside in the street it was twilight already: he tried to make out a scrap of torn paper upon the first door he came to—but it was too dark to read what it said. Taking a chance, he pushed the door open, and walked in . . .

He walked into a new world; and a new life.

In contrast to the blackness of the passage outside, the room was lit by many candles, which flickered in sconces around the mirrors upon the walls—mirrors that reflected the flames and redoubled them, so that the narrow dressing room seemed twice its size, and glittering with light. The golden glow threw up vivid splashes of color; a red gown that hung from a peg, a royal blue cloak flung on the back of a chair—a yellow petticoat, a green wrapper . . . Crimson feathers—a snowy-white tippet that looked like ermine but was not—a bright, silver headdress and a tiara tossed carelessly aside that sparkled as if the diamonds that encrusted it were genuine.

And the smell!— A smell that promised welcome, and excitement; combining orange peel, perfume and powder, scented soap, newly-ironed linen, and—above all—the unmistakable, tantalizing warmth of a woman's naked body . . .

Not one woman, but two: although for a brief, dazzling moment Gerard got the impression from the mirrored walls that there were four girls in the room, or even more.

But there were just two—two young ladies, half-undressed.

They stood, arrested in mid-action at the unexpected entrance of a strange young man; and in that split second, time stood still.

One girl, slightly taller than the other, had been ironing the yellow petticoat at a side table: there was a battered old stove in the corner, and upon this one of the flatirons was being heated, while its partner was in use upon the ruffles of the petticoat.

The other girl was bending over a cracked basin of water, in front of a looking glass: she had been washing herself, and was about to reach for a towel that lay nearby: but she too paused, with one hand outstretched, as she caught Gerard's eye in the reflection.

It was an embarrassing moment, for the girl with the flatiron—tall and dark, with raven-black hair that flowed down her back—was dressed only in a shift; and the shift was semi-transparent. From the glimmer of the candle-light that shone through the material, Gerard could see the outline of her full, curving bosom; the slender waist, the swelling invitation of her hips . . . She was extraordinarily beautiful, with a smoldering, passionate beauty that stirred his masculinity like a challenge.

Then he turned his gaze to the other young lady, and his heart stopped beating for an instant.

Where her companion was dark, this girl was red-haired; with shining copper curls that caught the candle-light in a hundred flecks of brilliance. Where the taller of the two was sultry and tempting, this girl's face was wide-eyed—eyes of deepest emerald green, like a kitten—but in those eyes such a depth of fire and flame that Gerald caught his breath. He had never seen any face so irresistible.

And she was literally half-undressed, for she had stripped to the waist in order to wash; clad in a white underskirt that fell from her hips as modestly as a bridal gown, but above this she was completely nude.

Gerard took in everything at one thrilling glance, as he gazed at her in the mirror . . . The incredible loveliness of her breasts; two perfect creamy spheres, with rose-pink nipples—no, not rose—a color more exotic with a hint of orange in it—and above, the slender column of her neck—her defiant chin, and her mouth, as sweet as a cherry, with lips parted in amazement as she drew breath to exclaim:

"You!—How dare you walk in without knocking? Who the devil d'you think you are, young man?"

At the same moment, she grabbed a woollen shawl and wrapped herself up in it; and the dark girl, moving at a more leisurely pace, picked up the green wrapper and slipped her arms into its sleeves.

"What do you want? Who are you?" she asked, in a deeper, huskier voice.

"I—I'm sorry—I beg your pardon—Mr. Maguire told me—I thought—" Gerard stammered, his head still in a whirl.

"Uncle Dermot? What about him?" persisted the red-head. "I'm sure he never told you to walk into a ladies' dressing room without so much as a by-your-leave!"

"I'm very sorry—I thought this was the gentlemen's dressing room—" Gerard tried to explain.

13

"Do we look like gentlemen to you?" asked the taller girl, raising an eyebrow with the hint of a smile.

"No—hardly—I mean to say—not in the very least—" Gerard assured her.

"There's no need to add impudence to your other faults," said her companion, tossing her head, and making sure that the shawl enveloped her completely.

Hearing voices, old Dermot Maguire pushed the door open wider, and followed Gerard into the room.

"What are you doing in here, my dear sir?" he asked—in the booming, sonorous voice that was beloved by audiences in all the theatres of Ireland . . . And, if he was to be believed, by half the crowned heads of Europe as well.

"I apologize, sir—I mistook the room—I couldn't decipher the paper upon the door—"

"It says 'Keep out'!" said the younger lady, crisply. "Plain enough, I should have thought?"

"No harm done," said old Dermot, benevolently. "At least you've already made the acquaintance of my family—the twin stars that shine in our theatrical firmament —the finest Portia and Nerissa I ever hope to see . . . And quite incomparable as Viola and Olivia—allow me to introduce you, sir."

The old gentleman drew each girl forward, in order of seniority; first the taller, black-haired beauty . . .

"My niece Miss Rosalie—this is a young gentleman come from England to join our happy band, and take the place of the late-lamented Mr O'Malley . . . And Rosalie's sister—Miss Coral . . ."

Coral . . . Gerard's mind flew back a few moments, to the revelation of her perfect breasts, and the mysterious color of her nipples, which were too vivid to be described as rose-pink . . . Coral—that was the very word for them—of course . . .

"I am honored to meet you both . . . Miss Rosalie—Miss Coral," he murmured, as they shook hands.

"From *England,* d'you say?" asked Coral with chilly disdain—as if her uncle had said "from an unknown isle of heathen savages."

"And why not? To be sure, the poor young man has to

14

come from somewhere—and it's my belief that he was sent to us by a blessed angel from above, to help us out of our dilemma!"

"How long have you been in Ireland, sir?" asked Rosalie, with rather more kindness in her tone than her sister had displayed.

"Only a few hours . . . I arrived by the packet-boat from Bristol today—and I immediately found myself in quite a dilemma also . . . !"

"Oh? And how was that, pray?" asked Rosalie, with interest.

Gerard hesitated; he could hardly tell her the whole story—it was not altogether suitable for the ears of two young ladies.

He could not tell her how he had left home—Rosewood Hall, near Guildford, in the county of Surrey; how he had run away with his wilful, pretty, and altogether maddening cousin Bella—eloping with her, as he hoped, to start a new life in Ireland . . . For Gerard's father, Sir George Mallory, had been quite set upon his enlisting in the army as an Ensign of Dragoons, and going off to fight in the Peninsular War . . . But Gerard had no ambition to become a soldier, and at the last moment, he had exchanged places with his sister Garnet—who had gone off in his stead, bag, baggage, uniform and all . . . But that was another story.

Upon arrival in Wexford, Bella had encountered an old beau, and had instantly thrown Gerard aside for his sake, leaving the youngster high and dry with no money, no prospects, and very little in the way of assets; he had nothing but the clothes he stood up in, a battered trunk that contained all his worldly goods and chattels, and a valise crammed with his favorite books of poetry—and some volumes of Shakespeare's plays.

It was a copy of *The Merchant of Venice* that had, in fact, introduced him to old Dermot Maguire, for while he was sitting in the "snug" of a Wexford hotel, trying to decide what on earth he should do next, the actor-manager of Maguire's celebrated troupe of thespians had struck up a conversation with him.

"The *Merchant*—?" Mr. Maguire had stared at him, dumbfounded. "Can I believe my eyes? You read Shakespeare? You know—you actually *know*—the *Merchant?*"

After another glass of ale, the old gentleman explained his own predicament.

"I was about to set out upon a grand tour of the land with my renowned company of players—we have a booking in Waterford, and another in Youghal . . . And now my leading juvenile has been taken from me at the eleventh hour, due to an over-indulgence in strong liquor and a misunderstanding with the local magistrates . . . He will not be able to take up the roles of Mercutio, Albany, Laertes or Bassanio for three months at the very earliest."

Half an hour later, the deal was struck; in the absence of the unfortunate and unreliable Mr. O'Malley, Gerard would join the company and undertake his roles: it was an arrangement that suited both parties admirably.

So now Gerard hesitated: wondering how much—or how little—of this strange story he needed to explain to the Misses Maguire.

"Explanations are not necessary," cut in Dermot, with an air of finality. "You know very well that we never ask questions of a newcomer—we don't seek to pry into anyone's background, my dear Rosalie—it's the future that concerns us, and I assure you, our future now is bright indeed!"

"Tell us one thing, though," Rosalie persisted. "The young gentleman's name . . . You haven't completed the introductions, Uncle."

"His name—? Ah—his name—" Dermot glanced at Gerard and knitted his brows for a moment. "Let me see now—his real name is of no interest to anyone—and it wouldn't look good on the playbills—too much like O'Malley for one thing, which could lead to confusion."

"Mr. Maguire suggested I should adopt a stage-name upon entering this new profession—and I confess, I should prefer to do so in any case—for personal reasons," Gerard added.

"This *new* profession?" Coral looked affronted. "Do

16

you mean to say you've no experience in the theatre, sir? You're a mere beginner?"

"I'm afraid so . . . But I'm very quick to learn, I do assure you," said Gerard, with a smile.

"Ha!" She turned away, as if in despair. "How will he ever learn the lines in time for the opening performance —never mind anything else!"

"Don't you be so sharp, dotey," her uncle reproved her. "For what *you* don't know is that the young man's a great lover of Shakespeare, and he has the entire works of the bard by heart already . . . ! So there!"

"Oh—well—I wouldn't say the *entire* works—" protested Gerard, rather appalled at such a claim on his behalf. "There's some I scarcely know at all—*Timon of Athens—Titus Andronicus—*"

"Oh, pooh—I don't call such stuff Shakespeare," said Mr. Maguire, dismissing them as beneath contempt. "Claptrap and togas—and they never bring in a penny piece at the box office . . . *Julius Caesar*—there's another disgrace now—a very piffling kind of piece—why, the leading performer gets killed off halfway through—what sort of drama d'ye call that, might I ask?"

"You still haven't told us the gentleman's name, Uncle," Rosalie reminded him. "Or doesn't he have a name yet?"

"Certainly he does—he's to be called Kean—it's just come to me—Mr. Gerard Kean, direct from the Drury Lane Theatre, London!"

"Kean—?" Coral looked indignant, "What's an English actor want with a good Irish name like that, I'd like to know?"

"Edmund Kean is playing in London at this very minute, and making the greatest success of his life there, so I'm told . . . 'Mr. Kean of Drury Lane'—yes, it'll look very well on the bills—yes, yes—that's sure to pull them in!" Old Dermot rubbed his hands, perfectly satisfied. "Now then, Mr. Gerard Kean—I'll show you where the gentlemen's dressing room is, and introduce you to your fellow actors—and afterward, perhaps you'd care to join me and my nieces for supper this evening? Nothing elaborate—a chop, and a pint of ale—but we'd be glad of your company, eh, girls? It will be a chance for us all to become better acquainted."

"Yes, indeed—that would be very pleasant," said Rosalie, with a glint of mischief. "Wouldn't it, Coral?"

"I'm sorry—I shan't make one of the party," said Coral carelessly, fidgeting with a hairbrush on the dressing table, "for I was about to wash my hair when you interrupted us—and I shan't be fit to be seen until it's dry."

"Well, my dear, that's up to you entirely, of course—we shall have to make do without you, as best we can," said Rosalie, and flashed a brief smile at Gerard that made the blood stir within him.

He had never, in his entire life, met two such provocative, exciting, and altogether adorable girls . . . He could not wait to get to know them better. If Miss Coral chose to be off-hand and unfriendly—so much the worse for her; he would devote his attentions to Miss Rosalie, who appeared to be very much more welcoming in every way.

By the middle of the evening, Gerard's brain was spinning with all the new information that he had been given —the names and faces of ten or fifteen gentlemen who would be his colleagues in the company—the part he would be required to play, and the costumes he must wear—the route to the little boardinghouse where he was to stay, along with some of the other members of the troupe—"You can have poor Mr. O'Malley's bedroom—no problem there, for that gentleman will not be needing it for some time to come, alas!"—and then the way to another, slightly grander establishment, where Mr. Maguire and his nieces were staying in shabby splendor within a suite of three rooms upon the first floor. But at last Gerard found himself sitting at supper with Mr. Dermot Maguire opposite him at the table, and Miss Rosalie Maguire seated beside him, on his right hand.

"May I offer you a lamb chop?" she inquired politely. "Some potatoes? A spoonful of greens?"

"Why—yes—thank you. I suddenly realize I have quite an appetite, Miss Maguire—for I haven't eaten since breakfast."

18

"You poor thing—you must be famished," said Rosalie kindly, and filled his plate liberally. "I expect you have been too much occupied with that—ah—*dilemma* you mentioned to us earlier ... whatever it might have been?"

"Rosalie my dear, I told you before—we never pry!" her uncle reprimanded her.

"Oh, it's no great secret," said Gerard. "I left my home and family—to start a new life in Ireland—but things did not turn out quite as I anticipated, that's all."

"You left home—alone? Or with a companion?" Rosalie probed gently.

Gerard looked at her quickly: could she have seen him earlier in the day—when he was with Bella?

"What makes you say that?" he hedged. "You saw me with—someone else—perhaps?"

"You—and a young lady—?" Rosalie continued in the same easy tone.

"So you *did* see us!" Gerard flushed, feeling a little self-conscious.

Rosalie laughed—a deep, full-throated ripple of laughter.

"I never saw you before in my life," she confessed. "But it wasn't hard to put two and two together—and take a shot in the dark!"

"Rosalie—for shame! You've no right to embarrass Mr. Kean so ... !" said old Dermot—but there was a twitch of amusement at the corner of his lips.

"Oh, I won't say another word ... It's plain to see you've been crossed in love, Mr. Kean—and I'm very sorry to hear it, I'm sure ... We must all be very kind to you and do our best to help you mend your broken heart ..."

As she spoke, her knee touched against his—very lightly, under the table. Gerard started; was it accidental? Without stopping to think he returned the pressure—and felt a faint but definite response before Rosalie's leg moved away.

At once the excitement tingled again in his loins, and he shifted uncomfortably in the chair, feeling his breeches tighten ... Heartbroken, indeed. Not a bit of it ...

The sensation reminded him, inevitably, of Bella ...

19

But he found to his surprise that he could think of his pretty cousin now without regrets. He was a young man, with a young man's natural instincts, and at Rosalie's feather-light touch—mingled with thoughts of his past encounters with Bella—he felt his muscles hardening instinctively, and a high tide of passion surged within him.

He remembered very clearly the first time he had truly experienced the mysteries of love; the first time he had been initiated into those most secret rites. Oh, he had romped with the pretty housemaids at home on several occasions; and thought himself no end of a young dog when he lost his virginity during a roll in the hay . . . But then he had discovered what else love might be, one afternoon in the old schoolroom at Rosewood.

He had been bored, and amusing himself with a book of poetry; and pretty, ringletted Bella had walked in and found him there—and set to work to amuse herself with his education.

She made him read aloud to her—love-poems, of course—and when she tired of this, she began to turn the erotic phrases to more practical advantage; offering her bosom to his inquiring hand, and smiling invitingly.

"Well, Gerard?" she had whispered.

Almost unable to believe what was happening, he replied hoarsely:

"You smell like a summer's day, Bella . . . You smell like sunshine and June roses . . ."

"Come to me, then, darling . . ." Her voice was soft and low. "Come and gather my roses—while ye may . . ."

And as he moved closer, her practised fingers set to work, unbuttoning his shirt.

Slowly—almost as if she were trying to make each moment last as long as possible—she proceeded to remove each garment from him; his shirt and jacket first, and then she slid to the floor to remove his shoes. Still moving at a leisurely pace, she rolled down his stockings one at a time, and pulled them off. She tickled his feet—oh, very gently —and then allowed her hands to slide up his calves, and over his knees on to his breeches; and daringly—shamelessly—ran her fingertips up the inside of his thighs,

20

arousing him to such heights of excitement that he found difficulty in breathing.

And when she unbuttoned the waistband of his breeches, and let them fall open—when she followed this by probing within, loosening his thin cotton drawers, slipping them down, and down, until he was completely exposed and defenseless—his young manhood stood throbbing impatiently, almost directly before her shining lips . . . And then she kissed him; and he thought he would die with such a confusion of joy, and outrage, and sheer, wicked, sinful delight . . .

"Now, my dearest," she breathed, as she rose to her feet. "One good turn deserves another, they say—and you shall do for me all that I have done for you . . . Come—begin by unfastening my bodice . . ."

With clumsy, trembling hands, he managed to unlace her corsage, and watched—transfixed—as her lovely breasts tumbled from their restraining ribbons and laces; two dazzling—white spheres, shining like twin moons in a new heaven . . .

Heaven and earth fell topsy-turvy as he continued to undress this bewitching creature; her gown, her petticoats dropping one by one—her sheer silk underclothes seeming almost to melt away, until she lay back upon the faded Turkey carpet—quite nude . . . And the old schoolroom had never known such a thorough tuition, or such a willing pupil.

"Remember—do as I showed you . . . Kiss me—everywhere . . ." she instructed him, and rolled round in a series of constantly-changing postures, to enable him to follow her coaching more easily.

He bent low, and covered her breasts with kisses—and her warm belly—and the softly-curling hair that veiled her Mount of Venus . . .

"Yes, yes—" she urged him. "More—more—"

Then she held out her arms to pull him closer still—lifting him higher as she did so, and opening her creamy thighs beneath him. Gerard found himself entering paradise; and there was no serpent to banish him from this Garden of Eden.

Or was there——?

Later, as he came to know Cousin Bella rather better, he began to realize how fickle and perverse she could be; she had taught him the art of love, as she might teach her lapdog new tricks—and tired of him as quickly, when a more appealing diversion came along; finally abandoning him for ever, for the sake of a more experienced wooer.

Remembering all this, Gerard looked across at Rosalie now, by his side at the dinner table, and thought he recognized in her smiling eyes a warmth, a kindness—a generosity he had never known from Cousin Bella . . . And besides, there was her beautiful sister Coral—he could never forget her . . .

Oh, yes—Gerard felt more and more certain that he was going to enjoy his new life with the Maguire company. What did it matter if he was only—as Coral had described him—a "mere beginner?" It seemed that he was going to have his traditional share of beginner's luck; he was sure of that.

In a back bedroom, on the other side of a pair of folding doors, Coral sat upon the edge of her bed, with her auburn hair wrapped in a towel, waiting for it to dry . . . And as she waited, she listened to the murmur of conversation that floated dimly through the doors, and felt angry with herself for having been so stupid.

Why did she have to wash her hair this evening? It would have been so easy to put it off till tomorrow—she could have got up early in the morning and seen to it before breakfast, couldn't she? Why hadn't she changed her plans, in order to have supper with Rosalie and Uncle Dermot—and Mr. Kean . . . ?

As she thought of the newcomer, she bit her lip . . . She pictured that moment all over again, when he had walked into the dressing room . . .

The first time Coral set eyes on Gerard—she had been half-naked; yes, but in that instant, as their eyes met in the glass, she might just as well have been completely naked—her entire body exposed to his gaze.

She felt his eyes upon her, burning down and destroying such feeble defenses as she had—she saw the way he looked at her body, and at the same moment she felt

22

her breasts shiver with excitement, her nipples suddenly standing firm, quivering and quick to respond—as if his glance had been an actual physical contact . . . As if he had laid his hands upon her bosom, as if his fingers had teased and tickled—

Then she had felt a wave of madness; a kind of heady intoxication, and she wondered for a moment if she were going to faint . . . But she had pulled herself together, and rebuked the stranger for walking in without warning . . . Good heavens, what on earth was wrong with her?

It was not that she was over-prudish or shy: having been on the stage since she was a child, she was accustomed to dressing or undressing in the presence of others —not that she ever flaunted herself in front of men; she always did her best to remain modestly covered, remembering what her mother had told her, and the nuns at the convent—but the life she led had taught her to take a realistic outlook upon such things.

So why should she feel so completely overwhelmed— when this young man looked at her? What was this sensation of helplessness that seemed to possess her, under that steady, relentless stare?

Even now—at the sound of his voice—his words only half-heard through the bedroom door—her hands shook, and her knees turned to water. What was happening to her?

It wasn't even as if she *liked* him, either . . . Liked him? She couldn't stand him! For one thing, he was English— that was enough to damn him in her eyes. Hadn't the English, since time out of mind, been raping and pillaging Ireland under their tyrannical rule? As a good patriotic Irish girl, Coral felt nothing but hatred and contempt for the bullying Britishers from over the water . . . And Gerard Kean hailed from England—so that damned him utterly.

Then again—he was not a true Christian. Oh, he might call himself a Christian—they mostly did—but what sort of religion did he practise, without so much as a rosary in his pocket, or a "Hail, Mary" on his lips—and wickedly proclaiming defiance of the Holy Father in Rome? In some civilized countries like Spain, men of Gerard Kean's

23

persuasion had been put to torture for their blasphemies—or sent to the stake, to burn in hell for all eternity—and quite right too . . . That would teach him a lesson . . . She tried to imagine young Gerard Kean, stripped and sweating as he turned upon a spit—*stripped* . . . She pictured his body, and felt a sudden choking pang of emotion—an indescribable feeling at the very center of her being, such as she had never known before . . . Quickly she put the mental picture out of her thoughts; what right had he to break into her mind and heart, upsetting her in this way?

What right had he in Ireland at all? How dare he join Uncle Dermot's company and set himself up as an actor? He—with no experience on the boards, daring to undertake the role of Bassanio, no less . . . And tomorrow she would have to endure the humiliation of rehearsal with him—herself as Portia, listening to his voice as he spoke all those pretty speeches that Shakespeare put into his mouth—she must hear him pay court to her, praising her, declaring his love for her . . .

Catching the sound of his voice as he laughed within the next room, she put her hands over her ears in a sudden fit of anger. She hated Mr. Gerard Kean, and everything about him—and she wished with all her heart that she would never have to see him or hear him again . . .

(2)

Stage Fright

The next day dawned bright and fair, and promptly at ten o'clock in the morning the company met upon the stage of the theatre for their first rehearsal with the new juvenile gentleman.

Coral only had three scenes with him—the casket scene, where he was supposed to choose her picture from a leaden box, and so win her hand as his bride—the trial scene, where she disguised herself as the young judge to save the life of his friend Antonio—and the garden scene, where the lovers were reunited.

It was a long, slow business, for Bassanio/Gerard had to be taught every little trick of the trade. He had never set foot upon a stage before—and that was painfully apparent.

"No, no, my dear sir!" Dermot interrupted him for the hundredth time. "Kneel upon your downstage knee—and gesture with your upstage hand!"

"I'm sorry, sir," mumbled Gerard, looking and sounding very ill-at-ease. "I'd do it willingly, only—what does downstage mean? What is upstage?"

The rest of the company hid their smiles—or their impatience—and waited as Dermot explained:

"The stage, Mr. Kean, has a *rake* to it . . . That is to say, in plain language, it slopes—haven't you noticed? It slopes down gently from the back wall to the floats—"

"Floats?"

"Footlights! That row of wicks, floating in those little pools of tallow, Mr. Kean—when they're alight, they illuminate the stage, so the audience can see what you're doing . . ."

"Always supposing you're doing anything at all!" said Coral, with honey-sweetness in her tone. "Which remains to be seen . . ."

"Don't interrupt, miss!" retorted Dermot. "Where had I got to? Oh—the rake—yes—hadn't you realized that the stage is built on a slope?"

"I thought perhaps the foundations had subsided somewhere," said Gerard, and there was a ripple of laughter that was hastily suppressed.

"Heaven give me strength, boy . . ." boomed Dermot, but he persisted. "That's another way in which we help the audience to see you. If the stage was flat—you would be swallowed up, half out of sight, each time you walked away from the floats . . . The playgoers in the pit would only see you up to your knees—or up to your waist, for those in the front rows!"

"And what a *waste* that would be," murmured the company's comedian, Mr. Walter Wilkins under his breath. "Got a good pair of calves on him—show up well in tights—popular with the females, eh, Miss Coral?"

"Hold your tongue, Walter—I'm not in the mood for your bad jokes today," retorted Coral, sharply.

"Oho! So that's the way the wind blows, eh?" Mr. Walter Wilkins pursed his lips, and made his eyes very round, but said no more.

"So you see, Mr. Kean—upstage is *here*—at the back wall—and downstage is *here,* at the floats. And when you gesture, it must always be with your upstage hand—otherwise, you'll throw your downstage shoulder forward and mask yourself from the audience, d'ye see . . . ? And when you kneel, you kneel on the downstage knee, for the same reason—so as not to turn away from your public, but expose yourself to them as much as possible . . . Do you understand?"

"I think so, sir," said Gerard. "I'll try again, shall I?"

"If you please. Places, everyone—let's go back to the top of the scene—Portia—give him the first speech once more . . ."

Coral sighed, took a deep breath, and began again:

"I pray you, tarry—pause a day or two . . ."

So the rehearsals dragged on—not just for a day or two, but for several days, and poor Gerard did his best to learn his business as an actor.

It was a slow process and he began to wonder if he'd made a mistake in accepting Mr. Maguire's offer in the first place.

One afternoon, when yet another weary rehearsal was over, and the company had been dismissed, he stayed behind on the stage, going over his lines, and trying to master the acoustics of the theatre.

One light burned fitfully in the wings—for Mr. Maguire was not extravagant, and saved upon the cost of candles as much as possible, pinching out every unnecessary flame between his finger and thumb the moment the rehearsal had ended. Gerard had been allowed one taper to see his way across the stage, and had promised faithfully to extinguish it as soon as he had finished.

With his nostrils full of the reek of candlefat, blundering about in the shadows of the empty theatre, he declaimed as best he could:

". . . But thou, thou meagre lead
Which rather threat'nest than doth promise aught,
Thy plainness—"

He broke off, temporarily defeated, struggling for the words.

"Thy plainness . . . What comes after that? *Thy plainness—"*

"Thy plainness moves me more than eloquence . . ." said Coral, emerging from the wings.

"Oh! Yes—thank you—I had it on the tip of my tongue—"

"Where it will not do much good, I'm afraid, Mr. Kean.

You must be word-perfect by Friday, you know . . . You only have two days left to get up your lines."

"I know *that* only too well," groaned Gerard. "It's very strange—I thought I knew this play inside-out, but now it comes to acting the part—there are so many other things I have to remember—the moves, the business—it puts the words clean out of my head."

"Would you like me to go through the scene with you again? We might as well—since I'm here," said Coral off-handedly.

"Would you really? That's very good of you—I thought you'd gone home to your lodgings with Miss Rosalie," said Gerard.

"No—I—er—I had to stay behind to finish sewing up a hem . . . I was on my way out when I heard your voice . . . Very well, Mr. Kean—continue from *'Thy plainness moves me . . .'* "

She stepped closer, taking up their positions in the casket scene, and as soon as she moved near him, she felt that old, bewildering wave of giddiness and excitement beginning again . . . Why should he have this effect upon her? He—of all people! She tried to concentrate on the words he was speaking . . .

"Thy plainness moves me more than eloquence,
And here choose I! Joy be the consequence . . ."

That was her cue. She sailed into the next speech:

"How all the other passions fleet to air . . ."—the speech had concluded with the words she had never understood before; never felt until now:

"Oh, love, be moderate—allay thy ecstasy;
In measure rain thy joy, scant this excess.
I feel too much thy blessing! Make it less,
For fear I surfeit . . ."

Yes, that was it exactly—love's ecstasy—and she feared to surfeit . . . But that was arrant nonsense; love—? She did not love this Englishman; how could she love him? She had never loved anyone in her life—apart from her parents, and her uncle, and her sister, perhaps . . . If she were to fall in love with someone, as Shakespeare described love, it would not be with a pompous, clipped-accented, self-satisfied young English actor who didn't even know how to deliver a line without tripping over the words, and couldn't walk across the stage without stumbling into the scenery.

"Go on!" she added impatiently. "That's your cue— *'For fear I surfeit . . .'* It's you now."

"Oh—yes . . ." He glanced at her, uncertainly, and suddenly stretched out and grasped her by the hand. "Is this where I take hold of you—?"

At the contact between them, Coral felt a sudden extraordinary sensation; almost as if she had been struck by lightning—her skin burned, and her whole body seemed to have caught fire . . . And she knew from the look in Gerard's eyes that he had felt it, too.

Snatching her hand away, she said quickly: *"No . . . !* That—comes later . . . This is where you open the casket."

"Oh, yes, of course—I'm sorry . . . It's very good of you to help me like this . . . I'm most grateful for your kindness, Miss Maguire."

Trying to recover her composure, she answered—a little too quickly, and a little too breathlessly: "There's nothing to be grateful for, Mr. Kean. If you don't know your lines, you will give me the wrong cues, and then *my* performance will suffer . . . That is all that concerns me."

"I see . . ." He looked at her—a sidelong look, as if he would have liked to say something more—but he changed his mind, and continued with the scene:

"What find I here? Fair Portia's counterfeit . . ."

And so he continued to struggle through the long speeches, hammering the words into his brain to the best of his ability.

Upon the night before the first performance, Mr. Maguire called the company together for a dress rehearsal. There was a frenzy of tacking and stitching, ironing and pressing, and the cast prepared to don their costumes at last.

In the gentlemen's dressing room, chaos reigned—at least, it seemed so to Gerard. He found himself squeezed into the darkest, most inconvenient corner, far from any candlelight or helpful mirror, gazing dubiously at the garments that had been presented to him by Mr. Maguire

. . . A pair of flesh-colored tights, a pair of absurd boots with the tops rolled down and a dandelion of yellow wool stitched to each instep—a pleated white shirt and ruff, and, to wear over all the rest, a tunic of bottle-green velvet, with the nap almost worn away entirely in places. There were some odd accessories, such as a pair of gloves, a belt, and a shapeless object on a long strap that seemed to serve no recognizable function whatsoever . . . And the whole ensemble filled Gerard with the gravest possible misgivings.

The long, crowded dressing room was abuzz with noise, as a dozen assorted actors carried on a dozen conversations at once—or, more accurately, a dozen uninterrupted monologues to which no one was listening—and Gerard glanced around nervously as his colleagues, without the least concern, peeled off their everyday, 1811 clothes, and prepared to cram themselves into the absurd and archaic apparel of some era that approximated roughly to the sixteenth or seventeenth century.

Bulging paunches were squeezed into brocaded trunks; hairy thighs plunged into threadbare and often-darned tights in every color of the rainbow. The room smelled to high heaven of old clothes, stale greasepaint, and rough, male sweat; and Gerard's heart quailed within him.

Having once gazed up and found himself staring at someone's naked posterior which arose like a full moon only a few inches from his amazed face, he tried to make himself as inconspicuous as possible, burying his nose in his copy of the play, and going over his words again for the ninety-ninth time.

Deliberately, he waited until the last actor—the low comedian, Walter Wilkins—was making his way out, in the costume of "Launcelot Gobbo" (a clown-like pattern of lozenges on his doublet, and a ridiculous scarecrow mop of orange hair standing on end, under a pointed dunce's cap) before he began, reluctantly, to change his clothes.

"Come along, sir—look sharp—you'll miss your first entrance—" Walter warned him.

"Yes—yes—I'll be with you very soon—I'm just coming," said Gerard, pulling off his jacket and unbuttoning his shirt, as the door closed.

When he was undressed, he picked over the pile of garments, wondering what to put on first, and finally settled for the flesh-colored tights. It felt extremely odd to pull them over his legs—he hauled at them, trying to get the wrinkles out as best he could—and tugged the top up to his waist . . . His masculinity was outlined clearly under the close-fitting material, much to his dismay, but he calculated that the long tunic would cover his loins and hide this embarrassing display. Rapidly, he continued to robe himself, and as he was stepping into the ridiculous boots, he heard Mr. Wilkins, calling from below: "Mr. Kean, sir—you're wanted on stage—your cue!"

He grabbed the flat, shapeless cap, jammed it on his head, and ran for the stairs.

When he arrived on stage, old Dermot Maguire wagged a reproving finger at him, shaking the shaggy gray locks that surrounded his balding pate.

"Never—*never*—be late for your entrance, young man . . . Commit any other sin in the calendar if you must, but never keep your public waiting! Come—begin—we have wasted enough time already."

The rehearsal began; Gerard felt acutely uncomfortable in his costume, unhappily aware that beneath the bottle green velvet his lower limbs were all but naked—and trying to dodge a very unpleasant draught that seemed to take a fiendish delight in blowing up the long skirts of his tunic.

However, nobody commented on the wrinkles in his tights, or his ill-fitting ruff, and he consoled himself with the thought that he probably looked no more bizarre than all the other men around him.

Then came his first scene with Portia—and as Coral set foot upon the stage, followed by Rosalie, as her companion Nerissa—Gerard felt his pulses quicken, and he held his breath.

Coral, in an Elizabethan gown of peacock-blue taffeta, was the loveliest sight he had ever seen. Her glowing red hair caught and coiled up in a rope of tiny pearls, her head high against a stiffened lace collar that framed her beauty—she was the perfect heroine for Shakespeare's poetry. Desperately, he tried to do her justice, remem-

31

bering his words, his moves—determined not to let her down.

In the moment when he had to declare his love for her, when he reached the words:

"... *And claim her with a loving kiss.*
Fair lady—by your leave—"

He took her hand in his, and raised her fingertips to his lips in a courtly gesture.

"No, no—too gentlemanly by half, my dear boy—you must woo her with passion—more passion, Mr. Kean ... Take the lady in your arms and embrace her with some spirit—as if you meant what you said ... Show us a loving kiss now!" commanded Mr. Maguire, from the side of the stage, where he had half an eye on the play, and most of his attention upon a set of false whiskers—oily black, for the character of Shylock—which he was endeavoring to stick on with spirit gum.

"Yes, sir—very well—"

Nothing loath, Gerard began again, and this time took Coral in his arms, as instructed.

As he felt her slender waist beneath his hands, and drew her close, he could tell that she was tense and hesitant—a wild young animal, who feared to be caught in a trap. Gently, he pressed her closer still, until his chest touched her ripe, round breasts; through the bottle green velvet, and the peacock-blue taffeta, he was very aware of her warm young body against his own, and he bent his head, bringing his lips down to her sweet mouth, with its slightly-parted lips of cherry-red ...

"*Fair lady—by your leave* . . ." he repeated—and kissed her.

As their lips met, time stood still.

In that instant, they had no secrets from one another; it was as if their embrace had been eternal—as if they had known each other since time began—and as if they would love one another long after time came to an end. They forgot the play, and their roles in the play, they were oblivious of their fellow actors and actresses, the stage, the theatre—everything but their joy in discovering one another.

At last Coral recollected who she was, and where she

was—and was uncomfortably aware of Rosalie, a few feet away, watching them with undisguised interest.

"Not so close—" she breathed, putting her hand lightly on Gerard's arm to move him a little further away. "You don't understand—we must only *play* at love—"

"Play at love? Never!" he whispered, for her ears only.

"Ssh! You have missed your next line," she interrupted swiftly; and led him back into his speech. But she could not take her eyes from his face; and her eyes were dark and glistening with ardor to match his own.

It was a magic moment, and for a few more speeches the scene skimmed along as if they were in a dream together—pure poetry, and pure delight. But then when she reached the words:

". . . This house, those servants, and this same myself
Are yours, my lord . . . I give them with this ring—"

Old Maguire interrupted again: "Now kneel, boy— kneel, so she can slip the ring on your finger. And remember what I told you—*downstage* knee—!"

The spell was broken, and the fairy-tale shattered. For Gerard did as he was told, and knelt—"exposing himself to the public" (as he had been told) as much as possible.

Exposing himself indeed, for as he knelt upon one knee, the velvet tunic slid open, and parted to reveal him —as if completely naked from the waist down—in his wretched flesh-colored tights; and the flimsy material clung to him so closely that every inch of his masculinity was revealed, in all its pride—wildly excited as he had become, after that brief, passionate embrace.

A gasp and a titter from the rest of the company on stage, swiftly alerted Coral, and as she gazed down at her suitor, in wide-eyed dismay, he reached his next unfortunate line . . .

"Only my blood speaks to you in my veins—"

And the suppressed amusement broke into open ribaldry at Gerard's obvious discomfiture. Coral, with her cheeks flaming, snapped:

"How dare you—! I'll never forgive you for making a fool of me, Mr. Kean—*never!"*

With that, she slapped his face with such force that he lost his balance and sat down heavily—then turned on

33

her heel, and ran offstage, up to her dressing room, with the laughter still ringing in her ears.

"What's that—? What happened?" asked Mr. Maguire, his attention deflected at last from the ticklish problems of false hair and spirit-gum. "Where's the girl gone to? What's got into everyone at all, this morning?"

As Gerard scrambled to his feet, red-faced, and tugging down his tunic as tightly as possible around his thighs, Walter Wilkins interposed cheerfully: "The leading lady has a fit of the vapors, sir—and the leading man has a spot of trouble with his costume."

"For pity's sake—do we have to hold up rehearsals for such a little thing as that?" demanded the actor-manager testily.

"Begging your pardon, sir, but 'twasn't a little thing at all—far from it . . ." murmured Walter, with an expression of angelic innocence—and the assembled company broke into another guffaw.

Gerard's complexion deepened from scarlet to crimson, and he stuttered: "I'm sorry—I didn't mean—I couldn't help—"

"Oh, cut to the next scene, and get on with it," boomed Mr. Maguire. "Act Three, Scene Three—a street in Venice . . . Who has the first speech? Come along, look alive—who are we waiting for now?"

"You, Uncle," Rosalie reminded him. "You open the scene . . . And since I'm not wanted—I think I'll go and see if I can do anything to help Coral—excuse me."

She slipped away, as old Shylock—wearing only half a beard—stepped out on to the stage, declaiming: *"Gaoler, look to him—tell not me of mercy . . ."*

Meanwhile Gerard took refuge in the wings, wishing he could disappear altogether. A kindly hand touched him on the shoulder, and Walter whispered in his ear: "Cheer up, my young bucko—they'll all have forgotten about it in ten minutes' time. And if they don't—well, it won't hurt your reputation, I promise you! By the end of the tour, you'll have all the young ladies of Southern Ireland pestering you with bouquets and billets-doux, just you wait and see."

This was no consolation to Gerard, who did not care

34

what any other young ladies might think of him; he was only concerned with the disastrous effect of his recent embarrassment upon one person.

"Miss Coral—what must she feel about me now?" he began anxiously.

"Oho—so *that's* what troubles you . . . Well, she's in no doubt as to the way *you* feel about *her*, that's certain! Dearie me—why on earth didn't you wear your codpiece?" he asked Gerard.

"Codpiece? What's that?" Slowly light began to dawn. "Oh—do you mean that funny-looking contraption, like a purse on a strap? I couldn't imagine what it was for . . ."

"It's not unlike a purse in some ways, lad," said Walter, with a twinkle in his eye. "Be off to the dressing room now—and put your valuables in it, for safety's sake . . . Get on with you!"

So Gerard climbed the staircase to the gentlemen's dressing room at the top of the theatre, and—after a couple of false starts that had him tying himself in knots—he discovered how to fasten the belt of the velvet codpiece around his waist, with the padded pouch tucked between his legs—concealing, but at the same time, slyly exaggerating the contours of his anatomy.

As he stepped back and surveyed his reflection in the flyblown mirror, he heard girls' voices, and stopped short—listening . . .

"Cheer up, dearest—it's not the end of the world you know . . . Why are you getting in such a frenzy about it?"

That was the voice of Rosalie; he recognized her at once, those husky tones were unmistakable.

"I've never been so humiliated—so *disappointed* in anyone—" replied Coral: and she sounded as if she were on the verge of tears.

Gerard looked about the room, perplexed. He was quite alone, and yet the girls appeared to be so close . . . Then he realized that their voices were coming from the open grating of an ancient ventilation shaft: for the dressing rooms were totally enclosed, with no windows, and this was a feeble attempt to introduce a breath of air. The girls' room, immediately below, must open on to the same shaft, and their conversation carried up the echoing flue with surprising clarity.

He knew he should not be eavesdropping, but wild horses would not have dragged him away at this moment.

"Disappointed—in Mr. Kean?" Rosalie sounded amused, and Gerard could imagine the characteristic raised eyebrow . . . "From the brief glimpse I got—I'd say you had no cause for disappointment . . . 'Anticipation' would be the word I'd choose."

"Rosalie, for shame! How can you make such jokes—?" Coral protested. "You know very well what I mean . . . Mr. Kean may be an Englishman and a snob and every sort of pompous ass—but at least I supposed him to have the manners of a gentleman . . . I'd never have expected him to indulge in such—such animal behavior! And in front of the whole company, too—it's so mortifying . . ."

"Poor Coral . . ." Rosalie's voice was softer now. "You will try to fight against the facts of life, won't you? When it's only human nature after all—the same for Mr. Kean as for you or me—and every man and woman ever born . . . He couldn't *help* feeling attracted to you, you know; just as you can't help feeling attracted to *him* . . . Only you don't show it in such a spectacular manner, that's all."

"Me? Attracted to that young man? Never! What makes you think such a thing?" demanded Coral, indignantly.

"Is it me you're trying to deceive? Or yourself . . . ? You wouldn't be in the state you are now, if you weren't halfway head-over-heels about the lad . . . Come on—admit it!"

Gerard held his breath, hardly able to believe his ears, and waited on tenterhooks for Coral's reply.

There was a long, long pause, then she said—lightly, and almost off-handedly:

"Oh . . . He's good-looking enough, I suppose—in his way . . . But what of it? D'you think I'd ever be such a fool as to let myself fall in love with an *Englishman?*"

Rosalie laughed: and a moment later, Coral joined her.

They changed the subject, discussing the repairs that needed to be made to their costumes before the first night—and Gerard went out of the room and made his way down to the stage again, with his head in a whirl.

The first night . . . A mere twenty-four hours away now. When Gerard stopped to think that, this time tomorrow, he would be setting foot upon the stage in front of a paying audience for the first time, his stomach seemed to turn over, and his knees trembled.

He knew his lines by now, thank goodness; he even had a fairly good idea of the moves and business that Dermot Maguire had drummed into him all the week. And he would certainly not make any careless mistakes in future, when putting on his costume. So why did he feel this overwhelming sense of terror at the prospect of acting his part in the play?

That night he hardly slept at all; he lay in the bed that had been originally rented to his predecessor, Mr. O'Malley, and went over the words of Bassanio in his head, again and again . . . He heard the slow hours crawling by, marked by the chimes of a clock somewhere in the vicinity; he tossed and turned, sweating with nervous apprehension. He even wondered wildly if this was what had led Mr. O'Malley toward his unhappy over-indulgence in alcohol—he could well understand how such miserable terror could drive any man to drink.

When daylight came, he looked at himself in the glass as he washed his face—the pallid skin, the worried wrinkles on his brow, the purple shadows beneath his eyes . . . Could this be the man who was to capture Portia's heart —and the hearts of all the playgoers in Wexford?

He refused breakfast, except for a few gulps of strong black coffee, and set out for the theatre and one final rehearsal.

When he reached the main entrance, he found that he was not the first to arrive; Dermot Maguire had forestalled him, and the playbills for tonight's performance, which had proudly blazoned the name of O'Malley (admittedly several lines lower down than the name of Maguire, and in considerably smaller type) now had stickers pasted over them.

Hand-lettered, the new amendment proclaimed: "Tonight—the Irish premiere of England's leading juvenile—

37

direct from the Drury Lane Theatre—Mr. Gerard Kean!"

Gerard's heart sank into his boots, and a cold sweat broke out all over his body.

Surely, when the citizens of Wexford clapped eyes upon him tonight, and realized just how raw and inexperienced he was, they would tear the playhouse down and demand their money back—or worse? He had visions of them besieging the stage door—a lynch mob, denouncing him as an impostor, every man eager to hang him from the nearest gallows tree.

For two pins, he would have turned tail, and run back to his lodgings—there to collect together his bookbag and his battered trunk, and flee to some other town before it was too late . . .

Then a resonant voice hailed him: "Well, my boy—are you in good heart? Looking forward to making your grand debut? That's the spirit!"

Dermot Maguire stepped out of the box office, and slapped him on the back, steering him round the corner to the stage-door, and keeping up a running monologue about his own first essays as an actor, more than half a century ago.

It was too late already. There was no escape now.

The day passed like a nightmare: he was in a private hell of misery, and no one could get through to him. Faces seemed to come and go from a mist of utter despair, and voices spoke to him: sometimes kindly—

"I remember my very first appearance on any stage—I scored a personal triumph, believe me . . ." (This was Dermot again, of course.) "Mind you, I'm not saying you should set your sights as high as that—inborn genius is a gift of the gods, we can't all be so fortunate—but I dare say you'll do well enough, provided you don't forget your words . . ."

Sometimes, the voices spoke in blank verse, as he staggered uncertainly through a final rehearsal: he heard Coral, very clear but very far away, as if she were speaking from another world, and he could not hope to reach her:

"The quality of mercy is not strained—
It droppeth as the gentle rain from heaven . . ."

And sometimes the voices were ready with practical advice: Walter Wilkins suddenly loomed up from nowhere, counselling:

"Always resort to the chamber pot, laddie, before your entrance cue . . . Nothing's worse than being caught short in the middle of a long speech."

The minutes ticked away; if the night before had seemed to drag, now time hurried by on wings—all too soon it was evening, and Gerard found himself in the dressing room for the last time, with Walter and Dermot fussing over him, taking turns to initiate him into the mysteries of painting his face.

"A spot of white—there—you see?—at the end of the nose, my boy—it lifts it, no question of that—you don't want shadows under your nose, or the audience might think you're Jewish," said Dermot, who was almost unrecognizable under an olive-green makeup, curling false whiskers, and a wig of oily-black ringlets.

"And a red dot in the corner of each eye—" said Walter. "Like so—it gives you a *sparkling* look—and you need all the sparkle you can get tonight . . ."

"Don't forget a dab of rouge on the lobes of the ears . . . It makes you look younger," added Dermot, grabbing a rabbit's foot and setting to work: overlooking the fact that Gerard was already the youngest actor in the company by several years in any case.

Then they went away, and for a few moments he was alone; feeling much too young, and totally lacking in any sparkle whatsoever. He shut his eyes, and waited for death's merciful release.

The sound of the door opening did nothing to cheer him: he pretended he was asleep, and hoped the latest visitor or well-wisher—whoever it was—would simply go away and leave him to suffer in silence.

"Mr. Kean . . ." Coral's voice was as soft as her breath at his ear.

He opened his eyes, and saw before him in the mirror, Coral's reflection, as she stood behind his chair; leaning forward to say quietly:

"I hope you don't mind me disturbing you . . . ?"

"No—of course not, Miss Maguire—what is it?"

39

He struggled to his feet, automatically adjusting his costume, and turned to face her.

She seemed a little shy; usually so self-possessed, he wondered at the change in her manner.

"I—it's nothing really—only just—I wanted—I thought perhaps . . . Well, this is your first performance, after all, so . . . I felt I should wish you success tonight."

"Oh—!" Her unaccustomed bashfulness was infectious; he did not know how to respond, and stammered foolishly. "Thank you . . . Yes—well—er—thank you indeed—I mean—"

Abruptly, she cut through his inarticulate murmurs and darted forward, kissing him swiftly on the lips.

The kiss lasted for the merest fraction of a second; then she withdrew, explaining: "That was for good luck . . . It's an old theatrical custom . . . I'll see you on the green."

She moved to the door, as he repeated stupidly:

"The—the *green*—? Where—?"

"The stage, you goose . . . Don't worry—you'll pick up all our phrases in time . . . And don't be nervous about tonight—I'll do my best to help you all I can."

She threw him a flashing, generous smile, and was gone.

Slowly he sank back into his chair, trying to make sense of what she had said . . . Could it be that Rosalie was right after all? Did Coral really have a secret tenderness for him?

He looked at his reflection again, and found that—for the first time in several days—he was actually smiling. Impulsively, he picked up a scrap of damp sponge and wiped the unnecessary daubs of rouge from the lobes of his ears. Dammit, he wasn't *that* young . . . !

Somewhere below, a voice cried hoarsely:

"Five minutes, please . . . Beginners on stage—five minutes!"

He took a deep breath, and squared his shoulders. This was it—his great moment. Perhaps after all he wasn't going to disgrace himself totally . . .

At which point the door opened yet again, and a complete stranger walked in: a young man in his mid-twenties, with a blue-black stubble on his chin, and uncombed, unruly hair.

"Mr. Kean?" asked the newcomer—almost like a challenge.

"Yes?—" he said, at a loss.

"I thought so . . . Take your clothes off, Mr. Kean—I want them."

(3)

A Waiting-Gentleman

As he spoke, the young man was rapidly unwinding a grubby muffler from his throat, and unbuttoning his greatcoat.

"What—? Who are you—what do you mean by—"

"Don't argue—do as I say!" The young man threw his jacket into one corner, unbuckled his belt, and dropped his breeches without the least trace of concern. Standing in his shirttails, he added curtly:

"The name's O'Malley—Rory O'Malley . . . I play Bassanio in this piece—you won't be required to go on after all." He scowled, and jerked his thumb at Gerard who was standing dumbfounded. "D'ye hear what I said? Get undressed, can't you?"

Slowly—helplessly—Gerard began to obey: there was a dangerous quality in Mr. O'Malley that suggested it would be wiser not to start an argument. From his wide, aggressive temples to the cleft of his pointed, jutting chin Mr. O'Malley's appearance spelled trouble . . . And from the whiff of Irish whisky on his breath—when he moved closer to take the garments as Gerard discarded them—

it seemed that he had been fortifying himself in readiness for this evening's performance.

When Dermot bustled breathlessly into the dressing room a moment later, Rory O'Malley was stark naked, waiting impatiently for Gerard to peel off the flesh-colored tights.

"Rory—is it really you? They told me below you'd turned up again like Lazarus from the dead, but I couldn't believe my ears—three months in gaol, I thought you'd be—"

"That's what the old fool of a magistrate said, sure enough." Rory drummed his fingers angrily on the back of a chair. "Look sharp, man, for God's sake!"

"But what are you doing here? Don't tell me you broke out of prison—"

"Not I . . . I happen to have friends in high places; influence at court, as you might say . . . The magistrate's wife is a dear good creature, and a close personal friend of mine—she interceded on my behalf—persuaded the old bastard to change his mind and grant my appeal—and I was let out an hour ago, a free man . . . It's as well for you, Maguire, that I have some admirers . . ."

Rory stretched his arms, flexing his powerful biceps and eyeing his reflection in the glass with satisfaction: while Gerard stepped out of the tights at last and handed them over.

The two young men were in marked contrast as they stood side by side, both stripped to the buff; each one an example of masculine beauty that any sculptor would have envied . . . Rory—tough, heavily-muscled, with dark, wiry thatch on his broad chest and belly; and Gerard—slim, lighter and easier in movement, with fair curls and a down of body-hair that shone almost like gold in the candlelight.

They looked at each other for a moment—measuring one another, like adversaries before a fight. Then Dermot broke the silence, saying irritably: "Heavens above, gentlemen—get yourselves dressed—the audience is growing restive . . . ! I'll make an announcement that you have returned to take over your role by popular request, Rory—"

43

"What about me?" asked Gerard.

"Oh—you—yes, of course—find yourself a doublet and hose—and a cloak—there should be some odd bits and pieces in the wardrobe somewhere . . . You can walk on and off as a waiting-gentleman, and swell the crowd scenes . . ."

And the old man hurried downstairs to address the waiting public.

So that was what happened: Gerard made his stage debut, not in a leading role, but as one of a nameless crowd, shuffling on and off whenever he was told to move —following his fellow actors and hoping for the best, without uttering one single word, and without making the slightest mark upon the drama.

At one point, when he had a long wait between scenes, he found himself in the wings, watching Bassanio declaring his love for Portia . . .

"Madam, you have bereft me of all words—
Only my blood speaks to you in my veins . . ."

Rory was kneeling on one knee and gazing adoringly up at Coral. Nobody laughed at all: the scene was expertly handled, by two experienced professionals, and Gerard could only admire their skill . . . Admire—and suffer a secret, unhappy twinge of jealousy . . .

He cursed himself for his stupidity; all day long, he'd been aching for the chance to escape—he would have given anything not to have to play Bassanio tonight. And now that the chance had come his way—his wishes had come true—what was the result? He resented Mr. Rory O'Malley, and felt jealous of him.

When the play was over, when the actors had taken their bows, and the audience had taken their leave— there was another, unforeseen difficulty. For when Mr. O'Malley returned to his lodgings, to discover that his bedchamber had been sublet in his absence to Mr. Kean —he was very far from pleased.

"We didn't know you were coming back—what else was I to do?" Gerard asked, as they discussed the situation.

"You'll have to find somewhere else, man—I was here first, after all," retorted Rory. "And I've been sleeping on a confounded hard bed these past few nights—I'm determined to rest easy tonight."

"I can't find lodgings at this hour—" Gerard argued. "It's far too late—"

"There's no problem at all," said the landlady, following them into the room. "Will you give me a hand, the pair of you?—to bring down an old mattress I have here—I'll make up another bed on the floor, and you'll both be as snug as two bugs in a rug, so you will."

Reluctantly, they were forced to accept this solution, without very good grace, and for the rest of their stay in Wexford, Mr. O'Malley and Mr. Kean shared a bedroom —spoke as little as possible—and ignored one another whenever they could do so.

"Thank God it's only till the end of the week," said Rory O'Malley to Walter Wilkins, over a glass of whisky next day. "Then we move on to Waterford—and I'll have a room to myself in that fair city—or I'll know the reason why!"

When the Wexford engagement came to an end, the Maguire company packed themselves up, and set out on the road westward, covering the forty miles to Waterford in various conveyances: the Maguire family in a decrepit carriage that seemed forever on the point of falling to pieces—some of the others by pony-and-trap, or in an open carriage (praying for fine weather on the journey)— some taking the public stagecoach—and the costumes and scenery following behind, very slowly, in a pair of ancient farm wagons.

Gerard travelled as cheaply as possible, by the public stage, and found himself seated next to Walter Wilkins. They kept up a conversation for the first hour or two; Walter had a fund of amusing anecdotes from his early days in the business, when he was a clown with a touring circus. Gradually the other passengers dozed off, and at last Gerard and Walter were the only two left awake.

Realizing this, Walter dug him in the ribs, and muttered:

"A word in your ear, laddie . . . Let me give you a piece of advice—watch out for the O'Malley . . . You've made a bitter black enemy of that one, I'm warning you!"

"An enemy—? I've done nothing—I hardly know the man—" said Gerard, in dismay. "We shared a room for a while, that's all—"

"All the same, he's jealous of you, and he's spoiling for a fight," said Walter, drawing down the corners of his long, expressive mouth, with a grimace of foreboding. "You keep out of his way, my lad, if you know what's good for you."

"But why should he be jealous—?" Gerard had a sudden thought, and added: "You mean—he's an admirer of Miss Coral—is that it?"

"Good God no—! Rory O'Malley admires no one but Rory O'Malley—the first time he saw his face in a glass, it was the start of a lifelong love affair . . ."

Gerard smiled, despite himself. "I understood from what he said that he was something of a ladies' man?"

"Oh, he goes through the motions from time to time—for the sake of his health, more than anything else, I suspect . . . And always with a lady who's flattered by his attentions—he dearly loves an appreciative audience, you see." Walter threw a sidelong glance at Gerard and said: "But I take it—you *are* an admirer of Miss Coral? Am I right?"

"Oh—well—as to that—I think she's a very fine young actress," said Gerard, awkwardly. "I have the greatest admiration for her Portia, you understand."

"Oh, yes, indeed—and you're not the only one!" grinned Walter. "No—when I said you'd made Rory jealous, I referred to the fact that you were rash enough to step into his shoes and understudy him as Bassanio— and you're younger and better looking—and you even had the brazen impudence to sleep in his bed! Mark my words—he'll be looking for an excuse to call you out before long."

"Call me out—?"

"Pick a fight with you—try to teach you a lesson in the art of fisticuffs! Just you watch out for him, because he has the deuce of a temper—especially when he's got a jar or two inside him . . . So beware!"

Gerard pondered this information unhappily, thinking back to his boyhood days at Rosewood, when his father had tried—without much success—to have him instructed in the art of self-defense . . . If only he had paid more attention to the lessons at the time!

When at last the coach arrived in Waterford, Gerard cheered up a little and looked about him with interest. Eternally optimistic, he hoped that Rory O'Malley would find no cause to pick a quarrel with him; and now they were no longer sharing lodgings, he would do his best to keep out of that gentleman's way.

He liked what he saw of the city, from the window of the coach; as at Wexford, there was a lot of shipping here—but where Wexford had been a busy seaport, Waterford was inland, straddling the river Suir, with vessels that travelled up the estuary, from Waterford harbor to the south. It was a much bigger place than Wexford, with an air of bustling excitement that appealed to Gerard immediately; he remembered some old prints of Paris that his French governess had once shown him—and the sight of the traffic on the broad quays along the riverbank reminded him somehow of that city. His spirits rose: life seemed all at once to be looking rather brighter.

When he and Walter alighted, they carried their baggage to the little hotel where Walter had advised Gerard to stay . . . And there they found a surprise awaiting them, for the first person they met in the saloon, on the ground floor, was Rory O'Malley. He sat in a wooden chair, tilted on to its back legs, with a glass in his hand—and his expression was unwelcoming.

"Oh, God—don't tell me the entire company is booking in here as well?" he demanded rhetorically.

"Can't speak for the others, Rory—but we're certainly going to dig ourselves in—I always stay here whenever I'm in Waterford," said Walter carelessly.

"I suppose it's a free country," grumbled Rory, and turned his back on them.

Once they had been allotted rooms and unpacked their luggage, Walter and Gerard returned to the saloon again in search of some food, and Walter ordered a substantial meal of fried eggs, fried bacon, and soda bread, washed down with lashings of a beverage hitherto unknown to Gerard—a bitter, dark brown beer called porter. He didn't care for his first sip very much, but he soon acquired the taste for it, like most of the other actors in the company . . . with the possible exception of Mr. O'Malley, who preferred to stick to whisky—and who, at this moment, was doing exactly that.

The saloon was filling up by now with many of the local citizens, and some of them recognized Walter and Rory, and struck up a conversation with them. What plays were they to perform upon this visit? Any good murders? Any ghosts? Had they any new actors in the troupe?

Rory threw a moist, mischievous glance across the table at Gerard, and said: "New actors forsooth? We present for your edification the greatest, the newest, the most splendid actor of this generation . . . All the way from England, no less—allow me to present my illustrious colleague—Mr. Gerard Kean!"

"Kean—?" A murmur ran round the crowded room . . . It was a familiar name, sure enough.

"From England, eh?" One young blade set down his tankard and said bluntly: "What are you doing here, then, Mr. Kean? If you're an Englishman—why aren't you fighting in the war against Bonaparte, like all the rest of your countrymen?"

It was an uncomfortable moment, and the noisy saloon suddenly hushed to hear Gerard's answer.

"Bonaparte—? Oh, no—not I!" He tried to shrug it off as a joke. "I'm an actor, you see—not a soldier . . ."

They exchanged glances, and his attacker began again: "An actor, you say? Sure you carry an actor's name, right enough—but I've never heard tell of you before . . . Gerard Kean—would that be any relation to Mr. *Edmund* Kean, now?"

Gerard hesitated, unwilling to lie, but unsure what stories old Dermot might have put about already. As he tried to frame a reply, Rory broke in with a winning smile:

"Of course the boy's related to Kean—that's why we hired him . . . He's going to follow the great man and take all Ireland by storm—and all England too, no doubt! 'Gerard Kean of Drury Lane'—that's what it says on the bills!"

The murmuring in the room grew to a rumble, and the chief prosecutor spoke up again. "Then how is it we never heard of you—for didn't Edmund Kean meet and marry a girl from this very city, less than a year ago? Mary Chambers—the leading lady of Beverley's touring company . . . ? Tell us, Mr. Kean—why don't you go and stay with the Chambers', if you're one of the family?"

Gerard realized that this was the trap which Rory had deliberately set for him, and tried hard to find an answer. He was saved by Walter Wilkins, who swallowed a mouthful of egg and bacon and said quickly: "Oh, it's a very distant connection—he don't wish to presume upon it, you understand—second cousin, twice removed—ain't that so, Gerard?"

"But nevertheless—a celebrated tragedian, just like his cousin, by all accounts . . . Go on, Gerard—stand up and give us a taste of your quality," Rory urged him on with a malicious gleam in his eye. " '*Once more unto the breach*,' perhaps? Or '*To be or not to be—?*' Let's hear you raise the roof, my boy!"

This was a challenge indeed, and Gerard knew there was no way to escape it. Slowly, he rose to his feet, and fixed Rory with a long, level gaze. Then—quietly at first, but with burning intensity, he began Bassanio's first great speech:

"In Belmont is a lady, richly left . . ."

It was the speech in which he told of his love for Portia, whom he had seen from afar, and to whom he intended to pay court. He forgot about the crowd of strangers that surrounded him: he forgot where he was, or who he was—all his concentration was focused upon one single point . . . This was one of Rory's key-speeches in the play, and he was determined to beat him at his own game.

For a few moments, he ceased to be Gerard, and became Bassanio, speaking from the heart and telling of his devotion to the fair lady of Belmont: and the customers in the crowded saloon listened as if spellbound until he reached the last line:

". . . That I should questionless be fortunate."

Then he stopped: and the silence that followed was

broken by the sound of one pair of hands clapping—an example quickly followed by the entire room.

Everyone looked round: in the doorway stood Coral and Rosalie with old Dermot a pace behind them. And it was Coral who had led the applause.

Under cover of the noise, Walter leaned across to ask Rory: "Well, old boy? Are you satisfied now?"

Rory O'Malley grunted, and turned away, his face darkening.

"This is an unexpected welcome, Mr. Kean," said Dermot Maguire, advancing into the room. "What's the idea? A sample of our program, to attract an audience? Well, the box office is now open, gentlemen—seats are obtainable at all prices!"

Rosalie smiled at Gerard: "Congratulations, Mr. Kean —you obviously have a flair for publicity—I'd never have expected it!"

Coral tugged at the old man's arm, saying under her breath: "Now the public have heard Mr. Kean, they will come to hear him again at the theatre, uncle . . . You *did* say you would give him a role in the next play, did you not?"

"Eh?—oh—yes—to be sure . . . Mr. Kean—come to see me in my dressing room after tonight's performance, and we'll find you a speaking part. You'll be a regular acquisition to our little band—eh, Walter? Don't you agree, Rory?"

Walter—with a mouthful of soda bread—could only nod enthusiastically: Rory pretended not to hear.

That night, when Coral left the theatre on her way back to the hotel, as she stepped into the darkened street, a figure detached itself from the shadows, and she exclaimed:

"Oh—Mr. Kean—I did not see you at first—you startled me . . ."

"I'm sorry: I have been waiting for you since the play ended . . . I hoped you might allow me to escort you back to the hotel."

"That is kind of you indeed—but you need not have troubled—I know the way perfectly well—"

"But it is late, and I don't like to think of you walking

alone at night . . . Besides—I wanted to talk to you . . . To thank you."

"Thank me—?" They fell into step together, and it seemed perfectly natural for her to take his arm. "For what, pray?"

"For putting in a word on my behalf with your Uncle. He says I am to have an important role in the next play —he hasn't yet decided which it is to be, but that doesn't matter . . . I owe it to you, Miss Coral."

"I'm quite sure it is no more than you deserve . . . You are becoming quite proficient as an actor, and in so short a time, too—everyone says it is really remarkable."

They turned out of a side street, on to the quay by the river. It was even darker here, with the blackness broken only by occasional flickering lamps—and the distant lights of the boats an anchor, dancing on the water.

"I am not concerned with what *everyone* says of me, Miss Coral . . . I only care for your opinion—what do *you* say of me?"

He stopped, and turned to face her. She looked up at him: he suddenly seemed very close to her, and his face —faintly gleaming in the half-light—was more handsome than ever.

"I say—you are extremely promising—" she began, hesitantly.

"I would promise you anything in the wide world— yes, and keep my promise too, or die in the attempt," he told her simply.

She heard her heart pounding, and the words came with difficulty as she said: "I meant—promising—as an actor—"

"And you know I meant nothing of the sort . . . To the devil with acting, Miss Coral—it's not important to me— nothing else is important to me, except you . . ."

"Mr. Kean—I don't know what to say to you—"

His strong arms were round her waist, and she felt the intimate pressure of his body against her own.

"Say nothing . . . There is nothing to be said—'only my blood speaks to you in my veins' . . ." he quoted softly; and then his mouth was upon hers, and her lips parted in the joyous revelation of a kiss.

51

It was just as it had been the first time, when they embraced on stage; so right, so instinctive, as if they belonged together . . . And yet this time it was also different —more exciting, with a new ardor that set her pulses racing. He held her more closely to him, and she felt as if she would fall—as if all her powers of self-protection and defense were vanquished utterly—as if she must throw herself upon him helplessly, subservient to his strength, his will, his passion . . .

Almost dizzily, she gave herself up to him; and emboldened by this, he pursued his advances with yet more fervor. Her head was swimming—the lights of the boats seemed to reel crazily around her in the darkness—she had never known such ecstasy . . .

And then she became aware of a new urgency in his manner; his hands moved upon her body, unfastening her mantle, his fingers straying within, exploring her waist, her bosom, the bodice of her dress—

Caught up in a wild confusion, that mingled panic and desire, she realized he was going beyond all restraint—he bent his head low, seeking to put his sweet, warm mouth upon her breasts—and suddenly she knew she had to stop him at once, or be lost forever.

"*No—!*" she gasped. "No—let me go—stop—please stop—"

With every ounce of determination she could muster, she pulled herself free from him, and cried breathlessly: "I should have known better than to trust you . . . Good night, Mr. Kean—and goodbye!"

She fastened her dress and pulled her mantle about her, then turned and ran off along the quay, and the sound of her footsteps along the cobblestones faded into the darkness.

(4)

First Night

When Coral got back to the little hotel room that she shared with her sister, she found Rosalie already in bed—and looking rather worried.

"Where have you been? I was beginning to be anxious."

"I walked home from the theatre—that's all." Coral tried to keep her face turned away as she started to undress, trusting that the flickering light of the bedside candle would not illuminate her too brightly.

"You walked home—? It took you long enough, in all conscience . . . Did you get lost, or what?"

Rosalie sat up, her arms round her knees, and studied her younger sister as she pulled off her dress, still keeping her back to the candlelight.

"No—I—I wasn't hurrying . . ." Quickly, Coral dropped her half-petticoat over her hips, and stepped out of it, trying to get through the process of undressing as soon as possible, so she might be hidden in merciful darkness.

"I don't understand . . . Look at me, Coral . . . Tell me what you've been up to."

Still Coral refused to turn round, as she pulled her final garment over her head—a flimsy cotton shift. Shaking her auburn curls loose, she replied; "I've been up to nothing at all. Now blow out the candle and let's get some sleep."

"Not yet . . . Look at me, will you? Turn around, and look me in the face—d'you hear?"

Reluctantly, biting her lips, Coral was forced to obey.

She stood naked, her slender, shapely figure picked out lovingly by the golden glow of the flame: two perfect breasts tip-tilted at their coral-pink nipples, and one leg slightly bent at the knee, so that the coppery fleece of the triangle between her thighs was half-hidden in modest shadow . . .

And on her pretty face the tell-tale glitter of tears.

"Why were you crying? Tell me . . . Who's been upsetting you?"

"Oh—does it matter?" Coral made an impatient move toward the old wardrobe, to fetch her nightgown, but Rosalie stopped her, catching her by the wrist.

"Not yet . . . I want to know the truth . . . It was Gerard, wasn't it? He made you cry?"

Coral nodded, almost angrily, adding: "But I don't want to talk about it . . . I've finished with Mr. Gerard Kean—once and for all. Now let me get to bed, for I'm very tired."

Swiftly, she found her nightgown and slipped it on, then pulled back the covers and climbed into the big double bed. Rosalie licked her finger and thumb, and pinched out the flame of the candle, so the reek of the burnt-out wick shouldn't keep them awake.

In the darkness, she was aware of Coral lying with her back to her, her whole body still tense and unhappy. Gently, she slid one hand round her waist, and drew her closer.

"Tell me about it," she said softly. "Don't try to shut up your feelings . . . You'll be happier afterward."

A long pause in the cosy darkness, and then Coral

54

shifted uncertainly, her hips finding a comfortable resting-place in her sister's lap; they curled up together as they had so often, since they were children.

"Well . . ." she said at last. "He was waiting for me—he offered to walk me home—I thought it was good-natured of him, so I said yes."

"Of course. And then what?"

"Then we—we began talking—and he started telling me how he felt about me . . ."

"Did he say he loved you?"

"He never spoke of love . . . But he said—I was the only important thing in his life—nothing else mattered—that's what he told me . . . And then—then he kissed me."

"And—?"

"And—it was wonderful . . . It was like nothing I ever knew before—"

"Oh, my baby—" Rosalie smiled to herself, holding her sister very close. "It *is* like nothing else on earth—a man's love—"

"But it didn't end there, you see . . . He began to get more—well—passionate, I suppose . . . He became very impatient, and tried to unfasten my clothes—eh—he wanted to kiss my bosom, Rosalie!—"

"What's wrong with that, then? Why wouldn't you let him?"

Horrified, Coral drew away, and lay on her back—her spine rigid, and her legs tightly together.

"Rosalie, for shame—you know very well why not . . . It would have been the first step toward mortal sin! Remember what the nuns told us at the convent—"

"Ah, those old dears didn't know the half of it, bless their hearts," chuckled Rosalie. "If Gerard loves you—and you love him, I'm sure of that—what's wrong with sharing your pleasures and making the most of those gifts which the good Lord has given you?"

"I won't listen to you!" gasped Coral. "What would poor Mama say is she could hear you now? We promised her we'd stay pure in thought and deed—or she'd never have let us go off to join Uncle Dermot's troupe—"

"Poor Mama must have had her moments of weakness, dearest—well, we know she did, or we wouldn't be here today," Rosalie pointed out, reasonably enough.

This was too much for Coral, who rolled over once more, keeping as far from her sister as possible, and saying in a horrified tone: "I think the devil himself gets into you sometimes, Rosalie Maguire . . . May you be forgiven for speaking so of our dear mother . . . Now hold your tongue, for I'll not say another word to you!"

Rosalie sighed: and the two girls settled down for the night.

So the weeks passed by, and the winter rolled on; and Coral watched Gerard each day at rehearsals, and saw that he was watching her too . . . And she tossed her head and tried to put him out of her mind . . . But it wasn't easy.

Dermot Maguire was as good as his word, and when they began to prepare their next production—*King Lear*—he summoned the entire company on stage and allotted them their roles.

"I myself shall undertake the King, naturally . . . It's a taxing ordeal, but I believe I may be able to give a good account of myself—thanks to the grace of God and a natural understanding of the character . . . I, too, have suffered the agonies of betrayal and injustice in my time; but I also have the courage and stamina to sustain me in my endeavors—"

"Not to mention two dozen bottles of porter under his dressing-table," whispered Walter Wilkins, who was sitting next to Gerard.

"As to the remainder of the *dramatis personae*—Coral will of course by my Cordelia, with Rosalie as Goneril, and Mrs. Mountford as Regan . . . Will one of you be so good as to rouse Mrs. Mountford? She appears to have nodded off again."

Mrs. Mountford, an elderly and imposing lady who undertook all the female character roles in the plays, was nudged awake, and automatically resumed her work on the grubby square of embroidery which she carried with her at all times.

"Regan? Yes, Mr. Maguire—thank you—that's the

one where I put out somebody's eyes, isn't it? Yes, that will be very nice."

"Walter—you'll play Kent, as usual . . ."

Gerard frowned, and turned to the comedian. "Surely you'd be better suited to play the Fool?—"

"What do you mean? There's no foolery in this piece—it's all high drama," answered Walter.

"Oh, but you're mistaken—I've read it a hundred times—the King has a jester who travels with him—one he calls his Fool—"

"That's the worst of studying your Shakespeare on the printed page," said old Dermot, loftily. "The play as written is too crude—too primitive for modern tastes. Fortunately, a very great author, Mr. Nahum Tate, has edited it for the stage—the character of the Fool has been removed, and Cordelia marries her true love at the end, and it all comes out very prettily . . . Audiences dearly enjoy a happy ending, Mr. Kean—Shakespeare didn't understand that."

Gerard decided in future to keep his opinion to himself, and Dermot continued: "Mr. O'Malley shall give us his Edmund, naturally—and you, Mr. Kean, shall have your chance to delight us as his half-brother, Edgar . . ."

"That's a good part, laddie," said Walter encouragingly. "Very showy, that is—you have to run stark mad halfway through, and appear as poor Tom o' Bedlam, dressed in rags and tatters—it always gets a very big ovation, I can tell you."

"Not too many tatters in your costume, I hope, Mr. Kean?" suggested Rory O'Malley, with a gleam in his eye. "We don't want to risk another exhibition like the one you gave at the last dress rehearsal . . . Of course, I wasn't there myself, but the story spread like wildfire—and I shouldn't like to think of you shocking our leading lady once again!"

Gerard colored furiously; and looked away. O'Malley never lost any opportunity to get in a gibe at his expense, trying to humiliate him in front of Coral and Rosalie.

Rehearsals began immediately; but there was a lot of work to be done upon the play, and it was decided that they should not open *King Lear* in Waterford after all.

57

Instead, it would be added to their repertoire at the next town they visited—Cappoquin, still further westward, on the River Blackwater.

It was a long journey, when they finally took to the road again; this time Gerard decided not to waste his hard-earned pay on the fares of a stagecoach, but travelled for nothing in the old farm carts, with the scenery and costumes. As the day dragged on, and the rickety vehicles bumped and clattered over potholes and furrowed country roads, he began to wish he had not been so economical. He thought of Walter and the rest, riding in comparative luxury, miles ahead, and envied them all heartily.

When at last he reached Cappoquin his spirits sank still lower—for this was not really a town at all, but an overgrown village; a sleepy hamlet with a church, a general store, and a cluster of houses that huddled round the main crossroads, by the bridge over the river.

The "theatre" was nothing of the sort; a tumbledown old building at the water's edge—something between a barn and a boathouse, with rough wooden benches for the audience, and a makeshift platform erected at one end, to serve as a stage. The dressing room was a long low hut divided by an old sheet that protected the ladies from the eyes of the gentlemen. Trestle tables, one or two cracked mirrors, and some rustic stools that would have seemed more at home in a cowshed . . . That was the extent of the backstage amenities at Cappoquin.

"Come, my boys—look alive!" Dermot instructed the younger men in the company. "Get the scenery unloaded and set up on stage, as quick as you can . . . Then when that's done you may go out and find yourselves lodgings. There are no hotels in this town, I fear; it will be a case of knocking upon doors and asking if they can rent you a bed for the night."

Dermot had taken care to arrange accommodation for himself and his nieces above the General Store, when he originally fixed the engagement; and now the Maguire family took themselves off to settle in and unpack their belongings at their leisure.

The actors worked as fast as possible, for there was not

58

much time to spare; they had to get the scenery into place, find themselves somewhere to stay, and be back in time for the performance at eight o'clock.

"Will there be any audience here at all?" Gerard asked Walter, as they struggled to hoist painted flats and rig up various tattered strips of hessian which did duty as wings.

"Oh, you'll be surprised—it's a great occasion in these parts when the actors come to town. All the folk from the farms hereabouts will be making their way to Cappoquin tonight, laddie . . . All eager to applaud your debut in a speaking role."

"Don't remind me of that—I'm trying not to think of it," groaned Gerard.

In fact, he was not so nervous as he had been at Wexford; these weeks of experience as a "waiting-gentleman" had accustomed him to the terrors of setting foot on stage—and in any event, he hardly felt that the eyes of the world would be upon him, here in Cappoquin.

"Oh, you'll do very well, I'm sure of that . . ." Walter glanced round and added: "There's not much left to do now—I think I'll just slip away and fix up my digs for the night . . . I'll see you on the green, dear boy—later!"

One by one, various members of the troupe were making their excuses and slipping away, and soon Gerard looked up from a particularly stubborn nail that refused to drive straight in to the timbered back wall—to find that he was alone on stage, except for one other actor . . . Rory O'Malley.

At the same instant, Rory looked round also, and made the identical discovery.

"So—they've deserted us," he glowered. "Lazy hounds . . . Everyone sloping off to have a bite and drink before tonight's performance, I suppose—while we're left to do all the work!"

"There's still the main backcloth to put up, as well—that's going to be a long job—" began Gerard.

"I've no doubt you'll manage it well enough; you're a strapping youngster," said Rory patronizingly. "Well—I shall leave you to it—for I must be on my way as well—"

"Oh, no, you don't!" Gerard moved rapidly, blocking the exit before Rory could make his escape. "How do you suppose I can fasten that scenery in place all by myself? You'll stay and help me or there'll be no backcloth in *King Lear* tonight!"

Rory scowled but he knew that Gerard was right; the task would require two pairs of hands to carry it out, at the very least . . . And Mr. Maguire would have something to say if Lear's kingdom was not complete when he returned for the first entrance.

Grudgingly, he conceded: "Oh, very well, five minutes, mind . . . But no longer—for I've no wish to find myself sleeping under a haystack tonight!"

Between them, they lugged the long roll of canvas into position and began to string it up as best they could—displaying a lurid and improbable landscape of what appeared to be the pineclad Scottish Highlands in a heavy thunderstorm. Gerard considered privately that it might have passed muster—at a pinch—in *Macbeth,* but it seemed rather out of place in *Lear.* However, since the only other backcloth available was the interior of an elegant drawing room with a chandelier painted overhead, there wasn't much point in worrying about that.

H contented himself with tying off ropes and banging in nails, to get the job finished as quickly as possible.

"Well now . . ." mumbled Rory, with his mouth full of nails. "I suppose this must be a great moment for you—your first night in a leading role, eh?"

"Yes," said Gerard shortly, wishing he would keep quiet.

"But no doubt you're hoping to impress the fair Cordelia with your excellence as a performer?" Rory continued.

"I don't know what you mean . . . Is this rope tight enough?—"

"It'll do." Rory threw a very superficial glance over his shoulder. "What I mean is we all know you've been casting cow-eyed looks at the girl, these past weeks, which I may tell you she completely despises, by the by . . . So let me warn you, you're not likely to make a great deal of impression upon the lady tonight, even if you play the mad scene with such passion that your rags and tatters fall off and you exhibit your privates to the public!"

"I'm getting very tired of that joke by now," said Gerard, between his teeth. "Can't you please give it a rest?"

"Oh, I'm not joking, Mr. Kean—I'm in earnest," Rory protested. "I'm simply telling you for your own good—don't waste your time trying to win Miss Coral Maguire by your manly charms for she ain't interested . . . Quite frankly, young shavers like you, still wet behind the ears, don't appeal to her."

Gerard straightened up, clenching his fists dangerously.

"And what do you mean by that?"

"I mean that I know pretty well what her tastes are when it comes to a tumble between the sheets," smiled Rory, with his chin stuck out aggressively. "For I've been there myself, d'ye see—on several occasions . . ."

"You're a damned liar!" shouted Gerard, and threw himself at his adversary.

This was what Rory had been waiting for, and he was ready for Gerard's onslaught.

As they grappled together, Rory stuck his foot out; Gerard tripped and fell, bringing Rory down with him. They rolled over on the dusty stage, and Rory achieved the upper hand, raining blows upon Gerard's face as he sat astride him.

Desperately, Gerard tried to ward off the flailing fists, and wished he could remember what he had learned in his unsuccessful boxing lessons in the gun room at Rosewood . . . Something about a feint—a defense—and a sudden lunge . . .

With the strength of desperation, he made a wild stab at this maneuver, and caught Rory off balance: landing a straight left to the young man's jaw. Rory rocked back, taken off guard, and Gerard followed up his advantage with a right and another left hook—and had the satisfaction of seeing Rory go backward like a ninepin.

At once, Gerard flung himself upon him before he could draw breath, and they rolled over once again—this time, alas! into the painted wooden flats at the side of the stage.

The whole structure—already uncertainly fastened—swung loose, ripping away from its moorings, and toppling sideways against the backcloth, which was still only half secured.

It descended with a crash that sent a great cloud of dust up from the boards, momentarily choking and blinding both the combatants.

"Jesus . . ." breathed Rory, when he could speak. "Will you look at that? What the devil is old Dermot going to say?"

Appalled by the magnitude of the disaster, they immediately abandoned their differences as they struggled to put things right.

"God help us, we've no time at all—and the old villain will flay us alive if he finds the stage like this . . . Quick—give us a hand here!"

Their fight was forgotten, and they worked together like Trojans, sweating and straining to rebuild the scenery as fast as possible. It was—it had to be—a makeshift job at best, with only two workmen to do the duties of a dozen . . . But at last their efforts were rewarded, and they stepped back, looking up at the re-erected setting, and took a long breath.

"It'll do," pronounced Rory. Then he glanced round at Gerard, standing beside him. "And so will you, I reckon . . ."

"What?" Gerard was almost dazed, and could not take this in for a moment.

"Maybe I had the wrong opinion of you at first . . . You're not such a damned scoundrel as I thought, after all." Rory looked him up and down—and grinned suddenly. "You've got the makings of a glorious black eye there, too—you're going to need a whole lot of grease-paint to cover that up tonight . . . How do I look?"

"Well—your nose is bleeding and you've got a lump the size of a hen's egg on the side of your jaw . . ."

"That's where you punched me, you young swine! God, you swing a fist like a sledgehammer when you really try —it took me completely by surprise, I can tell you!" Rory slapped Gerard on the back. "No hard feelings, eh? Come on—let's go and get washed up, and then I'll buy you a drink . . . I reckon we could both do with one."

In the snug, at the side of the General Store, they swallowed two glasses of home-brewed ale, and then decided to tackle the next problem—finding somewhere to sleep.

"My good man," Rory addressed the black-coated and half-witted potboy who had served their drinks. "Do you know of any lodgings in the neighborhood? This gentleman and I are in need of two rooms for the night."

The potboy shook his head glumly, and made some inarticulate noises that seemed to indicate that all the available accommodation in Cappoquin had already been snapped up by other members of the Maguire company.

"Are you sure? There must be *somewhere* left—come on, boy—think again!" Rory slipped a coin into the lad's hand.

Slowly, a smile broke upon the youngster's face, like the sun rising through thick cloud, and he began to nod. There was, it seemed, one house where they might be welcome after all . . . His old granny lived just up the road, no more than half a mile away . . . She would probably be glad of their company, he told them.

Hopefully, they set out, and after a certain amount of difficulty they found the place; a tiny, tumbledown cottage, huddling under an old oak tree.

Rory knocked at the door, and an elderly lady, whose black woollen shawl threw her silver hair into sharp relief, asked what they wanted.

"Rooms, is it? And who was after telling you I had rooms to let at all? Me grandson Michael . . . ? That Micky, he's soft in the head—you shouldn't have listened to him—I'm a poor lone widow-woman with no one to look after me, and . . ."

She broke off, and seemed to be communing with her thoughts.

"He did say you would have room for us—" suggested Rory.

"Well, so I have, to be sure, but at this very minute . . ." She suddenly made up her mind, and flashed them a smile. "There's just the *one* room, you understand —you wouldn't mind sharing?"

They exchanged glances, and Rory shrugged.

"We've done it before, I suppose we can do it again, if needs must . . . May we see the room, ma'am?"

"Indeed and you cannot, I'm sorry to say—for at this minute it's in such a state I'd be ashamed for you to set eyes on it, so I would . . . But come you back at the end of the evening, and by then I'll have everything spick and span for the two of you . . ."

So with this they had to be content; beggars, indeed, could hardly be choosers. In any case, there was no time to look further—for they were due back at the theatre, for the first performance of *King Lear*.

The next hour or two passed by in a blur to Gerard; he found himself crammed into the dressing room among his fellow actors, disguising the beginnings of a black eye with greasepaint as best he could, and struggling into Edgar's costume—muttering his words under his breath as his cue approached.

He half hoped that Coral might come, as she had done before, to give him a good luck kiss before the play began, but she kept her distance, and when he saw her at the other side of the stage she turned aside, as if deliberately avoiding his eye.

He remembered unhappily what Rory had said, about "tumbling between the sheets," and wondered if it could possibly be true. Then the curtains rattled noisily apart, and the tragedy began to unfold—and he forgot everything else.

Walter had been quite correct; the old building was packed with spectators, and they formed an appreciative audience. Perhaps the language mystified them from time to time, but they caught the gist of the story well enough, and even threw in kindly and helpful comments upon the action.

When Rory, as the illegitimate Edmund, declaimed: *"Now, gods, stand up for bastards!"* they cheered lustily (bastardy was a common condition in these rural areas, and it was not often that they heard themselves spoken of so favorably); and when Goneril and Regan both turned the aging king out into the winter wind and weather, someone shouted:

"Oooh, you're a pair of prize bitches, so y'are!"

(Luckily Mrs. Mountford, who was slightly deaf, took this as a cry of acclaim, and curtsied politely.)

The play was going well, until the storm scene was reached. There stood old Dermot, ranting against the elements at the center of the stage; in the wings, Rory rattled a thunder-sheet and Walter shook a box full of dried peas, to mimic the driving rain.

"Blow winds, and crack your cheeks—!" roared Dermot, striding the stage with awesome majesty. *"You cataracts and hurricanes, spout . . . !"* And he flung himself back, as if fighting against the full force of the storm, clutching at the scenery for support.

It was unfortunate that he should have picked upon the same ramshackle flat that had already been dislodged once by Rory and Gerard. Hastily repaired, and tied up with an improvised series of knotted ropes, the edifice toppled once more—slipped sideways—unhooked the backcloth—and brought down the entire landscape, Scottish Highlands, pine trees and all, with an almighty crash, just as Dermot reached the lines:

"And thou—all-shaking thunder—
Smite flat the thick rotundity o' the world . . ."

And his own thick rotundity was completely blotted out by yet another explosion of dust.

There was a moment of absolute stillness, and then the entire audience rose to their feet, shouting and applauding so loudly that the old building seemed in danger of collapse. Quite simply, it was the best stage effect that Cappoquin had ever seen, and the rustic playgoers were generous in their approval.

It was several minutes before Dermot could make himself heard and several more before the offending scenery could be hauled up and fastened once again; then the old gentleman bowed with enormous dignity, saying:

"With your kind permission, ladies and gentlemen, I will now proceed . . ."

And the show went on.

A long time later—half a lifetime, it seemed to the exhausted Gerard—he and Rory staggered out of the theatre, having given the most triumphant première of *King*

Lear ever known in South-Western Ireland, and having celebrated this feat with several glasses of strong local ale in the dressing room.

"Thank God he never knew who it was that put the scenery up so badly," said Gerard.

"Ah, he's so proud of himself this night, I don't suppose he even remembers what happened," said Rory, then stopped, digging Gerard in the ribs. "Ssh! Look who's there . . ."

Ahead of them was the General Store, and a shaft of lamplight shone out from the open side-door . . . Silhouetted in the doorway stood Coral Maguire, looking out into the night, and waiting.

The light behind her shone through her nightgown, and the thin wrapper she had thrown over her shoulders; although she herself was unaware of it, every curve of her lovely body was thrown up in startling clarity—she might as well have been completely naked.

Rory took a deep breath, and cleared his throat to speak.

"Who's there?" she asked, peering into the darkness. "Is it you, Mr. Kean?"

Gerard glanced uncertainly at Rory, who caught his breath, and whispered: "I'm not here . . . It's you she's waiting for . . . I'll be off to our lodgings, my boy . . . And I wish you the very best of luck."

With that, he slipped away into the shadows and was gone. Gerard advanced cautiously, saying: "Yes, Miss Coral, I'm here . . . Did you want to see me?"

"I hoped I might catch you when you left the theatre. I would have come to the dressing room to find you, but you were drinking with your companions, and well, I did not wish to intrude."

He reached the doorway, and she stood back slightly.

"Can you come inside for one moment? There is something I wish to say to you," she explained.

He needed no second bidding; and she led the way into the little back parlor behind the shop, a stuffy room, crammed with furniture.

"Everyone else has gone to bed but I waited up especially . . . Won't you sit down, Mr. Kean?"

"Call me Gerard, please."

"Very well then, Gerard . . . And you may call me Coral. After all, now we are fellow artistes, there is no need for formality between us, is there?"

"I hope not indeed." Impulsively, he took her hand between his own; she did not pull back, but regarded him with a steady, direct gaze. "What is it you wish to tell me?"

"Simply—that I am sorry if I have been unfair to you, Gerard," she said, carefully. He felt sure that she had been practising this speech; it came out as if it were well-rehearsed. "Since our last unfortunate meeting—you may have noticed that I have been avoiding you."

"I had noticed . . . And I regretted it deeply."

"I'm sorry. Looking back, I realize that you were not altogether in possession of yourself on that occasion and I would like to overlook it and start again—as friends."

"Friends?"

"And colleagues . . . for that is the other thing I must say to you—how very much I admired your performance this evening—"

"Coral, I must interrupt you—I shall always be honored to call myself your colleague, but your friend I can never be . . ."

"What do you mean?"

In reply, he leaned forward, and put one arm around her shoulders, coaxing her a little nearer.

"Friendship is too cold a word for the feeling that I hold for you . . . That feeling is love . . ." He slid both hands behind her, drawing her toward him, and added: "I think I loved you from the first moment I saw you . . . And I know that I will love you until the day I die, dearest Coral."

She felt herself grow weak; the old, seductive power was working upon her, and she knew that she was falling under its spell. Desperately, she tried to control herself; this wasn't at all the way that she had intended their meeting to develop . . . And yet had she, secretly, in her heart, expected something like this to happen?

She had told herself over and over during the evening that she must make an effort to bridge the gap between them—so they could live and work together in future, without constraint—and she hoped they might forget the past and begin again, like two sensible people . . .

But who cared about being sensible, when his hands were upon her, and she could feel the heady excitement of his body pressing close against her, and the rough, male aroma of his skin prickling her nostrils, and his mouth descending upon hers . . .

At this moment she forgot everything—forgot what the nuns had warned her, forgot her mother's advice, even forgot what Rosalie had said . . . She was adrift in a deep, warm sea of love, far out of her depth, and the current of his passion played upon her heedlessly, swaying her this way and that—totally lost and enraptured.

Even when his darting, urgent tongue penetrated her lips, and she submitted joyfully to him—she could think of nothing but the ecstasy of the moment.

Even when the fingers of his right hand travelled across her bosom, slipping within the fragile fabric of her night-gown, stroking her breasts, touching her nipples with such thrilling, intimate touches that her whole being tingled from head to toe . . .

Even then, she could not, would not stop him; she gave herself up to love, and surrendered herself unconditionally, as he kissed her again and again, until her head swam, and she was almost faint with desire.

And then he moved his left hand, under her nightdress and on to her knee and above; inexorably sliding higher yet, along her thigh and higher still . . .

"You filthy, deceitful beast!"

The words were torn from her in a wail of fury, and at the same instant she gave him a box on the ears with such force that he almost fell off the sofa.

"Get out of here, you dirty devil before I call my uncle to you!" she railed at him.

Before he could defend himself, or utter a word of protest, she followed this up by kicking him in the shins, and scrambling to her feet.

"Go on, get out—you—you young *lecher!*" she panted and she ran out of the room and up the narrow staircase.

Fifteen minutes later, Gerard dragged himself up an-

68

other and even narrower staircase; and was shown into the room which he was to share with Rory.

"You'll sleep well tonight, God save you—it's a fine luxurious bed, so it is—the old fella slept here all his life and never knew a minute's illness till the day he died . . ." said their elderly landlady. "And I'll call you in the morning as soon as the sun comes up . . .Good night to you both."

She shut the door behind her, and Gerard gazed unhappily at the prospect before him. A double bed; and Rory was already stretched out in possession of it.

"I know—I don't like it any more than you do, my boy, but there's no help for it . . . It's either double up, or one of us sleeps on the floor—and there's not even a rug to keep the bare boards from striking cold on your bum!" sighed Rory. "Come on—in you get—and hope to God you don't have a habit of snoring."

Uneasily, Gerard stripped down to his nightshirt, and clambered into bed beside him; Rory blew out the candle, and darkness enveloped them.

Gerard shut his eyes, and felt the room rotating slowly beneath him, as if he were on a huge wheel that turned with the motion of the earth . . . Though whether his giddiness arose from the beer he had drunk, or the box on the ears that had set his head spinning, he could not be sure.

Beside him, he heard Rory's heavy breathing, and then Rory's voice asking inquisitively: "She asked you in to say good-night, I suppose?"

"I went in for a few moments, yes . . ." said Gerard, shortly.

"Yes, of course. And then what happened? Did she give you a kiss? A sample of her favors?"

"Oh, drop it, can't you?" Gerard snapped angrily. "It's none of your damn business . . ."

"Which means you didn't get anywhere . . . Well, I can't say I'm surprised—it's happened to the best of us, my boy," sighed Rory. "Even yours truly . . . Personally, I think there's something wrong with the wench!"

"You mean, you didn't—um—tumble between the sheets?"

"No such luck. Did she box your ears? I thought so. I've had a taste of her temper myself before now. They talk about women fighting to defend their honor—but she doesn't just fight . . . It's more like a pitched battle!"

"That's true." In the darkness, Gerard rubbed the side of his face reflectively. "Well—at least I'm not the only one she detests . . . That's some consolation, I suppose."

"Oh, she's the same with everybody. It all goes back to her upbringing, I fancy. The convent school she went to, and the way her mother lectured her; no wonder she has such a hatred for the idea of lovemaking."

"You mean her mother was a pious, respectable woman?"

Rory chuckled. "I wouldn't say that, exactly! Pious, perhaps, but not so respectable, unless you call it respectable to run off with a no-good gypsy tinker, and bear him two daughters without the blessing of the holy church!"

"What? You mean—they—they're not—"

"Legitimate? Not they! When the rogue finally packed up and left her, the wretched woman collapsed; her brother took pity on her and welcomed her back . . . Though he was the only one in the Maguire family to do so, being a bit of a vagabond himself."

"Old Dermot?"

"Of course. He took the girls into his troupe as soon as they were old enough to leave home; and not long after that, the poor mother turned her toes up and was gathered to her eternal rest."

"And that's why Coral is so strong against sin?"

"I've always imagined so. Mind, it didn't work out that way with her sister, though—Rosalie's a very different kettle of fish," mused Rory, and Gerard could tell that he was smiling to himself.

"What do you mean by that? Certainly she seems altogether more easy-going . . ."

"Easy—aye, that's the word for Rosalie. Many's the time I—" Rory caught himself up, and decided to change the subject. "But we can't lie awake all night talking. We'd better get some sleep."

70

"I suppose you're right. Anyway, thank you for telling me about Coral and Rosalie. It's given me plenty to think about."

"Much good may it do you." Rory rolled on to his side, and there was a long silence which he broke at last, saying irritably: "I need to take a piss . . . That's what comes of drinking so much ale instead of sticking to good honest whisky."

He roused himself, then stopped to ask:

"When the old biddy showed you up, did you happen ask her where the jakes is in this house . . . ? No, no more did I—halfway down the garden, if I know anything . . . Maybe I'll just open the window and—"

"There might be a chamber-pot under the bed," Gerard suggested.

"A good thought—I'll investigate."

Gerard heard Rory scramble out of bed and drop to his knees, groping beneath the counterpane.

"No—I can't find any chinaware—nothing but a great wooden box, an open box, what the devil's in here, I wonder?"

A short pause, and then a strangulated exclamation followed:

"Mother of God! Light the candle, quickly! There's a dead body laid out under here!"

Seconds later, in the fitful light from the candle held in Gerard's shaking hand, they saw the serene features of a very old man, lying peacefully in his open coffin, with pennies upon his eyelids.

"She *said* it used to be the old fella's bed . . ." gasped Rory. "No wonder the potboy was all in black —this must have been his grandda!"

(5)

Undress Rehearsal

This proved to be no more than the truth; the old man had passed away only a few hours before they knocked at the cottage door and his widow, realizing that she could earn a few extra shillings, had made this hasty re-arrangement in order to accommodate them.

It was one of Gerard's first lessons in the hard economic facts of life; and it brought home to him how narrow the borderline was, which separated a bare sufficiency from starvation, for most of the people in this remote corner of Ireland.

By the following night, the coffin had been decently laid to rest, and a simple wake had been celebrated so the two young actors were able to sleep in their bed without any unforeseen company . . . But it was an incident which stayed deeply rooted in Gerard's memory for a long, long time.

And yet, although these rustic villagers lived on the edge of penury, they were all eager to spend their hard-won savings on visits to the play: *King Lear* ran its course, and was succeeded by a revival of *The Merchant* and the good folk of Cappoquin flocked in to see these dramas of life, death and high romance, night after night, with the utmost enthusiasm.

Spring came early to the south-west that year, and soon the hedgerows were bright with primrose and celandine, and not long after, the copses and thickets along the river were shimmering with bluebells, like a haze of wood-smoke between the trees.

It was warm enough to take rowboats out on the water; for the makeshift theatre stood right upon the river's edge, and several of the younger members of the company "borrowed" the small craft that lay moored up against the towpath.

One sunny afternoon, when rehearsals were over (Dermot had decided to add another piece to the repertoire, and was setting the actors to work on *Romeo and Juliet),* Gerard was loitering by the water, playing ducks and drakes with a handful of flat pebbles, watching them skim across the surface in a series of long hops.

"Well done!" approved a soft husky voice and he spun on his heel to find Rosalie a few yards away, watching him.

Coral stood a pace behind her sister, unsmiling; she remarked in a careless, off-hand manner: "Oh, yes, Mr. Kean is very adept at childish games, I'm sure."

Gerard shifted from one foot to the other, saying: "I was merely passing the time . . . I have nothing to do, until the performance this evening."

A shout of laughter echoed back clearly across the water, where a boat-load of actors were setting off on a fishing trip with more optimism than experience to guide them.

"You should have taken a rod and set out with your companions. You might have landed a salmon for supper," said Rosalie.

"Poaching, you mean? Yes, I'm sure Mr. Kean would be most proficient at that, too," Coral agreed pleasantly.

"I didn't feel like making one of the party," Gerard explained, then added daringly: "Unless, of course, you two ladies would care to take a turn on the river? I would be very happy to act as your boatman."

Rosalie looked at Coral, and said quickly: "Why don't you go, Coral? I should really get back to our rooms and comb out Uncle Dermot's wig before tonight."

"No! Thank you—I have no wish to accompany Mr. Kean . . . I have many other little tasks which will keep me busy, I assure you: I've no time for such a hazardous enterprise."

"Hazardous? You need have no fear, Coral, I'm pretty expert at managing a boat, you can trust me . . ."

"Trust you, Mr. Kean? . . . I think not."

With that, Coral turned and set off toward the General Store, without looking back.

Seeing Gerard's disappointment, Rosalie said impulsively: "Cheer up, Gerard, don't look so crestfallen . . . I've changed my mind; Uncle's Shylock ringlets can wait! I'll come with you—if I may."

So they embarked, and Gerard, true to his word, steered the rowboat skilfully out from the shore, in the opposite direction from that taken by the fishing party.

Upstream, the Blackwater grew narrower, and as they wound their way along the twists and turns of the river, the banks overshadowed them, thickset with tall trees. Rosalie pulled her shawl closer about her; there was a chilly breeze coming off the water, and she pointed to the opposite bank.

"There's a patch of sunlight! Why don't you pull in over there and rest for a moment for I'm sure you must be quite tired after your exertions."

Gerard followed the suggestion, and made the boat fast alongside a clump of willows that hung over the bank, in a pale-green curtain of young leaves.

"That's much more comfortable: it's warmer here, in the sun," said Rosalie, leaning back at her ease.

"Why, did you feel cold?"

"A little . . . But I'm very cozy now, I assure you. We're sheltered here, out of the breeze."

"I'm sorry, I hadn't noticed; rowing is warm work," Gerard explained, shifting the oars.

"Take your jacket off if you're uncomfortable," said Rosalie.

74

"May I?" He began to struggle out of the sleeves awkwardly.

"Of course . . ." She watched him, smiling, then said more quietly: "You don't look as if you are enjoying this little expedition very much, you know . . . I'm afraid I'm a poor substitute for my sister aren't I?"

"No—not at all—" Gerard started to protest.

"Don't pretend . . . I know very well that you've lost your heart to Coral, and she won't have you . . . I am sorry—I really am."

Gerard sighed: "I suppose every one in the company knows . . . I've made a fool of myself, haven't I?"

"Not at all. Come and sit here by me, and tell me all about it."

Rosalie slid across to one side of the boat, rocking it gently on the shallow water; it rocked more wildly as Gerard accepted the invitation and moved up to join her.

"There's not much point in talking about it really, for I love her, and she doesn't love me and that's an end to it," he said, wriggling to make a space for himself upon the narrow seat.

He was suddenly very aware of the warmth of her body through her thin print dress, as he squeezed close to her and the magical, musky scent of her skin.

"Poor Gerard . . . Coral's always had a very decided will of her own; it will take a patient man to win her over."

To make more room, she slipped one arm behind him, and it seemed quite natural for him to do likewise; so they found themselves sitting with their arms around one another's waists almost as a matter of course.

"Can't you give me some advice on how I should behave? How I might try to change her attitude toward me?"

"I wish I could . . . I can only say that you will need perseverance . . . 'If at first you don't succeed'— well, you know the old adage as well as I do."

"But to try and *fail*—to fail as miserably as I have done . . . I think I have made her hate me forever, and it's all my own fault," Gerard confessed. "Once—twice— she has let me kiss her—but on both occasions I have

75

lost my head; her kisses were so intoxicating, I completely forgot myself and got carried away—I mean—I—oh, it's hard to explain . . ."

"I think I know what you mean," Rosalie assured him gravely.

"I expect you must consider me to be a very contemptible—very immoral person," he said, unable to meet her steady gaze.

"I don't consider you to be anything of the kind," she said. "I understand your feelings very well indeed and I feel sorry you should be in such torment."

"That's how it is exactly—*torment* . . ." he agreed quickly. "Wanting her—all the time—and knowing it's hopeless."

"Poor Gerard," she said again, and her arm tightened about him, drawing him closer still: her rose-red lips came to meet his mouth, and she kissed him—gently at first, then with more and more ardor, as sympathy was overtaken by a more positive emotion.

Gerard clung to her, welcoming this unexpected tenderness, and yet fearing that she would soon repel his advances and draw away.

But she did not: their kisses redoubled, and he found himself exploring the soft contours of her throat, her shoulders, her full, ripe breasts. He hardly dared to breathe, as he let his hand travel down her slender waist, and on to the treasures of her hips—her thighs . . . With reckless abandon, he found his way beneath her long skirts, and proceeded toward the most secret places of her body, expecting at every moment that she would say "No—stop—you must not—"

Instead, he encountered no resistance, and when he looked into her eyes, she was smiling at him, and whispering:

"Yes . . . Yes, Gerard . . . Oh, yes . . ."

Even then, he could scarcely believe she meant what she said; as he faltered, uncertainly, she added on the softest breath:

"You need someone, my dear, and so do I . . ."

With loving care, she unfastened the belt of his breeches, and eased his restraining clothes from him; with equal skill, she brought him to a pitch of desire, and then when he could contain himself no longer, she gathered him in her arms, and they came together in a wild onrush of passion that set the little boat rocking so violently that it almost seemed they must capsize . . .

Afterward, as they lay together, drawing long, tranquil breaths of satisfaction, she ruffled his hair with one lazy forefinger and said:

"This was a wonderful interlude, for both of us . . . But you know, don't you, that it can never happen again . . . For you love Coral, and although I think you are a dear, delightful boy, I don't love you . . . So no one must ever know, and it will never be repeated . . . But don't forget this afternoon, Gerard . . . Or me."

"I will remember you, always;" he said truthfully.

"Yes . . . Now let us dress ourselves, and make ourselves respectable." She gave a low, throaty chuckle as she cast an eye over his shamelessly dishevelled appearance: "And then you shall row us back to the theatre—for it would never do if we were late for the play!"

Soon after this unlooked-for and altogether unique incident, Dermot Maguire announced to the company that they had exhausted the potential box office capacity of Cappoquin and the immediate neighborhood. It was time to move on again; along the River Blackwater, to the little fishing port of Youghal . . . (Pronounced, Gerard soon discovered, "Yawl.") The coast was hardly more than ten miles away, and this was one of their easiest journeys.

A pretty one, too, following the curves of the river until at last they could smell the tang of salt in the air, and saw the gulls wheeling and swooping overhead, their white wings flashing in the morning sunlight.

Youghal was a dignified town, with a long history stretching back to Tudor times: Sir Walter Raleigh, it was said, had lived here; it was even reported that he had brought the very first potatoes back to the town after his voyage to America, and cultivated them in his garden at Myrtle Grove.

Nowadays Youghal was busy and colorful, with its fleet of fishing boats along the harbor wall; and the main street was thronged with well-to-do merchants and their wives, together with a number of families from the big houses round about, who had come in to visit the shops and do their marketing.

Old Dermot rubbed his hands in anticipation: "We'll do very well here, I'm sure of it . . . *Romeo* will be a famous success, and take the town by storm."

For the old actor, *Romeo* was something of a respite; after his labors in the *Merchant* and *Lear*, he only appeared as Friar Lawrence, giving himself a comparatively carefree evening. Rory, of course, was to play Romeo, opposite Coral's Juliet, and Gerard was being coached in the role of Mercutio.

One small problem was that Gerard had no experience of stage-fights; he had never handled a sword in his life. However, Dermot said he'd very soon pick up the rudiments of the art, and told Rory to give him a few lessons.

Thus it was that, on their first free afternoon in Youghal, the two young men repaired to the flat sandy beach which stretched for five miles beyond the town, to a spot where they could practice undisturbed.

Stripped to the waist, with two willow branches, which Rory had plucked from the hedges along the way to serve as foils, they faced one another on the wide, empty sands, and Gerard commenced his first lesson in swordsmanship.

It was a slow process; the various positions had to be learned by heart, and time and again they rehearsed the unvarying sequence—"Thrust, parry, lunge"—while time and again Gerard made some mistake or other, and the whole lengthy business had to be repeated.

Gradually he began to improve, and eventually they were able to speed up the whole procedure, until their carefully-rehearsed ritual sprang to life at last, and they began to fight with gusto.

"Have at you—!" yelled Rory, with a new light blazing in his eye, as Gerard automatically parried a blow and deflected it. "Ah, you would, would you—take that—!"

The willow branches danced and flashed like duelling whips, and suddenly Gerard realized that Rory was no longer rehearsing—this battle was in deadly earnest!

He stepped back a pace, wary of the flying tip of the

oncoming rod—and Rory pressed home his advantage, landing a swift, stinging blow across his upper chest that left a thin red weal.

"Hey—hold on—steady—" Gerard protested indignantly; but he could see from the fixed expression on Rory's face that there was no stopping him now.

He fought back defiantly, and recovered some of the ground he had lost; but this only seemed to inflame Rory's temper.

"I'll have you begging for mercy before I've done with you—" he panted, lunging again and again; and Gerard was forced to retreat once more.

By now they had moved some way down the beach, and were at the sea's edge, but still Rory drove them on until Gerard felt the shock of cold waves breaking over his ankles. Still backing, trying to dodge sideways to avoid another painful lash, he slipped and fell—and instantly, as he tumbled back into the foaming surf, Rory flung himself upon him. Dropping the weapon he had been wielding, he made for Gerard's throat, both hands spread wide—

"For God's sake, what's wrong with you?" Gerard gasped, feeling Rory's powerful fingers close around his windpipe.

And then a huge wave broke over them, and they were both submerged in a rush of icy water.

As the undertow ebbed away, Rory scrambled to his feet, half-laughing, half-embarrassed.

"Sorry, I didn't intend us to take a cold bath . . ." he spluttered, shaking the water from his hair.

"What on earth was the matter? You nearly throttled me!" Gerard followed him back on to the sandy beach.

"I know . . . I couldn't help it—I—I suddenly saw red . . ."

A few minutes later, when they had stripped off their wet clothes and spread them out to dry—drying their own muscular bodies at the same time, with arms and legs outstretched like starfish on the beach—Rory tried to explain: "It happens to me sometimes . . . I should have warned you. When I start to fight—even a sham fight, something clicks inside my head, and, I don't know how

79

it is, I feel I have to go on—and *win* . . . I *have* to win, at all costs, you see . . . It's as if there were some demon within me, driving me on . . ."

Gerard rubbed some sand from his face with the back of his wrist, and said:

"It's as well for me that we got a ducking then, for I believe that demon of yours would have half-killed me, if the wave hadn't stopped the fight."

When they returned to town at last, they made their way to the Market Hall, where the Maguire company were to give their performances; and Gerard was surprised to find Rosalie and Coral on the stage, engaged in a musical rehearsal.

Coral was singing, in a clear, sweet soprano, while Rosalie accompanied her upon an old harpsichord.

"What's this?" he asked Rory. "There are no songs in *Romeo,* surely?"

Dermot emerged from behind a pile of benches, and cut in: "It's by way of an additional divertissement between the acts . . . This is a town full of cultivated gentlefolk—a song recital always goes down well with this type of audience, and my girls are so very accomplished . . ."

At this point the music came to an end, and Gerard applauded politely, saying: "I did not know you had these hidden talents, ladies."

"Praise from Mr. Kean is praise indeed," said Coral, without deigning to look at him.

"Oh, they're musical prodigies, no doubt of that . . . And a few songs break up the sad business of the play very nicely . . . It makes what you might call a little *interlude* . . ."

At this word, Gerard glanced swiftly at Rosalie but she was busy turning over a pile of music, and appeared not to be listening.

"While you've been practising your scales, we've been practising our swordplay," said Rory, jumping up on to the stage.

"You look as if you'd been rolling on the beach—your clothes are a disgrace," said Coral.

80

"Ah, that's because we had a minor accident, and fell into the sea!" Rory explained. "But it's only salt water; it won't do us any harm."

"You've been for a dip in the ocean?" Rosalie looked up eagerly. "Oh—I wish we could go swimming, don't you, Coral? I dearly love the sea, and we so rarely get the chance."

"Well-brought-up young ladies don't indulge in such tomboy tricks," snorted old Dermot, from the back of the hall— and took himself off to the box office, where he had been busy with the playbills for the forthcoming première.

"Look here—why not?" asked Rory abruptly, once the old man was out of earshot. "I tell you what—why don't we all go for a picnic on the sands, on our next free day? We'll take a basket of victuals and a bottle of wine, and have a little holiday for once—Just the four of us!"

"I'd like nothing better," said Gerard; then looked at the two girls. "But—how do the others feel about it?"

"A bathing party?" Rosalie's eyes were sparkling. "I'd love to! Oh, Coral—do say yes!"

"We'll be very prim and proper, I swear it," Rory urged her. "Nothing that could raise a blush to the most fastidious feminine cheek— I give you my word."

Coral's thoughts were racing: she longed to go with them—she knew that if she refused, they would go without her, and she would sit in the hotel all day, wishing she had not been so foolish . . . Of course it did sound extremely unladylike—a bathing party, in mixed company . . . But at the same time it sounded so attractive; and besides Rosalie would be there to chaperon her, after all . . .

"Very well," she said at last, with an effort to appear casual. "I don't really mind one way or the other. If you want to go, Rosalie—I suppose I might as well come along."

"Splendid!" Rory approved heartily. "And as a special treat, to round the day off—when the play is over, Gerard and I will take you both to supper at the hotel, how's that?"

"You're very generous, all of a sudden," said Rosalie. "I'm quite overwhelmed by such lavish hospitality—how can we refuse?"

So it was arranged; and on the first possible day, when the sun shone from a cloudless blue sky, and all the conditions seemed favorable, the little party of four set out for the beach.

Coral tried to seem calm, and kept up a flow of small-talk as they walked across the wide expanse of sand, but secretly she was feeling nervous and strangely excited. Gerard carried the picnic basket, while Rory had a huge carpet bag, stuffed with towels and sheets, borrowed (unofficially) from the hotel where they were staying. The sheets, Coral knew, were for them to wrap themselves up in, from head to foot, after their dip in the sea; partly to shelter them from the brisk sea winds, but also—and most importantly—to shield them modestly from one another's gaze.

She glanced back over her shoulder; the town lay far behind them, and there was nothing and no one in sight . . . Nothing but the tracks of four pairs of footprints on the sandy shore.

"There are some rocks just ahead of us," said Rosalie at the same moment. "I don't think we need go any further—do you?"

Promptly, the two men set down their luggage, and Rory spread one towel for the girls to sit upon, like a rug.

"Shall we bathe first and take our lunch afterward?" Rosalie asked.

Quickly, Coral broke in: "Oh, let's eat first—I'm quite hungry—"

"You'll have an even better appetite after your dip in the briny," said Rory. "Besides—it's a great mistake to go swimming too soon after a meal."

"I'm not in any special hurry—" began Coral, in a small voice; but Rosalie overruled her:

"No, Rory's quite right—swim first, and eat later," she said. "Come along, let's get undressed."

The system was very simple: the girls retreated a little higher up the beach with their backs to the sea, and began slowly to divest themselves of their garments.

"Give us a shout when you're in the water!" Rosalie called, over her shoulder.

"And don't you dare to turn round and play Peeping Tom!" Coral added.

The two men moved down by some small rocks at the water's edge and swiftly peeled off their clothes: then they ran into the sea, and swam out until they were some way from the shore.

"All right now—you can come on in!" called Rory, at the top of his voice.

Coral shivered—though whether she was cold, or for some other reason, she could not tell. Slowly, she turned, and found Rosalie—also completely naked—standing beside her, waving enthusiastically to the two boys, far out to sea.

"Rosalie—how can you!" Coral exclaimed, profoundly shocked, crossing her arms to cover her own body as well as she could.

"Oh, don't be such a goose—they're too far off to see anything—and even if they did, what does it matter? We're here to enjoy ourselves for once—do stop fussing!"

Rosalia ran down into the water, lifting her feet high like a young deer. Once into the waves, she threw herself full-length, splashing and calling: "Come along—it's heavenly!"

More slowly, Coral followed: the water struck very cold, and she hesitated, up to her knees, reluctant to go further.

Then she saw Gerard—a hundred yards away, but she knew that he was looking at her . . . Instantly, she plunged into the icy waves, to hide herself from his eyes.

The shock took her breath away for a moment, and then she saw Rosalie spashing beside her, and suddenly felt a thrill of intense happiness and excitement.

With a crow of delight, she spluttered: "You're right —it *is*—it's simply heavenly—!"

"I'm going to swim further out—it's too shallow here," said Rosalie, and Coral followed her.

Very soon, she noticed that Rory and Gerard were turning back to meet them; and again she felt a spasm of

—what was it? Fear? Excitement? Or some strange emotion she could not identify?

She tried to reassure herself; only her head was protruding above the water—it was really perfectly proper . . . She glanced at Gerard as he approached, his strong arms thrashing through the waves, and tried to behave nonchalantly.

"The water's cold, but refreshing—don't you agree?" she asked.

He stopped swimming, only a few feet away, and stood upright, with the water reaching his chest. His eyes were fixed—not upon her face, but at some point a little lower down, as he replied smilingly:

"It's quite perfect—cool, and clear."

Clear . . . ? She glanced down, and found that she was not so well-protected from his gaze as she had imagined. Quickly, she moved away, turning her back on him— only to find herself face to face with Rory, who suddenly surfaced only a few inches away, puffing and blowing after an underwater swim.

"Enjoying yourself?" he asked, when he recoverd his breath.

"I—why—yes, I am!" she replied, and suddenly realized that this was the truth. She was enjoying herself so much—nothing else seemed to matter. "Rosalie—I'll challenge you to a race—to the rocks and back!" she exclaimed happily, and hurled herself forward into the water once more.

They struck out for the rocks, side by side, and Coral's slighter, more agile figure was just taking the lead when she stopped short.

They were being watched.

Seated upon the rocks was a stranger; a young man with a smart bottle-green tailcoat, and a shining black tophat. He had pointed moustaches, and a small, curling beard—almost as black and as oily (although a hundred times more fashionable) as the beard Dermot wore as Shylock . . . And he was watching the two nude girls swimming toward him, with obvious pleasure.

When they stopped swimming, and their feet touched the bottom of the sea bed, they began to stand up instinctively—only to realize the they were now in such shallow water that they were scarcely waist deep. Immediately, they both plunged down into the sea once more, in outraged modesty.

The stranger smiled politely and raised his tophat in an elegant, ironic gesture.

"What are you doing here staring at us? Go away!" Rosalie began angrily.

"I was admiring the beauties of nature," said the gentleman, in a marked foreign accent which Coral could not identify at first.

"How dare you!" she exclaimed. "Have you no manners!"

"What's all this? Who's this spying on us?" asked Rory, and Coral looked round to find that he and Gerard had followed them in to shore.

"Don't you see you're not welcome here?" continued Rosalie.

"I'm so sorry—am I spoiling your little party?" the stranger asked, smiling again. "Forgive me, please."

"You take yourself off—go on, sling your hook, or you'll be sorry!" said Rory threateningly. "Come on, Gerard, let's see the swine off."

Completely undeterred by their own nudity, he and Gerard began to walk up out of the water, advancing upon the intruder. Coral had one hasty glimpse of Gerard's body as he emerged, his handsome chest, the light hair on his legs, now darkened by the sea water that clung to him; the still-darker bush of hair at the base of his stomach, and his lusty manhood swinging between his legs.

Quickly, she turned her back, gazing out to sea, and tried to blot the image from her mind.

"All right—all right—I am going . . . Do not trouble yourselves, gentlemen—I did not realize that this was a private beach," said the newcomer, gathering himself up and retreating diplomatically. "And, my dear young ladies, pray forgive this intrusion . . . My apologies to you both and my profound admiration!"

"Damn his impudence," growled Rory, watching him go. "I'd have liked to give him a good thrashing . . ."

"Well no harm's done," said Rosalie, with a tiny smile. "And you must admit, he *was* rather gallant . . . In his way . . ."

"Gallant?" snorted Gerard. "Those Frenchies are all the same—you can't trust the villains . . ."

(French! Coral realized at once that Gerard was right; that was why the accent had sounded faintly familiar—one of the oldest nuns in the convent, Mother St. Denis, had come from Paris originally.)

"I bow to your superior knowledge," said Rosalie respectfully. "But now, might I suggest you go in search of some towels, gentlemen? For the air is growing quite chilly and you are both very much exposed . . ."

Gerard and Rory looked at one another and realized how true this observation was; reddening, they both mumbled apologies, and set off hastily up the beach.

The rest of the day passed pleasantly and uneventfully; decorously wrapped in sheets, like guests at an ancient Roman banquet, the four swimmers made short work of their picnic. The bottle of wine was passed from hand to hand, and they all became happily relaxed.

"What a pity we can't stay here forever . . ." mused Rosalie, lying back upon the warm sand, on one elbow.

"Couldn't we come here every day?" Coral asked.

"We could rehearse here, just as well as in the Market Hall, I'm sure!"

"An undress rehearsal, perhaps?" suggested Gerard, tentatively and even Coral smiled.

The tedious business of getting back into everyday clothes was accomplished with a certain amount of hilarity; indeed, when Rory playfully tossed Gerard's breeches over the rocks, so that he had to go scrambling after them in his drawers, with his shirt tails flapping, Coral even unbent sufficiently to giggle a little.

When they returned to town, in time to play the evening performance at the Market Hall, the two young men and the two young ladies parted on the best of terms. Everything seemed set fair for a very enjoyable supper party after the play.

Then, quite out of the blue, everything changed.

When Coral and Rosalie came offstage after the final

curtain, they found Mrs. Mountford waiting for them in the dressing room, wreathed in smiles and carrying a huge bouquet of expensive flowers on either arm.

"These were handed in for you both five minutes ago, my dears," she explained. "Addressed to 'the Misses Maguire'—one each!"

Flattered and surprised, the girls scanned the accompanying cards, and read two identical messages: "Apologies and admiration . . . May I make amends by giving you both dinner tonight?" And the messages were signed with the initials: "P. la R."

As a general rule, the girls would never consent to accept any invitation from a total stranger, particularly a stranger as bold and shameless as the Frenchman upon the seashore.

When Dermot knocked and entered, they were still discussing the foreigner's effrontery; but to their surprise, their uncle seemed unperturbed.

"Yes, yes—I know all about it—I've just this minute been introduced to the gentleman, at the front of house."

"You know all about him spying on us?" Coral began, but Rosalie swiftly nudged her and interrupted:

"Uncle means he knows about the *invitation* . . ." (For old Dermot would have been very shocked if he had discovered that his nieces had ventured out in a mixed swimming party.) "Who is this gentleman, pray? Where does he come from?"

"From Paris, I'm told—though heaven alone knows what he's doing in this part of the world. Still, he's a great connoisseur of the arts, he tells me, and what's more, he's a personal friend of some of the local dignitaries . . . Why, he's even been loaned the use of a suite of rooms in the old Clock Gate, right in the middle of town!"

The girls stared at one another: he must indeed be a visitor of some importance for the Clock Gate was the most imposing building in Youghal; four stories high, it straddled the narrow main street, surmounted by an imposing clock, lantern and weather vane.

"And he's admired your performances tonight so very much, especially your song recital, that he's insisting upon paying his respects, and taking you both to dinner. Well, since he's obviously a person of quality, there can be no harm in that, so I've given my permission . . . In any case, as long as you're both together, there's safey in numbers, so they say."

"Oh, but Uncle, we promised Gerard and Rory—" Coral tried to explain.

Dermot waved this aside: "Pooh, those young rascals can entertain you at any time . . . You don't get invited out by Monsieur Paul la Roche every night of the week! Besides, if you make yourselves pleasant to the gentleman, and he speaks favorably of you to all his friends and acquaintances in town—it's sure to be very good for business."

There was no escaping it; the girls made themselves ready, and then went to break the news to Rory and Gerard, who were waiting for them backstage.

Rory was immediately angry; how dare they break their promise and for the sake of that peeping, prying Frenchie, of all people? For two pins he'd go round to see the man and call him out for a duel.

Gerard was no happier about it, but he realized that there was no use in fighting against the inevitable; he contented himself by hoping they might postpone their own engagement until another evening, and concluded: "Come along, Rory, old fellow, let's accept our defeat gracefully, and I'll buy you a glass of good Irish whisky."

"Defeat? Never!" glared Rory, but the mention of whisky mollified him a little, and, he suffered himself to be led away, still grumbling.

Half an hour later, the girls presented themselves, as requested, at the Clock Gate, and were shown upstairs by a manservant to a nobly-appointed dining room upon the first floor.

Their host was awaiting them with every sign of impatience, and now he bowed low and kissed their hands, saying how enchanted he was that they should deign to honor him so.

Another servant took their wraps; a third poured glasses of wine and very soon after, they were seated at the long oval dining table, which reflected the crystal and silverware on its dark polished surface.

"I hope you can find it in your hearts to forgive me for my boorish behavior this morning," said Paul la Roche, with fervent sincerity, looking from one to the other.

He had thick black lashes which ringed his melting brown eyes, and both girls felt it was impossible to withhold forgiveness from him.

"I had been strolling along the shore, and I suddenly espied two visions in the water, at first I truly believed the old legend had come true, and that I had stumbled upon two beautiful mermaidens . . . Until those two angry mer-*men* came to your rescue!"

The girls smiled, despite themselves, as the Frenchman told his own version of the story: in retrospect, Rory and Gerard did appear a little ridiculous plunging out of the water so truculently, in a high dudgeon and a state of nature.

"And of course at that time I had no idea who you might be . . . It was not until this evening, at the play, that I learned the truth, that my two lovely mermaids were none other than the brilliant and famous Maguire sisters!"

"Famous?" Rosalie repeated. "You mean you'd already heard of us?"

"Hasn't the report of your beauty and talent spread throughout the whole of Ireland?" asked Paul la Roche —a remark which appeared to answer her question but did not. "Ah, here is the first course of our little repast . . . Allow me to wish you both *bon appetit.*"

The meal was perfection; from the soup, to the fish, to the roast duck, each and every dish was exquisitely cooked, and Coral complimented their host upon such excellence.

"You are too kind," smiled Monsieur la Roche. "I shall pass on your comments to Henri, my chef . . . He travels everywhere with me, you see."

"You must be a very important man," said Coral, feeling a little light-headed, after a day of such high spirits.

89

"Do tell us who you are, and what you are doing here in Ireland?"

"Oh, my dear young lady, there is nothing to tell . . . I am a traveller, nothing more. I enjoy exploring new places, meeting new friends, discovering unexpected treasures. As I have done tonight," he added, with a gallant inclination of the head to each of the girls.

As they began on the last course—a water-ice, delicately flavored with peaches and decorated with luscious hothouse grapes, they heard a faint, discordant note from the street below: two late revellers on their way home, raising their voices in song . . .

"Let the toast pass—drink to the lass—
I warrant she'll prove an excuse for the glass . . ."

Paul la Roche smiled faintly, and shrugged:

"Someone else has been celebrating, it seems, but not too wisely."

The girls exchange glances; they recognized those inharmonious duettists only too well . . .

After the meal came the coffee; and after coffee, M. la Roche suggested charmingly that they might feel more comfortable in the withdrawing room on the floor above. They mounted the carpeted stairway to the second story, and found a cozy boudoir awaiting them—so softly and luxuriously furnished that it had an almost feminine air about it.

Their host motioned them to a long curving sofa, plumping up two velvet cushions for their extra comfort; and when they were seated, one at either end, he surprised them slightly by taking his place between them, in the middle.

"There! That is very pleasant, is it not?" he asked. "Now we can sit and talk at our ease."

As he spoke, he stretched out left and right, and once more kissed their hands in turn.

"Such a wealth of beauty surrounds me—I am quite at a loss," he commented disarmingly. "You have heard of the tale of the stupid ass, midway between two bundles of hay? They say the wretched creature was so tortured by indecision—he starved to death . . ."

Rosalie lowered her eyes, very conscious that he had

not released her hand, but was pressing it slightly as he addressed her.

"I am quite sure that *you* would never allow yourself to starve, under any circumstances, m'sieur," she said demurely.

"You know, you are absolutely right?" He chuckled, and squeezed her hand again. "I do not believe I should . . ."

Then he turned to Coral, and began: "Tell me, mam'-selle, do you also think I am the sort of man who—"

And at that moment, there was yet another interruption.

They heard feet pounding up the stairs, and a swift knock at the door, followed by the murmur of muffled voices.

"Nom de dieu—what is it?" cried la Roche, rather vexed.

The door opened, and the first manservant appeared, saying:

"Pardon me, sir, but there's a gentleman here; he's asking to speak to the young ladies—I told him you did not wish to be disturbed—"

Behind him, a booming voice said majestically:

"Stuff and nonsense, man—this is a matter of urgency!"

And old Dermot Maguire stepped into the room.

"Monsieur Maguire, I am delighted to see you again," began M. la Roche, with more courtesy than frankness.

"I'm sorry to trouble you, sir, but I must take my girls home—we've got work to do tonight!"

"Work? *Tonight?*" Coral and Rosalie rose to their feet. "What do you mean, uncle?"

"Re-casting—re-rehearsing—new lines to learn, new moves—new everything . . . We've got to turn to and start on *Romeo* all over again!"

"Why? What's happened?" asked Rosalie.

"Those young fools, O'Malley and Kean, went out carousing, and got themselves into a tavern brawl . . . And the upshot is, Rory O'Malley's acquired a broken arm, and won't be in any state to fight a duel tomorrow night!"

"Oh, no, what are you going to do?"

"We'll have to put Gerard Kean in to replace him—there's no alternative . . . So you must come back to the hotel at once; Coral—you'll have to sit up all night if necessary, to teach him the role."

Coral felt her cheeks flaming, and felt sure that everyone must notice her discomfiture . . .

To rehearse—to enact Juliet to Gerard's Romeo—to play romantic scenes together, without ever betraying her innermost feelings . . . If he ever discovered how much she loved him—how could she possibly endure it?

(6)

Exits and Entrances

The rest of that night passed like a dream for Coral; at
moments, a happy dream, almost too exquisite to bear
and yet sometimes it turned into nightmare, as she strove
to fight off the overwhelming temptation of Gerard's
charm, Gerard's vibrant personality, Gerard's physical
presence.

As the long hours ticked by, and night turned into
morning, Coral rehearsed Juliet's love scenes with her
new Romeo, over and over again.

They sat in the little parlor of Youghal's staid, family
hotel, and the impassioned speeches rang out incongru-
ously against the heavy panelled walls, and the faded
etchings of forgotten memorials.

Gerard sat at one side of the center tables, with the
copy of the play before him, desperately striving to be-
labor his fuddled brain and commit the lines to memory:
Coral sat opposite—the width of the table, covered by a
plum-colored chenille cloth, between them.

She tried not to look into his face, or let their glances

meet, as she recited those heartbreaking words, over and over again:

"My bounty is as boundless as the sea,
My love is deep; the more I give to thee,
The more I have—for both are infinite . . ."

And Gerard stumbled and stammered as he responded with the answering speech:

". . . I am afeared,
Being in night, all this is but a dream . . ."

As he spoke, he fixed his gaze upon her, and at that instant she looked straight into his eyes and held her breath, certain that the pounding of her heart, the depth of her feeling for him, must be pitifully obvious.

And yet, almost wanting it to be so; almost wishing that they could throw aside all play-acting and be honest with one another. Why could she not say simply: "I love you, Gerard—I'm yours," throwing all caution to the winds, and giving herself to him entirely?

She knew why not. She knew she could not trust him, because she could not trust herself. Once she dropped all barriers and became completely defenseless, she would be at his mercy; she knew that his arms would be about her, his hands everywhere upon her, his tongue fervently at her lips, and . . . And other intimacies she did not dare to contemplate.

Torn by her longing for him, and her instinctive fear of the consequences, she tried to put all such thoughts out of her mind; but it was far from easy, as she found herself repeating in a trembling voice:

"I have no joy of this contract tonight,
It is too rash, too unadvised, too sudden . . ."

At this point, the door opened, and they were joined by an unexpected arrival—Rory O'Malley, with his right arm tied up in a sling, and the whiff of Irish whisky still hanging about him.

"Back already?" Gerard asked, pleased for an excuse to break off from his studies. "I thought that doctor would keep you at his surgery half the night."

"He did . . . It's nearly three o'clock already," said Rory. "And he's put me through hell itself, if you'll pardon the expression, Coral, but at least he's set the bone

94

and put it in a splint with half a mile of bandages, and God knows what besides. I'm trussed up like a fowl ready for roasting, and totally unable to use my right hand at all—"

He spoke rapidly, with a strange feverish excitement, and Coral wondered if he were still a little drunk: but he seemed coherent enough, as he continued: "Old Dermot told me to make myself useful by coming in to help you with your rehearsal, Gerard. He says I can tell you the moves and business as we go along . . . And I dare say he has it in mind that as long as I'm here, his lovely niece will be well chaperoned, eh?"

He winked at Coral, who flushed, and looked away.

"Well, be that as it may, let's start from the beginning, my friends. Come now—Act One, Scene One—Romeo's first entrance . . ."

The mood of romance was totally shattered; and Coral did not know whether to be glad or sorry.

Dawn broke at last through the dusty windows of the parlor, but it was later still when Coral, yawning and half-drugged with fatigue, finally took refuge in her bed; the bed she shared, as always, with Rosalie.

"What? What time is it?" Rosalie stirred, waking reluctantly, and rubbing the sleep from her eyes.

"Nearly seven o'clock . . . Uncle Dermot's called a full rehearsal for ten o'clock, so I've less than three hours to get some rest . . ." Coral pulled her clothes off, too exhausted to hang them up, but letting them lie where they fell.

"What sort of progress is Gerard making?" yawned Rosalie.

"Oh, he's learning the words, slowly but surely . . . I only wish he could learn them with any other Juliet in the world; I'd give anything not to have to play the part with him."

She curled up in the warm bed, not even bothering for once to put on a nightgown; and Rosalie took her tired, warm body in her arms.

"What's wrong with poor Gerard? He's a nice enough boy . . . I can't think why you keep up this fight against him."

"I *must!* You know that . . . If I once forgot myself, and let him, let him, well, I needn't tell you what I mean. He's like all men; only worse than most!"

Rosalie gave a quiet, throaty chuckle, and rocked her sister gently as if she were a baby again.

"Worse than most, because you love him . . . Isn't that the truth?"

"No . . . Yes . . . I don't know . . ." Her head was spinning; she was beyond argument.

"I still say you should let yourself go a little—meet him half-way—discover what his love really means, and how much love you have to give in return."

"The more I give—to thee—the more I have . . ." Coral repeated automatically. "No, no—I won't listen to any more—let me go to sleep, Rosalie . . ."

She closed her eyes, longing for restful oblivion, and added in her last waking moment: "If you're such a champion of Mr. Kean, why don't you take on Juliet instead of me? I'm sure you'd make a fine partnership, and you'd save me a lot of unhappiness."

"Dearest, I'd do it gladly, only . . . I haven't the time to spare—Monsieur La Roche insists on seeing me again this morning—at the earliest possible moment. He wants to go walking with me and to take me for a drive in his carriage, and then perhaps we might go sailing together, for he says he can borrow a yacht belonging to a friend of his . . . I'm afraid Monsieur La Roche is determined to occupy every possible second of my time."

She hesitated; but as Coral said nothing, she continued: "He's a strange man—I don't understand him—he's certainly something of a mystery. But you can't help liking him, can you—when he's making himself so very agreeable? Coral, what do you think, honestly?"

But there was no reply. Coral was already fast asleep.

It was certainly true that Monsieur La Roche was a mystery man. During the following days, he pursued Rosalie with more and more devoted attentions, and soon came to know her very well indeed.

And yet, what did she know about him? What did any of them know?

They saw that he was wealthy, and that he had the

manners and bearing of an aristocrat: although he gave himself no title, but let himself be known as a plain "monsieur" or even, in the Republican fashion, *"citoyen."*

"It means 'citizen,' you know," Gerard explained to Rory one morning, in a break during rehearsals.

Rory had been painstakingly putting Gerard through his paces in the duelling scenes: now that Gerard had been promoted to the leading role, "Mercutio" had been taken over by Walter Wilkins (for there was no comic relief in this starcrossed tragedy) and Walter was finding it hard to discipline himself to the carefully arranged patterns of the sword fights. A born clown, he tended to trust to the mood of the moment, and ad lib both words and actions, as often as not, which is why they had now taken a temporary respite in the middle of rehearsal.

"Walter's only scratched the lobe of your ear with the edge of his rapier," Rory assured Gerard. "No harm done —it'll soon stop bleeding. I don't think you'll need a plaster on it."

"Just as well," Gerard grumbled. "Fine troupe we'd look—Romeo with one ear plastered, and Capulet in a sling . . . We should be like wounded soldiers back from the wars."

Rory frowned: "Don't remind me! I know I can't play one of the young gallants, when I'm tied up like this, but to descend from Romeo, to Juliet's *father,* it's positively humiliating!"

Gerard wasn't listening: his thoughts were still running on Monsieur Paul La Roche.

"I suppose that could be one reason why he's welcomed in this country when we're officially at war with France. If he's really a deposed aristocrat who fled from the terror of the guillotine, and sought refuge across the water . . ."

"At war with France?" Rory laughed shortly. "Who says so? *England* may have her quarrels with the French but this is Ireland, and there's an old bond between us, as two good Catholic nations."

"What do you mean by that? England—Ireland—it's all one and the same—"

"If you'll believe that, you'll believe anything." Rory

shifted, easing his aching arm into a more comfortable position. "Listen to me, my lad . . . I've a shrewd idea why Monsieur La Roche is here at all—and it's not for the reason you suppose . . . You know that Napoleon Bonaparte has been casting wistful glances at this emerald isle over the water; remember, he even tried landing some French troops here not so long ago—trusting to the sympathies of our loyal patriots to join forces with them against you Britishers!"

"Oh, I take no interest in politics," said Gerard, uneasily. "It's one of the reasons I left home—wars and victories aren't in my line."

"No, don't interrupt, hear me out . . . *That* attempt proved to be a failure, but what if the mighty Bonaparte plans to have another try? What if he's sent one of his high-ranking diplomats over here—incognito—to prepare the ground for another coup? The last time was too hasty; but if Monsieur La Roche were to make himself agreeable to all the local worthies in these parts, and win their sympathy, and their allegiance to the Catholic cause?"

"You really believe that's his game? He's an emissary from Napoleon?"

"It's the only explanation I can think of," said Rory.

"Good God. That means he's an enemy of my country and here we are treating the man like an honored friend. What the devil ought I to do about it, Rory?"

Rory grinned and tapped the side of his nose.

"Forget I spoke—turn a blind eye—it's all supposition, anyway, and I *could* be wrong. Though I rather doubt it!"

But there were two facts about Monsieur La Roche which had been established beyond any question: he had influence in high places, and (as Rosalie Maguire would have been the first to admit) he also had an immense amount of fascination, the most shameless physical magnetism and he always seemed to get his own way.

The following week, the Maguire company moved still further westward, to the noble city of Cork.

This was the largest city Gerard had yet seen since he came to Ireland; and he was very impressed. It had a ramshackle elegance, and a lively, cosmopolitan air: built upon the River Lee, with an endless flotilla of water traffic that came right up into the heart of the city, and travellers from every corner of the land or even further afield, congregated here.

There was a fine old theatre, too, where they were to present the first performance of *Romeo and Juliet*. Gerard felt a real thrill of excitement when he set foot upon the stage, and looked up at the curtained rows of boxes that embraced the proscenium from the pit to the gallery as gay and glittering as a fairy palace.

This, he realized, was the theatre he had been waiting for.

The final rehearsal took place, and the playbills were posted for the première: with Gerard's name in suitably large type though it may be worth noting that this was probably the only production in the history of the drama to be billed as follows:

MR. DERMOT MAGUIRE as FRIAR LAURENCE—
In *Romeo and Juliet*—
with the assistance of Mr. Gerard Kean and
Miss Coral Maguire

However, the old actor-manager did at least pay some small tribute to Gerard's contribution to the play, by inviting him, together with Rory, to share his own dressing room for once, instead of pigging it with the riffraff in the general men's room: Gerard, on account of his status in the piece, and Rory, because of his injured arm, sensibly enough, for it would have been disastrous if the fracture were to be accidentally jostled in the crush, before it had had time to heal.

So it was that, half an hour before the curtain was due to rise, the three actors sat at the long dressing table, staring at their faces in the mirror and putting on their greasepaint, when there was a knock at the door.

"Are you decent?" called Coral's voice.

"Yes, yes, come in, my dear," boomed Dermot.

Coral entered; already costumed for her first entrance, and looking breathtakingly lovely in Juliet's long gown

99

of apple-green, and a close-fitting cap, covered with pearls.

"Excuse me. I came in to wish you all good luck and—and I've a message for Gerard," she said shyly. "From someone in the audience."

"For me?" he repeated, in surprise.

"Don't tell me you have friends in front tonight?" asked Rory. "I thought you were a stranger in these parts?"

"So I am—I know no one here—except—" He thought of Cousin Bella, fleetingly; the Delaneys lived in County Cork, he remembered. But no—he shook his head. "No, nobody at all, really . . . Who can it be?"

Coral explained: "It's Monsieur La Roche. He's left Youghal and followed us here to Cork. Wasn't that nice of him? He's taken lodgings in a house by the river, and he wishes to invite you to dine with him after the performance to celebrate your dèbut as Romeo."

"Good heavens, it's kind of him, but I scarcely know the man."

Coral smiled: "You're not to be the only dinner guest. He's already invited Rosalie and me. So I expect he included you to make up the numbers."

"And to escort the girls—yes, yes, very proper—La Roche always behaves with perfect decorum, no doubt of that," agreed Dermot, pulling on a tonsured wig for his role as the Friar.

"What about me? Don't I get an invitation?" demanded Rory.

"I'm sure you'll be asked at another time," Coral reassured him. "When your poor arm's mended, and you can eat your supper without having to feed left-handed and spill half the soup over the tablecloth!" Then she leaned forward quickly, and kissed Gerard lightly on the cheek, adding: "That's for luck . . . I'll see you later."

And she was gone. Gerard's spirits rose; slowly, Coral's attitude toward him was changing again; ever since that day on the beach, she had seemed warmer, more affectionate. He began to revive his hopes, after all.

Perhaps it was this encouragement that set his performance as Romeo off to a flying start: certainly he acted better than ever before, and the fashionable audience applauded enthusiastically. He was both poetic and passionate, tender and fiery, by turns; and his Juliet matched him in her sweet sincerity. It seemed almost as if the two leading artistes had been born to play these roles, they enacted them so faithfully.

At the end they received a deserved ovation, and had to come back many times before the curtain, bowing and smiling; afterward old Dermot congratulated his niece then said to Gerard: "Yes, yes—you did pretty well, boy—pretty well for a beginner . . . But we'll call a rehearsal tomorrow, and I'll correct some of your faults . . . You haven't the *experience* yet, you see—the tricks of the trade. And it's these little touches that make all the difference between a pleasing performance like yours, and a *great* performance, like . . ." He left the sentence unfinished, from a natural modesty, and concluded: "But don't fret yourself, I'll soon lick you into shape, tomorrow morning."

Monsieur La Roche was courtesy itself, and sent a carriage to the stage door to bring his guests back to his lodgings after the play; and during the short journey, Coral touched Gerard's right hand, saying: "Take no notice of Uncle—he's only jealous because he knows he's too old to play Romeo any more . . . Isn't that so, Rosalie?"

Rosalie, squeezed on to the cushioned carriage seat on Gerard's left, agreed: "And whatever you do, don't listen to all the nonsense he'll tell you tomorrow . . . For it's your youth and your naturalness the audience applauded tonight—don't spoil it all with that stale bag of tricks Uncle Dermot will try to teach you!"

She pressed his other hand as she spoke, and he felt the prickling of desire; to be enclosed in the half darkness of a closed carriage, with the two most beautiful girls in all Ireland, feeling the soft pressure of their thighs against him . . . He wished that the drive could go on forever.

But their journey was all too short; and the carriage pulled up very soon, outside a handsome townhouse at the end of Cork's most fashionable promenade, the Mardyke—a mile-long walk overlooking the river, almost covered like an arcade by two lines of spreading elm trees.

"He certainly lives in style," said Coral, gazing up at the house as they alighted. "I wonder where he gets all his money."

Gerard remembered Rory's theory but kept silent.

The house was as stylish inside as out; the dinner, again prepared with devotion by the talented Monsieur Henri, was beyond criticism. ("My personal chef—he travels with me everywhere," Monsieur La Roche explained to Gerard.) The food was perfection, and each course was accompanied by a different wine, to emphasize its own particular excellence.

By the time the little party had retired, according to custom, to a comfortable withdrawing room upon the first floor, they were all exceedingly relaxed . . . Almost, perhaps, a little too relaxed.

There was another large, billowing sofa here just as there had been at the Clock Gate in Youghal: dimly, Coral found herself wondering whether Monsieur La Roche travelled with his own personal sofa, too?

But no. The other had been dark green, she seemed to remember, and this one was blue—pale blue, like the sky—like the cloudless sky above, the day she and Gerard went swimming. And they sat on the beach afterward, laughing and joking, as they were doing now. Only then, of course, she had been undressed, except for the sheet she was wrapped up in; and then Gerard was undressed too. And at one moment she had seen him quite naked, and had felt a strange breathless excitement such as she had never known in her life before.

But the oddest thing of all was that she felt the beginnings of this very same excitement *now*. Here and now, in this fashionable, tasteful sitting room after a wonderful meal and only just a *little* too much wine, perhaps she could still feel the most extraordinary stirrings of some nameless sensation, deep within her.

She shook her head, trying to clear her muzzy thoughts, and focus upon the scene.

She felt sure that this could not be the same sofa as

before; not only was it a different color but the other one was big enough to seat three people, she remembered. And this sofa was so very big—it actually seated four.

Admittedly, it was rather crowded, with four people upon it: or perhaps they were not all actually sitting *on* the sofa for although she had Rosalie next to her, Rosalie seemed to be half-lying, half-sitting upon the lap of Monsieur Paul La Roche. Which wasn't very ladylike, was it? And at the same time, she discovered that Gerard had established himself at her other side and he was leaning over her, with one arm around her waist.

She blinked, and tried to understand what was happening. What were they all doing here? How long had they been lying together in this carefree state of confusion?

"What—what *time* is it, Monsieur?" She heard herself pronouncing the words with great care, as if she were on stage.

"Call me Paul," he said: and his long, dark lashes and smiling brown eyes really were very attractive. "We don't stand on ceremony here, *cherie*."

"Paul, then . . . Tell me the time, Paul—"

"There is no such thing as time. Time has been abolished. We have all the time in the world," he purred, in his silky Parisian accent.

She smiled back at him. What a delightful man he was. And he behaved so beautifully . . . It seemed both beautiful and natural for him to reach out a hand and touch her face. As his fingertips travelled from her cheek to her mouth, she found herself kissing them, as a matter of course.

And then his hand moved down to her throat, to her bosom. It cupped one of her breasts, in the most friendly way in the world, and stayed there, stroking her nipple, very gently.

For a fleeting moment, she wondered if Rosalie might be displeased by this display of simple affection? But Rosalie turned her head and noticed what was happening and she merely smiled, in the kindest possible way. And she, too, leaned across and kissed Coral on the lips and at the same time, she drew Gerard closer into the magic

103

circle of their warmth and love, and ran her hand over his knee, along his thigh.

Coral sighed with happiness and snuggled closer still, imagining that their bodies were all melting together into one sweet embrace; she put her arms about Gerard, holding him fast. They were under a spell, and they must never break it. She looked up to find Gerard's face, a little misty, a little undefined, but full of love, gazing down at her, with such tenderness.

Some mysterious witchcraft was at work. She felt her loins growing weak, and the tugging undertow flowed again like a strong tide, making her want Gerard so desperately. This was how it had been at the beach, only then of course she was undressed. But, she reflected in a moment of bewilderment, surely it was all happening again? She felt as if she were half-undressed already. As she drowned in the depths of Gerard's eyes, and abandoned herself to him utterly, she was aware that somewhere, gentle hands were at work upon her clothes—unlacing, unfastening . . .

And then a wave of darkness overtook her, and she knew no more.

When at last she came to, she could not imagine where she was; neither could she remember how she got there.

She was quite nude; she could tell that much, without even opening her eyes. And she was lying in a soft, warm bed. In the hotel, perhaps? For it was a double bed, and she could feel Rosalie lying beside her, their bodies touching.

But no—this wasn't the hotel. This bed was far too luxurious, and the sheets were of finest satin. With a little shock, she realized she must still be in Monsieur La Roche's house—*Paul's* house. Rosalie must have undressed her and put her to bed: yes, she thought she could almost remember that happening. She stretched out, and her hands met warm, naked flesh.

Of course, Rosalie did not have a nightdress either; they hadn't planned to stay here.

She found she was touching Rosalie's stomach; her fingers moved, and she encountered Rosalie's navel, and below that, the beginnings of her silky, soft body hair. But wait—this wasn't soft or silky; it was coarse and wiry—a thick bush of hair. Exploring further, she made a horrifying discovery, and almost cried out in alarm.

The person sleeping beside her was a man; and a man in a state of considerable physical excitement! She let go, as if his warm, erect flesh had scorched her, and turned her head to look into the face upon the pillow.

With his eyes still shut, Gerard licked his lips, and put his arms around her, pulling her into a sleepy embrace.

For a brief instant she almost succumbed to the flood of desire that overwhemed her but at the same moment, Gerard whispered thickly: *"Bella—come to me—"*

The spell was broken. She pushed him away, recoiling so quickly that she nearly fell out of the bed. The sheets and blankets tumbled aside, and Gerard woke up, staring at her foggily, as if she were a vision.

Which indeed she was; a vision of unclad loveliness from her round, sweet breasts, flushed with palest pink, to the coppery curls of hair that veiled her secret treasure, she was completely revealed to his gaze. Slowly he sat upright disregarding the fact of his own nakedness: and she looked back at his handsome body, and longed for his embrace but it was too late for that now.

"How—what—where are we?" he asked huskily. "Am I dreaming?"

"No . . ." In this moment of total and utter frankness, she did not even feel ashamed to be seen undressed. Only one thing mattered now. "Tell me the truth, Gerard . . . last night, did you—did we—?"

She could not finish the question; and to her surprise she saw a deeper colour glow in his cheeks.

"No . . . I did nothing—I could not have done anything . . . I had too much to drink—I must have collapsed completely. I don't know who put me to bed," he muttered, shamefaced.

"I can guess . . . *They* did it—Rosalie and Paul—I think I remember now—they began to—to undress me— oh, Gerard, what a terrible trick to play on us both."

"But why? I don't understand."

105

"I believe Rosalie hoped—I mean, she thought perhaps that if—" Coral too was blushing now. She realized what Rosalie's plan had been, but she would have died rather than explain it to Gerard. She broke off, angrily: "How monstrous, how sinful—I'll never forgive her for this!"

Gerard said reassuringly: "It's not a sin for we did nothing. All we've done is lie together and look and there can be no harm in *looking,* surely?"

"No-o-o . . ." she replied doubtfully; but she could not take her eyes from his body, and the lusty staff of his manhood, which so clearly expressed his desire as he gazed upon her. "I—I've never seen any man like that, before . . ."

"Don't be afraid," he said, very softly. "Come closer, dearest Coral. Come here to me."

Then she remembered what he had said in his sleep, and scrambled out of the bed.

"Indeed I will not . . . !" she announced. "Looking's one thing, touching is something else, and I know *that's* a sin, sure enough. And anyway—*who's Bella?*"

"Bella?" He stared at her blankly.

"You mentioned the name just before you woke. 'Come to me, Bella,' you said, so who is she? A lady-friend, I suppose?"

"She's my cousin. I thought I was in love with her once but I soon found out I was not. You can forget Bella—I forgot her long ago—no, don't get dressed, don't go away."

For Coral had turned her back on him, and was now busy putting on her clothes which she found laid out in a neat pile, thoughtfully folded by Rosalie, ready for the morning. How *dared* Rosalie behave so wickedly?

Gerard tried to argue, but in vain; for at this moment they were interrupted by a gentle rapping at the door, and a servant's voice asking:

"Would you like tea or coffee, Mr. Kean, sir?"

Coral froze, and put her finger to her lips but the voice continued:

"And what would *Mrs.* Kean prefer?"

"Ah—well—thank you—we'll both have coffee," Gerard called out, with as much dignity as he could muster.

"Very good, sir. By the way, Monsieur La Roche presents his apologies, he has had to leave the house, early this morning. He begs you will excuse him, and wishes you *au revoir* . . ."

The mystery man was sustaining his reputation; without any explanation, he had simply vanished, leaving two of his guests to enjoy the hospitality of his bedroom. (And having been thoughtful enough to provide an alias for Coral, as far as the staff were concerned.)

Gerard and Coral dressed, breakfasted, and left the house as discreetly as possible. With a hazy memory of the etiquette for departing guests, Gerard even managed to tip the butler half a guinea, which he could ill afford and they made their way back to the hotel where most of the Maguire company were staying.

They exchanged few words upon the walk back across the city; their enforced intimacy seemed to have created a new awkwardness between them, rather than bringing them together. And yet, once, at a street corner, they saw a little encounter that touched them both: a young man, leaving his house to go to work, turned to kiss his wife goodbye at the door—his newly-wed wife, to judge by the way they clung together, as if they would never be parted.

Gerard and Coral looked at one another and found they were both smiling a little.

When they reached the hotel, Coral expected trouble and Gerard was prepared to face an indignant elderly uncle, demanding to know what he meant by damaging a young lady's spotless reputation. But they were fortunate; Dermot had overslept, and so was still blissfully unaware of the events of the previous night. Coral thanked her lucky stars and slipped up to her room—she wondered at what point Rosalie had left the party, and imagined she would find her tucked up in bed, waiting for her with a knowing smile.

But the bed had not been slept in and a moment later, she made an even more amazing discovery. All Rosalie's clothes—her luggage, her personal belongings—everything of hers had disappeared from the bedroom.

She hurried along the passage and knocked upon Gerard's door.

He opened it at once, and could see at a glance that she was very upset.

"What's the matter? What's wrong?" he asked.

"Rosalie's not here—she's gone—and she's taken everything with her." Coral began. "Where can she be?"

As if in reply to this question, Rory appeared on the staircase behind them.

"So there you both are at last," he said. "Don't tell me what you've been up to all night, for I'll ask no questions but there's going to be the devil to pay when your Uncle sees *this*. I found it left below at the porter's desk—it's addressed to us all."

"This" was a letter very hastily penned by Rosalie, the night before.

"Dear everybody—I don't know if you will ever forgive me, for I do know I'm letting you all down and particularly Uncle Dermot. But as you've probably guessed by now, I'm in love. I've met the one man in the world I want to marry; and by the time you read this, we will both be far away in a ship on our way to France."

"To *France?*" Coral repeated helplessly.

"Under the circumstances, it's impossible for Paul to be married here in Ireland, so he's taking me back to his own country, and there we shall start our new life together. I hope that one day, before very long, I may see you all again; and I wish you all the luck in the world. Don't think too badly of me. I am very happy."

Rory added: "There's a sort of a postscript at the end. She signs her name, and sends her love, and then says 'Dear Coral—I hope you had a good night,'—whatever *that* may mean!"

Coral bit her lip and said nothing: she was still trying to take in all the implications of this shattering news. What ever would Uncle Dermot say?

Uncle Dermot, when the news was broken to him over breakfast, as tactfully as possible, had a great deal to say.

He blamed himself for trusting that French rapscallion in the first place—anyone with half an eye could see that the fellow was no gentleman. He prayed to the Mother of

God and all the blessed saints in heaven that the man would not betray his poor, weak-willed and trusting niece, but at least do the right thing and make an honest woman of her. He launched into a speech that he half-remembered from a long-dead melodrama, which included references to trust and honor and loyalty and virtue, and a lot more words in a similar vein.

Above all, and he thumped his fist on the communal breakfast table at this point, making the teacups rattle, above all, he demanded to know, having replaced his Romeo and Mercutio at very short notice, where now, he asked in thunderous tones, was he to find a new Lady Capulet, at no notice at all?

The company around the table exchanged glances; they were one woman short, certainly, and there seemed to be no solution to this problem.

"We need another lady, sure enough," agreed Rory.

Upon this, the door of the breakfast room swung open, and a blonde enchantress swept in to join them, her face wreathed in smiles, her ringlets bobbing merrily beneath her bonnet.

"Gerard *darling!*" she exclaimed with delight, and descended upon that bewildered gentleman, embracing him rapturously.

"Oh—good heavens—yes—hello—" he stammered, very much aware of Coral, at his side, watching this little reunion with frozen amazement.

"How wonderful to find you again, after all this long time!" cried the newcomer. "I happened to be at the play last night, by the merest chance, and there you were! Well, naturally I made inquiries, and a very agreeable gentleman in the box office told me where you were staying, Gerard dear, so this morning I got up bright and early, and here I am. What a blissful surprise!"

"Yes, indeed," mumbled Gerard unhappily.

"And with all your clever, clever friends, too—aren't you going to introduce me?"

"Of course—um—ladies and gentlemen—may I present—my cousin—Miss Bella Delaney . . ."

"Of the Cork Delaneys, you know," Bella smiled. "We only live half a dozen miles out of the city—at Delaney

House—but you'll soon see that for yourself, won't you, Gerard?"

"Will I? What do you mean?"

"Of course you will for I'm here to collect you in the carriage and take you home to meet the rest of the family . . . You're coming to stay with us, my darling cousin and I won't take no for an answer!"

The silence that followed was broken by the noise of the door slamming as Coral made her departure from the room.

In Gerard's ears, it echoed like the crack of doom . . .

(7)

Love Scenes

"Pardon me, madam——" began Dermot, feeling it was time he took charge of the proceedings again, "we are in the midst of a professional crisis at this moment."

"Oh, really?" Bella looked at the old actor blankly, as if he were speaking Chinese. "What a shame . . ."

Gerard hastened to introduce Dermot and establish his importance in the situation.

"Miss Delaney——Mr. Dermot Maguire."

"Founder, only begetter, and leading actor of the Maguire Touring Company," added Dermot, sonorously, extending his hand.

"I'm charmed to meet you," said Bella gaily. "Now I come to think of it——I believe I spotted you in the play last night."

"*Spotted* me? Spotted *me?*" Dermot's complexion began to purple dangerously, and Gerard decided to create a diversion.

"What time is our rehearsal called, sir?" he inquired. "Ten-thirty? Excellent——I shall be there but in the meantime, I'll take my cousin out for a walk, and explain the circumstances to her."

"But I'm here to carry you off to Delaney House to see Papa and Mama——" Bella began.

"Some other time, Bella," Gerard interrupted firmly. "At this moment, you and I are going for a little walk. Come along!"

As the door closed behind them, Dermot was still spluttering: "Extraordinary young person . . . Did you hear what she said, Wilkins? *She believed she spotted me* when I was giving my Friar Laurence to a packed house."

"Never mind that now, Mr. Maguire," said Walter Wilkins, soothingly. "We must decide what we're to do this evening or you won't be able to give your Friar Laurence at all!"

"That's very true," Dermot sighed, and looked balefully at the assembled troupe, seated around the table.

"Rosalie gone, Coral fled to her room, heaven knows why."

"It's the shock of learning the news of her sister's elopement, no doubt," said Mrs. Mountford, who had resumed work upon her eternal embroidery at if she hadn't a care in the world. "Poor child. She's very like me in that respect—sensitive, you know."

"Hmm . . ." Dermot regarded the elderly actress dubiously then added: "Nevertheless, the fact remains that we are embarrassed by a shortage of female artistes. Could we play *Romeo* without Lady Capulet? If we cut most of the Capulet scenes altogether, and add a few ad lib commentaries, to explain what is going on for the benefit of our audience?"

"It'll make a very short piece," said Rory. "I tell you what—I could give a benefit performance—excerpts from my most celebrated roles—"

"No, thank you, Mr. O'Malley," said Dermot with steely politeness. "If a series of solo recitations becomes necessary, I shall, of course, step into the breach myself. But I dare say we can fill up the evening with the addition of some extra musical interludes—Coral shall sing an extended recital."

"And who is to play for her?" Walter pointed out the

112

flaw in this solution. "When Rosalie left us—we did not only lose Lady Capulet—we also lost Coral's accompanist. No, no, we'd do better to try and enlist a new actress into the company, to take Rosalie's place."

"And where are we to find an experienced Lady Capulet, in the middle of Cork, might I ask?" demanded Dermot. "This isn't one of the artistic capitals of the world, you know—we're not in Dublin now!"

Walter looked knowing, and closed one eye.

"You leave that to me, sir," he said confidently. "I happen to know that Beverley's Travelling Theatre is in town—preparing to embark on another tour."

"*Beverley's?*" Dermot bristled at the name of his chief rival. "That raree-show? Those mountebanks? Would you insult me by comparing their performances with ours?"

"No, no, not for a moment—but they do have a certain young lady—Miss Pike—who might be able to step into Rosalie's shoes, at a pinch—"

"*Pinch* is the word—" snorted Rory. "She's got feet as big as a blacksmith's hands, and her shoes are the size of ferry boats . . ."

"Be that as it may—she could easily take on Lady C. for us—not to mention Nerissa and Goneril and the rest. And I heard a whisper that she's had a tiff with Mr. Beverley just the other day, so she might be very agreeable to a change of management."

"Mr. Wilkins—I shall rely on you to make a tactful approach to Miss Pike at the earliest possible moment," said Dermot. "But as far as musical accomplishment is concerned, does the young lady perform on the harpsichord?"

"I think not. Still, we can't expect miracles." Walter scratched his head. "And—wait a bit—it seems to me I heard young Gerard mention something once, when we were traveling in the coach together. I believe he is proficient at the pianoforte. Perhaps he might be prevailed upon?"

"He might indeed. I shall tackle him when he returns. Thank you, Mr. Wilkins—you've been extremely helpful."

At that moment, the future accompanist was climbing the hill of Shandon, with his pretty cousin on his arm, unaware of the new responsibility that awaited him.

"Where are we going, Bella?" he asked. "I mustn't be away too long—I told you, I have to be back by ten-thirty without fail."

"Oh, you and your funny old theatricals!" Bella laughed, squeezing his hand. "As if all that mattered two hoots!"

"But it does matter—of course it does—"

"What matters is that you and I have found one another again—and this time I shall take good care not to let you go," she purred.

"I don't know what you mean by that. How is your friend, Mr. O'Brian?" he asked, remembering the flashy gentleman with a cigar who had stolen Bella away from him the moment they arrived in Wexford.

"Michael? Oh, pooh, I never see him nowadays—you can forget all about him . . . it's you I care about, Gerard dear; and nobody else. Indeed, I confess I must have been blind not to realize it before—I never quite noticed how handsome you are until I saw you upon the stage last night. And when you shinned up that balcony, well! Your legs looked very splendid, in those tights you were wearing. I declare, you've grown up into a real fine figure of a man, in this past year."

Gerard cleared his throat and changed the subject. "You still haven't told me where we are going now. Where are you taking me?" he asked.

"Why—*here,* of course! For we've just arrived." Bella stopped and pointed upward, at the tower of a church that loomed up before them, on the summit of Shandon hill. "St. Mary's . . Have you never heard tell of the bells of St. Mary's? Why, they're world-famous—every visitor to Cork has to come and admire the bells."

Gerard was rather relieved to hear that their objective was something as proper as the inspection of a church, and allowed Bella to lead the way into the edifice.

The church itself was fine enough, but Bella wasted no time upon that; she made straight for the stairs, and proceeded to the first floor, where a black-robed sexton bobbed and muttered a pious greeting, as he busied himself with the keys of the carillon—long wooden slats, like giant piano keys, attached to a series of wires that disappeared through the ceiling, connecting with the belfry above. As the sexton thumped each key with his fist, an answering bell sounded high overhead, and they heard a well-known hymn-tune ringing out through the morning air.

"Come with me, Gerard dear—and I'll show you where the bells are," Bella said, and started off up yet another flight of stairs.

These stairs were soon replaced by a series of open wooden ladders, and Gerard found himself climbing up into a dusty loft, in semi-darkness, where the great peal of bells hung, rocking and reverberating only a few feet away.

The sound seemed to vibrate in his head; he could hardly think clearly, with the endless jangling and clanging that beat upon his ears.

Bella looked at him and laughed; and he could see her lips shaping the words: "It's thrilling, isn't it?"

They were quite alone up there in the belfry; alone in a whirlpool of deafening sound and then she put her arms round him and held him tightly.

"Kiss me," she commanded; he saw, rather than heard what she said and her lips closed upon his.

For a moment he responded, feeling the surge of noise, and the sudden excitement in his blood, mingling together.

He felt her hands, like two soft snares, fastening upon him, and her little wet tongue darting impudently into his mouth. Yes, there was excitement in the embrace, certainly, and a kind of recklessness, but beyond that—
Nothing.

To his own surprise, he felt no answering tension in his loins; he no longer desired this pretty, playful, unreliable woman.

He broke the embrace at last, and she looked up at him, puzzled.

"What is it? What's wrong, beloved?" she asked.

"We can't talk here," he said.

"It's too noisy for you? Very well." She took his hand, and guided him up one last flight of wooden steps, to a little door and opened it.

Sunlight hit him in the face almost like a blow: and a moment later they were outside the tower, standing together on a flat roof, high in the clear summer sky. Beneath them, the warm gray stones throbbed with the last notes of the carillon, and then the hymn ended, and the echoes died away into silence at last.

They stood by the parapet, looking down at the street, and the old almshouses far below.

"It feels almost like flying," murmured Bella. "Oh, Gerard, I'm so happy that you are here."

She slid her hand around his waist, hugging him.

"As soon as you can get yourself out of that absurd theatre company, you shall come to stay at Delaney House for as long as you like. Now I have found you, I mean to keep you for always!" she smiled.

"No, Bella. That can't be," he said.

"What do you mean? They can find another actor, I'm sure—and anyway, what need have you to worry about cheap fair ground folk like that? You should never have got mixed up with such riffraff—"

"I was glad enough to join them, when you threw me over," Gerard reminded her, not unkindly. "Our paths have separated widely since then, Bella—we can't come together again."

"Can we not?" she looked at him challengingly, a mischevious sparkle in her eye, and let her hand travel, very lightly, down to the front of his breeches, stroking him provocatively.

"No. We cannot," he said, and removed her hand. "For I must tell you, there is another girl in my life now, and I love her with all my heart."

"What? Who?" Bella rapped out the two syllables like pistol shots.

"You saw her last night and this morning, very briefly, Miss Maguire—Coral . . . The girl who plays Juliet to my Romeo."

"An *actress?*" Bella laughed, as if she could not believe her ears. "You—letting yourself be ensnared by a person of that class? I don't believe it—and I won't permit it either!"

He frowned. "You're talking rubbish, Bella—you know nothing about Coral—and it's none of your business anyway."

"Oh, indeed it is! I tell you, you're coming to Delaney House—to me! This has quite decided me—I shall save you from the consequence of your folly, my dear . . . Tonight, after the play, I will be outside the theatre in a closed carriage. You will meet me there, and then we shall drive home together. But me no buts, for I am completely determined. It's for your own good, dearest cousin."

"And what if I refuse?"

"You will not do that." Bella smiled sweetly. "You *dare* not . . . For if you were so stupid, I should be forced to write a long letter to my Uncle George, telling him everything."

"*What?*" It was Gerard's turn to be shocked now.

"No doubt he still believes that you have gone overseas, to fight against Boney—serving in the Army, as an Ensign . . . am I right? Yes, I thought as much. How do you suppose your father will feel, when he learns the truth about his wicked, wayward son and heir. The runaway—the deserter?"

"You wouldn't?"

"Oh, but I would . . . I *shall*—if you do not do as I say, and come to me tonight. For I will have you, Gerard, make no mistake about that."

And he saw, from the look in her eye, that she meant what she said. He imagined the shame and humiliation that his father would suffer from such a revelation; it would break the old man's spirit. For a split second, he contemplated how easy it would be to lift his pretty cousin off her feet and topple her gently over the stone parapet, letting her fall head-first to the pavement below.

But then another hymn-tune began to ring out, and he came to his senses. He nodded helplessly, and shrugged. It was time to go.

When he got back to the theatre, old Dermot broached the subject of his musical talents, and Gerard had to admit that he had studied the pianoforte with his last governess —music and French were the only two accomplishments he had picked up from that long-departed lady, Mademoiselle Michot.

"Excellent, excellent," the old actor clapped him on the back. "Then you shall substitute for Rosalie, as accompanist to her sister—Coral, my dear—come and show Mr. Kean your music, so you may practice together, while I introduce our new recruit to the remainder of the company."

For the illustrous Miss Florence Pike had expressed her willingness to join the Maguire company, and informed them that she would be word-perfect in her role as Lady Capulet in time for the evening's performance.

Gerard and Coral repaired to the greenroom, where the harpsichord was kept during its time offstage, and began to look through the tattered sheets of music together.

"I hope my fingers aren't too stiff—it's some time since I last touched the keyboard," Gerard excused himself. "But I'll do my best not to let you down."

"Really?" said Coral, with a little, careless laugh. "That will make a very welcome change, certainly."

"What do you mean?" He realized that she was in a bad mood; she refused to look at him, but turned the yellowing pages quickly and irritably.

"You know very well what I mean, Mr. Kean," she retorted. "Or if you do not, you must have an extremely short memory."

"Oh, come now, you're not angry with me because of what my cousin Bella said this morning."

"Angry? I'm sure it's no concern of mine what you or your cousin may do. I take no interest in your family affairs."

"I assure you—"

"But I will say *this*—" she went on without waiting for him to defend himself. "I am sorry to find that you are such a poor liar, Mr. Kean. Having told me that you parted from your cousin long ago, and had no more to do with her—it was so simple for you to be caught out in that silly falsehood. For here she is—living not far away—and the two of you kissing and carrying on like lovebirds, for everyone to see."

"Coral, listen to me. I did not know Bella Delaney was here—I had not seen her since I first came to Ireland, and I have no intention of ever seeing her again. Does that satisfy you?"

"Me, sir? What has it to do with me? I dare say you will be meeting the lady and taking her out to supper after the play tonight—well, that's entirely up to you—I beg you not to put yourself out on my account."

"I swear to you—I will not meet Bella tonight." Gerard clenched his fists, realizing that he had to keep his word now. "Whatever happens, I will not see her."

"Suit yourself. Now may we rehearse the music?" And Coral placed a song-copy upon the harpsichord. "We'll begin with this one, I think."

It was an old song, and well-loved: *Drink to Me Only*—with the plaintive air that carried Ben Jonson's words along, like petals borne away on an eddying stream.

"Drink to me only with thine eyes,
And I will pledge with mine.
Or leave a kiss but in the cup
And I'll not look for wine . . ."

As Gerard played, he felt a sense of calm and certainty flow through him—into his fingertips, and out through the harpsichord's keys: the accompaniment met and married the sweet notes of Coral's voice and became one perfect harmony.

She was aware of it too, and for the first time she let herself glance at him, seated beside her; their eyes met, and as the song ended, she smiled.

". . . But might I of Jove's nectar sip,
I would not change—for thine . . ."

As the last words died away, he added quietly: "Tonight—you and I will have supper at the best restaurant we can find in the town."

She nodded: it was going to be all right after all.

"Thank you, Gerard," she said. "I shall look forward to that."

When at last Gerard returned to the dressing room, he found Rory, half-costumed as old Capulet, and in a state of deepest gloom.

"I'm not looking forward to it," he muttered. "I can tell you that much, before we go any further!"

"Why, what's the trouble?"

"She does not know the lines, for one thing. And it's no good saying she'll be word-perfect by the time the curtain goes up, for she won't. For another thing, she's no beauty, and I can't abide her leaning on me, the way she does."

"Poor creature, she *is* rather on the plain side—"

"Plain? She has a face like a carthorse, and hooves to match!"

"She can't help that, can she? Be fair to the lady—"

"Oh, I'd forgive her her looks and her clod-hopping feet—which she always manages to plant on my toes in every scene. But what I can *not* forgive is that the wretched hag has been eating raw onions for breakfast! It's enough to asphyxiate you every time she opens her mouth!"

Gerard laughed: "Bear up, old fellow—they say onions are good for you—the vapor of an onion is a sovereign remedy, I'm told, for keeping infection away."

"I tell you, Gerard, the breath of that woman would keep *anybody* away. And besides, there's worse trouble than that in store."

"Worse still? It must be serious indeed." Gerard tried to look suitably solemn.

"I'm not joking, lad. We're in for a rare old reception tonight, by my guess. Be prepared to fight for your life, every inch of the way."

"What are you talking about?"

"You wait and see . . . you're still pretty new at this game; you've never faced an angry audience yet, one that's out for blood. Well, we all have to suffer some time."

Gerard stared at his companion, completely mystified. "I don't understand."

"You will . . . Flossie Pike comes from the Beverleys,

don't she? Old Dermot and Walter have lured her away between them, with promises of better pay and no more sword-swallowing."

"What?"

"Oh, didn't you hear? Flossie started out at the Puck Fair—the one and only lady sword-swallower, she was —and Beverley still made her keep it up as a special attraction between the acts, in front of the curtain. That was what finally tipped the scales, when Dermot promised her she'd never have to swallow another length of naked steel as long as she stayed with the Maguires!"

"Indeed. It must have been an inducement, I do see that."

"But that's not what I'm talking about. How do you think old Bev and his crowd are going to feel, once they learn Flossie's left them in the lurch—and gone over to the enemy? They're going to be out for revenge, my boy —and no mistake!"

"But what can they do?"

"They'll find ways of making life unbearable, believe me. They'll do all they can to wreck this place tonight or my name's not Rory O'Malley."

"Oh, I think you're exaggerating."

"Do you indeed? You wait till some bright spark starts throwing dead cats or half-bricks this evening—wait till one of those flying weapons lands in the middle of your forehead, and pole-axes you—you'll be sorry you ever doubted me then, so you will."

Gerard smiled, and rubbed his jaw reflectively.

"You never know . . . it might be a relief in some ways . . . At least it would get me out of the devilish scrape I'm in at the moment."

And he went on to tell Rory of the dilemma that Bella had forced upon him: he was determined to reject her advances entirely, and prove his love for Coral by taking her to supper tonight . . . but at the same time, he was all too well aware of the revenge Bella could take if he spurned her.

"That gorgeous cousin of yours? And you're prepared to give her the cold shoulder? Shame upon you, Gerard—

for I tell you, I could find it in my heart to pleasure the sweet creature myself . . ."

"Well, I—" Gerard hesitated, and eyed Rory speculatively. "Do you really mean that?"

"As heaven is my witness; I'd like nothing better than five minutes alone with that one, in a private place . . ."

"How about in a closed carriage?" Gerard began to smile. "Rory, if you mean what you say, you could do me a very great favor tonight . . . and if you manage to give the lady satisfaction, she might decide to forget all her plans regarding me, and turn her attentions upon you instead . . ."

"Are you serious?" Rory was beginning to brighten up now, as well.

"Never more serious in my life. Coral's the only girl for me—and the sooner I can shake off Cousin Bella, the better I shall be pleased."

"Then you can rely on me. By Jesus, I do believe I'm going to enjoy myself this evening after all!"

But Rory was being over-optimistic.

To begin with—all his worst fears about the performance proved to be well-founded.

Miss Florence Pike essayed her first attempt at Lady Capulet with unbounded confidence, but she had not learned her words, and was forced to improvise, time and again, throwing in speeches from other plays, or relying on the inspiration of the moment to carry her through. With confusing results.

The audience grew restive; and Gerard realized that Rory's predictions were all too accurate when he heard a low, angry murmur rising from the pit. Later, there were cat-calls from the gallery, and a general din broke out. It seemed as if half the audience were hissing and booing, and the other half were shouting at them in an attempt to restore order. Between the two factions, the unhappy cast could hardly make themselves heard at all.

Dermot decreed that, in these distressing circumstances, there should be no musical interlude tonight; Coral and Gerard had rehearsed their song cycle in vain—these witless ruffians were not worthy of their artistry.

122

Then came the first missile: an over-ripe tomato, in the middle of a scene between the Capulet family and the nurse. Whether it was intended for Miss Pike, no one knew; but it sailed past Lady Capulet and landed on the Nurse's apron, where it splattered in a scarlet sunburst.

Mrs. Mountford looked down, and reacted in surprise, then with outraged dignity. Stepping forward, she announced majestically:

"If *any* of you ever *dares* to do such a thing again, I shall be very, *very* displeased."

And she resumed the scene with splendid equanimity.

But it didn't stop there. It soon became clear that the rowdy element were not concentrating their fury upon the unfortunate Miss Pike alone; the entire company were the target for their attack, and scene after scene limped along, accompanied by a barrage of rotten vegetables and even worse eggs.

When Romeo and Juliet were reunited at the moment of death, in the last act, some humorist at the back of the pit tossed a bouquet at the leading lady's feet. But it was a bouquet made of dandelions.

Coral, about to utter her last words, glanced down automatically, saw the posy and felt encouraged for a brief instant, before a ribald voice shouted: "Go on, darling, pick it up and piss the bed!" Then she realized that she had been rewarded with a handful of weeds, and almost broke down. Gerard, already lying motionless upon the funeral bier, stiffened angrily, and might even have jumped up to go and seek out the originator of this latest insult, but Dermot, as the holy Friar, clutched his shoulder in a grip of steel and whispered under his breath:

"Patience, boy, patience."

Somehow the play dragged to an end, and the curtain fell to a renewed barrage of abuse.

There were no curtain calls.

In the leading men's dressing room, Rory was tugging off his costume, flinging aside doublet and hose, and wasting no time in changing back to his own clothes.

"What did I tell you?" he asked Gerard. "I knew it

123

would be a massacre. The sooner we pack up and leave town after tonight's little disaster, the better."

Dermot, following Gerard in to the room, tried to be philosophical.

"I've known better audiences, but I've also known worse. They listened quite attentively to some of my soliloquies; that shows a certain amount of taste and discrimination."

"They were getting their breath back to shout all the louder next time Flossie Pike showed her face," muttered Rory. "Gerard, come and help me on with my jacket, will you? I'm helpless with this damned sling on my arm."

"What? Leaving already?" Dermot inquired, as Gerard assisted Rory to dress. "You seem to be in a great hurry to quit the theatre tonight."

"I—er—I have an assignation," said Rory, and grinned at Gerard's reflection in the glass as he made for the door, shrugging into his cloak.

"Wait—just a moment—what are you going to say to her?" Gerard called after him; but Rory was halfway down the echoing stone stairs already.

Out in the darkness behind the stage door, the closed carriage waited. A cloaked and hooded figure hurried out and climbed into the vehicle; and the coachman promptly cracked his whip and drove off into the night.

It was pitch black inside, with all the blinds tightly drawn; and Bella could not see her travelling-companion —but what of that?

Triumphantly, she gathered him into her embrace.

"I knew you wouldn't disappoint me," she murmured in her ear, and her mouth moved swiftly across his cheek, to his chin—his lips.

They kissed, and this time her ardor was returned with a passion that surprised and excited her.

She pressed her body to his, feeling the carriage rocking under them as they bowled over uneven cobblestones, and letting the erratic motion fling them together again and again: her desire mounting at every renewed contact.

"My dearest—oh, my dear, dear cousin," she breathed, entwining her arms about his broad shoulders—broader,

124

indeed than she had remembered. And his strong, muscular arms.

But what was this? She discovered that his right arm was tied up in a sling.

"What have you done? Are you wounded?" she asked.

Her fellow passenger did not reply, but kissed her again, more violently than before. And at the same instant, she had a sudden image in her mind—the actor who had played Lord Capulet the night before had worn a sling on his right arm.

She remembered him vividly; he had had broad shoulders too, and a rugged lusty torso but surely he had been a much older man, with grey hair and a grizzledgray beard?

It was unfortunate for Rory, and for Gerard, as well, as it turned out, that Bella did not stop to reflect that the hair and beard might both have been artificial; it never occurred to her that the man in her arms need not be any older than she was herself, a fiery young gallant, intent on conquest.

All she could think was that she had been deceived by Gerard, and tricked into an encounter with a lustful, elderly man. True, he was no fumbling amateur at the art of love, but then, neither was she.

"You're not Gerard," she whispered at last, with honeyed sweetness. "You're teasing me, whoever you are. Tell me your name, sir."

"My name's O'Malley," came the reply in the darkness. "Rory O'Malley—and I'm desperate for your favors, madam. Take me with you, and let's have sport this night. For I've been living like a blessed monk ever since I met with the accident that broke my arm."

"Oh, how very sad for you," she cooed. "You have one arm out of action altogether? Well, then, you must let me do all I can to make you feel a little more comfortable. No, no—don't struggle—let *me* do everything."

She knew how long the drive out to Delaney House would take, and she timed the course of their amorous entanglement down to the last second; she would not permit him to do more than lie back, imprisoned in her embrace —each time he began to fumble with her bodice, or try to slide his one free hand on to her knee, she reprimanded him gently:

"No, no—not yet—time for that later, my dear," she assured him.

And all the while, she redoubled her own efforts, unbuttoning his shirt, slipping her hand inside, stroking his chest, tracing the line of his body-hair with a feathery forefinger, and teasing his nipples as he longed to tease and tickle hers; his body rigid with impatience, awaiting the promised moment of deliverance when he would have her, naked, beneath him

Slowly she persevered, holding him off with one hand, and continuing the skillful process of undressing him with the other. She pushed down his breeches, and pulled aside his shirt, finding her way to the part of his body that seemed now to be on fire with passion.

"Oh, you're a little witch, so you are," he groaned. "Steady—steady now—don't touch me like that, or—"

He wriggled spasmodically, in the grip of an overmastering sensation of desire, feeling that he might explode at any moment.

"By God, if I had the use of both my arms here and now, I'd—I'd—"

"Yes, Mr. O'Malley? What would you do?" she asked, in a clear, sharp voice that stung like a lash. "You'd cut a fine figure of a man, I'm sure—as you do at this moment!"

And with that she gave him a sudden push that sent him reeling back into the corner of the carriage. At the same instant, the coach pulled up with a clatter of hooves, and Bella made a dive for the door handle.

As she climbed down into the stableyard at Delaney Hall, she called up to the coachman on the box: "You may show our passenger the gate, and set him off on the road back to the city, Manahan. It will be a long walk, but the exercise will do him good."

Then she disappeared quickly, leaving the door wide open, and the cruel lamplight flooding in—illuminating the humiliated and helpless figure of Rory O'Malley, his breeches about his ankles, his shirt up around his neck, rolling on his back in the corner of the carriage.

126

Hearing the sound of the coachman jumping down, Rory began desperately tugging at his clothes, trying, with only one hand, to cover himself and regain some sort of modesty before he was discovered.

Meanwhile, back at the threatre, Gerard waited in the dressing room for Coral to come and join him. Dermot had left some time ago; everyone else seemed to have gone but still she did not appear.

At last he went in search of her, and found her in the ladies' dressing room—alone. Half-undressed, in her bright green wrapper, her copper-colored hair tumbling, and her head buried in her hands.

"Coral?" he began, wondering if she were ill. "It's getting very late."

"Go away. I don't want you to see me like this," she said in a muffled voice, and he realized that she was in tears.

"My darling—" He crossed the room in two long strides, and put his hands on her shoulder. "Don't—please don't cry—"

"Oh, go away—leave me alone, do—I'll be all right presently."

"But what is it? Was it the boos and cat-calls tonight? It was frightening, I know, but it's over now—"

"It was the—the *dandelions . . .*"

She gestured vaguely along the dressing table, and Gerard saw that she had set the bunch of gaudy yellow flowers in an empty bottle as a defiant gesture.

"I pretended to the others—Mrs. Mountford and Miss Pike—that I didn't care at all . . . But I did care, Gerard. I was so ashamed. I've never lost an audience before, like that—never so badly. I wished I were dead."

She was sobbing like a child now, and she lifted her face to him, with the tear-stains upon her lovely cheeks, and her eyes washed clean and clear. Green eyes, green as the depths of a secret pool beneath a grove of willows.

Like a child, he comforted her, taking her head upon his shoulder, and coaxing her gently.

"It doesn't matter. It's not important. You couldn't have held that audience—no one could. As Rory said, they were out for blood. It was Beverley's crowd, determined to make trouble—it was not directed personally against you or me or any of us—it was a fight to destroy the whole Maguire company. But we're not going to let them destroy us, are we, my love? Of course not—because you are the best actress in Ireland, and they'll be at your feet again in no time at all—and they'll be throwing you roses then. Just you wait and see!"

She looked up at him solemnly, and said:

"Only in *Ireland?*"

He laughed, and held her to his heart, saying: "The best actress in Ireland, England, Europe—the whole wide world! And the most beautiful woman . . . And the love of my life."

He bent his head, and kissed her—on the cheek, as if to remove all traces of her tears: and she turned her face up to him, so that their lips met.

This was a kiss like no other that Coral had ever known; gentle, and yet with all the strength of deep, true affection. She knew that he meant what he said; he loved her—as she loved him—and suddenly she forgot her unhappiness—the tears and terrors of the evening fled away, and she was only aware of Gerard holding her in his arms. Gerard's steadfast love and kindness, now and forever.

"It is true," she said at last. "The love of your life. Oh, Gerard, I am so happy."

He kissed her again and again, drawing her into an embrace that seemed as if their bodies melted together and became one—and she felt such an overwhelming sense of certainty and peace, she wanted to show him some special tenderness—to repay his love in the most natural way in the world.

"Gerard," she whispered, on the softest breath imaginable. "I belong to you. I am yours."

As she spoke, she slipped her arms out of the wrapper, and he saw that she was wearing nothing underneath it but her plain half-petticoat.

"My darling girl . . ." He did not trust himself to speak: realizing that she was giving herself to him—body and soul.

"I'm yours," she repeated, and spread out her hands to

him—still with a childlike simplicity. "Hold me, Gerard, and never let me go."

For now she had no doubts at all: she knew that this was the man who had been put into the world especially for her, there would never be another. Her hands were trembling as he gathered her in his arms once more; but she was not afraid. She was only aware of a tremendous excitement that seemed to spread from the deepest center of her being and sweep across her whole body, like a raging fever in her blood. She could feel her heart beating, so loudly, she felt sure Gerard must hear it too, the strong, demanding rhythm increasing—increasing.

She was aware of his hands upon her; she was aware that the half-petticoat was slipping away, and that too was perfectly right, and as it should be, for now she was completely naked, concealing nothing and witholding nothing; naked with him, as they had been together for one whole night. Only that time they had done nothing but look, without touching and now their bodies touched, tingled, stroked, embraced one another, each new caress leading on to more and more wonderful delights. It was as if all the promises of love she had ever dreamed of were about to come true in one unbelievable moment— now—here—tonight—

Suddenly she was aware that he had stopped short, and that his head was raised: he seemed to be sniffing the air, and she was reminded of a young stallion she had once seen, when it scented danger.

"What is it?" she asked.

"Smoke . . . don't you smell it? Something's burning," he said.

Now the acrid tang of wood-smoke was in her nose too; like a bonfire—but what was a bonfire doing here, in the theatre?

Gerard pressed her hand once, and said: "Wait—"

He made for the door and flung it open. Immediately, a thick cloud of blinding smoke billowed into the dressing room, and she heard the roar of flames, somewhere below.

"God help us," said Gerard quietly. "Those villains have taken their revenge. The theatre is on fire."

(8)

Alarums Offstage

Coughing a little, as the killing smoke got into his throat, Gerard shut the door quickly, and said:

"Get dressed as fast as you can . . . I don't know how much time we have."

Coral thanked heaven, as she hurried into her clothes, that her experience of quick-changes between scenes had given her plenty of practice. Even at this moment of crisis, her fingers flew, and in a few seconds she had pulled on her undergarments, and slipped a dress over her head.

"Don't waste time fastening it up—you can attend to that later," said Gerard.

Meanwhile, he had been dousing two make-up towels in the basin of water that stood nearby, and now, wringing out the damp clothes, he passed one to her.

"Put that over your mouth, so the fumes won't suffocate you and stay close by me."

Once more he opened the door, and they plunged straight out into the fog of smoke as it rushed to meet them.

Coral felt her eyes sting with tears, and clung on to his

arm desperately: she could not see which way to go. He urged her along the passage.

"We'll try the stairs——" he began, then hesitated.

From the head of the stairwell, they could hear the menacing rumble of the fire blazing on a lower floor, and the wall of smoke was fitfully illuminated by the hellish glare of flames.

"Too risky. We must find another way," Gerard decided. "Come back here."

Along the corridor, he remembered seeing an old window—almost black with grime, and permanently unopened. Now he raised his forearm and struck the glass smartly.

The panes shattered, and with another blow he knocked out the rickety frame.

"Where?" Coral gasped, trying not to breathe the choking fumes that swirled around them.

"On to the roof. It's our only hope," he said shortly. "I'll go first, then you follow. Don't be afraid—I won't let you fall."

To her dismay, he scrambled out of the gaping hole where the window had been, hung for a moment by his fingertips, then disappeared. She put a hand to her throat, stifling a scream, then nerved herself to peer out into the darkness.

There was a flat roof, some ten feet below—it looked a horribly long way down, but Gerard was standing there, holding up his arms to encourage her.

"Jump down as I did—I will catch you," he called.

Behind her, the crackle of the blaze seemed to be growing louder; and the night air smelled sweet and pure outside. She had no alternative but to obey. Scrambling over the frame as best she could, she clutched at the sill and let herself down until her arms were stretched at full-length—and beneath her feet she could feel empty space. Shuddering, she whispered under her breath:

"Holy Mary, mother of God—help me now——"

And let go.

A brief instant of terror as she fell into blackness, and then—heaven be praised! She was in Gerard's arms, and he lowered her gently to her feet.

131

"Now where?" she asked, when she could speak.

"Over the rooftops, among the chimney pots, till we find a way down again."

He took her hand in his, and led her on a perilous journey that seemed as if it would never end; over coping-stones, balancing on narrow ledges, slipping and sliding down sloping tiled roofs—with the perpetual threat of a horrifying drop to the ground, far below. After one sickening glance downward, she resolved only to look ahead—and tried to forget what lay in wait if she should lose her footing.

But Gerard guided her safely, and at last they reached an open attic-window, and he helped her clamber inside.

The attic itself was in semi-darkness, and she could dimly perceive the shape of a double bed, and—oh, horrors!—the pale shapes of two figures coupling upon the sheets. A girl's voice cried out in alarm, a man swore an obscene oath, and fumbled for the candle upon the bed-side table.

As a flame leapt up and the room was illuminated, Coral averted her eyes from the two naked bodies, still entangled in the act of love.

Gerard stammered an apology and tried to explain—"The theatre—on fire—escaping for our lives—rooftops—window—"

"Go to hell!" snarled the man, and flung an empty bottle at Gerard's head.

They needed no second bidding, but fled through the door, and down an unfamiliar staircase, to the street.

"Go to hell . . ." The words echoed ominously in Coral's ears, over and over again; she was alive—she was safe—but she had stood upon the brink of hell, and but for God's grace she would have finished up in its depths.

The next morning, and for the second day running, the assembled Maguire company sat around the breakfast table in the commercial hotel, and their mood was one of black despair.

Dermot outlined the situation as best he could.

"As far as I can make out—Gerard and Coral were still upstairs in the theatre when the fire started, after everyone else had left." He frowned, querying this for the first time. "How was it you both stayed behind, so late?"

Gerard glanced around, and was relieved to find that Coral was not present at this company meeting, for some reason.

"I—we were rehearsing—" he lied. "Going over our lines, you understand."

"Ah—good lad—conscientious as ever . . . Well, it's a mercy you were there, or else the whole theatre would have been a smouldering ruin by now—the whole street, perhaps!" He turned back to the company. "For after Gerard and my niece managed to escape through an upper window, they raised the alarm, and the fire brigade was soon upon the scene. They managed to put out the flames eventually, before it had spread throughout the entire building. And they also discovered the cause of the fire."

"Beverley's hired thugs," muttered Rory. "That's obvious."

"We can never prove it—but I'm inclined to agree. The villains must have sneaked in when they thought the coast was clear or hung about after the play till everyone had left. Anyhow, there were traces of oil and tar scattered about. They intended the whole place to blaze up like an inferno."

"But the theatre itself has been saved?" asked Walter Wilkins.

"It will be closed for repairs for some time to come, I fancy—there's a great hole in the stage, and the front curtains are burnt to cinders. But yes—it can be restored, and it will reopen next season, I've no doubt."

"And—how about *us?*" Rory voiced the question that was in everyone's mind.

Dermot spread his hands wide, and let his head sag hopelessly.

"Ah . . . As to *that* . . ." His voice cracked: Gerard found himself wondering whether he was witnessing one of the old actor's better performances of a tragic hero but reprimanded himself when he saw that there were real tears in Dermot's eyes. "As to that—we have lost everything. Costumes, curtains, back-cloths, wings—all our properties—every single item that has ever graced our stage . . . Everything has been destroyed."

"What are we to do, Mr. Maguire?" asked Mrs. Mountford.

"We acknowledge defeat, dear lady . . . I have striven to battle against the slings and arrows of outrageous fortune—I have borne with patient suffering all the whips and scorns of time—but now I must admit that I am beaten."

He announced the arrangements for winding up the company; such money as had been taken at last night's performance would be divided among them all—and then they would make their way back across the country as best they could, to retire to Dublin, and lick their wounds. Somehow—some time—he hoped that he would be able to gather together his loyal band of artists once more, and begin again.

As the actors dispersed, in an unhappy silence, Gerard met Coral in the front hall; she seemed to have been out for a walk, and was exchanging a greeting with the hall-porter.

When she saw Gerard, her smile faded and she held out a letter to him.

"This arrived for you, by special messenger, the first thing this morning," she said.

He recognized Bella's spiky, ill-formed handwriting, and thrust the letter into his pocket, saying: "I'll read it later."

"From your cousin, I expect?" she asked politely.

"Scolding me for not meeting her last night—or bidding me farewell forever . . . It doesn't matter, either way; we have no more to say to one another."

"No—perhaps not . . . Just as you and I have no more to say, either," she added quietly.

"What?" he stared at her, wondering if he had heard her correctly.

"Sit down for a moment, Gerard. For I must explain to you."

She led him to a quiet corner, where a potted palm

shielded a small sofa in an alcove, and they could talk undisturbed.

"I don't understand—what are you saying?" he asked.

"Simply that we must not see one another again—except when it is necessary, in the way of business—if we are ever to act together, for instance."

"Your Uncle just told us all that the company has been disbanded. We can't go on."

"Yes, so he told me when I first woke up this morning—before I went out. But we may possibly find ourselves on the same stage at some future date—who knows? If we do—I shall try to think of you as a fellow-artiste, and treat you as such. But nothing more."

"Coral, what is all this nonsense? I love you—you love me—last night we both knew that without any shadow of a doubt—"

"Last night we allowed ourselves to be snared by Satan's wicked wiles. I was as much in the wrong as you—I admit that—and if it had not been for the fire in the theatre, I would have been seduced into sin. Today I should have been a scarlet woman. Oh, Gerard—just think—that fire was sent by God Almighty to keep us from falling from grace. It was a sign from heaven of the purgatory that would be in store for us both, if we had succumbed to temptation."

Gerard gazed at her for a long moment, and saw that she was in deadly earnest.

"You really believe all that, don't you?" he asked at last.

"Of course." She lifted her chin. "Oh, I know you're only a poor Protestant, and you don't understand the rules—so perhaps it would be easier for you to transgress, in your invincible ignorance. But I *do* know—and that's what the Father reminded me, not half an hour since."

"Father—?"

"The parish priest at the church around the corner," Coral enlightened him. "I had to go and make my confession for what we did last night—"

"What we *nearly* did—"

"No! We may have been saved on the brink of mortal

135

sin, but what we did was shame enough—we were more than halfway down the primrose path when the blessed saints intervened—"

"Yes—damn their interference. And just as we were enjoying those primroses so much." Gerard reflected bitterly.

"Hold your tongue, Gerard—for I won't listen to such wickedness! And now the Father has given me instructions that I *must* not let myself be drawn into temptation again. He says I have to avoid the occasion of sin, you see —and the occasion of sin is you. So from now on—we must go our separate ways. I'm sure you will understand that."

"I understand nothing of the sort—you and your Catholic rigmarole—we love one another, my dear girl—that's all I know or care about—"

"Ssh! I won't hear another word!" She rose to her feet. "If you love me as you say you do—then leave me in peace. For if I were foolish enough to listen to your sweet words and your easy promises—I would be lost forever."

And with that, she swept past him, and walked upstairs without a backward glance.

Slowly, and in deep depression, Gerard followed her up the staircase, and made his way to the bedroom which he shared with Rory.

He found Rory attempting as best he could, with one hand to pack up his clothes and his belongings before leaving the hotel.

"Here's a fine slap in the eye," he grumbled, cramming a pair of boots into an already overcrowded valise. "Here's a sudden end to fame and fortune. I sometimes think the fates have their knife into me—it seems to be one damned disaster after another. Breaking my arm, being booed off the stage, tricked and tormented by that cousin of yours last night—and a ten-mile walk back to town into the bargain. And now this happens, on top of everything else!"

"Oh—I forgot to ask you, Rory, in the excitement of the fire and all that followed—what *did* happen to you last night?"

136

Rory told him, as briefly as possible, only omitting some of the more embarrassing details; but then concluded: "The most infuriating part of all is that I really have taken a fancy to the wretched girl. God, I'd have given anything for a night with her—she's so full of fire and spunk—she really knows how to put a chap on his mettle—"

"But surely you'd never look at her again, after the way she treated you?"

"Well . . ." Rory paused, and gave a half smile. "I don't know . . . In some ways it'd be more exciting than ever, if she . . . Oh, but what's the use? We'll never see her again, I'm quite sure of that."

As he resumed his packing, Gerard recalled the letter that Bella had sent him, and tore it open, scanning the contents quickly.

"Dear Gerard *Kean*—as I shall think of you from now on, for you are certainly not fit to be connected to me by family ties in future. You are a low, treacherous hound, and I despise you. I also despise your poor fool of a friend, who got what he deserved: I only wish I could have made you suffer at the same time. Remember that I warned you what I should do if you disappointed me: I have the paper and ink here now, all ready for me to write to poor dear Uncle George, and tell him of your infamous conduct. But shall I do it—or shan't I . . . ? That will be your punishment, Master Gerard; the agonies of uncertainty. For you will never know whether I have told your father the dreadful truth—or not. I do hope that you will let this question torment you for many a long, sleepless night."

And the letter was signed by: "Your loving cousin no longer—Bella."

Gerard crumpled the letter and stuffed it back into his pocket angrily; then began upon his own packing.

In the end, he and Rory travelled to Dublin in the same stagecoach as Dermot and Coral. Rory pointed out that it was worth paying the fare, even if it took up most of the little cash they had left, in order to get to the capital as fast as possible.

There were plenty of theatres there, and opportunities

for young actors . . . they would find work again very soon, he felt sure.

Gerard was less optimistic; and the journey itself became a long, slow penance, as they bumped over the hundred and sixty miles of country roads between Cork and Dublin in the russet twilight of the dying summer. To make things worse, Coral tried to pretend that Gerard no longer existed; she only spoke to him when she had to, sitting on the far side of the carriage, gazing out of the window at the changing color of the leaves on the trees, and never once meeting his eye.

He watched her and cursed her and cursed the pious priests who had schooled her so strictly. He even tried to hate her; but that he could not do—for as he stared at her beautiful profile, and the pert, tilted tip of her nose— the lovely curves of her breasts that had once been his alone—the slim, seductive sweep of her long legs from thigh to ankle—he knew that he still loved her desperately, and that he always would.

Somewhere in her heart of hearts, he felt sure that she loved him too, and waited hungrily for some sign— some ray of hope—but it never came.

When they arrived in Dublin, Dermot recommended the young men to a lodging-house he knew well, and always stayed at—in a little alley off Merchants Quay, only a stone's throw from the River Liffey.

"Oh, Uncle—I'm sure that the boys don't want to come and lodge with us—they'll be far happier in some place of their own—and besides, Mrs. Riley may not have room enough for all four of us."

"We can but enquire," said Dermot. "After all, you need a roof over your head, don't you, gentlemen? And speaking for myself—I feel that as long as we four stick together—the sooner there might be a chance of getting our little company upon the road once more."

So they all went in to meet Mrs. Riley—a plump, garrulous woman with her hair forever tumbling about her face in untidy corkscrew curls, and such a rapid flow of chatter that she could hardly catch her breath between sentences.

"Oh, if it isn't Mr. Dermot and his beautiful nieces—no, only *one* beautiful niece this time—and where's Miss Rosalie got to at all? Is she still off play-acting somewhere? Well, may the holy Mother of God be with her wherever she is—Miss Coral, it's a joy to see you again, dotey—for I look on you as if you were my own long-lost daughter, so I do—and who have we here? Two of the acting gentlemen, is it? Good day to you, Mr. O'Malley—and good day to you, whatever your name is —for I'm pleased to make your acquaintance—if it's rooms you're wanting, you're in luck this day, for haven't I just had to turn out a poor miserable lump of a showman for not paying his rent? Him and his wife and his three ugly daughters—they go round the country telling fortunes, but they'll never have a fortune of their own to tell, and that's a fact—they travelled a mangy old parrot with them that picked cards out of a hat and sang a bawdy song—and I had to give them their marching orders only yesterday, so come you upstairs this minute and you shall see the set of rooms, God love you—though I must be honest with you and admit that the smell of that parrot-cage lingers on something shocking—but I swear to God it'll be all right once I've opened the window and rearranged the atmosphere!"

So Gerard found himself once again sharing a bed with Rory, knowing that in a small room just on the other side of the wall, Coral herself was lying on a narrow cot beneath the window. He sometimes wondered if she too spent sleepless nights as he did, gazing up at the frosty stars, and remembering.

The winter evenings drew in, and they set out to scrape a living from the busy city. True, there were theatres all around; but there were a lot of actors in Dublin, and jobs were not easy to come by. When Rory's broken arm was totally healed, he obtained a small part in a production of *As You Like It,* as Charles the Wrestler; and by his influence, persuaded the manager to take Gerard on as a walking-gentleman of the court, and understudy to Orlando.

Dermot struggled to recoup his finances—doing anything and everything from playing cards (for stakes he could not afford to lose) to wheedling small loans out of more fortunate cronies—and, on occasion, giving recitals of old poems in a bar-parlor, and then passing round the hat.

As for Coral, well, Gerard hardly ever saw her; she left Mrs. Riley's house early every morning, and did not return till late at night. She never said where she was going, but he had the vague impression that she might be working in a shop, perhaps—and that she would not wish him to know about it.

And then, one cold day, when the east wind blew in off the Irish Sea, scouring the riverside quays mercilessly, Gerard and Rory were making their way to a rehearsal at the theatre, when a carriage pulled up at the curb, and a voice hailed them.

"*Nom de Dieu!*—this is a pleasant surprise!"

The newcomer sprang out, shaking them warmly by the hand; and paid off the cab-driver.

"Thank you, my good man—now I have met my friends, I will walk instead. *Messieurs—comment allez-vous?* I hope you are well?"

It was Paul La Roche; looking more elegant—more expensively turned out—than ever.

"Monsieur La Roche—what are you doing here?" asked Gerard, and Rory chimed in: "Where's Rosalie? Is she with you?"

"One thing at a time, my dear sirs! Please call me Paul—remember? We are on first-name terms, are we not?"

"Paul then—but where are you staying? I don't believe Dermot and Coral know that you are back in Ireland," said Gerard.

"No, of course not—for I did not know where to get in touch with them. Rosalie, alas, is still in Paris; I had to come over at short notice—on a matter of business. I travelled alone—it is more convenient, I find—and one can move more swiftly."

"So you are here all by yourself?" asked Rory.

"Entirely . . . I have not even brought my invaluable

Henri this time—you remember Henri, my chef? I decided to leave him in Paris, to look after my lovely wife . . . But this is a very happy encounter—tell me, how is old Monsieur Maguire—and how is Coral?"

He fell into step with them, and they continued to stroll along Grafton Street. The two actors exchanged glances uneasily.

"Oh—Coral's pretty well," replied Gerard after a moment. "We don't see much of her these days."

"No? She is very busy, I expect—performing in some splendid role here in Dublin? I was looking for her name on the playbills, but so far. . . ."

"She—er—she's not exactly performing at the moment," said Gerard, and Rory added quickly:

"She's what we call *resting*, you understand—between engagements."

"Oh, I see . . . well, you must give me her address, so I may pay my respects to her, and to her uncle—I have many messages for them both from Rosalie—"

They turned the corner into St. Stephen's Green at this point, and Paul broke off, at the sound of a clear, sweet soprano voice. They all stopped—and looked . . .

Coral was standing alone, under the leafless branches of a tree, singing a sad little ballad of love betrayed. For an instant, Gerard thought she had taken leave of her senses—and then he realised that there was a begging-bowl at her feet, and that she was singing to any passer-by who might spare a penny for her song.

She saw them at the same instant, and broke off; the music dying on her lips. A quick flush of shame mounted in her cheeks, and she picked up the bowl from the pavement, and prepared to make her escape.

"Coral—*cherie*—don't go . . . Rosalie sent me to find you," Paul called out; and that arrested her. As she hesitated uncertainly—"Come," he added, in a softer tone. "I think perhaps you had better all come and have lunch with me, so that we can exchange our news."

They ran Dermot to earth in the snug of a shabby saloon ten minutes later, and then Paul whisked them all away to his very luxurious hotel. There he ordered a meal to be served in a private dining room, and sat listening while they pieced together the story of their misfortunes.

"But this is incredible!" he exclaimed at last. "I cannot permit you to continue in such circumstances . . . You must collect your company together again and prepare a new play. I have money enough to hire a theatre—to pay for costumes and scenery and salaries. And I also have many good friends here in the city—friends with influence in high places. I am sure I can raise plenty of support for your venture—come, dear Mr. Maguire—what is your next play to be?"

Dermot's head was bowed as if in prayer, listening to these words of hope and encouragement; and when he looked up, Gerard saw there was a new light in his eye.

"On this happy occasion—" he said, in a voice choked with emotion, "what else can I offer but the greatest play ever written? I will give you of my very best, Monsieur . . . I shall give you *Hamlet* . . ."

Gerard saw Coral's face fall, and wondered why: then he realized. The old gentleman was proposing to play the gloomy Dane himself; regardless of the fact that he was some forty years too old for the part.

There was a long silence; no one dared to speak. At last, Coral ventured, very carefully: "You don't think perhaps, Uncle—that this time—*King Lear* might be more acceptable?"

"*Lear?* Bah! We've just given our *Lear*. No, no—I am quite determined—it's *Hamlet* next, the finest play in the world, the most poetic role."

He looked around from face to face, and slowly read the message that was written in all their expressions; it was a poignant moment.

Dermot looked down at his hands, and studied them carefully; perhaps he noticed the brown marks of age upon the skin, or the way the veins stood out, or the thickening joints at each knuckle. Whatever it was that he saw he knew that his time had come, and he continued smoothly, as if he had not been interrupted: "I myself," he said, "will play King Claudius, naturally . . . as for the Prince of Denmark—well, that can be decided

142

later—Rory—or Gerard—I'll have to think it over at my leisure."

Then he took a deep breath, and followed up this unprecedented announcement by saying:

"You see, my friends, I've been giving a great deal of thought to this particular play recently and I've come to a very interesting conclusion. I have decided that, above all, this is a play about *kingship*."

So the decision was made. In many ways it was an excellent choice; there was no doubt that Dermot would make a fine Claudius, and steal every scene in which he appeared. Again, it presented no problems from the distaff side; Coral would give her Ophelia, and Mrs. Mountford would be recruited as Queen Gertrude. The only question that remained unanswered was the casting of the title role.

As the days passed, Dermot appeared to be unable to make up his mind; now he seemed to favor Rory, now he came down on the side of Gerard. One of them, certainly, would play the Prince, and the other would be given Laertes. But which?

The situation was becoming uncomfortable; Gerard and Rory, for so long the best of friends, found themselves in competition, and became increasingly irritable. Coral could see what was happening, and tried to restore a sense of calm, by saying:

"I know Uncle Dermot—he's unable to decide because deep down he doesn't want to decide. He may say he's interested in playing Claudius, but we all know that secretly he can't bear to give up Hamlet. That's why he's keeping you both dangling on a string."

It seemed all too likely but it did not help the two leading-men in their rivalry.

One evening, Paul La Roche summoned Gerard to meet him at his hotel for a drink before dinner and Gerard's heart leaped; he assumed that he had been selected to play the title role, and this was a confidential way of breaking the news.

But he was quite wrong; having set the wheels in motion, Paul was content to let the production take shape without interference from him. His intention in asking

143

Gerard to join him for a private conversation was something very different.

"Irish whisky—I hope that is what you like?" he said, pouring two generous measures. "Do you take water with it, perhaps?"

"No, no—I'll drink it as it is, thank you."

"As it is, then . . . *votre santé* . . . or *slainte,* as the Irish say . . ." He raised his glass, and added casually: "But of course when it comes to Irish you are as much of a foreigner as I, or so I am informed."

"What? I'm sorry—I don't quite follow."

"Monsieur Maguire let me into your little secret just the other day—he tells me that Kean is not your real name, and that you are in fact an Englishman. That is why I invited you here this evening—for this news interested me very much . . . We have something in common, it seems."

Gerard stared at him. "I still don't understand what you are saying . . ."

"Your country is at war with France, *n'est-ce pas?* Your armies under the great Duke of Wellington are doing their best to chase the Emperor Napoleon Bonaparte out of Portugal and Spain."

"Well—yes—but—"

"So it follows that you yourself are an enemy of Bonaparte—no?" Paul La Roche smiled faintly, and sipped his whisky. "Do not worry, my friend . . . You are not alone in that . . ."

Gerard tried to piece together the information that was being given to him.

"You mean—*you*—? But I thought—I always assumed that was why you keep travelling from France to Ireland on 'business,' as you call it. I imagined that you were acting as the Emperor's agent trying to raise public opinion in support of France, against the English—"

Paul gazed into his glass for a moment, then said: "There is such a thing—you know?—as a double agent. Oh, yes, I am a trusted member of the Emperor's confidential cabinet, one of his most respected advisers. And I can pass freely into this country, for I am accepted by the British as a French aristocrat, fleeing from the tyranny of the republic. And the beauty of it is, this is *all* true, sadly true. My father was Count André de la Roche and he met his death upon the guillotine. So I ask you, Mr. Kean—or Mr. Mallory—to whom do you think I owe my loyalty? If you were in my place—which side would you be working for?"

Gerard did not reply; his thoughts were in a maze. Noticing this, Paul shrugged and smiled again.

"It is no matter . . . I wondered—after what old Maguire let slip—if perhaps you yourself might be here for some deeper purpose. Sent by your countrymen, to find out information? But no, I think I have misinterpreted the situation. You are a fine young actor and nothing more. So let us forget all I have said. It might be that I was only jesting, after all."

When Gerard returned to the lodging house that night, he had a great deal to think about; and perhaps that is why he was not in a very tolerant mood when he found Rory in the bedroom, pacing the floor with a script in his hand, and declaiming: *"To be or not to be—that is the question . . ."*

"And what's the answer?" Gerard broke in impatiently. "You've been told you're playing the role—is that it? While my back was turned—Dermot's promised you that you'll play *Hamlet*—"

"Not exactly," said Rory, smiling. "But I don't think there's much doubt that he will, before long. After all, I am the more experienced actor—he'd hardly entrust Shakespeare's finest role to a comparative beginner."

"Experience doesn't matter—it's sincerity that counts," retorted Gerard. "I've just been informed by Monsieur La Roche that I am a fine young actor—and since he's the one holding the purse-strings—"

"Sincerity counts, does it?" exclaimed Rory, flinging down his script. "What's so sincere about crawling to the management—licking the Frenchie's boots, to land the role—I call that disgusting—"

"How dare you accuse me of—" Gerard began: and stepped back a pace as Rory advanced upon him threateningly, his eyes ablaze.

"Don't you take that tone with me, you young dog!"

he shouted, raising his fists. "I'll thrash you any day of the week—"

A tattoo of thumping upon the wall of the next bedroom startled both men; Coral had overheard the argument through the thin partition, and was telling them to behave themselves.

They broke off, and looked at the wall then at one another. Suddenly, a grin lit up Rory's sullen face, and his expression changed as if by magic.

"Sorry . . . I'm in a black mood, and no mistake."

"And so am I. It's all the fault of Old Dermot—shillyshallying like this—"

"It's not only that. Do you want to know why I'm spoiling for a fight—and so are you? It's women that's the cause of it all," said Rory, lowering his voice discreetly.

"Women?"

"The lack of them, rather . . . I haven't had a girl for this past month and there's you going half-crazy for love of that one in the next room . . . We're both in a bad way, old son—and all for the sake of a quick tumble between the sheets."

Gerard sighed. "You may be right there . . . but it can't be helped—"

"Don't talk such nonsense. How much money d'you have on you this minute? Listen to me, lad—we'll pool our resources, and I'll take you visiting. We'll pay a call on a certain young lady I know, who lives not five minutes' walk from here. A very *obliging* young lady."

Gerard began to argue—he didn't want to go with a whore—he wasn't in the market for love that required payment—he'd prefer to stay at home and let Rory go on his own—

Rory refused to be put off. It was what they both needed; and once they had satisfied their physical needs, they would feel all the better for it. Then they could stop sparring, and be better friends than before.

Gradually, Gerard let himself be talked into it.

So that night, he followed Rory into a shabby bedroom in Bartholomew Lane, one of the most notorious streets in Dublin. By the light of a pink-shaded lamp, he appraised the girl who sat on the unmade bed—a girl in a negligée of ragged lace, with too much rouge on her cheeks, and an aura of cheap perfume hanging over her like a cloud.

"This is Deirdre," said Rory. "Say good evening, old fellow—and get your clothes off."

"Manners!" The girl slapped Rory on the wrist. "There's no need to be *vulgar* . . ."

Gerard eyed her, and decided that he might have done worse. She was fairly young, and though her eyes were cold and hard, her painted mouth was attractive—and so for her figure.

She stood up, and let the negligée fall to the floor: now she was totally nude, and he let his eyes roam over her full, ripe breasts—her gently-curving belly—and the valley between her legs, which, he noticed with surprise, was quite uncovered by hair.

"She shaves herself," Rory murmured in his ear. "She thinks it's more refined, would you believe it?"

"What are you whispering about?" Deirdre asked. "Look sharp, young 'un—or your friend'll be ready before you—and you don't want to get the left-overs, do you now?"

Gerard began slowly to undress, noting that Rory was already half-naked, and obviously eager for action. It was the first time Gerard had seen another man in a state of excitement, since he was a young boy, spying on the stable-lad who lay with his sister, Garnet, on the banks of the fishpond at Rosewood, after they had been swimming together. Suddenly Gerard felt shy, and looked away, saying: "Which of us—I mean—who will—that is to say, I don't mind waiting in another room."

"Sure, there's no other room here—what do you think this is, the Grand Hotel?" asked Deirdre, and came toward him, smiling. "It's all for one and one for all in this establishment—ain't that so, darling?" she added, with a wink at Rory.

By this time Rory had stripped completely, and they both watched Gerard as he began reluctantly to unfasten his breeches.

He fumbled with the buttons, feeling foolish and ill-at

ease under their scrutiny. He wished fervently that he had never agreed to accompany Rory on this expedition, and remembered Coral, who would now be at their lodgings alone ... and longed to be with her.

But at that point, Deirdre pounced upon him and Rory grabbed his arms—between them they hauled him on to the bed, pulling his clothes off despite his protests.

"Stop being bashful, my old cock-sparrow—" Rory cried, dragging down his breeches.

"Never mind the sparrow," giggled Deirdre, "let's see his."

Her hands flew to his drawers, swiftly exposing his most private parts; her supple fingers encouraging him to join in the fun. Helpless, Gerard found himself being rolled over on to his back, being teased and tickled by practised hands that were swift to arouse his lust; he began to laugh, and, for the moment, he forgot all about Coral.

For a while, the trio sported on the bed like young animals at play; hands grasping thighs, mouths upon breasts, fingers probing, groping, exploring, as they changed places in a swift sequence of movements that built steadily from one shameless position to another.

"Go on—give it to me—give me all you've got—" panted the girl, wrapping her legs around Gerard's waist: and he found himself entering her on a rising tide of excitement. They lay upon their sides, and he realized that Rory was behind her now, his knees pressed hard against Gerard's thighs, and his loins fastened close to Deirdre's generously-rounded hips.

"Yes, yes—both of you—both at once—" she gasped breathlessly. "Oh, God—the size of them—you'll destroy me altogether between you—but don't stop—don't stop —keep at it, boys—"

Gerard realized as the sexual crescendo mounted to a climax that she had contrived to accommodate them both in different ways; he even fancied that he could feel Rory's sturdy member thrusting away in a counter-rhythm, as if in response to his own accelerating tempo.

And then he reached the supreme moment all too soon, and the long triumphant spasms of relief spurted from him in a glorious torrent of satisfaction.

When it was over, he lay back, temporarily exhausted: and listened to Rory's impatient unfulfilled grunts of desire—for he had not yet been able to reach the same pitch of frenzy.

"What's the matter, lovey? Can't you get off the mark?" Deirdre asked, and added in a more menacing tone: "Do I have to get strict with you, mister?"

Gerard heard Rory growl, deep in his throat: "You know what I need—give me my punishment."

"Here and now?" She pulled away from Rory, and he turned his head, burying his face in the dirty sheets of the bed, and lying on his stomach, his arms outstretched, as if he had been crucified.

Gerard could not think at first what was happening, but then he saw Deirdre return to the bed, carrying a riding whip with a leather thong.

"Have you been a bad boy?" she asked, and her voice cut like a steel blade.

Crack! The lash descended across Rory's buttocks, raising a stinging weal: Gerard was about to protest, seeing his friend writhe under the blow in obvious pain. But was it pain or pleasure?

"Yes—I've been very bad—punish me again—get him to hold me down while you teach me a lesson—" Rory groaned.

"Well, sonny-boy? Do you want to help me to school him?" Deirdre invited Gerard mockingly.

"No—no, I can't—I won't do that. I've had all I want —I must go now."

And Gerard scrambled into his clothes as fast as possible, unwilling to stay and be a witness to Rory's humiliation. He left his share of the money on the mantelpiece and hurried from the room, hearing the sounds of the blows falling on naked flesh behind him—and hearing in his head, long after, the sounds of Rory's grovelling defeat—and final triumph.

Now at last he realized what made Rory O'Malley so short-tempered and aggressive; why he was always going out of his way to pick fights wherever he went. He had claimed that he had the will to win—but Gerard understood now that he also had the urge to lose. He gained perverse satisfaction from being beaten—morally, as well as physically; he wanted to suffer, and he went out to welcome his own degradation.

Gerard sympathized—but he could never put himself in Rory's situation, or fully comprehend the strange pattern of his desires. For Gerard, the pleasures of the body were something joyous and uncomplicated, and he thanked God that he did not share Rory's tortured appetites.

It was late when he finally let himself into their little bedroom at Mrs. Riley's lodging house; and later still when he awoke next morning after a deep, dreamless sleep. He found himself alone in the bed; Rory had not returned at all, last night.

At breakfast, he was unusually quiet; and Coral, as usual, said very little. Dermot and the landlady shared the talk between them; and even Dermot's determined efforts to speak had to give way before Mrs. Riley's endless flow of chatter.

"And where's Mr. O'Malley this morning, I wonder? Not in his bed?—now that's a strange thing, for didn't the two of you go out on the town last night? Sure you told me when you left that you were both off to visit an old friend—so what happened to Mr. O'Malley at all? Did he decide to stay overnight in his friend's house and let you come home alone?"

"Something of the sort," mumbled Gerard, and out of the corner of his eye he saw Coral raise her head and look at him suspiciously.

"I just hope to goodness the dear man hasn't been getting himself into any trouble," Mrs. Riley rattled on. "For God help me, I had an officer of the law here this morning before 'twas daylight, banging on the door and rousing decent people from their beds. 'And what are you wanting at this hour, man dear?' I asked the constable, and says he to me, 'I believe you have some theatrical gentlemen staying here, Mrs. Riley,' says he. 'Tell me now, would there be two young men in that line who might have gone out late last night and not returned home?' 'Nothing of the sort,' says I, for of course at that time I imagined that you were all tucked up snug in your beds like plums in a Christmas pie. I sent the Barney off with a flea in his ear, saying that we'd no one missing at all."

"But why did they want to know?" Dermot inquired: and she swept him away with the full flood of her reply.

"Seemingly there was some disgraceful goings-on last night down in Bartholomew Lane and there's a wicked sinful street if ever I heard of one. Some young woman no better than she should be entertaining two young actors in her room—the shameless hussy! And there was some trouble and terrible carryings-on—I didn't ask for details, for fear that I might poison my ears with the listening. Well, it can't have been *you,* Mr. Kean, for I declare you're always a perfect gentleman, and in any case I know full well you were sleeping alone last night in your own bed, like a Christian. But I wonder now, could Mr. O'Malley have got into bad company and gone astray?"

"Perhaps both our perfect Christian gentlemen went astray together last night," said Coral, flatly: and her glance was a direct accusation. "For I woke when I heard you come in, Mr. Kean—and I heard the clock chime three . . . plenty of time for the two of you to get into trouble before that . . ."

Gerard pushed back his chair and stood up.

"I've had all I want, thank you, Mrs. Riley," he said. "If you'll excuse me, I'll just slip up to my room . . ."

With that, he made his escape to the bedroom and discovered that Rory had returned while they were all at breakfast, and was now slumped across the bed, with a bruise the size of a pigeon's egg over his eye.

"Good God, man—you look terrible!" Gerard exclaimed. "What's been happening to you?"

Rory struggled to sit up, and tried to keep his voice steady as he replied: "After you left . . . well, you saw how things were with me, I'm not making any excuses—I know what I like, and I'm prepared to pay for it . . . But while she had me at her mercy, the little bitch, her pimp walked in on us, and started making himself objectionable . . . laughing at me, and—insulting me. Well, I wasn't going to stand for that—you know what I'm like when I see red. I let fly and he hit me in the face and—and I knocked him down. The damnable part was he struck his head on the fireplace, old son. I thought at first he'd knocked himself unconscious, but it was worse than that."

"Worse?"

"I'm in the hell of a mess, Gerard—Deirdre was screaming like a banshee, and then someone called for the Barneys—so I just grabbed my clothes, and—and I made a run for it . . . She don't know my name, but she knows I'm an actor—it won't be long before they track me down . . . can you lend me some money? For I'll have to take to the road, as fast as possible, and try to get away."

"But *why?* The pimp—what happened—"

"I told you, he hit his head, cracked his skull open. He's a dead man, Gerard and they'll say I killed him. If they catch me, it'll be a hanging matter."

(9)

The Curtain Falls

A hanging matter . . . Gerard sat on the bed beside Rory, his thoughts racing.

"What shall you do?"

"Once I get out of this damned city, I'll be in the clear —just let me have a day's start on them, and they won't see me for dust."

"But where will you go?"

"I'll make my way straight across country, to the West Coast . . . For I've friends and relations, in Galway—'tis the place of my birth, and I'll be safe there. Only God grant me good fortune to make the journey."

Gerard pulled a leather purse from his breeches pocket, and emptied it on to the rumpled sheets . . . A few golden guineas rolled out, and he pressed them into Rory's hands.

"Take these—take all the money I've got; no, don't argue—for I can earn more, and your state is desperate. I think I have some silver too, in my topcoat—"

He glanced at the back of the door, expecting to see his topcoat hanging there—but it was gone.

"Where the devil?" Then he remembered, and slapped his forehead angrily: "Fool that I am—I came away from that whore's lodgings in such a rush, I left my coat behind!"

Rory grimaced: "One thing's certain—you can hardly go back to fetch it now . . . For they'd lock you up for questioning till you told them all you knew of me."

"Don't worry—I shall never do that. The coat's of no importance—let it go."

Rory pocketed the guineas, then took Gerard's hand and Gerard could feel the moisture of his sweating palm.

"You're a true friend, so you are and I'll never forget what you've done for me . . . I will repay you all I owe some day, in God's good time."

They clasped hands for a moment longer, then Rory rose to his feet.

"Now I must be on my way, for the sooner I make a start, the happier I shall feel."

"What shall I say to old Dermot—?" Gerard began.

"Tell him what you like—tell him the truth—it's all over for me now." Rory grabbed his cloak, dragged a long muffler round his throat, and pulled it up over his chin, half-masking his face. "And . . . wish me luck."

"You know I do."

The door opened, and Rory was gone.

Gerard sat thinking over the situation for a few moments, then roused himself to go downstairs and break the news to Dermot—and to Coral.

He found them sitting at the breakfast table as he had left them, and Coral looked up in some surprise.

"You're still here?" she asked. "I was sure I heard the front door open and close just now—I thought you must have gone out."

"Not I . . . It was Rory you heard."

"He's back? For this relief, much thanks! I was beginning to be afraid he'd met with some dreadful accident," began Dermot.

"He had . . . And he's not here any longer." Gerard tried to explain as best he could. "Rory came in, but he's gone out again . . . And he won't be coming back."

"What's that? What are you saying?" frowned Dermot.

"We've a rehearsal called for ten o'clock—the assembled company—"

"Rory will not be among them . . . He sends his compliments, and asks me to make his apologies. He has had to leave town, unexpectedly."

Coral stood up: "I knew it—Mrs. Riley's guess was right—he's in some trouble with the law—"

"Is this true?" Dermot interrupted her. "So he did go last night, to Bartholomew Lane?"

"They *both* went there . . ." said Coral contemptuously. "Drinking and debauching—what beasts men are."

She moved across the little parlor, her head held high, concluding: "Don't tell me anything more, for I don't wish to hear the sordid details . . . I'm going to my room, Uncle."

When the door was shut, Gerard said quietly: "Perhaps that's as well for the fewer people who know the truth, the better. You see, sir, there was a fight last night."

"There always is, if Rory has anything to do with it. He's been caught in some drunken brawl again, is that it?"

"It's more serious than that. A man was killed, accidentally, in the course of the fight and they'll be after Rory for manslaughter . . . But he's not been caught—not yet, at any rate."

"*What?*" Dermot clasped his hands as if in prayer. "Dear God—what a terrible thing to happen—and at such a moment too . . . I was just about to make the announcement that he would be taking the title role in our play . . ."

"I see . . ." Gerard reflected on the vanity of human ambition: until half an hour ago, this news would have reduced him to the depths of gloom and jealousy but now it seemed curiously irrelevant. "That's unfortunate, of course, but—"

"Unfortunate? My dear young man, it means I have to reconsider the problem of casting the role all over again . . . *Hamlet*—without the prince? Oh, it's a bitter blow indeed."

Gerard looked at him, and felt like asking which was the more important—a man's life at stake—or the fortunes of an actor-manager? But he could see that Dermot was totally immersed in his own problems now, and decided to save his breath.

"I'll just go and make my peace with Coral," he said. "If you'll excuse me."

Up in her little bedroom, Coral was sitting with a mirror in one hand, and a comb in the other, arranging her glorious copper curls into a discreet chignon.

"Come in," she said, at the knock upon the door. "Oh —it's you, is it?"

"May I talk to you?" Gerard asked, coming in to the room.

"If you must . . . But I hope you'll be as brief as possible, for this promises to be a very busy day."

"What do you mean?"

"Had you forgotten that we have a rehearsal at ten o'clock? And no doubt the Barney officers will be here at any moment, wasting still more time with their tiresome questions about Rory . . . Oh, I could bang your silly heads together—how could you both be so stupid?"

Gerard broke in: "First of all—let me explain one thing to you. Rory is in very serious trouble, and has left town already. With luck, he will get away safely—thank God, there was only one witness to what happened last night, and she doesn't know his name."

"She? I thought as much. He was with some little drab, of course. Oh, what a fine pair of gentlemen you are—I hope you're proud of yourselves, going out to taste the delights of a place like Bartholomew Lane when everyone knows it's nothing but drinking-dens and brothels."

"Coral . . . Listen to me, please." Gerard dropped to one knee beside her chair, and gently took the comb and glass from her hands. "And look at me . . . I'm not proud of myself at all. And I would never have kept Rory company last night, if I had not been deeply unhappy— and lonely—myself."

"What do you mean?" She was looking at him now; her large green eyes, green as emeralds, searching his face.

"Unhappy because I had lost your love. And lonely because I had forfeited your friendship. Don't you under-

156

stand what torment I have been in, ever since we left Cork, because you've scarcely thrown me a word of a glance?"

"You know what we agreed—" she began uncomfortably.

"Forgive me—there was no agreement. You decided; I had no choice in the matter. I have had to endure the punishment of being banished from your side; but I have never stopped loving you for a single instant."

Impulsively, she put her hand upon his, saying: "Oh, Gerard, has it been such misery for you too?"

He took her hand between his own, and asked: "You admit it, then—that it is misery for both of us—to remain apart?"

"Yes—oh, yes—" she breathed. "All this while I have missed your company so much—loved you so deeply—wanted you so badly—"

"My dearest Coral . . . if you knew how much I want you—always—"

And then his arms were about her, and their bodies clung together in a hungry embrace—all the more fervent for having been so long denied them.

"It's true, it is really true," Coral thought, as her senses melted under the warmth of his kisses. "We do belong together—we were meant for one another—nothing else matters, only this."

She let herself go completely; as if she slipped down and down into the depths of their longing for each other, feeling his hands taking possession of her body, and welcoming the sure, strong passion that swept them both along, like a subterranean river. She knew that he was slowly beginning to undress her, and she gloried in it; she could not wait to be naked in his arms again, as she should be . . . She found herself, indeed, hurrying the moment of consummation along by helping him to pull off his jacket—slipping loose his cravat—unbuttoning his snowy-white shirt.

And then she stopped: and time stood still.

For there upon the collar was a gaudy smear of rouge and she realized that his shirt, his skin, was pungent with

157

some rank, vulgar perfume . . . The perfume of a whore.

Instantly, her violent hunger turned to rage, and she slapped his face hard, and pulled free of his embrace.

"How *could* you?" she demanded. "How could you come to me from that woman's bed with the smell of her still about you and the mark of her painted face on your linen? Keep away from me, you cheapjack Casanova!"

He tried to pull her into his arms again, but she eluded him skillfully, and dodged to the far side of the bed, adjusting her disarrayed garments.

"You say you love me but it's not love you want; it's nothing but filthy lust. You disgust me!"

Gerard scrambled to his feet, and followed her, maddened by her attack, and by his own feeling of guilt and worst of all by the desire for her beautiful body which completely overpowered him.

She saw the look in his eyes, and grabbed a candlestick from the bedside table, determined to put up a fight for her honor.

"Don't you *dare*," she panted.

His hands grasped her by the wrists, and he dragged her toward him: she aimed the candlestick at his head, and missed, the blow fell wide of the mark, striking him on the shoulder, overbalancing him, so that they tumbled sideways together on to the bed, kicking and struggling.

A hammering on the door interrupted them, at this critical moment.

"Coral! Coral, I say!" boomed Dermot "What in heaven's name d'you think you're playing at? Stop that noise you're making—the pictures are dancing on the walls down below! Give over your foolery this minute, and come downstairs, for there's a lot of serious work to be done."

Breathless, the two youngsters on the bed came to their senses, and sat up, without looking at one another.

"I have to go," Coral said in a low voice.

"I'll come with you," said Gerard.

"Suit yourself." She tossed her head, and discovered that her new chignon had come adrift in the fight, and that her riot of auburn curls had fallen loose about her shoulders. *"Oh!*—this is all your fault. I'll have to do my hair all over again."

As she rushed for the mirror and the comb, another and even worse realization struck her.

"And I'll have to go to confession now, on your account! Oh, I could murder you, Gerard Kean!"

Straightening his collar and cravat, Gerard murmured: "But I always understood that murder was a sin as well? Or is that just another example of my poor protestant ignorance?"

Dermot was waiting down in the parlor, and he cast a suspicious eye over them both as they came in. He knew that something had been going on, though he wasn't quite sure what it was: some childish squabble, no doubt. In any case, he had far more important things to worry about.

"I have decided," he announced. "In view of the unfortunate circumstances, with no suitable *Hamlet* readily available. I shall have to make the spreme sacrifice of giving up *Claudius* and taking on the title-role myself."

Gerard and Coral both began to speak at once and both fell silent.

"You have some comment you wish to make?" asked Dermot, with deceptive mildness.

"Well, sir—" Gerard started again. "I was wondering—couldn't *I* perhaps—what I mean is—I know I'm still pretty inexperienced, but—"

"I would never describe you as inexperienced," said Coral, between her teeth.

"But anyway—what I'm trying to say—people do seem to think I've improved a good deal lately."

"Allow me to be the judge of that, please," said Dermot with finality. "Coral, my dear, you were also about to say something, I think?"

"I was going to suggest . . . perhaps we ought to consult Monsieur La Roche before we go any further," said Coral. "After all, he *is* putting up the money. It may be that he would prefer to see you playing Claudius, Uncle."

"He's a sensible and courteous gentleman, and I'm quite sure he will raise no objections whatsoever; he

159

leaves all these artistic decisions to me," said Dermot. "Still—you may be right—I should perhaps inform him of this change of plan."

The rehearsal was therefore cancelled, while Mr. Maguire, together with his two young companions, presented himself at the Grand Hotel, and requested to see Monsieur La Roche.

They were shown into that gentleman's drawing room, and found him pacing the floor, a folded paper in his hand and a look of anxiety on his face—almost, one might have said, a look of fear.

"Good day, mademoiselle—messieurs," he said with automatic courtesy. "I'm sorry to say that you have come upon me at an unhappy hour. I have just received some very bad news."

"So—you have heard already of his disappearance?" Dermot asked.

"His disappearance? No, what are you saying? It is *she* who has disappeared. *Mille tonnerres,* if only I had been there!"

Dermot knitted his brows. "I don't follow you, sir—*she* has disappeared? Nothing of the sort—it's poor Mr. O'Malley who's in trouble—cut and run, with the law at his heels."

Paul motioned them to be seated, and said: "We talk at cross-purposes, I fear. I know nothing of your Mr. O'Malley and his troubles. For I have misfortune enough of my own . . . I am sorry that this news will come as something of a shock to you, m'sieur—and to you also, M'meselle Coral."

"What is it? Is it something to do with Rosalie?" Coral's face was suddenly drained of color. "Tell us at once."

"This is not easy for me." The Frenchman stood by the fireplace, his fingers drumming upon the mantelpiece as he spoke. "I must explain, as I hinted to Gerard recently, I have been playing a dangerous game, for some time past. On the one hand, I was sent to Ireland as personal emissary of the Emperor, on a series of secret missions. Upon the other hand—and I must beg of you never to speak of this again, outside this room—"

They exchanged uneasy glances, and promised not to betray his confidence.

"Very well . . . upon the other hand, as I say, I have also been secretly working with the British military intelligence to plot the overthrow of Bonaparte and his accursed Republic."

"What?" Coral was completely bewildered.

"Gerard will explain to you: my father died upon the guillotine. I am myself one of the hated 'aristos'—but to save my skin I pretended to renounce my family and turn traitor to my noble heritage. I gave up my title, and became a diplomat for the Corsican brigand . . . But all this while, I determined to do everything I could to bring about his downfall. Now—and in the most vicious way— Bonaparte has turned the tables upon me."

"How did he find out?" Gerard asked. "You say he trusted you."

Paul La Roche shrugged. "Spies can be set to spy upon each other. Someone has betrayed me; that is obvious. Today I received this letter."

He held out the paper and showed it to them.

"From Paris . . . an official ultimatum . . . The Emperor has given orders to the Minister of Police, General Savary . . . My wife, my dear Rosalie, has been arrested."

"Rosalie—oh, mother of God—" Coral gasped, her hand at her throat.

"I am informed that unless I return to France and put myself into the hands of the authorities, she will be imprisoned, kept in solitary confinement, and fed upon bread and water. She will only be released in exchange for me."

There was a long moment of silence, broken at last by a small, choking sound, as Coral tried to fight off the tears that threatened to overwhelm her.

"Are you certain the message is genuine?" Gerard asked at last. "Could this be a gigantic bluff to test you?"

Paul shook his head. "I know these men; it is no bluff. And now they know me, and all I have been trying to do. But *who,* I ask myself—who could have informed upon me?"

The answer was all too simple, although Paul was not to guess at it for some time to come.

A few weeks earlier, at a fashionable house in Paris, just off the Place des Vosges, Rosalie La Roche had sat alone in her salon, awaiting the bell which would inform her that supper was served.

She was not especially happy: the ecstatic honeymoon with Paul had flown by all too soon, but when he had to return to Ireland—"on business," as he told her—he left her installed in some degree of luxury at this elegant eighteenth-century house in a quiet side street.

She had everything she could wish for but she was alone. There were plenty of books to read, but her French was sketchy, and she could not be bothered to puzzle over them; there was a gilded harpsichord but she did not feel in the mood for music. So she sat, day after day; the servants waited upon her hand and foot—Paul had been so considerate that he even left his personal chef, Henri Clavel, to prepare her meals—and Rosalie waited upon her husband's return.

To make things worse, there was a certain item of news which she had only learned since Paul's absence, and she was impatient to share it with him. Still she sat alone, willing him to despatch his business, whatever it might be, and come home again.

To pass the time, she played at patience—"solitaire," as the French called it—laying out the cards again and again, and hoping that sooner or later they would come out. Only they never did.

The door opened, and she glanced up idly, expecting to see her little housemaid, telling her that it was time to dine.

But the newcomer was the chef himself—Henri.

Henri Clavel was a giant of a man; well over six foot tall, and massively built in proportion—in fact, he was even beginning to run to corpulence, and there was a telltale roll of fat under his chin, which bulged on to his greasy neckerchief.

She was surprised to see him in the salon; the kitchen

staff never left their subterranean quarters unless they were summoned particularly.

"Yes, Henri?" she asked. "What is it?"

He bowed an ironic bow, and kicked the door shut behind him at the same moment. Rosalie's eyes widened at this display of insolence.

"I have the honor to inform you, citizenness," he began, in a deep rumbling basso, "that you are to consider yourself from henceforth under house arrest."

She stared at him.

"Are you mad? You're talking nonsense—please go away—back to your kitchen."

"Oh, no, madame. I will never go back to the kitchen. I have a much more important function to perform from now on . . . I am to be your jailer."

She listened incredulously as he explained the situation; once he began to give her the facts, so many things became clear . . . No wonder Paul always appeared to be so wealthy, when he was being well-paid by both England and France for his services.

The French had trusted him, at first, but after the days of the revolution, and the Terror that succeeded it, the authorities knew better than to rely completely on anyone's loyalty. So Henri Clavel had been recruited to spy upon the spy; to accompany him everywhere, and report back on his every move.

At last the trap had been sprung and Rosalie realized with growing horror that she herself was to be the bait.

"You would keep me here as a prisoner until Paul gives himself up?" she asked huskily; and her fingers trembled upon the card table. "But that is insane and unfair; I knew nothing of any espionage, I swear to you."

"I believe you, my angel," said Henri, smiling and revealing a gleam of gold in his teeth. "But that's of no importance. All that matters is that I keep you safe until your fancy husband comes back, to pay the penalty for his crimes."

"He'll never do that!" she protested. "You can't expect him to—it would be like signing his own death warrant."

"That all depends which he values most highly." Henri's grin grew broader. "Your safety—or his own . . . Oh, I admit he might keep us waiting for a time, but I'm not going to grumble about that—I consider I've got the best of the bargain, to have you here, all to myself."

He moved closer, and she realized that his eyes were upon her bosom—the flimsy material caught up under her breasts in a high waistline, according to the latest fashion.

She rose, and moved aside, keeping the card table between them.

"If you dare to imagine you've any chance of winning my favors, let me tell you at once."

He interrupted her: reaching across the spindly table and grabbing her by her shoulders. "Dare, madame? I dare do anything I fancy—and who's to stop me?" he asked.

At the same moment he ripped at her corsage, and in one vicious movement her dress was torn in two, her exquisite creamy breasts laid open to his gaze.

"Stop! Listen to me," she began, backing away. "Let me tell you something that no one else knows . . . Not even my husband."

"Well?" He waited, wondering what she would say.

"I discovered recently since he left that I am with child. In the new year I shall give birth to our first baby. Now you understand why you must leave me alone."

Henri Clavel gave a coarse shout of laughter, and kicked the card table aside.

"And what difference do you suppose that makes to me?" he demanded; then taking a leisurely pace forward, he stretched out one massive hand, and pinched her left nipple, between his finger and thumb, so that she cried out in pain . . .

But of course Rosalie's friends and relatives at the Grand Hotel, some weeks later, suspected nothing of this. They only knew that Rosalie was in desperate trouble and they were determined to find some way in which they could help her.

"If I go back I shall certainly be executed as a spy and

a traitor," said Paul. "But if I stay here, what of Rosalie? Dear God, I cannot bear to think of it."

Coral had been silent for some time, her head bowed. Now at last she looked up and her expression was determined.

"You cannot risk going back to France, that's obvious," she said. "So I must go in your place."

"*You?*—but—"

"I shall rescue Rosalie from prison wherever she may be and help her to escape. Somehow I shall bring her home to Ireland."

The three men all began talking at once: this was surely madness. Paul tried to point out to her the risks she would be running, as a British citizen.

"I'll tell them all I'm a good Irish patriot ready to throw in my lot with the French against King George and his fat highness, the Prince Regent. You know better than anyone, Paul, how close the French and the Irish are at this moment."

Dermot added his voice in protest: "What's to become of the play if you abandon us now? I've already lost two of my leading performers."

He realized from their expressions that they were not in sympathy with this line of argument, and changed course. "Or if you don't care about that, what is to become of *you,* my child? Alone, in a foreign country where you only know a smattering of the language—"

"She won't be alone," Gerard cut in. "For I'll be with her. And I do have a reasonable grounding in French."

"*Never!*" Coral turned upon him with a look of withering contempt. "You're the last man in the world I'd choose as travelling companion. Besides, I don't need anyone—I shall make my own way. I can always sing for my supper—'Coral Maguire, the Irish Songbird'—I'll pick up a few crumbs as I go along."

Gerard objected hotly: "All the more reason to take me with you, as your accompanist, manager and interpreter."

But she refused to listen to him. She had made up her mind to undertake the journey alone, and she would brook no argument.

After this, things moved at a surprising rate, and as soon as Coral had furnished herself with the necessary luggage, a passport that gave her place of birth very clearly as the county of Kerry, in *Ireland,* and a supply of French money provided by Paul's good offices—she was ready to leave, the following day.

Once again, Paul's contacts came to the rescue, and he put her in touch with a seafaring man at Dun Laoghaire—the harbor a few miles outside the city. Captain Duffy owned a small fishing boat, and, for a modest consideration, he was prepared to run the risk of ferrying passengers secretly across to the French coast.

The operation had to be carried out at dead of night, and so, at about eleven o'clock, Coral sat wrapped in a warm travelling cloak, with her luggage beside her, under the shadow of the jetty.

Dermot had insisted on coming to see her off; Gerard had wanted to join the party, but Coral refused to permit this. Perhaps she would have found it even harder to bid farewell to her native land, if the man she loved had been there at the moment of parting. She caught herself up sharply; the man she *loved?* What was she thinking of? The man she loathed and detested above all others; in fact, she was glad to get away from him, and his wicked, insidious ways. She'd be far better off without him, surely—completely alone.

The wind off the sea was cold, and she found herself shivering.

"You're afraid . . ." said old Dermot, huddled beside her upon the rocky shoreline. "It's not too late to change your mind—give up this foolishness and come back."

"Never," said Coral resolutely. "Not until I can bring Rosalie back with me."

"You're walking into terrible danger," the old man persisted. "Not to mention leaving me high and dry with no Hamlet and no Ophelia either, and black ruin staring me in the face. It's a bad day indeed when the curtain falls on the Maguire company for the last time."

"You'll survive, uncle," said Coral. "Besides, think how pleased you will be when we come home again—

the entire Maguire family reunited. *What was that?"* She broke off, listening.

Yes—there it was again: the surreptitious ripple of muffled oars. Through the darkness, they could just make out the shape of a rowing boat moving in to shore, ready to take Coral to the fishing boat that was moored some way out. There was a crunch as the keel ran aground on the shingle.

"Miss Maguire?" whispered one of the two oarsmen, in a thick brogue. "Are you right now? For the tide's at the turn, and the Cap'n's waiting for you this minute."

"I'm coming," said Coral, and she kissed her Uncle once more. "Goodbye, dear Uncle—and try not to worry. It will all come right in the end—you wait and see. And —and give my love—no, my regards—give my regards to Mr. Kean."

With that, she stepped into the boat, and the two men pulled at the oars again. With a gentle lapping sound, all three disappeared into the black night like so many ghosts. Dermot sniffed and cleared his throat, trying to wave Coral farewell but she had vanished already.

After a few minutes, the boat reached Captain Duffy's ship, and made fast alongside. A rope ladder came down from above, and Coral braced herself to climb aboard.

"Off you go now," said the boatman encouragingly. "And don't bother about your luggage—himself will bring it up after you."

Determined not to show any weakness or indecision, Coral did her best to ignore the oily waters that sucked greedily below her feet, and the wet, slippery rungs of the swaying ladder. She clung on with all her might, and slowly dragged herself up to the level of the deck, where helpful arms lifted her over the side and carried her to safety.

A moment later, the second oarsman followed with her luggage upon his shoulder, depositing it on the deck and at once someone cried: "All aboard, sir! Ready to cast off!"

"Cast off and haul anchor!" came the answer; Coral heard a chain rattling up, and felt the lurch as the vessel swung round to meet the tide. Then she realized that the boatman who had carried her luggage was still standing beside her.

"I thought you would be rowing back to shore," she said. "Are you to sail with us across the Channel, then?"

"Did you really think I'd let you go alone?" responded a familiar voice—and an uncovered lantern suddenly illuminated his face for a brief second, before they were plunged into darkness again.

"*Gerard*—" she gasped.

He put his arm around her, and he could feel her body shaking, as he said: "I'm coming with you, my love—and you can't stop me . . . We're travelling on—together."

PART TWO
FRANCE

(1)

Walk on Strange Ground

A few minutes later, Coral and Gerard had been shown into a tiny cabin, with two bunks in it, and he set down her luggage.

She began to protest: "What are you doing here? I told you I didn't want you with me—you must go back."

"Too late, my love. We've set sail for the French coast now; you'd better get accustomed to the idea. Like it or not, I'm coming with you."

"You must be mad! You're English. If you set foot in France, you'll be seized and imprisoned as an enemy."

"That's all taken care of. I made sure I had a set of documents in the name of Gerard Kean, a native of Donegal, and a staunch Irish patriot! They're all signed, stamped and officially sealed—Paul La Roche saw to that."

"You got help from Paul?"

"Of course. He has money and influence; it wasn't difficult. Besides, he was as anxious as I was myself at the idea of you travelling alone. When I told him I intended to go along as your escort, he was overjoyed."

"*He* may have been—I'm not!" said Coral firmly, sitting down upon the single chair in the cabin, her elbows upon the one narrow table.

"Come—look on the bright side. You speak hardly any French, and I do have a nodding acquaintance with the language which could prove useful, could it not?"

"I'm not denying that . . . It's just—*you*—of all people." She broke off and looked at him, then quickly averted her face, "Well, you understand what I mean, surely."

"You mean that you are uncomfortable in my company because you know that we love one another?"

"I never said so!" she broke in hotly.

"But it's the truth—why bother to pretend?" He took her hand and added more gently: "All the more reason for us to travel together, my dearest . . . For you must realize that I'd never have known a moment's peace all the time you were away . . . I *had* to be with you, Coral."

She looked at him now: a long look, full into his eyes, and what she saw there seemed to reassure her.

"Oh, Gerard . . . I don't know what to say to you . . But I believe you mean to do the right thing . . . I hope so."

"Trust me," he said softly, and kissed the tip of her nose, very gently.

"I *want* to trust you . . . If only—"

She broke off, and left the sentence unfinished, but the thought remained in her heart. "If only I could trust myself."

A knock on the cabin door heralded the arrival of one of the fishermen with a tray; two bowls of steaming soup and a plate of bread. He urged them to make a good meal, for this would be their last chance to eat until they reached their destination. By way of beverage, he brought them two huge tankards of dark brown porter. Coral sipped the bitter brew, and made a face.

"Not to your taste?" Gerard inquired. "Think of it a medicine—it will keep your strength up. And no doubt it will be the last draught of good Irish ale that you'll encounter for many a long day."

So Coral persevered, and managed to swallow half the tankard before admitting defeat. Gerard gallantly disposed of the remainder, throwing it back in a couple of long swigs.

Whether it was the porter, or the warming effect of the food, Coral didn't know, but she realized she had stopped trembling at last, and was feeling more relaxed. Perhaps, secretly, she was reassured by Gerard's presence after all; and he had—so far—behaved in an exemplary fashion.

So far . . . But at last, when they had finished talking over their situation, and possible plans for the future, Gerard who had been sitting upon the edge of the lower bunk, stood up and stretched his arms, smothering a prodigious yawn.

"Oh—forgive me! I had not realized I was so tired. We must both get some sleep, or we shall be good for nothing tomorrow."

"Sleep?" Coral looked at him suspiciously. "What—here? Now? Both of us?"

"There are two bunks," Gerard pointed out. "Which do you prefer? The upper or the lower?"

"Oh—I don't know." She imagined herself scrambling into the upper bunk, while Gerard watched her from below, and corrected herself hastily: "The lower bunk, I think."

"Splendid. I'll hang my clothes over the back of your chair, if I may—and you may use the hook on the door."

"You don't imagine I shall *undress*—?" she asked, indignantly.

"I would advise you to remove your outer garments, at least—or they will be sadly crumpled by the morning. You don't wish to arrive in France looking like a scarecrow, do you?" He pulled off his jacket as he spoke, and began to unbutton his breeches. "That is what I intend to do, anyway."

Coral looked away hastily as he proceeded to disrobe.

"Perhaps you're right—that *would* be sensible. But you will please keep your back turned to me!" she insisted.

173

"As we did on the beach—last summer in Youghal—remember?" She could hear that he was smiling as he spoke.

"Yes . . . Something like that . . ." she said, breathing rather quickly, and turned to face the wall as she took off her cloak and began to unfasten her bodice.

It was a very confined space, and as she stepped out of her dress, she felt her arm collide with Gerard's back. Automatically, she glanced over her shoulder to apologize and found him in his shirttails, with his long muscular legs bare . . . As she herself was only dressed in her shift and underpetticoat, she felt very vulnerable.

"Aha!" Gerard reproved her playfully. *"Now* who's peeping, pray? For shame, that a young lady should be so inquisitive . . ."

She blushed hotly, stammering: "I never meant—I didn't look to see—"

"Of course you didn't," he smiled soothingly. "And why should you, in any case, when we have both seen each other completely naked on more than one occasion? Away with false prudery, let us fling off all conventions, like simple children of nature."

And he made as if to pull his shirt up above his head.

"No!" gasped Coral quickly. "If you are to undress any further, I must insist that you put out the light."

"Certainly, my lady, at your service!" he said, with mocking deference. There was a candle lantern upon the table, and he extinguished it immediately.

As soon as they were in darkness, Coral realized she had made a mistake. Trying to find her way to the door, to hang up her dress, her groping hands encountered Gerard's body, and her fingers touched firm male flesh. She recoiled hastily but now his hands had found her too, and he pulled her close.

"I *beg* your pardon—" murmured his voice in her ear. "This is a very incommodious dressing-room, to be sure . . . It seems we can't avoid colliding with one another."

She felt the warmth of his body against hers, and found her voice at last.

"Please—on second thoughts I'd like you to light the

lantern again, after all. I don't want to go to bed in the dark!"

"Ah—I'm afraid that's easier said than done. I'm not sure if I can find the confounded lamp now. Once you let go of something, it's hard to lay your hands on it again."

Impudently, as he spoke, he shifted his hold upon her, sliding his hands up from her slender waist to the curve of her breasts.

"Oh, you devil—" she breathed, struggling in his grasp. "I knew you'd start playing your tricks—let go of me this minute, or—"

A rat-tat upon the cabin door startled them both, and a deep voice cried:

"Miss Maguire? Mr. Kean? This is Captain Duffy— may I disturb you for one moment?"

Gerard let Coral go, and with a stifled exclamation she made a dive for the shelter of the lower bunk, scrambling for the modest cover of a blanket, while Gerard caught up the dress she had dropped.

When Captain Duffy opened the door, moonlight flooded into the little cabin over his shoulder; Coral was discreetly tucked up in bed, and Gerard was decently shielded from the waist down by the length of the dress that he carried over his arm.

"Excuse me, ma'am—sir—" began the Captain. "I just wanted to make sure you've got all you require for the night, and are making yourselves as comfortable as may be."

"Oh—yes, thank you, Captain," replied Gerard. "As you see, Miss Maguire is resting, about to snatch a little sleep, and I dare say I shall follow her example shortly."

"Aye—well, I trust you'll both sleep soundly. 'Tis a calm sea running this night, so you shouldn't be disturbed by the motion of the vessel. You have no complaints, Miss?"

Coral hesitated for a fraction of a second, then said in a small voice: "No, Captain. No complaints at all. But thank you for asking."

"Very good, ma'am . . . Good night to you and you, sir."

The Captain's silhouette withdrew, and the door closed again.

Coral's voice said: "I should have complained about your behavior. I should have asked him to throw you overboard!—and I will too, if you dare to take any more liberties."

"Don't worry," said Gerard. "I was only teasing you. We'd better both try to get to sleep while we can."

He hung up her dress on the back of the door, by the gleam of light that now filtered in at the one small porthole. Coral's eyes were beginning to grow accustomed to the gloom, and she could just make out Gerard's shape as he crossed to the bunks.

"Good night, my dearest girl," he said quietly, and touched her face for a brief moment with his fingertips, like a caress, before climbing into the upper bunk.

"Good night . . ." She could see one naked leg kicking in mid-air, only a few inches away, and asked suspiciously: "What are you doing?"

"Exercising my muscles! I've got cramp in the sole of my foot . . . Ouch!"

The leg withdrew, and she heard a thump overhead as he stretched out above her.

"Rosalie always used to say that meant you were going to walk on strange ground," Coral remembered.

"We both are . . ." Gerard's voice was thoughtful, as he added: "In fact . . . We both have a lot of ground still to cover—haven't we?"

As Captain Duffy had predicted, the voyage to France was calm and uneventful, and the next excitement for Gerard and Coral came with their first sight of the foreign shoreline as it loomed up through a morning mist.

"That's Le Havre," said the Captain, pointing out the shapes of rooftops, towers and steeples on the horizon. "We'll lower the rowboat and put you both ashore with Pat and Con. I may even take a turn on dry land meself later, I shouldn't wonder. If you fancy a taste of coffee in the middle of the morning with a drop of something stronger to fortify it. You could meet me at Mother Poulbot's kitchen at eleven o'clock."

"What? Where?"

"La Mère Poulbot, they call her . . . She runs the local inn—the 'Golden Lobster,' that's the name on the sign-board. But ask anyone for Mother Poulbot, and they'll direct you to the place."

"Captain—I still don't understand. If we're at war with France, how can it be that you pass to and fro so easily?" asked Gerard.

"Who's at war with France? The English!" Captain Duffy chuckled in his beard. "Loyal Irishmen are always welcome here for we bring good business to the local folk. You'll find Irish fishermen making themselves at home in Le Havre at any time."

"Business? You mean buying and selling fish?" asked Coral.

"Not your everyday cod or mackerel, ma'am. We have other fish to fry!" The Captain tapped his nose and closed one eye. "Brandy, ma'am—French brandy—that will always find willing customers in old Ireland! And especially if it can go the long way round, when the excise-man's back is turned."

So that was it . . . Smuggling people in and out of France was only a sideline for Captain Duffy: smuggling casks of brandy under cover of his hauls of fish was a far more profitable concern: and the inhabitants of Le Havre were only too keen to turn a blind eye to tiresome details like international politics, while such a thriving trade could be carried on.

"I'm afraid we shan't stay long enough in the town to take advantage of your kind invitation to coffee, Captain," said Gerard. "For we have business in Paris, and we must be on our way as soon as possible."

"Then you'll be wanting to catch the Rouen mail-coach," said the Captain. "It leaves from the main square on the stroke of ten. But remember—if you pass this way again, and you wish to take a trip back to the Emerald Isle, you've only to pass the word to Mother Poulbot, at the Golden Lobster . . .Any time you need a friend, remember me!"

Everything went like clockwork; the rowboat was lowered over the side, and Gerard helped Coral down the

177

rope-ladder. An hour later, the young couple found themselves squeezed into the corner of the mailcoach as it rattled over the cobblestones on its way out of Le Havre.

"I certainly won't forget Captain Duffy," said Gerard. "You never know when we might need a friend again—in a hurry."

The other occupants of the coach, petit-bourgeois merchants, shopkeepers and their plump wives, glanced curiously at them, intrigued by the sound of an unfamiliar language. Coral nudged Gerard, urging him to keep quiet.

"We're in a strange land now," she whispered. "Don't draw attention to yourself."

She imagined that the sharp-faced woman opposite, studying her with such open curiosity, must be about to denounce her as a foreigner—a spy—an enemy . . . not for the first time, she wriggled a little closer to Gerard, and thanked God that he had insisted upon accompanying her. How could she ever have survived this fearful journey alone?

She thought of Rosalie—friendless and isolated, imprisoned in Paris. The sooner they could reach the capital, and find her, the happier she would be.

At this very moment, as the mailcoach covered the winding road that followed the River Seine, Rosalie was lying in bed, a prisoner lapped in luxury; trapped, as she often reflected bitterly, within a gilded cage.

She rolled over and punched the pillows of her four-poster bed.

It was ironic; all her life she had been forced to struggle for her livelihood—and now here she was, living in a comfortable house, in elegant surroundings, with all she could want to eat and drink brought to her at regular intervals . . . Everything her heart could desire, in fact, except for two things, her loved ones—and her freedom.

She was well cared for by the servants; but she was never allowed to leave the house. As the weeks dragged on, she had begun to spend more and more time in bed. Her confinement, due in January, was growing nearer in any case; and what was the point of getting up—getting dressed—when there was nowhere to go and no one to see?

No one, that is, except Monsieur Henri Clavel—her jailer.

At first she had feared him; she had shrunk from his oily smile, and the occasional crude, impudent touch of his hand. The first time he had talked to her of her situation, he had made the position clear—underlining her humiliating helplessness by tearing her dress, and handling her breasts roughly.

But that was only to teach her a lesson, and since then he had behaved with more circumspection. Every day, he came to visit her; sometimes, she thought, to gloat over her predicament. Whatever she was doing, he forced his way into her boudoir. If she were dressing, he would stand there, openly staring at her half-naked body, his eyes glowing like live coals.

Once, she had been in a hip-bath before the fire, with her little maid, Melanie, pouring warm water over her shoulders. He had sent Melanie away with a snap of his fingers, and taken over the task—slowly and carefully continuing to let the trickle of water run over her shining skin, coursing down in tiny rivulets upon her breasts, and falling upon her naked thighs and swelling stomach. Making the action last as long as possible, she realized, and enjoying her discomfiture to the full.

She had tried pleading with him, but to no avail. She had tried unleashing her Irish temper, and railing at him but he was impervious to this, too. Now she had gradually come to accept him as a necessary evil as she accepted the bleak wintry weather, or the limitations imposed upon her by her pregnancy. She no longer hated him actively; she resented him passively, and suffered in silence.

Just as she did now, lying with her face in her pillow, when she heard the door click open, and heavy footsteps approach the bed. She knew his footfall at once; in any case, none of the other servants would invade her privacy without having been summoned. She sensed Henri standing beside the bed, and imagined his hungry gaze burning down upon her and she kept her eyes shut, pretending to be asleep.

"My angel . . ." he said at last in a vibrant basso that seemed to rumble from the pit of his stomach. "Are you awake?"

She ignored him, hoping that he might go away.

"Wake up . . . listen to me . . ." he continued after a moment. Then—"Open your eyes . . . look at me."

Still she would not budge.

"My God, but you're beautiful," he said at last, and she could not be sure whether he were addressing her, or talking to himself.

Another pause, and then there was a sequence of confused noises—a floorboard creaked, she heard the rustle of cloth—a thump upon the carpet, and another—could he be taking off his boots? Then further soft, anonymous sounds and all the while, the rhythm of Henri's own heavy breathing, as it gradually quickened into excitement.

"Go away and leave me alone," she said at last. "I'm not asleep now. What are you doing?"

A pause—her question had startled him, perhaps—and then the rhythmic noises continued. She raised her head and turned to look at him, and reacted with shock and revulsion.

He was standing very close to her, completely naked. Stripped, she saw what a giant of a man he was, his heavy body beginning to run to fat, with thick black hair upon his chest and belly—there was even a light animal-like pelt upon his shoulders; and his loins and legs were covered in coarse, matted fur. And he held his huge manhood in his hands, erect and throbbing with impatient lust like the lust in his bloodshot eyes as he stared down upon her prostrate body.

"Get out . . ." she said, trying to keep her voice steady. "You disgust me." He did not seem to hear: his gaze was fixed and terrifying.

Suddenly, one massive paw shot out and snatched at the bedclothes, pulling the sheets and blankets down. She lay motionless for a moment, her generously rounded hips only half-veiled by her flimsy nightgown. It had become twisted around her as she tossed and turned, riding up so that her buttocks were almost completely uncovered: and it was this spectacle that was riveting Henri's attention now.

"Keep away from me, you savage—" she exclaimed, and began to wriggle on to her knees, trying to evade him.

It was useless. In one bound, he had flung himself across her, pinning her down: the breath was almost knocked from her body by his vast weight, and she felt his hairy flesh pressed against her, smothering her in a clumsy embrace.

"Stop—no—let me go—" she panted.

He took not the least notice; one hand grasping her by the shoulders, forcing her down upon the bed, the other exploring her thighs, pulling her legs roughly apart.

She wanted to cry out, but what good would that do? No one would come to her rescue; and it was useless to appeal to his pity, for he had none. His carnal appetites were in command now, and he was deaf to all other considerations. Helplessly, she felt her struggles growing weaker, knowing that this brute male was about to violate her—

And then she did scream.

So suddenly, so strangely, that Henri Clavel was momentarily arrested by something in her voice.

"I will not hurt you if you lie still—" he began.

"You don't hurt me," she gasped, almost contemptuously, and set her teeth as another wave of pain engulfed her. "It's not *you* that makes me cry out; it is something far stronger than you could ever be."

"What are you saying?" He let go of her, mystified.

She arched her back, holding herself rigidly then gave a long sigh of shuddering relief as the contraction passed.

"Fetch a midwife—quickly!" she exclaimed. "You fool—don't you understand? It is the baby—it has begun —prematurely!"

Outside the bedroom windows, the wicked December wind rattled the shutters like shaking fists.

In Rouen, the same cruel wind flayed the passersby, as they hurried home to their firesides before the daylight failed.

Gerard and Coral had left the mailcoach at the old

marketplace and were struggling in the direction of the Cathedral, which loomed up above them against the darkening sky, a vast stone ship in full sail.

"There's a hotel," said Gerard, pointing to a swinging inn sign in the Rue Jeanne d'Arc. "I'll go in and ask if they have any rooms for the night . . . Leave all the talking to me, for heaven's sake."

"Wait!" Coral clutched his sleeve, and pointed.

Further along the street, she had seen a familiar sight; the façade of a building hung with lights. The Municipal Theatre.

"*You* go and see about the hotel; I'll come back and join you later," she said, her spirits rising. "*I* shall go and make inquiries about an engagement!"

"But you don't understand French—" Gerard protested.

"I understand the theatre," said Coral. "That's all that really matters. Just leave this to me!"

She left him at the entrance to the hotel, and made her way to the theatre, where she turned on her most bewitching smile and requesed the flunkey at the door to show her to the Manager's office immediately.

Her French may have been almost non-existent, but her smile was quite irresistible, and within three minutes, she was sitting before the Manager's desk.

Luckily, this worthy gentleman spoke a little English, and between them they managed some kind of communication.

"You wish for work in my theatre?" he asked courteously, studying her through a pair of owl-like spectacles. "What is it that you hope to do? To act? To dance?"

"To sing, m'sieur." Coral demonstrated, trilling out a series of roulades and arpeggios in her high, clear soprano. "You see? I really can sing!"

The Manager's eyes widened. "I do not dispute the fact, dear young lady . . . But who are you? Where do you come from?"

In answer, Coral produced some folded playbills from her reticule—announcements from various theatres where the Maguire company had performed, all with glowing tributes to "Coral Maguire, the Irish songbird"—accompanied by her equally musical sister, the illustrious Rosalie.

"You are here in France with your sister, actually?" inquired the Manager, peering over the top of his spectacles.

"Well—no—not at the moment. My sister and I have split up—parted—just temporarily, you understand. But I'm travelling with a young man instead."

"Ah, I understand—say no more," the Manager blinked fatuously, his head on one side, looking more owl-like than ever. *"L'amour, l'amour . . ."*

"Nothing of the sort," said Coral sharply. "He accompanies me on the pianoforte—and that's *all!"*

"Really? My heart bleeds for him—whoever he is," said the Manager, then continued in more businesslike tones: "This is the week before Christmas, and it is customary to mount some additional item of entertainment in our program. I will therefore be prepared to take you on for one week only—with your young accompanist— to provide a short musical interlude between the tragedy of *Phèdre* and the vaudeville afterpiece . . . Be here at ten tomorrow morning for rehearsal, if you please."

So Coral ran back to the hotel, and found Gerard, reporting eagerly on her success. He, too, was pleased with what he had accomplished; he had arranged to rent a pair of adjoining bedrooms upon the first floor of the hotel.

"They're not exactly opulent," he explained, showing Coral her room, "but they're clean and simple—and there's a view of the Cathedral along the street, and— um—"

He hesitated, with his hand upon a second, discreet door beside the wardrobe. "And where does *that* lead?" Coral asked, with a polite smile.

"Well—er—as a matter of fact—*my* room is just through there—"

"Quite so. And that door will remain locked, and *I* shall keep possession of the key—thank you." said Coral, her hand outstretched.

Reluctantly, Gerard handed the key over, muttering:

"I can see this is going to be a very miserable Christmas."

"Gerard—how can you say such a thing? Think of poor Rosalie, before you start complaining!"

"I *am* thinking of Rosalie . . . why can't we get on with our journey and catch another coach to Paris? Why do we have to waste a whole week here?"

"The money Paul La Roche gave me will not last two of us for very long," Coral pointed out. "But a week's salary from the theatre will be a useful nest-egg when we reach Paris . . . We can't afford to turn down any chance to pay our way."

In the event, the week at Rouen was a great success; the Irish—like the Scots—had always been popular in France, and the Manager seized every opportunity to publicize the visiting "Songbird." Two of the local police guards called at the theatre after the first performance, and asked to see their papers—but when Coral stoutly affirmed her detestation of England and all things English (and Gerard kept his mouth shut) the officers went away again, well satisfied.

The audiences were friendly and enthusiastic, and the Irish performers could undoubtedly have continued to appear for a second week, but Gerard explained that they had a pressing engagement in Paris, and must move on after Christmas.

Their last performance took place upon Christmas Eve, and they received a great ovation from the public at their final curtaincall. As they came off stage into the wings— and stepped aside to make way for the red-nosed comedians and pretty dancing girls who were to provide the closing vaudeville—Gerard said: "When we've collected our wages let's go out and celebrate with a really good meal at the café opposite our hotel. After all, Christmas comes but once a year."

"Yes, but . . . not yet," said Coral. "I want to ask you a favor, Gerard. There is a midnight mass at the Cathedral, and I *must* go to it but I don't like to go alone. Will you keep me company?"

"Well, you know I'm no Catholic—" Gerard began, and she silenced him swiftly, her hand upon his lips.

"Ssh! Was there ever a good Irish man who was *not* a

good Catholic?" she demanded. "But you can pretend, can't you? Keep an eye on me, and do as I do . . . it's all very simple."

So an hour later, they made their way into the crowded Cathedral; dazzling with candles, and thronged with worshippers.

One problem arose immediately; it became apparent at once that the devout French congregation was segregated by gender—the dark-shawled women all going to the left of the centre aisle, and the bareheaded men splitting off to the right. So Gerard and Coral were separated, and he could not rely on her to coach him in the unfamiliar ritual.

He could see her dimly, far away across a sea of heads but that wasn't much help. As he hesitated, wondering where he should go, a neighbor jostled him, and asked in the sing-song Normandy accent: "Aren't you the Irishman from the theatre? The one who plays the music for that pretty singer?"

"I am, sir—what of it?"

The man—a swarthy individual who might have been a tax-collector with beetling brows and a long, inquisitive nose—scratched his head.

"You look as if you'd never set foot in a holy church before . . . Are you *sure* you're an Irishman?"

"Of course I am," smiled Gerard, his heart sinking, and sketched the sign of the cross rapidly, as he had seen other worshippers doing. "God bless you, my friend."

The man scowled and stared, unsatisfied.

Gerard ducked away, trying to find a place as far from his troublesome stranger as possible.

In fact, the order of the service presented no great problem. Gerard took care to kneel when everyone else knelt, and stand when they all stood; when the Holy Communion was distributed (and he saw Coral go up to the altar rails to receive it, along with a large proportion of the women present) a great many of the men who had clearly been celebrating Christmas already, unwisely and all too well, did not go forward to participate, so Gerard was able to hang back, unnoticed in the throng.

At last the ceremony came to an end, and the huge

Cathedral began to empty. Gerard made his way toward the main doors, trying to find Coral in the crowd. Perhaps she was already outside, waiting for him.

A little way ahead, he noticed that every man was putting his hand into an ornate cup-shaped receptacle in a pillared niche. He guessed that this must be the Catholic version of the Protestant offertory-bag or poor-box, and fumbled in his pocket for a piece of silver, wishing to follow the general example.

It wasn't until he reached the stone pillar, and dropped his coin with a splash!—into what he discovered, too late, was a holy water stoup, that he realized his mistake. But it was impossible to rectify it.

Several men round about him were staring curiously, and as he hesitated, wondering whether to retrieve the coin from its watery resting-place, a bony hand clutched his wrist.

"I thought as much," snarled his long-nosed inquisitor. "I've had my eye on you all the while . . . You're no Irishman—send for the guard, someone! This man's a spy!"

(2)

Marry Me

Half a dozen yards away, in the press of people making for the doors, Coral heard angry shouts and saw the ring of hostile faces closing in around Gerard.

She could not understand the words they used, but their meaning was clear enough: Gerard was being accused of treachery, of spying. She saw him try to defend himself, arguing as best he could and then rough hands grabbed him by the shoulders, and as he struggled to get free, a heavy fist struck the side of his face. She gasped in horror as Gerard's head rocked back, and the mob jostled him up against a stone pillar. Above him, a wooden crucifix hung as a silent witness to the scene.

She realized Gerard could not escape the violence that was rapidly building up, and for a second she felt dizzy with fear. What could she do to help him?

The answer supplied itself instantly. She could faint! She was an actress, wasn't she? Very well, then, she would stage the best collapse ever seen on or off any stage!

She took a deep breath and uttered a high, wordless

cry: loud enough to cut through the clamor of voices, and set the vast spaces of the Cathedral nave ringing with a hundred echoes.

At once, all the faces turned in her direction. She followed up her advantage by emitting another wail, this time letting the sound die away in a strangulated sob, as if she were exhaling her final breath. At the same moment, she fluttered her eyelids, clutched her throat, and sank to the ground, apparently lifeless.

The diversion worked. Everyone's attention was diverted to this new drama, and the crowd suddenly began to push and shove toward Coral, eager to see what was happening.

Taking advantage of the momentary reprieve, Gerard wasted no time, but ducked under the arm of his principal attacker, and took to his heels. Within two seconds, he had wriggled out behind the backs of the staring onlookers, and reached the main door.

Meanwhile a babble broke out over and above Coral's head. She could not of course make out what anyone was saying to her, and decided to remain "unconscious" for as long as possible. Someone slapped her wrist, another fanned her face, a third thrust a pungent phial of smelling-salts under her nose, making her cough and splutter but still she kept her eyes shut.

Then she felt strong hands bearing her up, and realized that someone was making a path through the crowd, carrying her toward the doors.

The cool freshness of the night air on her brow, and the change in the murmuring sounds about her alerted her to the fact that they were outside at last; gently her rescuer deposited her upon the stone steps before the great west front.

Gradually she let herself "come to"—blinking a little—sighing—gazing round at a cluster of strange faces as if she were waking from a dream.

"*Qu'est qu'il y'a?*" asked a broad-shouldered farmer with a ruddy complexion, and she realized this was the man who had carried her out. "*Va mieux, maintenant?*"

She could not reply; she could only bite her lip, nod-

188

ding, putting on a brave face. Quickly she gathered herself togethter, struggling to her feet.

"Voulez-vous que je vous accompagnerai?" the man began.

She guessed that he was offering to escort her home, and shook her head with a dazzling smile, indicating that she was now fully recovered.

Then, before he could say anything further, she bowed graciously and set off along the street as rapidly as possible.

It wasn't until she reached the corner that she discovered she was going in the opposite direction from the hotel. But perhaps that was all to the good; she glanced back over her shoulder, and saw that the obliging farmer was still standing by the steps, amid the departing congregation, uncertain whether he should follow. She didn't want him or anyone else to go with her; she wanted to be quite alone.

Continuing round the block, she thought fast.

Where was Gerard now? Where would he go? She guessed that he must try to make for the hotel, and hoped she would meet him there. It was risky, but they had no choice—their luggage, their papers, most of their money was still in the hotel rooms, and they could not afford to abandon any of them.

She imagined that Gerard would have made his escape under cover of her "fainting fit" and prayed that he had thrown off any pursuit by now. Her instinct was to run—run as fast as her legs could carry her, back to the hotel, and Gerard but she must not draw attention to herself.

So she continued to walk briskly but still outwardly calm up one street, and down the next, keeping up a steady, circuitous course that finally brought her back to the Rue Jeanne d'Arc, and the hotel.

In the cafe opposite, the feast of Christmas was being celebrated in traditional fashion: through the window, Coral could see hundreds of laughing customers eating and drinking, keeping a score of white-aproned waiters on their toes, fetching and carrying the steaming dishes.

The hotel foyer was empty—perhaps the staff, too, had

joined the merry party across the road. Thankfully, Coral reached for the key to her room, from the row of pigeon-holes behind the desk. And her heart sank, for the key to Gerard's room was still there, too. He had not returned yet.

She went upstairs to her darkened bedroom and opened the shutters, looking down into the street at the festive scene across the way, at the endless procession of passers-by but there was no sign of Gerard.

She decided to go to bed, to try and rest while she had the chance, and so began to undress. One thought kept repeating in her mind, over and over—Where is Gerard? Is he safe? Where is he? God help him—*where is he?* She put on her nightgown, and turned down the covers of the bed but she could not settle yet. She paced the room, knowing that sleep was impossible, returning once again to the windows, and looking out for a familiar face in the crowd.

A tap upon the door made her gasp. She held her breath, wondering what she should do or say her few halting words of French totally deserting her.

The sound was repeated, and this time she realized that it came, not from the door to the passage, but the smaller, communicating door that led into Gerard's bedroom.

Almost running, she darted across and turned the key —half-laughing, half-crying with relief as Gerard stepped through the door.

"Oh, thank heaven—thank heaven—" she babbled, as he took her in his arms. "I was so afraid. I did not know what had happened to you—"

"I got away, thanks to you," he said: and she could see in the faint glow from the window that he was smiling. "I've been dodging round the back streets for the past half-hour, hoping I wasn't being followed. Then at last I took a chance and made my way here."

"I did the same thing—there was nowhere else to go. Oh, Gerard, thank God they didn't catch you. Hold me tight."

"It was a near thing." His arms were strong and reassuring about her, and she clung to him for warmth and comfort. "Someone in the cathedral had been watching me—he knew I was no Catholic, and he called me a foreign spy. I thought for a moment I would be lynched."

"What are we going to do? Suppose they come and find us here."

"They won't do that tonight. They'll go to the theatre tomorrow, perhaps—but by then we'll be on the road. We must leave the city as soon as it's light."

"We don't know when the coaches leave for Paris."

"We can't risk hanging about and asking questions. We'll go on foot this time."

A shout of laughter and a burst of music rose up from across the street; they both looked down at the crowded café, and Gerard said: "We were going out to celebrate tonight, remember? A Christmas celebration . . ."

"It doesn't matter. I'm not hungry—I couldn't eat anything—"

She touched his cheekbone cautiously, and added: "Your poor face . . . I saw that villain hit you—"

"It's nothing—only a bruise . . . but I am sorry. We've lost our supper party . . . I'll make it up to you soon, when we get to Paris."

"When we find Rosalie—we'll have our Christmas dinner then, won't we?"

"Of course we will . . . Now you must get to sleep, and so must I, for we have a long hard journey ahead of us."

He let her go, and moved toward his own room.

"Gerard . . ."

Her voice sounded thin and far away, as if it were the voice of a stranger.

"Yes?" He turned, at the open door.

"I—I'm still shaking . . . I've been so frightened . . . Don't leave me, Gerard—I don't want to be alone—tonight."

In silence, he shut the door, then came slowly back to her as she stood silhouetted against the window.

"My dearest—my dearest girl . . ." He took her face in his hands and kissed her; and she felt in that moment that she had come home again. It didn't matter that she was in a strange room, in a strange city, and in danger of her life . . . When Gerard held her and kissed her as he held and kissed her now—she knew that she was safe.

This was where she belonged; she need never be afraid or alone, ever again.

Now she could tell him what was in her heart—the truth she had longed to share with him, all these endless, empty months.

"I love you," she said at last.

"And I love you," he replied quietly. "And I will never leave you."

In one strong, easy movement, he slipped his arms around her and picked her up effortlessly, as if she were a child and carried her across to the bed that awaited them.

She lay upon her back, feeling the coolness of the sheets beneath her nightgown, and the beat of passion that was within her body, waiting for the chance to be released. Her heart beat fast, as she listened to the swift sound of Gerard undressing in the darkened room.

She realized that there was no turning back; they belonged together, now, tonight and always. Every drop of blood in her veins pulsed eagerly, and she ran her hands down the line of her body as if for the last time, for she knew that she would never be the same person after tonight, and that this body itself would never belong to her again, as long as she lived.

She felt the bed move when he stretched out beside her. He embraced her gently, and she welcomed the touch of his skin against her legs and arms, but . . .

"You don't need a nightgown," he said. "Let me help you off with it."

His sure, deft fingers pulled aside the ribbons at her breast, and unfastened them—then he eased her last remaining garment up—his hands upon her legs—her hips —her waist—her breasts—and he drew the gown over her head and tossed it lightly aside.

Now there was no barrier between them, of any kind. They kissed again and again; he used all the gentle skills he possessed to give her pleasure, soothing her and at the same time arousing her. When he slipped his hand down

192

to the secret places between her thighs, where no one had ever touched her until now, she shivered for a moment but it was a shiver of ecstasy, and not of fear.

Very slowly, without any kind of impatience, his supple fingers caressed her, played with her, stirred strange deep longings that she had never known before. His touch was as soft as thistledown; as smooth as silk but the passion he called forth within her was as strong and boundless as the ocean.

She began to rock gently to and fro in response to his fondling, and she felt herself growing moist with desire.

"I love you—I love you—I'm yours—" she whispered breathlessly, and rolled over to face him, pressing her body hungrily aganst his, aware of the hot, hard strength of his manhood between them.

Without breaking the ceaseless pattern of their lovemaking, he drew her gradually into an easier posture, and she felt his slim hips between her legs.

"Trust me—" he said—and then slipped forward in one firm, sinuous movement.

She caught her breath—for a split second she was afraid—she could not—it was too much to bear—and then . . .

It was as if she had waited for this moment all her life. This was the man she loved, and she unfolded like a flower, giving herself completely to him, as he gave himself to her. There was no doubt or question for either of them from now on.

The age-old magic of love took charge of them both, and they passed through all the successive stages of joy as the slow rhythm of their passion mounted to a frenzy.

She reached a pinnacle of excitement and delight such as she had never even imagined—letting go utterly, abandoning every thought or caution that had once been part of Coral; for now Coral and Gerard did not exist any longer. They were one person, one body, one soul—riding into paradise on endless waves of love. Waves that lapped around them, bore them up, carried them higher and yet higher, to a climax of perfection that left them both breathless and speechless and filled with wonder.

Gerard looked at her face, and her shining eyes of sea-green, and kissed her once more—a long, heartfelt kiss that arose from their shared satisfaction.

She looked up at him, and when at last she could speak, she whispered: "It's a kind of miracle . . ."

* * *

In Paris, another kind of miracle had just taken place. At five minutes past two a.m. on Christmas morning, 1812, Rosalie lay back upon her pillows and looked at the new-born infant in her arms. A boy—fair and blue eyed as a cherub. It had been a long, difficult confinement; three times the pains had begun, and twice they had stopped again. For a whole week, Rosalie had struggled to bring her child into the world, and now at last—on Christmas day—she had achieved her purpose triumphantly.

Paul would be pleased, she thought, when he heard the news. And as she sighed for Paul, so far away, and in such terrible trouble—a shadow fell across her bed.

She looked up, and recoiled instinctively.

Henri Clavel stood over her, looking down at the baby boy.

"What do you want now?" she asked, and her voice cracked with exhaustion. "Can't you ever leave me in peace?"

During the whole week, he had been in attendance; only leaving the bedchamber when he was turned out by the indignant midwife.

He shrugged, and put out one massive hand, touching the child's head with his fingertips.

"If you harm a single hair of his head, I shall kill you." said Rosalie evenly, and she meant what she said.

"I would never hurt the child . . . I don't mean to hurt *you*," said Henri.

He spread his huge fingers wide, and let them trail from the child's head on to Rosalie's breast for a lingering moment.

She looked up at him with contempt, and a sort of pity as if he were some kind of freak.

"For God's sake," she said dismissively. "Can't you

194

ever leave me in peace? I'm tired—don't you understand that? Leave me alone, please."

"As you wish."

He withdrew his hand slowly, then smiled, and she saw the flash of gold among his teeth.

"You have a fine son there . . . Congratulations, madame."

Then, to her surprise, he turned away and left the room. Could it be that the brute did have some human instincts after all?

She closed her eyes, hugging the child to her breast; and they both fell into a deep sleep.

The next morning, Gerard and Coral awoke at the first glimmer of dawn in the sky. Gerard sat up and stretched his arms, yawning.

"It's time we were on our way, my love."

"Already? I'm still so tired it feels like the middle of the night," she protested, slipping one arm around his waist as if to draw him back to her.

"That's because we didn't get much sleep after all," he smiled. "But we can't take any chances. We must leave Rouen as soon as possible—it's too dangerous for us to stay here now."

"You said something about *walking*," she remembered. "How far is it to Paris?"

"Oh—eighty—ninety miles perhaps," shrugged Gerard, climbing out of bed.

"Ninety miles? You're mad—we can't walk that far—"

"I don't intend to . . . There's somewhere rather nearer than that, which I have in mind."

As he scrambled into his clothes, Gerard explained: "When I was a child, in England, my sister and I had a governess, Mlle Michot."

"The one who taught you to speak French and play the pianoforte—well?"

"Well, I remember she lived at a place not far from Rouen . . . Somewhere along the river, she said, on the way to Paris—Les Andelys, it's called."

"Les what?"

"There are two villages together—Le Grand Andely

and Le Petit Andely. The name's so strange, it stuck in my head. And she used to talk of her home—a great mansion, she said, with a big garden running down to the river. Well, my plan is to go there and ask her to help us. She was always kind to me when I was a boy; I'm sure she will do all she can."

"Are you sure you can trust her?" Coral asked.

"I'm certain of it. She's bound to offer us hospitality —she'll let us stay in her grand house for a day or two, while we decide how to tackle the next stage of our journey. And she will be able to give us good advice, too."

When they crept downstairs, the hotel was very silent; everyone was still asleep except for a yawning *concierge* at the desk. Gerard peeled off some bank notes and paid for their week's board and lodging. The *concierge* offered coffee and croissants, but they could not stop, even for that. Outside, it was daylight already—a raw, gray December morning.

"Happy Christmas, my dearest," said Coral, as they set off. "I'm sorry I don't have a Christmas gift for you."

"Last night was the best Christmas gift in the world," said Gerard. "You gave me yourself—I could never hope for anything more generous."

Coral smiled back at him but her smile was a little uncertain.

Because it was the morning after a midnight feast, the city was almost deserted at this early hour, and they trudged on through empty streets until they found a signpost by the river that pointed to Paris and Les Andelys.

Once they passed a market-gardiner with a cart piled high with swedes and turnips, but for the most part they seemed to be the only two people left alive in a world of ghosts.

The last houses of Rouen fell away behind them, and they followed the winding road that echoed the curves of the Seine. It was a slow journey, for Gerard was weighed down with all their luggage, and as the day wore on, he had to stop more frequently to recover his energy and rub his aching and blistered palms.

The distance between Rouen and Les Andelys was twenty-five miles, and it took them most of the day to get there. They were cold and hungry and very tired indeed when at last they reached the little huddle of cottages and shops, dignified by the name of "Le Petit Andely."

It was dusk by now, and they peered through the thickening shadows, trying to find Mlle Michot's "great mansion."

"The biggest place is the inn," said Coral. "Perhaps your governess lives in the other half of the village, at Le Grand Andely."

"No, that can't be right," Gerard pointed out. "Because of the garden running down to the water's edge there's the river, right enough—Le Grand Andely is further off, inland."

"Well, I don't see any mansions hereabouts," said Coral. "In fact, there's nothing very welcoming about the place at all—no sign of life except for that mangy dog coming toward us."

As she said this, the dog, perhaps objecting to her description, began to bark indignantly, and advanced upon them threateningly.

"Go away, you brute—get back," said Gerard.

Coral flinched, as the dog made a mock attack upon them, barking and baring its yellow teeth. Another dog came around the corner to see what was going on, and gave tongue—then a third appeared from nowhere, adding to the clamor.

"Can't you get rid of them?" Coral asked, dodging behind Gerard.

"I wish I could! Even if they don't go for us, they're making such a racket, the villagers will soon be popping out to find out what the matter is, and they might ask awkward questions. Get away, you filthy hounds—go on—"

He picked up a stone, and made as if to throw it; the pack of curs paid no attention, but redoubled their noise.

At which point a small iron gate in a fence beside them creaked open, and a female voice shouted: *"Va t'en! Allez!"*

A pail of water shot past Gerard in the direction of the

197

mongrels, who immediately remembered pressing engagements elsewhere and took themselves off.

"Petits monstres . . ." grumbled the newcomer, an elderly woman in a plain sacking apron, and then she broke off, seeing that Gerard was staring at her.

"Mademoiselle—" he began. "It *is* Mlle Michot, isn't it?"

She searched his face, and her mouth fell open.

"Master Gerard . . ." she gasped. *"Sacré bleu—c'est un reve—"*

"I've come to find you . . . With a travelling companion, Coral—"

"From England?" The woman's gaunt face was pale. "Oh, *mon Dieu*—"

She looked up and down the little street, and made up her mind.

"Come in—come inside quickly," she ordered, and swept them through the gate.

Beyond, a narrow yard ran down to the river; at the water's edge was a small white-washed cottage, and she led the way indoors swiftly.

"We had a little trouble finding your house," Gerard began.

"Oh . . . Yes . . . There have been certain—changes," she said gruffly, drawing the curtains, and busying herself with the oil lamp.

Gerard and Coral exchanged glances; they both guessed that Mlle Michot's description of a "great mansion" with its riverside garden had been a harmless exaggeration, and said nothing more.

As the light from the lamp sprang up, Coral glanced round the small kitchen-parlor, with its dresser of gleaming china and its black oven where a fire glowed red and a pot of stew bubbled comfortably . . . It all looked—and smelled—very attractive.

As quickly and as briefly as possible, Gerard explained in French that he and Coral had come here on urgent business; they had to go to Paris, to find Coral's sister, who was in desperate trouble, and they had hoped to escape arrest by carrying Irish documents.

Their hostess pursed her lips doubtfully—she was not

optimistic about their chances. Besides—there was, it seemed, yet another problem.

"I am no longer Mlle Michot, Master Gerard. Since I returned from England, my situation has changed. I am now Madame Bernard, you understand?"

As she spoke, the door clicked open behind Coral, and a man with grizzled gray moustaches and a military air stepped into the room.

"Ah, *mon cheri!* Allow me to present my husband," the good lady rattled on. "This is Gaston . . . Gaston Bernard—Sergeant of Police . . ."

Coral gave a small cry of dismay, and Gerard gripped her arm urgently.

They all shook hands, and Madame Bernard continued: "My husband speaks no English, of course—so I shall explain to him that you are Americans—it is better so, I think . . . The Americans are good friends of France for they are also at war with the English!"

She exchanged a few rapid sentences with her husband, so fast that even Gerard could not follow what she said, then turned to her two visitors: "I have told him that you are to be our guests for one or two nights and that you are Mr. and Mrs. Mallory travelling from New York to Paris."

"Mr. and Mrs.—" Coral repeated, bewildered.

"Of course. For there is only one bedroom upstairs, and it would not be proper for you to share it, if you were not a married couple!" said Mme Bernard, briskly. "But you must be hungry, come, let us prepare for supper . . ."

Coral was inclined to argue, over her newly-acquired status as a married lady, but she realized that under the circumstances she did not have any choice. And besides, the stewpot smelled so *very* appetizing.

During supper, Sergeant Bernard asked Gerard several questions, and Coral could not understand what was going on; however, after two plates full of stew, and a couple of glasses of strong red wine, she did not care very much.

At last it was time for bed, and Mme Bernard showed them the way to the upper room, which was reached by a trapdoor and a wooden ladder. Gerard went first, carrying a lighted candle, with Coral following at his heels.

When the trapdoor was firmly shut, Coral asked: "What did the policeman ask you? Was he suspicious?"

"Not really. He was quite apologetic. He did not wish to trouble me, but he had a duty to perform. He hoped I would not take it amiss that we show him our travel documents."

"*What?*" Coral froze. "But that's impossible—he'll see we're not Americans at all."

"Don't worry, I told him I'd stupidly left our documents in our last hotel at Rouen—I said we'd go back and fetch them in a day or two, and he seemed quite satisfied with that."

"Well! He may be satisfied but I'm not!" Coral sat on the old-fashioned double bed, which was built into a recess in the wall, enclosed by a pair of folding cupboard doors.

"What do you mean?"

"What did you tell your Madame about me, Gerard? You said I was your 'travelling companion'—what does that mean, in French? I suppose you hinted that I was your mistress—is that it?"

"Certainly not! Why should I say such a thing?"

"Why should she put us both into a double bed, otherwise? Oh, you had it all arranged very conveniently, didn't you?" She kicked off her shoes, and began to roll down her stockings. "Now I've fallen from grace at last, you take it for granted I'll be happy to sleep with you again and again."

He caught her hand, kneeling beside her, his hand on her leg.

"And won't you be happy to sleep with me? Weren't you happy last night?"

She softened a little, and said: "You know I was . . . But that's not the point and kindly remove your hand from my knee, Mr. Kean! For I don't like being taken for granted!"

He continued to slide the stocking down her shapely leg, as he said: "That's something I will never do, my love. As for the double bed—it wasn't *my* idea to pass ourselves off as a married couple. But what else was poor

200

Madame to say? There's only the one bed here—no doubt she and her police sergeant will have to make do with a mattress on the kitchen floor, down below . . . I could hardly refuse her kind hospitality, coud I?"

He tickled the sole of her naked foot, and she drew away from him.

"Stop teasing, Gerard. And listen to me for I'm serious . . . I love you and I love it when you love me—you know that without my telling you. But you also know it's a mortal sin to make love like that—outside marriage . . . And I'm trusting you to do the right thing and regularize our situation as soon as possible."

"What are you saying, my darling? Regularize our situation?"

"I'm saying—make an honest woman of me, dearest, as Paul did when he ran off with Rosalie . . . Marry me, Gerard . . . Please!"

He sat back on his heels, baffled.

"How can I marry you? I would do it willingly this very minute but we can't marry without documents, and *that's* going to stir up a hornets' nest, by the look of things. And besides, the good Sergeant Bernard thinks we're married already, and on top of all that, I'm a Protestant, and you're a Catholic, and your church isn't likely to welcome me with open arms."

"Excuses!" Furiously, Coral planted her bare foot upon his chest and pushed, toppling him backward on to the bare plank floor. "I might have known you'd try and talk your way out of it . . . Well, just you listen to me, Gerard Kean or Mallory or whatever your name is—we may be married in the eyes of Sergeant Bernard, but we're not married in the eyes of God—and I'm not going to commit any further mortal sins with you, tonight or any other night!"

"I'm not sleeping on the floor, to please you or the Pope of Rome himself—" snorted Gerard, picking himself up. "I never heard such rubbish!"

"Rubbish, is it?" Coral pulled back the bedclothes, and picked up the bolster. "I'll not be unkind to you though goodness knows you don't deserve such consideration. We'll have this bolster between us tonight, running north and south down the bed, as a barricade. For I swear to you, until we're joined in Holy matrimony, you'll not lay a finger on me again!"

In Paris, Rosalie was wrestling with a similar problem. She knew that Henri still desired her—the way he followed her about, his eyes fixed upon her body, made that apparent. And yet he seemed to be trying to conquer his own temptations. It was as if once the child had been born he had come to look upon her in a different light.

When he touched her now, it was only with gentle forbearance, a mere caress. Most of the time he seemed content to keep at a distance and indulge his appetites by watching her as she lay in bed, nursing the baby or while she got up and dressed or, as now, when she took her bath.

It had become a regular ritual. Melanie was never allowed into the boudoir at bathtimes nowadays; once the shallow tub had been filled with water, and the towels laid out to warm by the fire, Melanie withdrew, and Henri Clavel assumed his role as Rosalie's master and her slave.

Sometimes this irritated her—sometimes it amused her. She found herself, occasionally, taking an especially long time as she undressed, unfastening each garment with maddening deliberation, and slowly letting each one slip from her body . . . Knowing that she was tantalizing his frustrated hunger all the more by doing so.

Well, why shouldn't she made him suffer? He was her jailer—he had made her suffer in the past—this was her chance to turn the tables.

So she drew off her flimsy silk wrapper very, very slowly, letting the material slide with a whisper from her shoulders clinging to the curve of her hips, slipping down the long sweep of thigh—calf—ankle. And then she spread her arms wide and turned to face him, with a mocking smile.

"Thank you, Henri," she said, and pointed her toe as she tested the temperature of the tub. "A little more hot water, if you please."

He lifted the porcelain ewer and obeyed. As he did so,

she moved past him so close, that her soft skin brushed against the back of his hairy wrist, and his hand shook slightly. A small splash of water lapped over the rim of the tub, on to the carpet.

"Clumsy . . ." she reprimanded him sweetly, and then turned her back on him, stooping to sit in the bath.

He watched the long arc of her spine as she bent from him, and the roundness of her buttocks, like two white peaches—and his throat constricted: he found it hard to breathe. Melanie had poured bath oil into the water, and a heady perfume arose in the clouds of steam, making him almost intoxicated.

She looked up at him with a sidelong smile, sensing what torment he must be suffering.

"You're very quiet today, Henri . . . Have you nothing to say to me?"

She leaned back, soaping her gorgeous breasts, half-covering their shining luster with winking bubbles of lather.

He grunted a non-committal reply, and tried to restrain himself, feeling the blood mounting in his loins, impatient for satisfaction.

"What's the matter? Aren't you feeling in a sociable mood? I can't understand you, Henri—sometimes you can be almost pleasant when you try, and at other times—"

She raised one long leg out of the tub, letting the droplets trickle down her thigh to the shining fleece of black curls that swirled and danced just below the surface of the water.

"What was I saying? Oh, yes, why are you so changeable, Henri? Friendly one day and the next you're so sullen and unapproachable—hand me a towel, would you?"

She stood up, shaking herself lightly, so that her breasts swung freely in response to her movements, and then stepped out of the bath, letting the water-drops sprinkle the carpet as she waited for the towel.

He placed it around her shoulders, and she wrapped herself in it completely—then he began to dry her, his great hands moving with surprising delicacy, patting, stroking, soothing.

She stood quite still under his ministrations, content to be treated like a precious object, gently wrapped in cotton wool. As a rule, he stopped when he had dried her back, but today he took longer than usual, and she became aware that his hands were moving further—one slipping round her waist, his arm enfolding her in a muscular embrace, the fingers spreading wide and exploring the opening between the two edges of the towel.

"Stop—at once—you have no right to do such—"

Her voice changed; suddenly she regretted that she had teased him. For he was an animal, there was no doubt of that—and sometimes a wild beast can forget its training and revert to primitive savagery. His left hand was under the towel now, groping for her breasts and his right hand was running down her stomach to the line of curls below, and probing further yet.

She stiffened, her body quivering.

"No—let go of me—I don't want—" She broke off, suddenly unable to speak coherently, feeling the excitement within her loins growing at his touch—"I—I don't want—" she began again, hesitantly.

"Don't lie to me . . ." he grunted, and the deep tones vibrated against her as she struggled in his arms. "You *want* . . . Oh, yes, madame—*you want me now.*"

She fought—not against him, but against herself. It was several months since she had seen Paul, and she was not able to accept a life of chastity and self-denial easily. Her body ached now—ached to welcome this rough invader. But this was madness; he was her enemy —she hated him—how could she stoop to such folly?

"Let me go," she repeated, weakly. "I am a married woman—I love my husband—I will not be untrue to him."

The towel slipped from her as she wriggled to escape, but she did not notice it—her defences were down already.

"Do you think he's true to *you?*" said Henri thickly, pulling her closer still. "He's had as many women as there are stars in the sky—sweethearts, mistresses—yes, and wives too!"

"Wives?" she stopped short, staring at him. "What do you mean? I am his wife!"

"So you are—but not the first! For he divorced the last one only a year ago. Didn't he tell you that?"

"Divorce?" Rosalie's world was tumbling around her. "But the Holy Church does not admit divorce—"

"The Church may not, but the Republic of France approves it well enough! He was divorced by the State—it's all the rage nowadays, my lady!"

"Then our marriage was no marriage, and my son was born out of wedlock . . . Oh, God help me!"

She broke down in a storm of bitter tears, while Henri embraced her, consoled her, caressed her, drew her down upon the carpet, and so at last, in her moment of deepest misery and despair, possessed her.

(3)

Under Lock and Key

The fire in Rosalie's boudoir had burned low; it was long past midnight, and the embers gave out a faint red glow that barely illuminated the room.

Rosalie lay in bed, upon her side, with her knees drawn up. At her back Henri Clavel slept heavily after his exertions, and she could feel his belly rising and falling, pushing against her spine with each long breath that he drew. His hairy legs were bent, tucked up under her own . . . She had a sudden poignant flash of memory, recalling how often she had slept like this with Coral—only then the positions were reversed, for Coral, as the younger sister, always curled up in Rosalie's lap at night.

It seemed a lifetime away, and she fought to repress the tears that came to her eyes, anxious to make no sound that might disturb her sleeping jailer.

He had not been unkind to her; he had not even been deliberately brutal—indeed, when she broke down and sobbed in a culmination of shame and exhaustion and bitter disillusion, he had tried to comfort her.

At first with words, soothing her like a child, telling

her that Paul La Roche had not deceived her—marriage by civil law, and divorce under the *Code Napoleon* were a commonplace now in the French social system. It was entirely *de rigueur*.

She shook her head, and sobbed: "He knew I would never consent if he had told me the truth—that is why he pretended that ours was a real marriage . . . Oh, I understand it only too well now—the private ceremony in this house rather than in a church—the half-drunk priest in his shabby vestments—was he some friend of Paul's, brought in to make up the charade? The sacrament itself —was that nothing but vile blasphemy?"

Henri shook his head, stroking her neck, drawing her into his huge embrace.

"There are many such priests about nowadays . . . They try to keep a balance between the demands of the State, and their own consciences. It is not easy for them."

She buried her face against his chest, crying: "I don't care about their consciences—Paul lied to me—he has deceived me—what will become of me now?"

"There, there . . . Gently, my angel . . ." Henri whispered in her ear, and his massive hands continued to caress her, running over her naked shoulders and stroking her as if she were a kitten.

In her misery, she welcomed the soothing touch and when it gradually aroused an answering warmth in her body, her tearful outburst subsided at last. Slowly, cautiously, Henri's exploring fingers dared to go further, and their embrace changed its character.

She knew that her own unhappiness and longing was clamoring for relief, and as she felt herself responding instinctively, eagerly, even—to his advances, she tried to blot out every other consideration, and give herself up to the pleasure of the moment.

For a little while at least she would forget everything else, and match her need to his. Hungry for love, she clung to this passionate giant, and allowed him to make free with her—unfolding her body to him without shame, leading him on to still wilder transports of desire.

Upon the carpet, in front of the dying fire, he had entered her at last. She lay face down upon the floor, with her legs spread wide, and let him take her in the way that pleased him best, like two beasts in rut.

When the first demands of their ardor were satisfied, he said quietly: "Come to bed . . . We have the whole night before us . . ."

So they moved to the canopied bed, and there continued their loveless love-making, as if under some strange compulsion to lose themselves for ever in a whirlpool of physical sensation.

Again and again he had mounted her, until they were breathless and speechless—satiated with the fulfilment of their craving. Then, and only then, he fell into a deep sleep; curled up behind her, holding her in a bear-like hug.

But Rosalie did not sleep. Her body was temporarily satisfied—she was sore and aching, but in some strange way at peace . . . And yet her mind still revolved endlessly on the dreadful situation she was in.

Had Paul deliberately cheated her? Did he mean to desert her now? She could not bring herself to believe this; she felt instinctively that he loved and cherished her, and that he had been driven to take recourse in a "mock-marriage" by his desperation to have her as his wife.

But her position here was impossible. She felt totally humiliated—totally helpless. At all costs, she had to break out of this sensual trap, and try to escape.

Slowly, with infinite caution, she disengaged herself from Henri's arms, and slid very carefully to the edge of the bed. Without making a sound, she tiptoed to the dressing table, where her clothes had been folded neatly by little Melanie, before her bath.

In the near darkness of the bedroom, she began to dress herself, and when that was done, she opened the door of the clothes closet, and took out a warm cloak and a shawl to go over her head. Then she glanced back at the dark mound in the bed but Henri had not stirred, and the rhythm of his breathing was unbroken.

She moved across to the chair where he had tossed down his clothes impatiently before going to bed. She knew where to find what she was looking for . . . There—

208

on a heavy iron ring at his belt—hung the keys to the house. The key to the front door.

Holding her breath, anxious not to make the slightest sound, she slid the ring slowly from the leather strap.

Once it was in her hand, she felt safe; but there was no time to waste—he might wake at any moment.

She crossed to the bedroom door and opened it, praying that it might not creak. A moment later, she was outside in the passage; she knew where she must go now, and what she had to do.

The adjoining room was used as the nursery, and the baby was asleep in his cot. She picked him up, still wrapped in blankets, so he should not be disturbed, and cradled him in her arms, under the long woollen shawl.

Then she set off down the staircase, testing each step with her foot, determined to make no sound.

At last she reached the hall below, and put the key into the lock and turned it. It was well oiled, and did not squeak. She slid back the bolts, one at a time, then turned the doorknob, and pulled.

A rush of cold night air hit her in the face, and she felt her child shiver in his sleep; but she could not stop now. She walked out into the darkness of the Paris streets, pulling the front door shut behind her, and:

"Madame La Roche!"

She almost screamed with terror, as a heavy hand fell upon her shoulder, and a dark lantern was suddenly uncovered, throwing a blinding light into her eyes.

"Au secours!—Attention! Au secours!"

The cry went up, and she knew all was lost. Alarmed by the sudden noise, the baby awoke, and began whimpering. Rosalie was in despair and yet she knew she could not give way, for the child's sake.

Lights went on inside the house; her captor, a sentry posted outside on the pavement, grabbed the key-ring from her, and re-opened the door, as the household assembled.

More uniformed guards came running, and everyone talked at once. Rosalie could not follow what they said, but the meaning was clear enough. She had been caught trying to break out, and must now expect some more severe punishment. But how had she got so far? How had she laid hands upon the keys?

The clamor died down as Henri, pulling on shirt and trousers, stumbled down the stairs, rubbing his eyes. He took in the scene at a glance, and stopped short.

The guard held out the keys and questioned Henri rapidly; Henri shrugged—he had no explanation—he must have fallen asleep.

Another torrent of French, and two of the guards seized Rosalie by the arms.

She turned to Henri, asking desperately: "What are they saying? What will happen to me?"

He would not look her in the face as he mumbled the reply: "You are no longer under house arrest, madame . . . You are to be transferred to prison where you will be kept in permanent captivity, under lock and key. I can do nothing to help you now."

The following morning, when the wintry sun rose upon the little village of Les Andelys, Coral wakened slowly from a sweet, happy dream, and tried to remember where she was.

She had been dreaming of Gerard, she knew that much . . . and he was here, only a few inches away from her, sharing this cosy double bed. It all came flooding back to her now—the little cottage by the river, the bed in the wall-cupboard—the bolster that lay between them, as a respectable barrier to ensure that they should not touch during the night.

She opened her eyes lazily, feeling strangely contented, with a thrilling glow deep in the center of her being . . . she had been dreaming that Gerard was making love to her, and the dream was so vivid—she could almost imagine the warmth of his hand upon her, pressed fondly upon that special, secret place between her thighs.

As she thought this, she felt an unmistakable tickling sensation, and the impudent trespassing of one familiar fingertip. This was no dream!

210

She stifled a little gasp and tried to move but the hand held her fast, pinning her down.

"Gerard!" she panted furiously. "Don't you dare—what do you think you're—*how* did you manage it?"

He chuckled and her heart melted at the sound of his cheery voice as he replied: "Oddly enough that damn bolster seems to have finished up on the floor. Do you suppose I could have kicked it out accidentally in my sleep?"

He continued to fondle her and she tried to forbid him to take such wicked liberties but her own desire betrayed her, and she could not resist him. While her lips formed the words: "No—no—stop—"

Her wanton limbs were saying: *"Yes—yes—go on—"*

And she found that her body seemed to move of its own accord; her arms slid around him, her mouth opened to greet his kiss, and she gave herself up to the joy of their mutual love.

When at last they lay at peace, entwined in a happy tangle of arms and legs, she whispered: "You are a devil, and I'm a lost soul—but I love you . . ."

"Then we're two of a kind, my darling, and we'll go to hell together so at least we shall never be lonely," he retorted lazily, and rolled over to kiss her again.

"You must not say such things, even as a joke," she reproved him. "For there's no joke about committing mortal sin—"

He did not reply, but let his moist lips travel gently down her throat, kissing her breasts, teasing and titillating her nipples until his quick tongue and playful love-bites made her shiver with ecstasy.

"No—stop—don't do that—you know I'm helpless when you do that to me—" she pleaded, shuddering in spasms of delight.

"All the better—then we can begin all over again—" he suggested, redoubling his efforts to demoralize her.

"No!" She summoned up all her will-power, and pushed him away, then tumbled out of bed before he could stop her.

"What's wrong?" he asked. "Come back to bed—you've taken all the bedclothes—"

211

She stood at a safe distance and looked down at him, as he lay there uncovered; his broad manly chest tapering down to a slim boyish waist and narrow hips—and his manhood half-aroused, eager for another bout of dalliance.

He looked like a young pagan god, she thought, come back to earth to rediscover the golden age.

She pulled herself up from such wanton musing; how could a good Christian girl indulge in these profane notions? It was true enough, as the nuns had told her so often, that the path to sin ran downhill, and it was all too easy to fall headlong.

"You *are* a devil," she repeated firmly. "And I'll not let you seduce me like that another time. For although it seems to have slipped your mind, Gerard Kean, we have work to do! We must get away from this place, and move on to Paris—to find Rosalie—as soon as possible!"

At breakfast, they explained to Madame Bernard that they had to continue their journey. The good Sergeant was already out and about on his business, and Madame told them that he was expecting them to return to Rouen today, to recover their missing documents—including their American passports!

"In that case, the sooner we make for Paris, the better," said Gerard.

"But when we don't come back Sergeant Bernard will become suspicious . . . and if he makes inquiries in Rouen . . ." Coral frowned, as a new thought occurred to her. "We wouldn't want you to get into any trouble on our account, madame."

Madame Bernard smiled, and turned to Gerard.

"You have picked a fine girl, Master Gerard . . . I am very happy for you both."

Gerard put his hand upon Coral's, and said: "Yes—I have been very lucky, madame. But it is true—if our arrival here makes difficulties for you now—"

"Have no fear. My husband does not know of any past connection between us, so he will not blame *me* if you disappear without explanation. But I think perhaps I can help you upon your way to Paris."

She went on to tell them of her plan.

It transpired that Madame had a certain cousin, Mlle

Marthe Michot, who lived in Neuilly-sur-Seine, almost at the gates of Paris, and made her living, as her cousin had done, by teaching. In fact, she was the head teacher of a small private school for young ladies, and Mme Bernard had written her a brief letter, explaining the situation.

"I have suggested that she should give you shelter for a little while, at least. In return, you may be able to offer your services and assist in teaching the pupils. You tell me you sing, m'meselle and I know Gerard plays upon the pianoforte quite proficiently, for I taught him myself. I have suggested to Cousin Marthe that you could both make yourselves useful by giving music lessons."

She handed them the letter, then added: "Also, I know of a local farmer who will be sending his vegetables to market in Paris this morning. I am sure if you meet him at the corner in half-an-hour, you will persuade him to let you ride in the back of his cart. It will be slow progress but very safe."

So, after a long and laborious journey along the country roads, Gerard and Coral arrived at last in Neuilly, and made their way without difficulty to the little school of Mlle Marthe Michot.

Mlle Michot was several years younger than her cousin; in her early thirties, Coral imagined; with a very prim expression and a frigid personality quite unlike the warm generosity of Mme Bernard.

Now she read Madame's letter in silence, while a clock ticked loudly in the chilly parlor. At last she put it down, and looked up, with a disapproving gaze. Her command of English was a little stiff, and carefully correct.

"My cousin does not inform me as to the nature of your business in Paris, Miss Maguire," she said at last. It seemed that she preferred to address Coral exclusively, ignoring Gerard altogether. 'However—that is, of course, no concern of mine. I am to accept you as visiting Americans, who have arrived in France on business."

"Connected with the tobacco industry, we thought," Gerard broke in eagerly. "After all, there is a flourishing trade in tobacco between France and the United States, so it's quite likely we—"

"An extremely offensive commodity!" Mlle Michot

sniffed. "I sincerely hope you do not indulge in such a vulgar habit? I need hardly say that tobacco is prohibited in *this* establishment."

"Oh—quite so—" Coral chimed in, appeasing her. "We wouldn't dream of such a thing, would we, Gerard?"

"I am relieved to hear it . . . My cousin requests me to give you board and lodging for a short period of time, in return for which, you will provide music lessons for the pupils of this school . . . As you will gather, the school is closed for the winter vacation at present, but the girls will be returning next week, and then I am prepared to take you both on trial, for one term. As for accommodation, you will follow me, please."

She rose, and led the way from the parlor to the back of the house, where classrooms gave way to dormitories.

"These are the ablutionary facilities for the senior girls," she explained curtly, indicating a communal washroom with one bathtub and several basins. "You will be required to share these facilities for your toilet arrangements, Miss Maguire . . . And you will sleep in the senior dormitory—in here . . ."

She flung open a door and revealed a long room divided into cubicles, each with a narrow cot under a snowy-white bedspread, and a small window opening on to the garden beyond. Coral was reminded of the cells which the nuns occupied at her convent school.

"I shall give you the bed at the far end, Miss Maguire —you will also be responsible for the discipline and obedience of the entire dormitory. There is, for example, a strict rule forbidding any talking after lights out, and you will see that this is enforced."

"Excuse me—" Gerard broke in again! "That's all very well, but what about me? I don't imagine you'll wish me to become a dormitory prefect, too?"

Mlle Michot froze him with a glance.

"There is no provision for *male* visitors in this establishment, sir," she announced. "You will be provided with a mattress and blankets in the garden shed . . . I sincerely hope you may be satisfied with the arrangement."

"Oh—well—er—if needs must, I suppose I shall have

to settle for that," said Gerard. "And what about—forgive me—my ablutionary facilities?"

She regarded him with distaste, then said flatly: "I understand that there is a stretch of the river frequented by young men, as a swimming place, not far away. I suggest you should bathe there—I can offer no alternative."

"In the winter?" Gerard began to protest.

She looked him up and down, and replied: "You appear to be in reasonable physical condition. A cold bath should do you no harm, from time to time."

And she turned and led the way back to the parlor, while Coral murmured under her breath: "It might even do you a lot of good!"

It was almost dark by now, and Gerard realized that it was too late to find alternative accommodation tonight: he had to make the best of these spartan conditions. After a simple supper which they shared with Mlle Michot in a silence broken only by the ticking of the clock (the schoolmistress having made it clear that she disapproved of conversation at mealtimes, since it hindered good digestion) Gerard found his way to the garden shed, and glumly set to work to make up a bed upon the floor.

He stripped off his jacket and breeches and settled down to sleep in his shirt, huddled up under two skimpy blankets on a straw-filled palliasse. But sleep was slow in coming, and he tossed and turned, thinking of Coral. He knew where her cot was, in the dormitory, and he remembered the line of windows that looked out onto the garden. At last he could stand it no longer; he threw aside the blankets, grabbed an empty wooden crate that he found under the gardener's workbench, and set forth into the night.

It was pitch-black outside, and he blundered into various obstacles, barking his shins on flower pots, colliding with tree trunks, walking into rose bushes and being scratched by thorny briars . . . But at last he found Coral's window, and put down the wooden crate on the flower bed below.

Then he climbed up and tapped the window pane with his fingertips.

215

He heard her gasp: "Who's there?"

"It's me . . . Were you awake?"

"Yes . . . What do you want?"

"I can't sleep either . . . Let's talk."

"We can't! She might hear—you know there's a rule against it."

"We're not two of her precious schoolgirls, for heaven's sake! Besides, we can whisper . . . Open the window, Coral, and let me in."

"No! You know I can't do that."

"I'm begging you to be kind. It's freezing cold in that shed—I shall die of frostbite."

"Don't exaggerate. Go back to sleep, Gerard . . . Good night."

"It's all very well for you, tucked up in a real bed, nice and warm—"

"It's *not* nice and warm—it's icy-cold in here, if you must know—"

"Then let me in, and we'll get warm together."

"You're mad—I can't possibly!"

"Please, Coral darling—I'm pleading with you . . . I want you."

"No, Gerard. I'm sorry."

"Don't you want me?"

"N—no, Gerard . . ."—a little uncertainly now.

"Remember Rouen? You asked me to stay with you then because you didn't want to be alone. And now I'm asking you, Coral. Don't leave me alone tonight."

A long pause and then he heard the joyous sound of bed-springs creaking. A moment later, the window slid up quietly.

She said nothing, but held out her hands to help him climb into the room.

"My dearest, dearest girl—" He threw his arms around her in a fond embrace. "My own true love—"

They tumbled upon the narrow bed together, and the bed-springs squealed in protest. His hands roamed over her body, pulling at her nightgown, uncovering her breasts and his sweet, soft lips closed upon her mouth, his tongue probing fervently, greedy for her kisses while his fingers strayed to her nipples, erect under his touch.

216

"Miss Maguire! This is an outrage upon decency!"

They were so intent upon one another, that they had not noticed the approach of Mlle Michot who now stood at the entrance of the cell-like cubicle, a lighted candle in her hands, a blanket wrapped tightly around her, and her hair plaited in two long braids.

"How dare you abuse my hospitality in this scandalous manner?" She held the candle high, and glared at them like an avenging angel. "As for you, young man—leave this room instantly!"

Gerard had no choice; truth to tell, his heart quailed under her accusing gaze—she really was a very formidable woman. He shot out of bed without any argument, and scrambled out of the window. His shirt tails flew up as he jumped down, so the last they saw of him was a nude backside, disappearing like the full moon when it is swallowed up on a cloudy night.

"Monstrous!" gasped Mlle Michot, and turned to Coral. "How could you permit such a thing?"

Coral knew that her only hope was an apology; and indeed she felt extremely guilty.

"I must ask you to forgive me, madame," she said in a small voice. "It was very wrong, I know. And I promise you it won't happen again."

"I wish I could believe you," said the teacher. "I trust you are properly ashamed of such behavior?"

"I am indeed and tomorrow, I'll go to confession and swear before a blessed priest that I'll never do such a thing again. Until we're married, that is."

So the following morning, Gerard and Coral both took themselves off to do penance, in their different ways. Coral at the confessional, and Gerard by taking a cold bath in the river.

Mlle Michot had recommended Coral to a certain priest at the nearby church, who spoke a little English: but it was still extremely difficult to make him understand.

She knelt in the stuffy half-darkness, with a slatted wooden louvre in front of her face, whispering to the elderly cleric whom she could dimly make out on the other side.

"Bless me, Father, for I have sinned . . ." she began automatically.

"Plus lentement, s'il vous plait!" he interrupted. "More slow, my little one—more slow, if you please."

She took a deep breath—nearly choking in the odor of stale incense and dusty curtains and plunged ahead: " . . . I accuse myself—of—of certain sins of the flesh . . . with a man . . ."

"Qu'est que c'est? The flesh?"

"Yes, Father . . . I committed a mortal sin—with this man . . ."

"A sin—yes, yes—how many times? Once? Twice?"

"More . . ." She could hardly utter the word, she felt so ashamed and confused.

"Speak loud, my child . . . I cannot hear you well . . . You committed mortal sin—which sin do you mean? What is this word—the 'flesh'? I do not understand you . . ."

She struggled to translate the word into French, and settled upon "body" instead.

"I think it's the—the *corpse,* Father . . . C-o-r-p-s, corpse . . . ?"

"Ah! Le cadavre! Mon dieu—vous avez tués quelqu'un?"

She could hear that he was suitably horrified, and hurried on: "Yes, Father—three or four times—"

The elderly *curé* nearly choked. "You did this terrible thing *three or four times?"*

"I don't really know . . . More, I think—"

"Morts? Yes, yes, I know *ils sont morts*—but I ask you—you have done this to three or four men?"

"Oh, no, Father—I only did it to one man—three or four times . . . He keeps asking me to do it again, you see."

When the parish priest finally got his voice back he repeated:

"This man—he ask you to kill him—many times?"

"Oh, no—I didn't *kill* him—I made love to him, Father!"

A long, long pause and then the priest's voice, shaking a little, said faintly: "Ah . . . Now I understand. You have committed mortal sin by loving a man . . . Very well, my child—try not to do it again, won't you?"

It was something of an anti-climax.

Meanwhile Gerard was having an adventure of a very different kind.

He found the bathing place easily enough; it was one of those freak winter days when the sun breaks through the cloud for a few hours and tricks everyone into imagining that spring is on the way already.

Encouraged by this unseasonable mildness, several young men had gathered to swim in the river Seine, and when Gerard arrived, he saw half a dozen lads pulling off their shirts and breeches, making ready to dive into the sparking water, one after the other.

There was a rough wooden structure, rather like a summer-house, under the trees at the water's edge, and most of the swimmers had left their clothes there. Gerard began to follow suit, though he was rather disconcerted to find that there was no other form of protection —no canvas awning (such as they were starting to use at the English seaside, to shield the bathing machines from the gaze of passersby) that he might hide behind.

Admittedly, his fellow bathers—rugged young men, all intent on plunging in for a dip in the chilly water—did not even cast a second glance at him as he undressed . . . But far more astonishing to his mind, was the fact that only a few yards away, several women were taking a genteel promenade by the river, and gazing at the naked bodies of the swimmers with open and undisguised interest.

Some of them were fairly obviously disreputable young women, who nudged one another and commented loudly upon the masculine physiques on display; but others were older ladies, to all outward appearance eminently respectable—one or two even being dignified matrons with schoolgirl daughters or nieces in tow. Gerard scratched his head: it was all very perplexing.

He decided finally that they ordered these matters rather differently in France, and so continued to disrobe unconcernedly, leaving his clothes within the shelter.

As he crossed the towpath and made his way to the water's edge, he heard a whisper of female comment behind him, but turned a deaf ear. Then he plunged headfirst into the air waves, and all other thoughts were immediately expelled from his mind.

At first the shock was considerable, and he regretted his hardihood—but once he had swum several strokes, the blood began coursing through his veins, and he started to enjoy himself. His fellow bathers called out to him cheerfully, and he waved back in response, before diving down and swimming underwater.

When he came up for air, the sunshine seemed dazzling, and he rolled over on to his back exulting in the brilliance of the light. He lay on top of the water, his arms stretched wide, and noticed that his sexual organs seemed to bob up through the surface as if they had a life of their own. No doubt the ladies who patrolled the shore were all equally gratified by the spectacle—but what of that? He didn't care.

And then he noticed one lady, standing apart from the others; quite still, with her gaze fixed upon him. He could not distinguish her features, for she wore a dark veil, but he knew without any doubt that she disregarded all the other swimmers—she had eyes only for him.

He smiled to himself, and wondered who she was, and what drove her to spy on masculine nudity in this fashion. As he was pondering on this, a wicked little breeze sprang up, and he shivered, plunging deeper into the water—and at the same instant, he noticed that the veiled lady's bonnet had been snatched from her head in the sudden gust, and tossed into the water.

It landed only a few feet away from him, and he grabbed it immediately, then—as the other swimmers gave an ironic shout of laughter—he popped it on his own head, and struck out for the shore.

The lady, obviously dismayed by this turn of events, retreated, and took refuge in the little shelter; then as Gerard climbed out of the water, shaking himself vigorously like a dog, she shrank still farther into the corner and found herself trapped.

Gerard, stark naked and dripping wet, bounded in,

and swept the hat from his head with a heroic gesture.

"Allow me, madame—"he began . . . and stopped short.

For her veil had also been disarrayed in the breeze, and she could no longer conceal her features . . . Mlle Michot stood with her eyes downcast, and her cheeks aflame with embarrassment.

"Why, Madame . . ." he said at last, with a mischevious grin. "You must forgive me for this outrage upon decency . . . next time I must remember to wear my gloves!"

And he returned the bonnet with a mocking bow. She took it, and murmured, still without looking at him: "Thank you, sir . . . may I suggest—there is no reason for you to mention this incident to Miss Maguire?"

He inclined his head courteously: "I think we understand one another, madame . . ." And before she could stop him, he raised her hand to his lips and kissed it swiftly. "It shall remain a secret between ourselves."

She snatched her hand away as if his lips had scalded her, and marched out of the shelter, replacing the bonnet on her head as she went—and trying to ignore the lewd cheer that arose from the young men in the water.

When Gerard rejoined Coral later, at the lunch table, she noticed that the headmistress raised no objection although he broke yet another rule by talking cheerfully throughout the meal. Afterward, she said: "Gerard, you shouldn't tease her so—we mustn't anger her any further: we have to keep on the right side of her."

"Don't worry," Gerard assured her. "Last night I was a little in awe of the dear lady, but today, for some reason, I'm not intimidated by her any more!"

Coral did not press him for any further explanation; she had far more important things on her mind.

This afternoon, she had decided to go and make some enquiries at Paul La Roche's house, at the address he had given them—just off the Place Des Vosges. Gerard insisted upon accompanying her, and they agreed to use up some of their remaining money by hiring a carriage into the city of Paris.

The sun was setting already, and the milder weather

brought down a thick mist that shrouded the gray buildings in a soft blur. It was difficult to see where they were going, but they peered out of the windows of the carriage and tried to make out the various streets and avenues they passed along.

The Emperor had instigated a vast program of rebuilding, and they saw many houses fenced about by scaffolding, and many highways that were being resurfaced with new paving-stones. The carriage rattled down the long hill of the Champs Elysees, and continued along the arcades of the Rue de Rivoli.

Coral glanced at some of the shop windows as they passed—brightly-lit and full of the latest fashions—and sighed, trying to put aside such frivolities. For at any moment now, they would reach Paul's house, and she hoped against hope that Rosalie would be there.

At last the carriage drew up; Gerard counted out what seemed to be a small fortune in banknotes, and the driver tipped his hat as he whipped up the horse and rolled away.

They looked at one another in some trepidation, and Gerard attacked the doorknocker.

A trim little maid answered their summons. In his best French, Gerard asked if Madame La Roche might be at home?

The maid looked askance, and bit her lip, then asked them to step inside.

They were shown up the stairs and left to wait in a little withdrawing-room upon the first floor. There was no doubt that this was Paul's house; his excellent taste showed itself in every detail of the furnishings. Coral sat upon the velvet chaise-longue, next to Gerard, and fumbled for his hand; he could feel that she was trembling.

"I can't help it," she whispered. "I am a little nervous."

Then the door opened once more, and a stranger walked in—a giant of a man, well over six feet tall, and heavily built in proportion. He looked at them suspiciously for a long moment, and then broke into a rumbling laugh.

222

"Mademoiselle Maguire? This is *formidable!*"

Coral stared at him then at Gerard, but he was equally bewildered.

"How do you know my name? I've never seen you before."

"But I have seen you, I think—in Ireland . . . You are madame's sister . . . And you, m'sieur—I fancy I noticed you there also, at one time."

They were totally mystified, and he enlightened them, displaying a gleam of gold as he smiled.

"I am Monsieur la Roche's chef—Henri Clavel, at your service . . . I had the honor of preparing more than one meal for you, I think, mademoiselle. And—like all servants—I made it my business to peep through from the kitchen quarters when you arrived . . . One likes to learn as much as possible below stairs, you understand."

Coral relaxed: "Henri! Of course . . . Paul spoke of you so often—thank goodness you are here; it's good to know we're among friends. But lately Paul had terrible news of Rosalie; that is why we are here— do tell us what has happened to her."

Henri looked left and right, as if afraid of eavesdroppers, then asked: "You are come to take her away to safety—is that correct?"

"Exactly," said Gerard eagerly. "We want to get her home to Ireland . . . will you help us?"

"Where is she?" Coral chimed in.

The chef put a finger to his lips, and said quietly:

"Wait. She is no longer here, but before I say any more, I must take care . . . There are spies everywhere, alas . . . You must stay here—I will be back very quickly, and then I will tell you everything."

He disappeared from the room with surprising speed, and Coral turned to Gerard eagerly.

"What a piece of luck! Fancy finding Henri here—I never thought of that—of course he will help us—he's always been a very good—"

She broke off, realizing from Gerard's expression that something was wrong.

"Why—Gerard—what is it? What's the matter?"

He began: "I'm not sure—I thought I heard—"

Then he got up and crossed to the door, and tried the handle. When he turned back to her, his face was grave.

"I was afraid of that . . . It's locked."

"Locked? I don't understand—what does it mean?"

"It means that we have walked straight into a trap, my love . . . And the enemy have got us where they want us—under lock and key . . ."

(4)

Black Rendezvous

Ever since Rosalie's attempted escape, Henri Clavel had been under suspicion by the authorities; they had permitted him to stay on for the time being, in charge of the La Roche household but he was well aware that he was on trial, and that they were keeping a close watch on him.

Now, therefore, he knew that he had no alternative. Since these two Irish spies had arrived, he had no choice but to hand them over to the police.

Having locked them safely in the drawing room, he hurried downstairs and reported to the guards who were whiling away their tedious tour of duty by flirting with the kitchenmaids.

Briefly, Henri explained the situation. The guards drew their pistols, loaded them (while one of the kitchenmaids put her hands over her ears and trembled on the verge of hysterics) then accompanied Henri upstairs to round up the prisoners.

Triumphantly, Henri unlocked the door and flung it open.

"Do your duty, officers—" he began . . , and broke off, in dismay.

The room was empty: and the window was wide open.

They all rushed across and looked out into the foggy night. The flat roof of the kitchen quarters was directly underneath—it was a ten-foot drop, but not impossible. And from that flat roof, there was an easy access to the outbuildings of the neighboring house, and a back alley beyond.

The younger of the two guards cursed fluently, and said: "While we were down below they were making their escape right above our heads."

The elder of the two looked at Henri darkly, and added: "They won't take kindly to what you've done, citizen . . . *Two* mistakes will be too much for them to overlook . . . There'll be trouble over this, you mark my words."

In a hired cab, clip-clopping back to Neuilly through the swirling mists, Coral tried not to cry—and Gerard put his arm round her shoulders.

"Cheer up, my love . . . Just think how fortunate we have been. Escaping from the blazing theatre in Cork was an excellent rehearsal for us—we managed to get out of that window and away as if we'd been cat-burglars! Luck was on our side."

"Yes, but to go through all that and for *nothing*. We're no better off than we were before—all we know for certain is that Rosalie isn't at Paul's house—she could be anywhere now!"

"Of course we only have Henri's word for that and he could have been lying," said Gerard thoughtfully.

"You mean she might still be there locked away in another room? But that's terrible because we daren't go back again, now they know who we are—oh, Gerard, what are we to do?"

He held her close, and drew her head on to his shoulder, talking soothingly.

"Don't worry, my dearest. I told you luck is with us—that is only a temporary setback. We'll find her very soon, I'm sure of it. I'll start making inquiries—we'll have news of Rosalie before very long—you wait and see."

The following week, Mlle Michot's Academy of Young Ladies reopened for the spring term, and temporarily Gerard and Coral had to put aside their quest for Rosalie and concentrate on the more immediate problems of earning their living.

Neither of them had ever taught music before, and they awaited the first lesson with some nervousness. Mlle Michot brought in half a dozen girls, and performed the introductions.

"Mlle Maguire who will give tuition in singing and Monsieur Kean, who will supervise your practice upon the pianoforte. The lesson will last for one hour; I trust you will take full advantage of these opportunities, young ladies, and work hard. Now I shall leave you together, to—er—"

"Sink or swim?" suggested Gerard innocently.

Mlle Michot flashed a furious glance at him, and departed, shutting the door with a little more force than was, perhaps, strictly necessary.

So the lesson began; to start with, Gerard accompanied Coral as she sang a series of exercises—scales and arpeggios—and then invited the pupils to follow her.

Gerard found it hard to concentrate upon the keyboard; the girls were all about sixteen years old, and extremely well-developed for their age. As they took deep breaths before embarking on their vocal gymnastics, he observed their full young bosoms swelling—rising and falling with such verve that they seemed likely to escape altogether from their tight bodices. It was hardly surprising if Gerard's fingers fumbled upon the keys from time to time, and struck a false note.

Coral glared at him: "Let us begin again, Mr. Kean . . . And this time we will try not to change key, if you please! Henriette shall sing the next solo, and show us what she can do."

Gerard translated this instruction into French, inviting the flaxen-haired and blue-eyed Henriette to "show him what she could do."

"*Avec plaisir, m'sieur,*" dimpled Henriette, with an impish smile—and took another deep breath that seemed likely to demolish her corsage entirely. Henriette's friend

227

Gabrielle was equally willing to display her talents but as a pianist rather than as a singer. So she took her place beside Gerard at the piano bench, and they continued the musical accompaniment in the form of a duet. Sometimes she too played a discordant note, and then it was Gerard's task to correct her, placing her soft fingers upon the correct keys. He noticed that Gabrielle gave him a sidelong glance from her lustrous brown eyes, and a moment later—could it be, or was he imagining it?—her knee, firm and warm under her thin muslin skirt, pressed lightly against his thigh.

He smiled to himself; he felt sure that he was going to enjoy the teaching profession after all. What was it Mlle Michot had said about "taking advantage of the opportunities" . . . ?

At the end of their first day, Gerard was politely but firmly shown the door; Coral would remain on the premises, to share the evening meal with staff and pupils. ("And afterward, Miss Maguire, you will kindly report to my study," Mlle Michot told her; "I wish to discuss your syllabus for the remainder of the term, in detail.") but Gerard had to find his own supper at a neighborhood *estaminet,* and then make his solitary way home, via the back gate, to the lonely palliasse in the garden shed.

Once again, he found it hard to settle down to rest. Memories of the young ladies kept returning to his mind's eye—Henriette, Gabrielle, Blanche—all so mischievous, and so alluring . . . And then he remembered Coral, and all the other faces fled from his thoughts.

Coral's unique copper curls tumbling loose over her creamy shoulders, when she let her hair down at night. Coral's deep green eyes, brimming with promise of excitement, of fulfillment, of love. Coral's perfect breasts, with their blushing nipples like miniature rosebuds . . . Coral's generous thighs; as soft and smooth as silk, parting to receive him.

He couldn't bear another moment of solitude; he had to be with her again. Swiftly, he retrieved the wooden crate that he needed as a foothold, and with shirttails flapping above his bare legs, made his way quietly and secretly through the darkened garden.

He was in luck; her window, he found, was partly open—perhaps she was waiting for him? It was the work of a moment to slide it open all the way; and in no time at all he had climbed through into the narrow cubicle.

He put out an exploratory hand in the blackness, and to his disappointment, discovered that the bed was empty. Where was she? Could she be in the bathroom, busy with what Mlle Michot would call "her ablutions"?

As he hesitated, wondering what to do, he heard an odd little noise—something between a whisper and a smothered laugh. He froze, remembering belatedly that the dormitory was no longer occupied by Coral alone, but now must be inhabited by a party of schoolgirls. He held his breath; surely they should be asleep by this time?

But obviously they were not. He listened intently, and heard other noises—suppressed giggles—more whispering —and then a sudden cry of dismay.

He could not distinguish the words, but the meaning was clear; a group of these mischievous young ladies was playing some kind of trick on one of their number —dragging her out of bed, by the sound of it, and carrying her off between them, despite her struggles of protest.

"Ssh! Ssh!" Someone had put a hand over her mouth, to judge by the frenzied, indistinct cries the poor girl was uttering: and the others hushed her, telling her to keep quiet, and threatening unspeakable reprisals if she did not hold her tongue.

The sounds began to fade away as the little raiding-party moved off. Unable to master his own curiosity, Gerard followed, picking his way cautiously through the empty dormitory, faintly illuminated by the row of windows along one side. The girls had disappeared by now into the washroom, and he could hear faint sounds of splashing—and renewed laughter.

With infinite care, he pushed the washroom door open and stopped short on the threshold, amazed at the scene that met his eyes.

There were two or three candles alight, and after the darkness outside, the room seemed brightly lit—almost dazzling.

229

But most dazzling of all was the spectacle of half a dozen girls in flimsy nightgowns—so flimsy that their lively, nubile bodies were clearly visible through the semi-transparent material—and in the midst of them was the lovely Henriette, spreadeagled, with arms and legs wide apart and entirely nude.

The other girls had pulled off her nightgown, and were about to duck her in the bathtub, which had been filled with water. Poor Henriette was being tormented and teased by countless prying fingers; they tickled her ribs so that she giggled helplessly even while she pleaded for mercy—they stroked her breasts, making her gasp and thresh about in involuntary spasms—they even toyed with the blonde fleece of curls that lay fully displayed between her legs, and there Gabrielle's wicked fingertips explored shamelessly, arousing Henriette to a frenzy of excitement.

Amidst waves of delirious pleasure and pain combined, Henriette's eyes suddenly opened wide, and she gasped in alarm: *"Attention—M'sieur Kean!"*

She had seen Gerard, half-undressed, standing in the doorway. For a frozen instant, no one moved—then Gabrielle, who was clearly the ring-leader, uttered one swift command. Immediately, Henriette was released, tumbling to the floor: and before Gerard realized what was happening, he found that he had taken her place as a prisoner.

He tried to escape, but it was impossible. These girls were strong and determined, and he was hopelessly outnumbered.

As they grabbed his arms and legs, dragging him toward the tub, Gabrielle made a sudden lunge and pulled up his shirt, beginning to tickle him as Henriette had been tickled a moment earlier. The other girls followed her example, and he could not resist the knowing, excruciating touch of their fingers. He struggled violently, but he knew that his efforts were in vain; at any moment they would pull down his drawers, and expose him, already desperately aroused.

In the midst of this breathless horseplay, they had all forgotten one thing and that was the necessity to keep quiet. Now they were laughing and calling out breathlessly to one another, and when the door slammed behind them, at first they did not even notice it . . . Until Mlle Michot cut through the hubbub, with a voice like ice.

"Mr. Kean! You will report to my office in the morning, before breakfast. Young ladies—go to your beds instantly! I shall deal with you all tomorrow."

The girls let go of Gerard at the very edge of the bathtub, and he tumbled into the icy water, splashing and spluttering, while the terrified girls scuttled off to their beds, and Mlle Michot stood in the doorway, with Coral—appalled and mortified at her shoulder.

Their interview next morning, in the chilly study, did not take very long.

Gerard tried to explain that he had been waylaid by the girls as a childish prank—taken by surprise, overpowered and made the butt of a practical joke.

Mlle Michot's face was stony as she sat at her desk and asked: "And what were you doing in the girls dormitory in the first place, Mr. Kean?"

"I—I came to find—I hoped to have a word with Miss Maguire . . . about the syllabus," he concluded feebly.

"Quite so . . . you leave me no alternative, sir—I shall have to dispense with your services. You will depart from this establishment at once. Miss Maguire can hardly be blamed for your behavior—she is at liberty to remain here if she wishes—"

"Thank you, m'meselle, but I do not wish to stay," said Coral; her cheeks were very pink, but her voice was steady. "If Mr. Kean goes—then I must go, too. We are travelling together, you see."

Mlle Michot shrugged slightly. "That is for you to decide . . . I am sorry things have turned out so unfortunately—I should never have allowed my cousin to persuade me to break the rule of a lifetime and employ a male teacher upon my staff—it was bound to lead to trouble."

Coral went off to pack her bags, but Gerard stayed behind for a moment longer, saying: "Don't be too hard on the young ladies, will you, M'meselle? Girls will be girls, you know—just as boys will be boys . . . and women—will be women."

She looked at him for a moment, then said: "You realize that I could have called in the police and reported the outrageous events that took place here last night? I would have been within my rights if I had demanded your arrest."

"No doubt you would," said Gerard quietly.

"But I did not do that—and I shall take no further action," she continued. "And I think you know why."

Gerard smiled suddenly, then leaned forward across the desk and kissed her once, quite gently, on her tired, lined cheek.

"Thank you," he said.

And the interview was over.

Coral and Gerard were on the move again: they began the long walk toward the center of Paris, with Gerard carrying their luggage, for they could not afford to throw money away on cabs now.

At first Coral remained very silent and aloof, although Gerard argued in his own defense: "It wasn't *my* fault that those infernal schoolgirls pounced on me last night—you don't suppose I *wanted* to be ducked in a cold bath, do you?"

She wouldn't answer, but tossed her head and walked on.

"How was I to know they would all be out of their beds, playing the fool?" he demanded. "I only came in through the window to find *you*—nobody else—"

"Yes, and now everyone in the school knows that! They all realize what you were up to—sneaking in to my bedroom, halfdressed . . . It's so humiliating."

"I don't suppose you'll ever meet any of them again—so what does it matter?"

"It matters to *me* . . . That you should be so careless of my reputation—of my feelings."

She increased her pace, and Gerard, laden down with the luggage, was hard pressed to keep up with her. He saved his breath for his labors, and the conversation languished.

232

Their immediate object was to find somewhere to stay, and eventually Gerard saw a notice in a window— *"Chambres à louer"*—"Rooms to let"—in a seedy establishment, not far from the Palais-Royal.

"At least this looks pretty down-at-heel—it's bound to be cheap," he suggested. "But all the same, I propose we tell the landlord that we're a married couple, and then we need only rent one room—it'll save us money—"

"Certainly not! Some things are more important than money!" snapped Coral indignantly, leading the way into the building.

The manager was sitting in the salon, reading a newspaper and picking his teeth with a quill. When he saw Coral, he brightened up immediately, disposed of the quill, and sprang to his feet, clicking his heels in a military fashion.

"Mademoiselle? A votre service—"

Coral left Gerard to do the talking, and Gerard launched into their story—they were Americans, visiting France on business—they wanted somewhere inexpensive to stay for a few nights, or perhaps longer.

"Une chambre?" asked the manager.

"Deux chambres!" Coral broke in: she knew that much French, at least.

Gerard tried to argue yet again, but Coral refused to listen to him. She tugged at her valise, from among the bags he was carrying, saying: "Give me my luggage . . . I'll take it up to *my* room!"

In the tug-of-war, the valise burst open, and a lot of Coral's personal belongings scattered on the floorboards, among them, several yellowing copies of songs, in music manuscript paper. The manager clicked his heels again and hastened to pick them up.

"Mademoiselle is a musician?" he inquired, handing them back with practised gallantry.

"Allow me to present Miss Coral Maguire—the American songbird!" Gerard announced. "This young lady is the toast of New York—the belle of Boston!"

"Enchantè, m'meselle," smiled the manager. "I am delighted that we have something in common—Emile

233

Schindler, of the Tivoli pleasure gardens . . . delighted to make your acquaintance."

With this, he made a low bow and kissed her hand. Gerard frowned slightly at this enthusiastic chivalry, and said: "Schindler? That doesn't sound a very French name, m'sieur?"

"I am originally from Alsace, you understand. Of mixed parentage—but in the world of entertainment, we are all gypsies, *n'est-ce pas?*"

"Oh, yes, I agree!" Coral was enchanted by this unexpected friendliness, and rattled on: "My own family have gypsy blood in their veins, back home in Irel—"

"In America, dearest," Gerard corrected her swiftly, digging his elbows in the ribs.

"Oh—in America! Yes, of course . . ." She changed the subject. "But now you have given up entertainment and gone in for hotel-keeping, M'sieur Schindler?"

"Not at all—I am happy to be able to pursue both careers; for I also run a café in the Tivoli gardens; a *bal-musette,* you understand?—with music and dancing—singers and acrobats . . . Perhaps one night you would honor us by giving a short recital of your songs, Mlle Maguire?"

Coral glanced at Gerard eagerly: "Yes—why not? It might be exactly what we need."

Gerard interrupted again, dismissively: "We must talk it over on some other occasion, m'sieur. If Miss Maguire can spare the time, it might be amusing but we have a very crowded schedule of engagements, you understand. Now—may we see our rooms?"

The rooms were shabby and depressing, and smelled of damp plaster and stale cooking but at least they were cheap. When they had unpacked, they set out once more to explore the city and try to decide what they should do next.

"I don't know why you didn't let me book an engagement to sing at M'sieur Schindler's cafe," Coral gumbled. "Heaven knows we need all the money we can earn—"

"It's always a mistake to appear eager; let him stew for a bit," said Gerard. "Besides I took an instant dislike

234

to the fellow. He's far too oily for my taste—all that lip-smacking and heel-clicking."

"I thought he was rather handsome," said Coral. "A little on the old side, perhaps—he must be at least thirty-five but a fine figure of a man. And so *polite!*"

But Gerard wasn't listening. By now they had reached the Palais-Royal, and he led the way into the inner courtyard.

An open square, with straight avenues of pollarded trees, was surrounded on all sides by tall gray buildings and beneath the buildings were a series of arcades, which housed countless shops and cheap eating-houses . . . and among the arches and pillars of these arcades was a little bevy of young women; some of them sitting beside wicker baskets of flowers, selling posies to the passersby—others offering reels of silk thread—holding out tiny phials of lavender-water or smelling-salts—toothbrushes, garters, sealing-wax—toys and trinkets of every kind.

"Oh—it's a market!" cried Coral, cheerfully.

"Yes, it's a market . . . and there's more on sale here than meets the eye. Wait here for a moment; I have an idea but I can't carry it out if we're together."

Without another word, he left her standing in one of the archways, and set off purposefully. Coral was bewildered; what was Gerard up to now?

She saw him picking his way through the busy throng —shaking his head as various girls tried to offer him their wares. Then she noticed that not all the young women of the Palais-Royal had baskets of goods for sale; some were standing idly in corners, doing nothing—leaning against a pillar, with their dresses pulled down so low in front that their bosoms were flauntingly displayed—others strolled languorously to and fro, idly fingering their clinging dresses, and contriving as if by accident to pull their skirts up high enough to show off a pretty ankle, or a shapely calf—or even more.

With a sudden flash of anger, Coral recognized what sort of women they were, and what sort of place Gerard had brought her to. So it was these brazen creatures that he had come to find! She watched him chatting and laughing with first one, and then another—he whispered a word in a shell-like ear, and then bent his head so that a luscious pair of painted lips could breathe a reply.

Coral clenched her fists: for two pins, she'd walk away and leave him—how *dare* he introduce her to such a den of vice, and then—worst of all—abandon her like this?

She noticed with alarm that an elderly gentleman with white moustaches and a monocle was eyeing her with interest, and realized with dismay that since she was doing nothing but loiter here, in this notorious place—he must obviously assume she was no better than the rest of the sinful crew.

Luckily, before he could accost her, Gerard returned, and steered her into one of the cafés.

"Sit down—don't argue—listen to me!" he ordered, and snapped his fingers at a waiter.

Over two glasses of wine, he explained his plan.

"Don't start giving me any more moral lectures, because in the first place you're wasting precious time, and in the second you're completely wrong . . . I didn't go seeking out those lights-o'-love for fun—I had a much more serious purpose in mind."

"What are you talking about?"

"We want to find Rosalie and the sooner the better—is that agreed?"

"Of course, but—"

"Very well, then . . . All we know is, that she is under arrest but we have no idea where. If she has been arrested, she will be in the hands of the police and who knows more about the doings of the police than the city's strumpets? I told those girls I want to find a young lady-friend of mine who's in trouble with the law."

"A lady-friend? Gerard!"

"Don't interrupt—that played on their sympathies; they're a sentimental lot . . . I explained that I need to find someone in the know—an informer with access to police secrets and for the price of a few francs, they told me how to find such a one . . . He's called Cock-Eyed Alphonse and they say that if I present myself tonight at 102, Rue de Vaugirard, I'll be sure to find him there."

"Is that where he lives?"

"No, it's a meeting-place he goes to—I don't know

what it is—another café of some sort, I suppose . . . the girls call it the 'Black Rendezvous'—I don't know why . . . anyway, that's where I shall be, at nine o'clock tonight —number 102, Rue de Vaugirard."

By a quarter to nine, he was on his way and Coral was alone in her dingy hotel bedroom.

She lay upon the bed, her hands behind her head, and stared at the cracks in the ceiling, and the dancing shadows set up by the flickering candle on the bedside table. She thought of Rosalie and prayed to the Holy Virgin for her sister's safety. She thought of Uncle Dermot, and felt a terrible pang of homesickness—Ireland seemed to be a long way away. She thought of Gerard, not very far away at all but going into the unknown for Rosalie's sake . . . For *her* sake . . . Perhaps facing horrifying dangers at this very moment!

She held the thought of Gerard in her heart, praying for him too, and for his safe return to her waiting arms.

A sudden tapping at the door startled her.

"Who's there?" she asked, sitting up.

"It's only me," said a thickly-accented voice. "Emile Schindler—may I come in? I have a little business proposition I wish to discuss with you."

She hurried to the door and opened it.

"Yes—of course—please come in," she said. "I'm sorry, I can't ask you to sit down—there's no chair—"

"Oh, how disgraceful. Remind me tomorrow and I will see to it that you have a chair . . . but how have you managed with nowhere to sit, this evening, m'meselle?"

"I was sitting on the bed," she began.

"Of course—just what I was about to suggest—let us *both* sit on the bed."

He dusted the threadbare counterpane with his handkerchief, and they sat side by side on the bed's edge.

"That's better . . . Now then, you tell me you are a singer, and I will be perfectly frank with you. I need a new attraction in my café—someone to draw the crowds. You are young and beautiful, and if your voice is as charming as your appearance, I am sure you will do very well."

"You are too kind, m'sieur!" Coral couldn't help feeling

a glow of pleasure; she knew he was flattering her, but what was the harm in that?

"Not at all. We are the servants of the public, and if you can give the public what they want—I shall pay you well. Very well indeed."

"I'm sure that sounds very nice, but I should have to talk it over with my—er—my pianist, Mr. Kean—of course."

"I do not see any necessity for that, my dear lady. I am not interested in hiring your Mr. Kean—musicians are plentiful, I have several already—this is to be an arrangement between you and me."

As he spoke, he leaned back, letting one arm fall casually behind her, and for a moment she wondered if he were quite as charming as he appeared to be. But she reminded herself—this was a simple business discussion, after all.

"I see—yes, well—I couldn't possibly leave Mr. Kean, I'm afraid—he and I are—so to speak—partners, and unless you'd be prepared to come to some arrangement with—"

"I'd be prepared to come to any arrangement with *you*, my little one," smiled Emile Schindler and she noticed there was a fine sheen of perspiration on his upper lip. "But you must forget this man Kean—he is no longer your partner—*I* shall be your partner from now on—"

He slipped his hand around her waist, and pulled her closer to him.

"You are the most beautiful creature in all Paris—I cannot resist your bewitching charms—I adore you, Coral Maguire—"

"No—please let go of me—I thought this was supposed to be a business proposition—"

"And so it is—I propose that we go into business as a partnership—I shall pay you many hundreds of francs to sing in my café every evening and make the customers happy—and every night you will come back here with me—and make *me* happy—"

He grabbed her roughly, and threw her back upon the bed, then launched himself upon her in a passionate assault.

She tried to fight him off, but he was overpowering her; as his thick wet mouth sought her lips, and she smelt his breath, reeking of brandy and garlic, she thought desperately: *"Gerard—help me—oh, dear God—where is Gerard?"*

At that precise moment, Gerard was ringing the doorbell of number 102, Rue de Vaugirard—on the other side of the city.

The door was opened by a smart manservant in footman's livery, who let him in without comment, merely saying: "In here, if you please, sir."

He was shown into a small anteroom where a large, elegant matron of uncertain age sat by the fire, stroking a small pugdog that lay upon her lap. She looked up at Gerard with mild surprise.

"Good evening . . . I don't believe I have had the pleasure of seeing you before, m'sieur? Is this your first visit?"

"Well—yes—that is to say—"

"Who recommended you to come here, may I ask?"

"A young lady at the Palais-Royal said that I would find what I was looking for."

The matron smiled faintly and said: "I am quite sure you will. But the name of the young lady?"

"She said I was just to tell you—Clo-clo sent me."

"Ah—Clo-clo—very well. That will be twelve francs, please—in advance."

"Twelve francs? But—"

He was about to object; the smile faded from the lady's lips, and the pugdog growled in its throat. Gerard decided that it would be a waste of time to haggle. If it cost twelve francs to enter this "black rendezvous"—so be it . . . If he obtained the information he sought, it would be worth the money. He peeled off a handful of notes, and the lady accepted them graciously.

"Thank you . . . Now you may go in . . . You are a little late in arriving, I warn you—play has already begun?"

Play? Was it then some sort of gambling house?

The matron summoned the footman, who took charge of Gerard, and led him along the narrow passage to another anteroom, and yet another—each a little darker than the one before. At last he said:

"*Entrez, m'sieur . . .*"

And he opened a pair of double doors, and ushered Gerard in.

The doors shut behind him and for a second Gerard wondered if he had been struck down by blindness, for the room was in total darkness. There was not a single gleam of light anywhere. So this was why they called it the "black rendezvous."

Uncertainly, he edged a step or two forward then paused, listening, and at once realized that he was not alone. He heard tiny sounds all around him; the noise of heavy breathing—of whispers—of soft feminine laughter —a man's abrupt oath, and the sound of a muffled collision. The room was full of people.

Gerard cleared his throat, and asked timidly:

"M'sieur Alphonse?"

At once a little zephyr of shushing broke out around him, and Gerard realized that conversation was out of place in this extraordinary situation.

Then a gentle, female hand touched his wrist, and clasped it and drew him forward. Another soft pair of hands found his face and turned him in another direction. He smelled perfume all about him, and the warm exciting scent of woman's flesh. From the darkness a sweet mouth nuzzled against his cheek, and moved unerringly to his lips, and a tongue danced against his tongue while hands, more hands, were travelling over his body—exploring, searching, unfastening, unbuttoning.

Now he understood what kind of place he had come to: and now it was too late to retreat, far too late, even if he had wanted to.

Determined arms encircled him, and he felt himself being slowly and surely undressed, his shirt pulled up from his breeches, his breeches gradually slipping down his thighs—the relentless hands came at him from all directions and he let himself sink helplessly into a multiple embrace, as a dozen arms and legs closed about him, and he gave himself up to the nameless excitement of the black rendezvous.

(5)

The Pleasure Gardens

Gerard's last rational thought was: "So this is what an orgy is like . . . "

He had always been vaguely fascinated by the idea of orgies—the very word had a greedy, salacious thrill about it somehow —and when he was still on tour in Ireland, he had heard tall tales from Rory O'Malley about the go-ings-on in certain disreputable houses in Dublin but this was his initiation into such mysteries.

But then all coherent thoughts fled, as he plunged into the warm mass of willing flesh that enfolded him.

He could see nothing—he knew nothing of his partners in the game—he could not tell whether he was being caressed by two, three or even four women. In total blindness, he was explored, aroused, devoured—and in ut-ter darkness, his own hands discovered breasts, buttocks, thighs; exploring, arousing and devouring in his turn.

This was complete freedom; without any inhibition or restraint he was at liberty to do whatever pleased him, and he exercised this freedom to the full—kissing and nibbling on scented nipples—letting his mouth slide over slippery skin, down and down—questing with lips and tongue in regions he had never entered before.

The pitch-black room was no longer hushed; he was aware of the sounds of sexual ecstasy all around him— panting, groaning, sighing—with occasional breathless words gasped in a paroxysm of delight—words of crude abandon, that Gerard had never been taught in his school-room French lessons, but whose meaning was startlingly plain.

Only one word was never mentioned in the Black Rendezvous; and that word was "love."

Twisting and twining between the pliant bodies, he found himself entering the inmost secrets of an unknown woman and as a dozen hands urged him on, he mounted to a swift climax, and found relief all too soon.

But the game could not end so quickly; there were many willing helpers only too eager to arouse him to new heights of passion, and he found himself being turned on to his back, lying on soft cushions, while gentle fingertips caressed the inside of his thighs, tickling and massaging him as he stiffened with fresh desire—and then a wet mouth came down upon his loins, and seduced him into strange and unimagined pleasures.

He could not even cry out with mingled joy and pain, as sharp white teeth nipped him gently—for yet another pair of lips opened upon his mouth, and another tongue plunged inquisitively within and he let himself be rolled over again in a tangle of arms and legs.

Another hand touched his calf, and moved up to fondle the back of his knee and further still, teasing and pro-voking—a larger hand, Gerard realized dimly, than all the rest. And he suddenly realized that the naked limbs behind him were muscular and hairy, and that a male member had joined the little group. He tried to shake off the intruder, but he was pinned down upon all sides, and could not free himself.

At that same moment, he was already beginning the spiralling ascent of yet another climax, and nothing else mattered. Again and again he spent himself in long, shud-dering spasms of frenzy. And when at last the transports subsided, he became aware that the probing male member was now very much more intrusive, and that he might well be ravished in his turn if he did not take evasive action.

With an effort, he disentangled himself, and wriggled clear of the bodies that pressed upon him from all sides.

"Excuse . . . Fresh air . . . Must go outside," he mumbled indistinctly, and gathered himself up, trying to reassemble his clothing as best he could.

He fled for the door or rather, in the direction that he imagined the door to be, and after several false starts, in which he encountered many other coupling figures, and collided with threshing limbs—he reached a haven of temporary calm in the faintly lit anteroom outside.

He leaned against the door, and tried to think clearly, after the wild excesses he had just experienced. He had come here to work—not to play—he tried to recall what his errand had been . . . Yes—of course—Rosalie—how could he have forgotten?

Behind his back, the door inched open again, and Gerard moved aside with an automatic apology.

A man followed him from the room; a man of about fifty, with graying hair caught up in an old-fashioned *queue* and fastened at the nape with a velvet bow. He glanced tentatively at Gerard, and said:

"Too warm for you in there, my friend? It can be rather suffocating on occasion . . ."

He looked Gerard up and down appraisingly, then added: "Come—let me show you the back entrance of the house; there is a little garden there, where you may regain your breath—follow me."

He took Gerard's arm in a purposeful grip, and Gerard was about to pull away—fairly sure that this was the anonymous figure who had tried to take advantage of him in the *melée*—

But at that moment the stranger smiled, and for the first time Gerard noticed his eyes. The man had a marked squint: and at once he remembered everything—Cock-Eyed Alphonse—of course!

"You are M'sieur Alphonse?" he asked.

"Aha—my reputation has run in advance of me, alas," sighed the other man. "Yes, sir—I am Alphonse Bertrand —what of it?"

"Only that—you are the very man I came here to meet."

M. Bertrand's smile grew broader, and his squint even more pronounced.

"I am delighted to hear it. In that case let us repair to the garden at once, my dear young man."

Steering Gerard by the arm, he led him along a shadowy corridor and out through another door into the garden.

It wasn't much of a garden; a small paved courtyard with one flickering lamp hanging above the door, and a dozen formal bay-trees in rubs. Facing them was a high wall, and above them the purple velvet of the night sky, unbroken by moon or stars. There was a little breeze, and the leaves of the bay trees whispered together uneasily . . . Gerard shivered.

"Now my dear boy—who sent you to me?" asked M. Bertrand. "Who was kind enough to arrange this little rendezvous?"

As he spoke, he released his hold upon Gerard's arm and pressed his hand instead.

"No one arranged a rendezvous, sir—I think perhaps you misunderstand me," said Gerard as politely as possible disengaging himself.

"I do hope not—explain yourself, my child," purred the older man.

"I am in Paris to find a friend of mine who has disappeared—"

M. Bertrand shrugged, and smiled again: "In these times, people disappear every day—it is sad, but one cannot cling to old friends; one must console oneself by making new ones . . . Forget him, my dear, and—"

"My friend is a lady, sir . . . Madame Paul la Roche." Gerard sensed the sudden suspicion in the man's reaction, and continued quickly: "She has been taken from her husband's house, I believe—but I don't know where she is now, except that I fear she may be in the hands of the police."

244

"And you believe I may be able to tell you which prison she is in?" Bertrand asked coldly.

"She is in *prison?*" Gerard was half-expecting this, but the news came as a shock, none the less.

"But of course—her husband is a traitor and an enemy of the State—where else would his wife be, but in prison? and now, my friend, before I tell you any more—perhaps it is time that *you* told *me* a few facts . . . Who are you? Where have you come from? It is clear from your accent that you are not a Frenchman. Come—the truth now!"

Gerard said defensively: "What if I do not choose to tell you?"

"Then you may be forced to do so. Do you not realize whom you are addressing? I am Alphonse Bertrand, Commissioner of Police."

With horror, Gerard realized that he had placed himself in this man's power.

"Excuse me—I have to go—" he began.

The grip on his arm this time was like a steel trap.

"Not so fast, my pretty young man. It is clear to me that you are a spy—and you will accompany me to police headquarters for interrogation."

His voice was purring again now, with a gloating relish; M. Alphonse Bertrand was going to enjoy himself. He continued in silky triumph: "Of course—if you are sensible, and are prepared to be—shall we say?—co-operative—I might yet be able to help you in some ways . . . It all depends, my dear, on how adaptable you are."

And he ran his other hand, very deliberately, up Gerard's leg, and squeezed . . .

As Gerard recoiled, trying desperately to think what he should do, there was a sudden clamor from inside the house: the sound of a warning shot—doors banging and men shouting: "Open—in the name of the law!"

A woman screamed, and several more began to shriek at the tops of their voices.

"*Damned idiots!*" Bertrand let go of Gerard and cursed. "They swore to me they would not raid this house until tomorrow night—devil take them!"

245

He adjusted his clothing, straightened his cravat, and threw a last warning over his shoulder as he made for the door: "Don't try telling any lies—I shall say I caught you as you were about to escape—follow me—"

Gerard acted in a flash. He kicked the Police Commissioner hard, sending him sprawling into the darkened corridor, and simultaneously slammed the door upon him. With seconds to spare, he raced for the garden wall, and jumped; fear must have put wings to his heels, for he managed to reach the top of the wall in one bound. He clung on, then with a mighty effort dragged himself up and over. A moment later he was free, running for dear life along an alleyway, and making his way back to safety—and Coral.

Coral, meanwhile, had endured an equally terrifying experience.

From the moment when Emile Schindler flung himself upon her, in the shabby hotel bedroom, she had fought with all her strength to fend him off.

"Take your hands from me, sir—let go—"

But he would not. Emile Schindler was not a particularly big man, but he was several stone heavier than Coral, and as he lay across her, she could hardly move.

With one brutal gesture, he tugged at the ribbons of her bodice, and ripped her dress open, so that her breasts were uncovered. His eyes gleamed, and he licked his lips, letting his thick fingers stray on to the perfect curves of her naked flesh—pinching her pink nipples—

"How dare you touch me—you—you *libertine*—"she cried furiously, drumming her fists against his chest.

He laughed, and said thickly: "That's it, my pretty wildcat—fight me if you will—I like a girl with spirit. But you'll tire of the battle long before I do, I promise you that!"

And ignoring her struggles, her began to unfasten her dress, leaning still closer, and forcing his mouth upon hers. Between terror and disgust, she bit his lip—hard!—and he flinched away: "You little witch—you'd stick your fangs in me, would you?"

He put his hand to his mouth, off-guard for a mo-

246

ment. This was Coral's chance; she stretched across to the bedside table and grabbed the brass candlestick. As she snatched it up, hot wax ran over her fingers, and the candle flame extinguished; then she brought the heavy object down in one resounding blow upon the man's skull.

He gave a little moan, and flopped back, motionless.

Coral's first thought was: "Oh, God—I've killed him...!"

In the dark, it was doubly unnerving. There was a faint glimmer of light from the window, and she could just make out his features as he lay across the bed, face upward, with his eyes wide and staring.

She put her ear to his chest . . . Thank heaven—his heart was beating—he was still breathing; she had only knocked him unconscious. Well, this was her opportunity to rid herself of the loathsome creature, and she had better make the most of it.

When Gerard finally stumbled home exhausted, about midnight, he found M. Emile Schindler, with a bandage round his head, hammering at Coral's bedroom door.

"What the deuce is going on?" Gerard asked.

M. Schindler had the grace to look slightly abashed.

"That young woman tried to murder me!" he complained indignantly. "She assaulted me with a blunt instrument and now she won't even open her door!"

"*What?* Coral, what's been happening?"

Gerard tried the door, but it would not budge.

"Oh, Gerard, is it really you? Where have you been all this while? I've waited for such ages—just a moment, while I shift the bedstead."

There was the noise of heavy furniture being dragged across the floor, and then at last the door opened.

Breathless but determined, wearing a dressing gown tightly buttoned up to her throat, Coral let Gerard in to her room.

"I had to barricade the door—that man was trying to —to rape me!" she said accusingly, as Emile followed Gerard in.

"Nothing of the sort!" Emile snorted. "I merely tried to behave in a friendly manner, and *this* is all the thanks

247

I get. She nearly brained me—when I came to I found myself lying in the passage . . . I could have bled to death for all she cared."

"You did *that?*" Gerard asked Coral, studying the landlord's bandaged head with some awe.

"I had to defend myself, didn't I? I caught him a wallop with the candlestick," she explained in a small voice. "And where were *you,* when I needed protection? What took you so long?"

"I'll tell you later . . . First of all, m'sieur—you'd better take yourself off— and think yourself lucky I wasn't here, otherwise you'd be unconscious still!"

"I don't see what concern it is of yours," grumbled the landlord sulkily. "You're only her pianist—I don't have to ask your permission every time I choose to pay attention to the young lady—"

"Just don't do it again, my good man—that's all." Gerard took him firmly by the collar and escorted him into the passage once more. "For the truth of the matter is—this young lady happens to be my wife!"

"What's that?" goggled Emile, and behind him, Gerard heard Coral gasp.

"You heard what I said. As I tried to explain this morning—we shall not be requiring two rooms after all; for I shall be occupying this room with my wife, and we do not encourage visitors . . . Two's company—three's a crowd."

"But—but—the young lady herself insisted upon two rooms—"

"We were having a family tiff this morning, but it's all forgotten now—isn't it, my dearest?" Gerard kissed Cora very firmly on the lips, and began to undress. "Let's get to bed, my love—our little disagreement is quite forgiven and forgotten . . . Good night, M'sieur Schindler—and sleep well!"

He shut the door in the man's face, turned back to Coral, and grinned; adding softly: "I don't think he'll trouble you again, somehow . . . "

"Oh, you clever devil," she sighed. "I might have known—you turn every situation to your advantage."

"Well now—which of us would you sooner go to bed

with?" he asked, impudently dropping his breeches and stepping out of them. "Him? Or me?"

She turned her back on him, and took off her dressing gown, then climbed into bed: she did not, it appeared, have very much choice.

One minute later, Gerard blew out the candle and scrambled in beside her. The bed was very narrow for two people, and she was not surprised to discover that he was naked.

"Don't think you're going to get your own way so easily," she warned him, and rolled away as far as possible . . . But that wasn't very far, and she could feel his body pressing warmly at her back, and his legs sliding close behind hers.

"Tell me what happened tonight, and what you have found out," she continued quickly. "I've been waiting all this time for news of Rosalie. Do you know where she is?"

"Yes—and no," he said. "Our fears were right—she is in police custody—but I haven't yet discovered where they are keeping her."

(He avoided the use of the word "prison," guessing that it would be too upsetting for Coral.)

"And that's all you know? Dear heaven, it took you long enough in all conscience—you've been gone over three hours, and that's all the news you've learned at the end of it? What have you been up to all this while?"

"It—it wasn't easy . . . I had to work at it—very hard." Gerard smothered a yawn. "I was nearly arrested too—though I managed to get away—but I really am rather tired . . . I'll tell you all the rest of it in the morning, my darling."

Coral thought for a while; and listened to Gerard's slow, rhythmic breathing, and felt the regular pressure of his broad chest against her shoulderblades—and the warm, tingling sensation of his strong thighs tucked behind her hips.

At last she said very softly: "I suppose *now*—you'll be wanting to make the most of the situation you've got me into . . . " She wriggled up against him a little, and added: "No doubt you'll insist on having your way with me . . . "

She turned to face him, and waited for his embrace.

"Gerard?"

Nothing happened. She put out an inquiring fingertip —and found that he was completely uninterested: worn out by his exertions, Gerard had fallen fast asleep.

"Men!" Coral said to herself furiously. "That's the worst of it—you never can rely on them at all!"

The following morning, when she woke up, she resolved not to let Gerard suspect her moment of weakness, and so slipped out of bed quickly, while he was still sleeping. By the time he opened his eyes, she was washed and dressed, and ready to begin the day.

"There's water in the washstand ewer," she told him. "It's cold—but that won't do you any harm. It might help to wake you up."

He sat up, rubbing his eyes; and she sat at the foot of the bed, and gazed at him critically.

"Sleeping like a lump you were, all night," she remarked. "Now perhaps you'll give me the details of what you were doing last evening, and why it tired you so much."

Still half asleep, Gerard began to relate the events of the previous night, and perhaps told her more than he had intended to, for when he finished, she exclaimed with vexation: "Are you trying to say that you spent your time in that black den of vice—with all those loose women?"

"Well—you see—I didn't know when I went in, what to expect—and by the time I *did* know—it was too late to back out . . . "

"You mean to tell me you were romping in the dark with a parcel of harlots—while I was alone here, fighting for my honor? You actually admit you committed fornication last night?"

"Be reasonable, my dearest—since you won't let me make love to you, I have to make do with whatever I can find by way of compensation—if you weren't so desperately proper, I'd never have dreamed of such— *ouch!*"

He broke off as the furious Coral took her revenge by pulling aside the bedclothes and emptying the jug of cold water over his head . . . It was not a promising start to the day.

When at last they went downstairs, Emile Schindler was already in the salon—wearing even more bandages round his head, rather like a turban.

"Very becoming, m'sieur," said Coral sweetly. "Who knows—perhaps you may start a new fashion?"

M. Schindler cleared his throat, and said loftily: "I have decided to overlook your extraordinary behavior, madame—no doubt you were distressed at your husband's absence . . . and I admit, I had slightly misunderstood the circumstances—so we will say no more about it. But I am still anxious to proceed with the business proposition I put to you last night."

"Eh? What's that?" Gerard asked, frowning.

"You mean—when you told me I should have to make your customers happy every evening, and then come here every night to make—"

"I mean that you should sing a selection of your songs at my café," Schindler interrupted hastily, with one eye on Gerard. "I think I told you, m'sieur—I manage an establishment at the Tivoli—the pleasure gardens, you know—a *café-concert*—and *bal musette* . . . and we are sadly in need of some new attraction to draw the crowds. I suggested to Madame that she should sing for us—with you yourself accompanying her at the pianoforte, naturally."

Gerard and Coral exchanged glances. Their money was running low, and they were in no position to pick and choose their engagements.

"Very well—when do we start?" Gerard asked.

"The sooner the better—why not tonight?"

"We shall have to spend more time in rehearsal," said Gerard. "We must arrange a little group of suitable songs."

"Of course—and I must prepare posters to announce your début—Miss Maguire, the American songbird—let me see, how is it spelled, this Maguire?"

Gerard said smoothly: "I think on the whole we'd prefer not to use my wife's full name. Just call her 'Mademoiselle Coral' and let her be a woman of mystery!"

As they went off to rehearse, he explained quietly to

Coral: "Don't forget Henri Clavel knows your name. We can't afford to take any chances."

"I suppose so. But—oh, Gerard—how are we ever going to find Rosalie now the police have arrested her? Where can she be?"

At that moment, Rosalie was only about a mile away, had they but known it. A little less than two miles from the Palais Royal, to the north-east, was the Prison of the Temple: a notorious building, whose name struck a chill into many a heart. It was here that the most important "enemies" of the Republic were housed; it was here that King Louis XVI had been held before his execution, twenty years earlier. Royalists, traitors, spies and *emigrés* of both sexes were kept here under conditions of utmost security; and it was here that Rosalie had been transported after her arrest.

Now she stood—as she had stood so many times since then—with her wrists shackled, her hair lank and unkempt, her dress torn and stained—awaiting interrogation by the most feared man in the prison . . . Chief of the secret police—the merciless Desmarets; especially hated, perhaps, on account of his thin smile and unfailing courtesy, even while supervising the most ghastly tortures.

"Good morning, Madame la Roche," he began genially. "And what have you to tell me today?"

"I have nothing to tell you, m'sieur—today or any other day." She kept her eyes fixed upon the floor. "I should have expected you to realize by now that I am telling the truth: I know nothing of my husband's work —I never met any of his associates—he never confided in me—I can tell you nothing at all."

"I am desolated to hear it, madame," responded Desmarets with a note of sincere regret in his voice. "For you must realize how much easier your punishment would be if you were to remember something—even some trivial detail—that might assist our investigations."

"I have nothing to say, m'sieur. I rarely speak to any one at all nowadays, except when you call me in here for these little tête-à-têtes . . . " She shrugged hopelessly.

"I have difficulty in understanding my cell mates and in any case they have nothing to say to me. I keep my own counsel, as a rule . . . I think they believe that I am deaf—or dumb—or mad . . . And perhaps they are not far wrong."

"But you have struck up an acquaintance with one of your fellow prisoners, I believe?" Desmarets consulted a paper on his desk. "You have been observed in conversation with a certain Mlle Duchatel?"

"Sophie Duchatel? Dear God—you call her a 'fellow prisoner'?" Now Rosalie looked up at last, with a spark of defiance. "I call her a child and I call her situation an outrage . . . She's not more than twleve years old—you've already murdered both her parents—"

"The citizen Duchatel and his wife were notorious royalists; their crimes against the State were numerous—they had to be put to death . . . "

"Why couldn't you let the child go? She's committed no crime."

"She might arouse sympathy in certain reactionary quarters—there could be trouble—we cannot afford to take such risks. Mlle Duchatel must be protected for her own sake . . . "

"Protected? Stuck in a cell with a dozen other prisoners —with no one to turn to for help? Her only happiness in life is when I let her nurse my baby; she is a good, careful girl, and she tends my child with all the care and love in her innocent heart."

"It is well for you that you have found a nursemaid in this girl—for you will need someone to look after the child from now on."

She looked at him, and at his smile her blood ran cold.

"What are you saying? Do you plan to murder me too?"

"My dear Madame La Roche—what an idea! No, indeed—I have a scheme in mind that may alleviate some of your distress, and even help to pass the time for you more amusingly . . . I remember you have told me repeatedly that you have no money—"

"That's the truth and God knows I've suffered because

of it. Some of the women in this stinking gaol have private means—they are able to bribe their keepers to let them have better accommodation—palatable food—a few luxuries—"

"I deplore the word 'bribe', but we will let that pass ... I have decided to grant you permission to earn a little money; only a few francs a week, but at least it may help to moderate your sufferings slightly ... And provide some necessary items for the baby, perhaps?"

"Earn money—I don't understand—"

"The child can remain in your cell, in the care of Mlle Duchatel; for you are to be sent to work in the prison laundry, Madame, for twelve hours, every day."

"The *laundry?*" She stared into his eyes, searching for some signs of pity. "I have heard the most horrible tales of the indignities the women suffer there—they say it is a hell upon earth—for the sake of my baby, I beg you monsieur, not to send me to work there—"

She broke off ... It was useless. His smile was as relentless as ever, as he folded the paper neatly upon his desk, and rang a bell for the jailer to take her away.

"I regret—the matter is already decided—you will begin work tomorrow ... Next, please!"

A few hours later, after the sun had gone down, the Tivoli Pleasure Gardens came to life—and a greater contrast to the dank horrors of the Temple Prison could hardly be imagined. It was as if the revolution, and all its terrors, were a million miles away, and the customers who thronged the gates of the little park, off the Rue St Lazare, had not a care in the world.

Within, Tivoli offered a fairyland of delight; cafés, dancehalls, fairground booths surrounded a maze of gravel walks bordered by evergreen trees, lighted arbors, even a miniature lake.

Candlelight and lanterns sparkled on every side; later, it was said, there would be a firework display. On the little sheet of water, young couples ventured to try their skill in rowboats and if that seemed too daunting, they could experiment with another breathtaking form of loco-

motion; for the latest dance was all the rage, and sometimes one might see as many as three hundred people all
swinging and swaying in time to the intoxicating one-
two-three beat of "la valse."

To Gerard and Coral, the sheer spectacle was overwhelming, and as they took their places on the little bandstand at the side of the café Schindler, they felt more than
a trifle nervous.

Emile made a brief announcement, and the song-recital
began with "Drink To Me Only" . . . an old favorite.

Favorite, that is to say, in Ireland, but unknown to
the Parisians. They listened politely enough, and they admired Coral's voice—and her slim figure, clearly outlined
in a classical white gown, with a velvet stole. But at the
end there was only a smattering of applause, and Gerard
whispered: "Try the French one next . . . 'Plaisir D'amour' . . . "

Coral had a few continental songs in her repertoire,
and now she launched into that regretful tribute to love's
philosophy.

> *"Plaisir d'amour—ne dure qu'un moment . . .*
> *Chagrin d'amour—dure toute la vie . . . "*

This time the listeners were caught and held by the
clear, wistful melody, and as the last note died away they
applauded heartily, and called for more.

But it had been decided that after each pair of songs,
the little orchestra should play for dancing, and now, on
cue, the musicians struck up yet another valse, and the
couples took the floor once again.

Gerard was about to discuss the next choice of items,
but he saw that Coral wasn't listening; her eyes were fixed
upon a girl who stood just below the bandstand, staring
up at her.

"What is it? Who are you looking at?" he asked.

"Don't you recognize her? The little maid who let us
in to Paul's house?"

Gerard looked again, and remembered the girl: remembered too how nervous and ill-at-ease she had seemed.

"Ignore her," he advised. "If she says anything, swear

you never saw her before in your life—she could be dangerous—"

"Don't be silly—this is our chance to find out about Rosalie!" said Coral, and before Gerard could stop her she had jumped down from the little platform, and addressed the girl.

"You were there—at Madame La Roche's house—' Coral began.

"Madame La Roche—oui—" Melanie, the little maid looked even more apprehensive now, and glanced over her shoulder.

"Then you must know I'm her sister—tell me where they have taken her, for God's sake—"

Several of the other customers were looking on curiously at this unexpected diversion, and Melanie became frightened by Coral's questions.

"Non—non—je vous en prie—" she pleaded desperately, trying to get away.

Coral stopped her, holding the girl's wrist, and Melanie began to protest, begging her to let go—

More and more people were watching and listening by now, and Gerard felt certain that at any moment there would be trouble. In the background, he thought he saw uniformed figures gathering—could it be the police, moving in to find out what was going on?

But at this point there was a sudden interruption. A tall young man, with elegant sideburns and the air of a dandy, stepped out of nowhere, and tapped Coral on the shoulder.

She turned—taken off-guard—and without a word he swept her into his arms and whirled her away to the insistent beat of the waltz. Coral struggled and protested, but in vain; over the man's shoulder, Gerard caught a glimpse of her face as she looked back, desperately signalling to him for help.

That was all he needed; with one leap he had gained the dancefloor, and was pushing his way through the waltzing throng. A second later, he had caught up with Coral and the unknown dandy. Now it was Gerard's turn to tap the intruder on the shoulder, and when he turned round, Gerard did not waste time on words.

Earnestly hoping he hadn't forgotten his far-off lessons in pugilism, he let fly with a right hook to the man's jaw. His adversary saw it coming, and dodged but not fast enough and the blow connected with the dandy's nose, causing it to bleed profusely all over his frilled shirt-front.

Gerard bowed politely, and explained in his best French: "My apologies, sir—but you were dancing with my wife . . . "

The other man pulled out a handkerchief and pressed it to his nose, then—aware of the excited crowd that had gathered around them instantly—he extracted a slip of pasteboard from his pocket and presented it to Gerard.

"My card, sir . . . You will do me the honor of meeting me at dawn tomorrow in the Bois de Boulogne . . . Pistols or epées?"

"What—pistols?—but—"

"Very well—pistols it shall be . . . I look forward to settling this affair to my satisfaction, under the code of the *duello*."

And with that he dabbed at his nose again, turned, and strode off, leaving Gerard speechless.

Duello . . . So he had just been challenged to a duel —pistols at dawn—and with a total stranger . . . He looked down at the card in his hand.

"Henri Martin . . . Lieutenant-Colonel, Grand Hussars . . . "

Dear God—as if it weren't bad enough, the fellow had to be a military officer—a professional swordsman!

He swung round, looking for Coral—for advice, or sympathy, or reassurance—and this was the worst moment of all.

Somehow Coral had slipped away in the confusion, and vanished among the milling crowds. She was nowhere to be seen.

(6)

Within the Temple

Immediately, Gerard began to search for her. He abandoned all thoughts of continuing the performance for how could he accompany a singer who had disappeared?

He started to make his way through the waltzing couples, looking on all sides for Coral but she was nowhere to be seen. If she had taken cover, he decided, she would instinctively head for the darkness beyond the illuminated area of the dancefloor; and so he turned away and began to explore the pleasure gardens beyond.

Away from the bright lights, the lawns and gravel walks seemed even darker than before, and he found himself peering into dense shadows, where drifting silhouettes emerged from the gloom for a moment, then faded into still deeper obscurity.

He was really worried now—what could have happened to Coral? She would not have gone so far in search of a hiding-place, surely?

He saw a shrubbery ahead, with some ornamental summer-houses among the trees, and plunged off the path to investigate. Out of nowhere, a black shape loomed up at him—then separated into two indignant lovers, interrupted at an intimate moment.

Mumbling an apology, Gerard blundered on, and then stopped short at the sound of a woman's voice, screaming in terror.

Could it be Coral? He wasn't sure but he broke into a run, and made for the source of the cries, within one of the little pavilions, built in the pagoda-like style of the fashionable "chinoiserie."

He burst in and the screams terminated abruptly. By the light of a flickering Chinese lantern, he saw a young woman lying back upon a divan—her clothes disarrayed, and large areas of her anatomy generously on display. The man with her had his breeches round his ankles, and now glared at Gerard over his shoulder, spitting out a curse, and ordering him to get out.

"Pardon me, sir—I thought—the cry of a lady in distress—"

The lady in question uttered a foul-mouthed verb, telling Gerard in effect to mind his own business.

Apparently her screams only added spice to their love-making, and were not meant to be taken seriously.

Gerard retreated, in some confusion: and continued his hopeless search . . . Where on earth could Coral have got to?

At the moment when Gerard rescued her from the arms of the total stranger who dragged her in to the dance, Coral had seen a familiar figure out of the corner of her eye. She whirled round, and recognized Melanie once again—the little maid from the La Roche household—who was standing, half-hidden among the crowds at the edge of the dancefloor.

As Coral met her gaze, she turned and fled; and this time Coral was determined not to lose her quarry. Heedless of Gerard's predicament, she set off in hot pursuit.

The girl had only a few yards start on her, and Coral was certain she could catch up. But she was thwarted by the numbers of passerby who continually blocked the way, and as she dodged and side-stepped, she realized the distance between them was increasing.

The girl reached the main gates that led into the Rue

St. Lazare, and glanced back for one moment to see if she were still being followed. This brief hesitation gave Coral a chance to make up the ground she had lost, and when Melanie, with a terrified gasp, rushed out into the street, Coral was almost within arm's length of her.

They continued their breathless pursuit along the busy road, dodging the pedestrians, and skipping from the newly-laid pavement on to the cobblestones of the roadway. A carriage and pair rattled past, swerving to avoid them by a narrow margin, and the driver cracked his whip angrily.

Coral flinched aside as the whip whistled past her—and when the carriage rolled away, she thought for one awful moment that the girl had vanished. But then she saw her, disappearing like a ghost into the dark mouth of an alleyway across the road.

Coral did not stop to wonder where she was going, but redoubled her speed, and raced after her.

The alley was a narrow passage beween two tall buildings, and very black indeed; but there was one glimmer of light above a doorway—a door that hung crazily, half off its hinges, with a crudely-painted legend daubed upon the fanlight—a message that Coral could not understand.

But the door was open; that gave her courage to go on. She went inside and found herself faced by a hanging bead-curtain—and pushed her way through. The curtain clattered and chattered as it swung to behind her, and within the filthy room, lit by one shaded lamp, an old crone looked up from the table where she sat, and beckoned her forward with a gap-toothed smile.

"Entrez—entrez, ma p'tite . . . N'ayez pas peur."

Somehow, Coral remembered enough of her occasional French lessons at the convent to realize that the old woman was telling her to come in, and saying that she need not be frightened . . . But where was the little maid?

A slight movement caught her eye, and she realized that the hanging curtain at the back of the room—tattered and black with age—probably masked a further doorway. The girl must be hiding there.

Coral took her seat at the table as the old woman had indicated, and studied her more closely. There was a faint family resemblance between them—perhaps this might be the girl's aunt—a great-aunt—or even her grandmother?

But the old hag was holding out her hand, and gesturing for Coral to do the same. Playing for time, and still trying to decide on her next move, Coral obeyed and to her dismay the old woman took her hand firmly in her bony grasp, and turned it over, palm-uppermost . . . Then she began to peer at it, bringing her beaky nose very close and screwing up her eyes.

She gasped and wheezed and poured out a torrent of words that Coral could not follow at all—she knew that her fortune was being told, but she could not make out anything that was said . . . Until suddenly the old woman paused—frowned even more fiercely—and then looked up, examining Coral's face with two red-rimmed, watery eyes.

"Danger . . . " she croaked hoarsely. "Danger incroyable . . . Danger de mort."

The words were familiar enough—"danger" and "death." Coral felt her heart pounding, and tried to stammer out a question—what did it mean?

Abruptly, the old woman let her hand drop and stood up.

"Je ne peux plus. C'est fini."

Clearly, the consultation was over. Bent almost double, the fortune-teller hobbled round the table, leaning upon a stick, and held out her hand again, awaiting payment.

Too late, Coral realized that she had no money with her, and tried to explain this to the old woman. She carried no purse—she had nothing.

The crone broke into a shrill scream of abuse, and flew at Coral, who tried to defend herself against the attack but the old woman was not trying to strike her. He clawlike fingers flew to Coral's bosom, and ripped at the bodice of her gown—Coral heard the thin material tear, and caught at the woman's wrists, but the damage was done.

Her breasts were uncovered and hanging between them, on a thin chain, was a silver crucifix . . . The only gift she had ever had from her mother. As the old hag tried to unfasten it, Coral struggled with her: "No—! You shan't have it—let go—"

The fortune-teller began to tug at the chain to snap it; the thin metal bit cruelly into Coral's neck, and the woman shouted: *"Melanie! Melanie—ici!"*

The curtain at the far end of the little room was pushed aside, and Coral saw the little maid reappear. Now she would be outnumbered—now she could be robbed, or even murdered, and no one would ever know. She opened her mouth to call for help but the cry died upon her lips, as she realized that Melanie had not come to the old woman's assistance but to stop her.

She dragged the old woman back, forcing her to let go of the crucifix: and a furious volley of French broke out as they shouted at one another. But now it was the fortune-teller who was outnumbered, and she realized she could not expect to have her way.

In a last explosion of rage, she hit the girl across the face repeatedly, knocking her to the floor and then snatching up her walking-stick and beating her about the shoulders, screaming abuse at her all the while.

It was over in a few seconds, and then the old harridan hobbled out, and the little room was silent except for the muffled sobbing of the little maid.

Appalled by the scene, Coral made a move to try and help the girl—she was, after all, little more than a child, she realized now—but at once Melanie pulled herself up and darted off behind the filthy curtain, like a frightened animal seeking shelter.

Coral made up her mind quickly, and followed her, pushing aside the curtain.

The room beyond was not much bigger than an alcove; a ragged mattress on the floor, with straw gaping from several holes, indicated that the girl used this as a sleeping-place. Melanie lay curled up, sobbing into the pile of old sacks which served as her pillow.

Quietly, Coral sat beside her, and put her hand on the girl's head, talking soothingly, telling her not to cry.

They could not talk to one another, and yet something in Coral's tone touched the girl's heart, and she suddenly rolled over, whimpering, and burying her face in her lap.

"There, there, my dear . . . everything will be all right."

Melanie needed someone to turn to, and from having been frightened of Coral originally, she now found in her something she felt she could trust. She pulled down the shoulders of her plain woolen dress, showing Coral the red weals that were already standing out across her pale flesh, asking for her sympathy.

Coral stroked her with cool hands, and gradually Melanie's tears ceased. She stared into Coral's eyes puzzled but no longer afraid, and suddenly with a simple, childish gesture, put up her face to be kissed.

Impulsively, Coral hugged and kissed her; then Melanie smiled faintly, and pointed to the torn bodice of Coral's dress, where two lovely breasts lay open to her gaze and, very lightly, brushed the tip of one pink nipple with her lips, in a shy expression of love.

Coral felt her nipples harden and quiver at the touch, and was about to restrain the child but at the same moment she realized what the embrace meant. On one level, this poor waif was comparing her own scarred shoulders to the attack that Coral too had suffered but on another, and more important level, she was reverting to babyhood, and seeking instinctive comfort.

So she did not recoil, but continued to stroke and caress the girl, who nuzzled contentedly at her breasts; and gradually as they clung together, they curled up upon the ragged mattress, holding one another close for warmth and reassurance.

Coral's last conscious thoughts, as she drifted off to sleep, were: ". . . I can never find my way back to the hotel at this time of night . . . I've stayed in places nearly as bad when we were on the road in Ireland, before now . . . and this poor child needs a little affection in her life. It won't hurt me to stay here till daylight."

Dawn came with a lemon-yellow glow of sunlight that broke through the Paris mist.

At the gates of the city, in the Bois de Boulogne, Gerard paced and waited—and worried about Coral and called himself a fool.

A fool to have lost her last night; he had continued his search at the Tivoli gardens until the small hours, without finding any trace of her.

And a fool to have obeyed the command of a stranger and presented himself at this lonesome and chilly place today, to fight a duel!

He knew nothing of duelling; his only experience had been with swords, when Rory taught him the stage-fights of *Romeo* . . . And this duel was to be fought with pistols; he'd never fired a pistol in his life.

Why hadn't he turned tail and taken himself off to the safety—and the anonymity—of that seedy hotel-room near the Palais-Royal? Oh, it would have been cowardly and dishonorable to refuse a challenge—he knew that— but he couldn't help reflecting that it would be far better to live as a coward than to die honorably, satisfying the self-esteem of some dandified officer! And no one need ever have known, either.

So why didn't he run away and hide from the danger? Why present himself at the appointed time and place— shivering with cold—half-expecting to be blown to pieces by a bullet at any moment?

The answer was—in a word—curiosity.

For Gerard's curiosity had got the better of him last night, when he examined the military gentleman's calling-card more closely.

One side was pringed with his name and rank—*"Henri Martin, Lieutenant-Colonel, Grand Hussars"*—but on the reverse side was a handwritten message.

There was a rough sketch map of the Bois de Boulogne, with a cross to show where the meeting-place would be, and a brief note—in English: "G—Do not fail me: I will explain when we meet—H."

It did not sound like the outraged challenge of a duel-list. And it was *in English* . . . Most mysterious of all, it was addressed to him as "G"—how did Henri Martin know his name was Gerard?

This was why, against all odds, Gerard had turned up at the meeting-place after all.

He was beginning to have second thoughts; the dawn was very cold and cheerless, and the mists among the stark trees were slow to clear. He shivered as he paced backward and forward—and wondered . . . was it a hoax? Was it a trap? Should he, even now, think again, and take himself off to safety before anything could happen?

But it was too late.

A tall, slim figure appeared through the swirling mists; his adversary, dressed all in black, with a tall hat and a military-style cape . . . and he was carrying a case of pistols.

Gerard took a deep breath as the man advanced to meet him.

"M. le Colonel—" he began, uncertainly. *"Bon jour . . ."*

The man's features relaxed into a grin.

"I think we can drop the French lingo now, don't you, old fellow?" he said briskly. "Lieutenant-Colonel Henri Martin doesn't exist, you see—allow me to introduce myself . . . Lord Harry Merton—delighted to meet you, old boy!"

Gerard stared, and stammered, as they shook hands: "You—you're English, too? But your card—the duel—the pistols—"

"All part of the charade, my dear chap; in case anyone happened to have their sharp little eyes on us . . . But I've taken careful precaution this morning, and the coast's clear. So what do you say to a cup of coffee and a cognac? We've got a lot to discuss, and I do dislike talking business on an empty stomach—what? Come along, Gerard—let's go and find some breakfast!"

Half an hour later, they sat at a café-table, opposite Gerard's Palais-Royal hotel, and the stranger began to tell his story.

"When I say we've got to talk business—I mean we've got to talk *my* business; because I'm in Paris in an official capacity, so to speak . . . Business, that is to say, for the dear old British Government."

Gerard, who was drinking coffee at that moment, spluttered and nearly choked: "You mean—you're here—as a British spy?" he asked.

"Would you very much mind lowering your voice just a little, my dear fellow? You're making me slightly nervous . . . Let's just say, I'm here to do a few odd jobs for our lords and masters in the War Office . . . Military intelligence and all that stuff."

Gerard studied the foppish young man sitting opposite him, with his fashionable sideboards and languid air: intelligence of any kind seemed improbable—and yet at a second glance he was aware of a cool, clear brain behind the superficial, good-natured nonsense. Lord Harry Merton was not quite such an ass as he liked to appear.

"But—you pass yourself off as a French Army Officer —how can you possibly expect anyone to accept you as a Frenchman?"

"I was lucky enough to grow up bi-lingual, don't you know—English papa, French *maman*—I've talked two languages ever since I was a tot . . . And if anyone asks, I've been sent home from the Peninsular, after the defeat by Wellington's troops at Cuidad Rodrigo last winter . . . Shell-shocked, and a dicky leg—what?"

"I see . . . and then—last night, at the Tivoli—"

"Last night, I was on the prowl—for reasons I won't bore you with now—and I happened to be passing by the bandstand when I heard you in conversation with that young lady. Deuced pretty creature, too, if I may say so . . . I heard you address one another by name—you didn't know anyone was listening, and you were being a trifle careless . . . All that eye-wash about being Yankees —by jove, I knew you were an Englishman as soon as you opened your mouth!"

"I suppose we have been rather foolish—" Gerard began.

"Well, no bones broken, luckily; I don't think anyone else spotted you. But of course I couldn't help taking an interest; and then, when your pretty Miss Coral started an argument with that little servant-girl, and began to attract a certain amount of attention, I said to myself: "Harry, old son," I said, 'Something must be done, and pretty sharp too—or there's going to be trouble.' So that's when I stepped in and whisked her off for a waltz around the floor, just to create a small diversion."

"I'm extremely grateful, sir—"

"Oh, pooh—don't call me, 'sir'—the name's Harry, I tell you. After all, it seems we're both in a similar plight, in some ways—I'm rather hoping we might be able to help one another . . . How about another *café-cognac?*"

By the time Coral walked up and saw the two men sitting drinking together, they had consumed three small cups of coffee each—and three large glasses of brandy.

She pulled a chair out and joined them, feeling highly indignant.

"So this is how you pass the time while I'm away, Gerard dear!" she said, with an over-bright smile. "Aren't you going to introduce me to your friend?"

Gerard hastily performed the introductions, explaining that he had been beside himself with worry, that he had spent most of the night searching for her, that he would no doubt have been searching still, had he not met Lord Harry Merton, who challenged him to a duel—and after that—

Coral cut across these explanations impatiently: "I'm very pleased to make His Lordship's acquaintance, but while you've both been amusing yourselves, I've been finding out some real news!"

"News?" repeated Lord Harry, sharply. "What do you mean?"

"News of my sister, sir. I don't know if Gerard has told you."

"Yes, yes—he says you are trying to find the unhappy Madame La Roche, but so far—"

"So far without success, but at last I've discovered where she is."

"What? How?" Gerard asked.

"Last night, I met that girl again—the maid whom we saw at Paul's house—her name's Melanie . . . I followed her, and persuaded her to trust me, and she told me all she knew. It wasn't very much, but at least we know now where Rosalie is being held . . . 'Within the Temple,' Melanie said—is there a prison called the Temple?"

Lord Harry's usually amiable face was grave as he replied: "There is indeed—and I would not wish my worst enemy to be sent there . . . Perhaps your sister may only have been housed there temporarily—with luck, she might have been moved on to another place of detention."

"Dear God . . . " Coral put her hand to her mouth. "How can we find out for certain? We must know the truth!"

"I think perhaps I may be able to assist you there, my dear lady," said Lord Harry quietly. "I do have—certain contacts . . . Friends of friends, you understand—some of them, even, inside the Temple prison—and others who can be relied upon to act as go-betweens . . . What time is it now? Give me a few hours to make inquiries, and we will all meet again in this café—at this same table—at six o'clock this evening. Then I shall give myself the pleasure of inviting you both to dine with me, and I will report to you anything I have discovered."

In fact, Rosalie had not been moved to another place of detention; but every night and every morning, she prayed that she might be granted such a reprieve. For the continuing horror of life in her present circumstances was becoming unendurable.

Being held as a prisoner at the Temple had been bad enough, and during all the time that she was forced to live like a caged animal, sharing her cell with half a dozen more or less crazy inmates, with no one to talk to but little Sophie Duchatel, desperately trying to feed and clothe and rear her baby son under such vile conditions —she had believed that she had reached the lowest depths of misery.

But that was before Police-Chief Desmarets ordered her to be sent to work each day in the prison laundry.

She knew now that he had chosen this punishment for her with careful and calculated deliberation, confident that it would be the quickest way to break her spirit and encourage her to talk.

So far, she had managed, somehow, to cling on to her sanity; and she had continued resolutely to maintain that she could tell him nothing, for she had nothing to tell. But she did not know how much longer she could go on.

Each day, the routine was the same; she and the other female prisoners were roused before dawn, and brought out of their cells.

Shivering with the cold that seemed to seep from the stones of the dank, black walls the women were forced to strip off all their clothes, under the leering and watchful eye of a fat, elderly warder who sat and stuffed his hands deep in his trouser-pockets as they undressed, and roused himself to secret ecstasies of excitement at the sight of their naked flesh.

The women ignored him: this was a trivial himiliation, by comparison with everything else they had to suffer—they were past caring about it.

When they were naked, they had to put on the one garment allowed them—as a feeble concession to decency —a single shift of cotton that hung from their shoulders like a shapeless sack. Then their ankles were shackled to a heavy chain, to stop them from attempting any escape, and in a long line, shuffling together hopelessly, with their bare feet already smarting and raw upon the hard stone floors—they were led across the open courtyard at the heart of the prison, and down a flight of steps into the basement.

Before she had ever set eyes upon the laundry, Rosalie had smelled it—the hot, wet smell of steam, and the stench of human bodies—urine and excrement—the odor that clung forever to the piles of soiled linen in huge baskets. And the nauseating, sickly smell of cheap, strong soap . . . and worse than all of these, the scent of fear; the scent of sweat, as the women huddled together, going about their business under the perpetual threat of pain and cruelty and degradation.

When she walked into the laundry room, deep in the prison cellars. Rosalie blinked—half-blinded by the stinging cloud of steam that assailed her eyes and nostrils. But by now she could almost carry out her tasks with her eyes shut; she was nothing but a tiny cogwheel in a huge machine; a machine that ground on relentlessly, day after day, crushing out humanity.

In their long line, chained by the ankles like galley-slaves, the women at a row of tubs, up to their elbows in scalding hot water; scrubbing, pounding, squeezing, wringing out the endless heaps of garments that had to be washed and washed and washed again, until the guards in charge were satisfied that the laundry was clean.

The guards were there at all times; five or six brawny men, stripped to the waist for they too were sweating, in the suffocating, humid atmosphere, and the rivers of sweat ran down their broad chests, and darkened their breeches.

The guards kept watch on the laundresses throughout the long day; and they were armed with whips.

If anyone made a mistake, she was whipped; the long, cruel lash cracked across her back, or her thighs, until she screamed with pain. If she screamed too loudly or too long, she was whipped again, to teach her to hold her tongue. If an item of laundry was not clean enough to satisfy the guards' high standards, she was whipped. If she used too much soap, or not enough, she was whipped. If anyone dared to complain or ask a question or pass a remark to her neighbor, she was whipped.

Small wonder, then, that Rosalie had now accustomed herself to remain silent. She never spoke to any of her workmates; she accepted every blow, every insult, every outrage in silence. She knew that some of her companions believed by now that she could neither speak nor hear, but she did not care about that; she tried to withdraw her mind from these horrifying surroundings, and fix all her thoughts and feelings upon her baby son, concentrating upon him so intensely, that nothing else could really matter.

For it wasn't only physical cruelties that they had to suffer; even worse, perhaps, were the physical indignities.

As the women worked, straining and striving over the scalding tubs, they spilled some of the washing water, inevitably. If they spilled too much, they were whipped again for their clumsiness; but on the whole the guards preferred to turn a blind eye to this particular crime—in fact, they even encouraged the laundresses to be careless with the hot water.

At first Rosalie could not understand why, but she soon discovered the reason. Each time one of the women accidentlally slopped some water over the edge of a tub, the single shift she wore would get wet—and as the day wore on, all the women would become soaked, their thin garments sodden with soapy water, clinging to their bodies.

By nightfall, when they were all stumbling and exhausted, staggering like drunkards from one task to the next, they might as well have been stark naked, for the shifts had become almost transparent, and each curve of their breasts, bellies, and thighs was completely revealed to the watching guards. Indeed, on occasion—if one of the more shapely women had managed to remain comparatively dry—the guards would correct this by contriving to splash a bucket of hot water over her, so that she finished up in the same state as all the others.

And that was when the real horrors began.

Stirred by the spectacle, by the line of near-naked females, helplessly shackled together, unable to retaliate, the guards would move in closer, brushing against their bodies deliberately, groping and squeezing, thrusting their coarse hands under their buttocks, pinching their breasts, invading the secret places between their thighs.

Of course, if any woman dared to protest, she was whipped.

Rosalie, who was one of the most comely women among the group of laundresses, was particularly vulnerable, and time and again she had to steel herself against these bestial attacks, and try with all her might to ignore them . . . But it wasn't easy.

On this particular day, each one of the guards seemed to take a special delight in thrusting himself against her as he passed, and every one seemed to try some new way of putting her to shame. She stood aloof—unspeaking, unmoving, letting them touch her and handle her as they would, counting the minutes until her twelve-hour sentence would be ended.

At last the time came; a whistle blew; the women moved back from the wash-tubs with a sigh of relief, and turned expectantly toward the flight of steps that held their cells and temporary respite. Another day was over.

But tonight there was a difference. Instead of marching them off immediately, the guards whispered together, and then the leader of the men came forward to Rosalie, and took a key from his pocket.

Before she knew what was happening, he had stooped down, and unlocked her ankle-fetters. She had been released from the line.

Not understanding, she watched in bewilderment as the other women were marched away up the stairs and out of sight. She noticed one or two of the laundresses looking back over their shoulders, giving her a pitying glance . . . And then at last she understood.

She tried to escape—she tried to make a run for the stairs—but it was hopeless. Her limbs were dragged down by the sodden shift she wore, her feet slipped on the soapy wet floor; she had not covered more than two yards when the men grabbed her.

She began to scream—a strange, rusty sound, for her voice was so rarely used nowadays—and the men laughed at the absurd noise she made. In any case, there was no one else to hear her.

A dozen strong hands pulled her down on to the wet floor, and she cried out with sheer primitive terror; clumsily, they tugged at her one wet garment and finally managed to peel it from her body, ripping it from her threshing limbs.

She was quite naked now, and she felt the stone floor striking cold beneath her skin. Sickened and almost numb with fear, she gave up the struggle.

When they pulled her legs apart roughly, she did not resist; she was afraid that if she put up any kind of fight, they might kill her.

Some of the men held her down; the rest were impatiently unfastening their black prison trousers, and she saw that they were already fully aroused.

Two men began to argue over which of them should take the initiative, and one man struck the other across the mouth—then, as the second reeled back, the first threw himself down upon her, and with no preamble, forced her to receive him.

272

She bit her lip until she tasted the salt sting of blood in her mouth, and tried to endure the pain of his assault.

The man who had been pushed aside—determined to be revenged—picked up a bucket of soapy water and emptied it over them both, as the onlookers laughed and jeered.

Rosalie closed her eyes, feeling the brutal force of the man tearing into her, and the wash of pungent suds enveloped their bodies, slippery and obscene, as they wrestled together . . . And she knew that when the first man was satisfied at last, he would give way to the second, who would be followed by a third, and a fourth, and so on until all the guards were exhausted.

She hoped that before they had finished with her, she might be dead . . . But she knew that she would not.

And then—and this was the final degradation, and the very worst—she felt within herself the first stirring of physical excitement; a hot craving grew within her loins, and she knew that her own body had betrayed her. These inhuman brutes had succeeded in stripping the ultimate shred of self-respect from her, they had managed at last to drag her down to their own level of mindless debauchery . . .

That was when she began to cry—soundlessly—choking upon the vile mixture of soapsuds, and male sweat, and filth, and her own bitter tears . . .

At six o'clock that evening, Coral and Gerard met Lord Harry Merton at the little café, as they had arranged.

He had hardly taken his place at the table before Coral asked eagerly: "Well, what news?"

He hesitated for a moment, then said: "I'm not sure . . . There *is*, I'm informed, a woman called Madame La Roche inside the Temple; she has been there for some time now, but you must remember it's a common enough name, and she could be a different woman entirely."

"What? But surely—"

"She does not seem to answer to the description you gave me . . . This Madame La Roche works in the prison

273

laundry; she's a deaf-mute—and she has her child with her."

Coral looked at Gerard, her hopes dwindling.

"No . . . That's not Rosalie . . . Are you sure there isn't *another* Madame La Roche? One who was there, but has now been transferred to another place, perhaps —as you suggested?"

"No, I made certain of that. This woman is the only La Roche they knew of at the Temple. And since she is quite clearly not your sister, I can only suppose there has been some mistake."

"Then—that means—we've wasted all this time and we're no nearer finding her . . . " Coral's lip trembled, and she had difficulty keeping her voice steady.

"Cheer up, my dearest," said Gerard quickly. "At least we've established one thing for certain—we know now that Rosalie is *not* in the Temple Prison, so we needn't trouble to look for her there."

Coral nodded miserably, unable to reply.

"But we'll carry on, don't worry—we'll find her, won't we, Harry?" Gerard continued.

"Let's hope so," said Lord Harry, equably. "And of course I'll be glad to give you any assistance I can . . . But in the meantime—" he poured himself a glass of wine from the carafe on the table: "Perhaps you will both be obliging enough to return the favor, and perform a small service for *me?*"

They stared at one another, and Gerard asked: "What do you mean? What kind of service?"

"I can't go into too many details, but there's a certain fellow I must intercept in the very near future—he's by way of being an errand boy, like myself, only it so happens, that he's on the other side of the game—if you follow me . . . "

"A French agent?"

"Let's call him a courier. He carries messages—documents—and I'm anxious to find out what's in those documents. Unfortunately, our paths have crossed once already, and he would undoubtedly remember me if we met again. That's why I propose that you two shall waylay him, on my behalf."

"Us? Oh, no—we're not secret agents—" began Gerard.

"I'm not even a loyal Britisher!" protested Coral. "I'm Irish, and proud of it!"

"Quite so, my dear lady but would you be quite so proud of it if your passports were to fall into the hands of the police? If you were both to be held for questioning? I think you might find that highly inconvenient . . . " His foppish manner was as light and foolish as ever, but suddenly his eyes were as sharp and cold as a rapier. "If I may say so—you're hardly in a position to refuse me, are you—what?"

Gerard said: "Look here—you've got us at a disadvantage, I admit that, and I'm prepared to throw in my lot with you, if I must . . . But leave Coral out of this— she has nothing to do with it, and—"

"Oh, but she has—forgive me, my dear Miss Maguire, but I really must insist!" Lord Harry beamed at her fatuously. "You see, for this particular job, I'm going to need both of you . . . "

"Both of us?" Coral repeated, helplessly. "But why?"

"Perhaps I should explain . . . This French errand boy I was telling you about—he's a capital fellow, very good at his job and all that, but luckily for me he does have one little weakness . . . "

Lord Harry raised Coral's hand to his lips and kissed it gallantly, as he concluded: "He has a taste for pretty women."

(7)

A Gentleman from Troyes

It was another trap even more terrifying than that moment when they had been imprisoned by Henri Clavel; and it was far more difficult, this time, to escape.

As the days passed, Coral and Gerard discussed the situation again and again; endlessly trying to discover some loophole that would enable them to wriggle out of it.

In the meantime, they continued to live at the Palais-Royal Hotel, and to perform each evening for the delight of the customers at the Tivoli Gardens. M. Schindler had been far from pleased by the extreme brevity of the song recital on the night of Coral's debut, although they explained to him that a total stranger—an officer of Hussars—had made ardent advances to Coral, and Gerard had been forced to go to her rescue, and help to shake him off.

"Are you mad?" Schindler snarled. "Your job is to please the public, m'mselle—if one of the customers wishes to dance with you, to buy you a drink or entertain you to supper—you will accept the invitation graciously

. . . Always provided the gentleman is wealthy enough to pay for his pleasure."

But he agreed to give them another chance, and the nightly entertainments were resumed. Gradually Coral became popular with the visitors at Tivoli, and acquired a regular following, who applauded and feted the "little American songbird."

There was only one grave disadvantage to all this; the more successful she became, and the more she appeared in the public eye, the more difficult it would be for them to continue their search for Rosalie without arousing suspicion . . . and the more impossible it was to shake off Lord Harry Merton.

They had at first thought of running away once more; moving on to another hotel, in a different district—starting all over again under other names. But Lord Harry would not let them slip through his fingers so easily.

Every day and night, when they least expected it, he would appear—sometimes at the café, or the hotel—sometimes among the crowds at the Pleasure Gardens. And always he assured them that their little "assignation" would take place very soon now.

"Perhaps tonight—or tomorrow—don't worry, I'll let you know the moment that the gentleman from Troyes arrives in the city."

"From—Troyes?" Gerard repeated.

"It's a town to the south-east of Paris . . . in an area where the Emperor's troops have been hard-pressed by the Allies. He has fought them off a couple of times, but they keep returning to the attack. They will not be satisfied until they have taken Paris, and kicked Napoleon from his throne."

"But what has this to do with the gentleman from Troyes?" Coral asked.

"Everything, my dear lady! This particular errand boy is one of the Emperor's most trusted messengers; when he returns to Paris, he will be carrying despatches from the front line . . . and it will be your task to obtain a sight of those despatches, on my behalf."

They argued, they pleaded, they tried to persuade

277

Lord Harry that they would be hopelessly inefficient as secret agents but he would not listen to their excuses. The job was vital, and they were the only people available to carry it out.

"It's a lucky coincidence," he added, with as admiring glance at Coral's copper-colored tresses, "that the gentleman from Troyes is particularly susceptible to redheads!"

Later, when they were alone together, Coral protested vigorously to Gerard: "It's all very well for you—you're not going to be used as bait on some shameful hook . . . but I'm the one that's going to be in real danger."

As she spoke, she remembered suddenly what the old fortune-teller had said after reading her palm: "Danger . . . Danger of death . . ."

She caught her breath; but she wouldn't tell Gerard about that. He would only laugh at her for being a superstitious fool. Instead she continued: "It's different for you—you're an Englishman, and no doubt you feel a proud glow at the idea of doing something to help your country win this miserable war . . . but why should I lift a finger to support King George and his fat bullyboy of a son?"

"Because we have no choice, my darling. Harry Merton has us in his clutches, and he's not going to let go until we obey orders."

"And what if I refuse?"

"He would report us to the police without a second thought. We're only pawns in his game, and he'd sacrifice us cheerfully if needs be."

"The devil . . ." Coral knew that Gerard was right; there was no way out. "For two pins I'd run off and leave him to stew in his crafty plots and plans . . ."

"And leave Rosalie alone with no hope of rescue? And would you leave me too?" Gerard asked, putting his arms around her gently.

"Oh, you're as artful as he is . . . Why did I ever let myself get mixed up with a pair of smooth-tongued English tricksters? You know very well I can never leave you now."

She put her lips to his, and they kissed; the kiss that sooner or later ended every argument and brought them together again in the happy union of love.

"When can we be married?" she asked, as soon as she could get her breath back. "For God's sake, Gerard, when will we be able to give up living in mortal sin and be restored to a state of grace?"

"Is it so very bad living in a state of disgrace?" Gerard teased her, with his hand exploring every inch of her body.

She sighed a long sigh, that mingled sadness and ecstasy: "Oh . . . you're such a heathen creature, you'll never understand, will you? What we're doing—what you're doing—now, this minute—is all wrong . . . so terribly *wrong*."

As he drew her down on to the bed in the little hotel room, he whispered in her ear: "It doesn't feel so terribly wrong to me. It feels perfectly right."

And while Coral abandoned herself to the joys of their shared love, she had to admit—it felt perfectly right to her, as well. How could something so exquisite—so God-given—be against His rules? It was all very perplexing.

"The moment we get back safely to Ireland when all our troubles are over, and we can live as we want to—we'll be married by the first priest who'll perform the office—I swear it," Gerard concluded, and then they clung together in a transport of joy, and there were no more words.

The following day, as they left the hotel on their way to the Rue St. Lazare, Lord Harry Merton was waiting for them at the café opposite, and beckoned them across to join him.

"We can't stop to talk now—we shall be late for the Tivoli," Coral began. "We've got a lot to do this evening."

"I'm afraid you must stop for a few moments at least, my dear lady because in actual fact you have more to do this evening than you imagine." He motioned to them to sit at the table beside him. "Tonight, if I may coin a phrase, is the night . . ."

They stared at him in dismay. So the moment that Coral dreaded had arrived at last.

"How do you know? How can you be sure? Where is he now—this gentleman from Troyes?" asked Gerard.

"I have contrived to let slip a morsel of information, which will certainly have reached his ears by this time. The information that I myself will be present at M. Schindler's café tonight. He won't be able to resist that!"

"He wants to meet you?"

"He wants to kill me," said Lord Harry simply. "The last time we crossed swords, I got the better of him, and he has been waiting to take his revenge ever since."

"But if he sees you at the café—"

"He will not see me . . . I shall take care of that. Instead my dear Miss Maguire—he will see *you* . . . And you will see him."

"But how shall I know him, among the crowds?"

"He is a good-looking man—very good-looking indeed —many a lady has lost her heart to him at first sight. He has curling black hair and gray eyes . . . but the most remarkable thing about him is that he has one snow-white tuft of hair in his left eyebrow. You cannot mistake that."

"And when I see him what am I to do?" Coral wanted to know.

"Have no fear—I've planned everything, down to the last detail. Now listen carefully, for we have not much time."

That night the Tivoli gardens seemed more popular than ever; by the light of innumerable lanterns, the visitors thronged the gravel walks, and strolled arm-in-arm through the shrubbery.

A firework display had been arranged, and already a great many people had taken up their places beside the ornamental lake, where they would get an uninterrupted view of the spectacle.

But there was still a great number of customers in M. Schindler's café, and, although Coral felt understandably nervous, her songs were received with high acclaim. Gerard could tell that she was uneasy; she hurried the tempo of the final encore, and her voice trembled ever so slightly on her top note.

As the crowd applauded wildly, someone threw a white rose which landed at Coral's feet, and she picked it up with a charming smile.

Under cover of the noise, Gerard said: "You were frightened I could tell. Don't worry—Lord Harry promised us that everything is under control—you will be safe. Besides, he could have been mistaken—there might even be a change of plan. Perhaps the gentleman from Troyes won't put in an appearance tonight, after all."

"Oh, he already has . . . I saw him very soon after I began to sing," Coral answered. "A dark man with one white fleck in his left eyebrow—there's no mistaking him . . . and it was he who tossed this rose to me."

"Where is he now?"

"Don't look round he's watching us . . . take your time, then turn ever so casually," said Coral. "At the table by the ornamental fountain . . . sitting alone."

Gerard managed to make his inspection appear accidental—then frowned.

"I see what Lord Harry meant. Damme, the fellow's handsome *and* he knows it. Look at him, smirking and self-satisfied. Give me that rose!"

Before she could protest, he had snapped the stem short, and pushed it into his own buttonhole, in a defiant gesture.

"Don't be a fool—you'll ruin everything—". Coral scolded him, in a whisper. "I've got to go and be nice to him."

"Just take care not to be *too* nice—that's all," grumbled Gerard. "Remember what Harry said and be sure you stick to the plan exactly."

"Don't worry—I will," said Coral. "You don't imagine I'm looking forward to this, do you?"

All the same, as she stepped down from the bandstand and made her way across the dancefloor, she felt a tiny tremor of excitement. The stranger certainly was extremely good-looking.

He watched her as she approached, and smiled.

"Good evening, sir," she said when she reached his table. "You must forgive me if I don't speak French—"

"You are from America, I understand? Very well, we will talk in your own language," said the stranger, and bowed gallantly to kiss her hand.

"You are very kind . . . I saw you throw me that flower—I was very flattered."

"It was a small tribute to your artistry as a singer." His English was carefully correct, with only the slightest trace of an accent, and somehow the occasional foreign note made him sound all the more attractive.

With growing alarm, Coral realized that his flashing smile—his cool gray eyes, fringed with long black lashes —were having the strangest effect upon her . . . The man really was irresistible!

"Will you do me the honor of taking a glass of champagne?"

He pulled out a chair, indicating the bottle upon the table, in its bucket of ice.

"That would be delightful." She accepted the invitation gracefully, and sat down.

As he poured another glass, he added: "I notice you are not, however, wearing my rose, after all?"

"Ah, no—I gave it to my pianist as a buttonhole—I do hope you are not offended? But I had to do something to placate him. He had asked me to have supper with him, and I refused. I'm afraid he was disappointed, but as I told him, I had a slight headache, and no appetite."

"I'm sorry to hear that—if I'd known you were not feeling well—"

"Oh, I think I am beginning to recover now. Champagne is such a wonderful restorative." She smiled at him over the rim of her glass, and he smiled back. Dear heaven those eyelashes—those piercing gray eyes! Coral's heart was melting within her, and she tried to pull herself together. "I expect—when I've had a little fresh air—I shall be completely revived."

"In that case, allow me to suggest a brief stroll in the gardens? Perhaps later you might care to view the firework display? There is a little secluded pavilion I know —it will be an admirable vantage-point. And if you regain your appetite, I could order a cold collation to be served to us there—In privacy."

"You are extremely hospitable, m'sieur—I'm sorry, I don't know your name—"

"Call me Jacques . . . And be so very kind as to let me call you Coral . . . For I felt sure as soon as I set eyes upon you that we would become friends—isn't that extraordinary?"

"Quite extraordinary," said Coral faintly.

She had just become aware of the pressure of his knee against hers under the table, and found herself breathing rather faster . . . This was going to be far, far more difficult than she had ever suspected; or—worse still—perhaps it was going to be all too easy.

She tried to ignore the overwhelming impact of his physical presence, and concentrate on the task in hand and upon Gerard . . . Yes, of course that was the answer—she must think only of Gerard.

"Shall we go?" she asked rather abruptly, setting down her empty glass. "I should be very sorry to miss the fireworks."

He offered her his arm at once, and they left the *bal musette,* and stepped out together into the soft night air. As they walked side by side, she noticed that he contrived to hold her closely—so closely that their thighs pressed together at every pace—his left leg moving against her right. She felt a thrill of pleasure stirring within her, and scolded herself. She must not weaken—she had to be strong!

Obviously Jacques knew his way about the Tivoli, for he soon left the other sightseers behind, and abandoned the main paths for a side alley.

It was darker among the trees, and once or twice Coral stumbled as they pressed on into the shrubbery. She might even have fallen, but his arm was strong, and he supported her by slipping it around her waist.

"Come . . ." he said, in a low, vibrant tone that sent a delicious shiver up her spine. "This is the place."

283

They had reached one of the little Chinese pavilions, and he held the door open for her to go inside. She hesitated for a second, uncertain whether she were confident enough to be able to proceed with the plan.

But there was no turning back now. She thanked him, and walked in.

There was a single lantern, where a candle flame leaped and twisted, and by the fitful light, Coral saw that as she had expected there was a wide divan, heaped with cushions. Beside the divan, a long low window stood open to the night.

"You see? We shall have an excellent view of the fireworks across the lake," said Jacques. "There is not long to wait, I think . . . we might as well maké ourselves comfortable. Shall we sit down?"

Coral obeyed and almost lost her balance again; the divan was very soft, and only a few inches above the floor. It was not easy to sit upright with nothing to lean against . . . and as Jacques flung himself down beside her, making the divan heave and rock, she found it even more difficult . . . Most difficult of all, perhaps, when he put his arm about her and pulled her down to join him.

With a little smothered cry, Coral let herself fall back on to the soft, yielding cushions.

She expected him to say something—to make some declaration of love, perhaps—and she had decided in advance that she would keep him talking as long as possible. Frenchmen were always great philosophers of *amour,* she had been led to believe, and they liked nothing better than long abstract discussions on the nature of passion.

But this Frenchman did not abide by the rules. He said nothing at all. Actions, it seemed, spoke far louder than words, where he was concerned.

He was already trying to undress her, without any preamble. She felt his hands moving purposefully over her dress, finding buttons and laces, and making short work of them.

"Oh!" She gave a genuine exclamation of dismay as he pulled apart her bodice, investigating the delights of her bosom with his long, supple fingers.

284

"Ssh—ssh—" he soothed her, and began to toy with her nipples.

"The braid on your cuffs—it scratched me—" she complained, trying to think what she should do next.

"That's easily remedied." Jacques threw her another dazzling smile which made her heart skip a beat, and proceeded to slip off his coat. "Perhaps we would both be more comfortable—if we were more *deshabillée*."

"Oh, sir—for shame!" She remembered the next move now. "Surely you don't suppose that I would ever be so bold as to look upon a gentleman—half-dressed?"

"If we are both in an equal state of undress, there can be no shame on either side," he argued, flinging his coat down at the side of the divan, under the window, and following it up by pulling off his boots. "Keep me company, my pretty Coral, and do as I do . . . We will set a new fashion in clothes—by wearing less and less!"

Suiting the action to the words, he began to unfasten his breeches.

"For pity's sake, sir—forbear!" she exclaimed, with a mixture of feigned modesty and very real alarm. "At least have the goodness to put out the light, and spare my blushes."

No sooner said than done; Jacques rolled across the divan, and extinguished the candle-lantern.

Now the pavilion was in darkness, except for the shadowy outline of the window frame and the faint blue patch of night sky beyond. Coral heard Jacques divest himself of his breeches, and prepared to struggle against his demands . . . Or against her own, shameful desires . . . She tried desperately to summon up the image of Gerard in her mind's eye. *Gerard*—where was he at this moment?

As if in response to her unspoken question, she saw the blur of movement above the low window frame. A man's arm and shoulder insinuated itself across the sill, fumbling among the heap of clothes Jacques had discarded.

Impulsively, terrified that Jacques would turn and see what was happening, Coral grabbed him with both arms, and pulled him to her.

"Come to me!" she exclaimed breathlessly.

He needed no second invitation; he was naked except for his frilled shirt, and she felt his body—muscular and hot, as he forced himself upon her.

With half her mind, she wanted to resist his advances and push him violently away—but she knew she had to keep him occupied until Gerard found what he was searching for.

And then again she could not deny that she was finding this amazing intimacy wickedly exciting.

He was as adept at love-making as he was handsome, and now for the first time he kissed her—full on the mouth, his tongue seeking hers, his lips opening upon her lips. She expected a violent attack, and braced herself . . . But to her amazement, now he had her in his arms, he was in no hurry. He took his time, letting tongue and lips play upon her with excruciating and painstaking deliberation . . . Slowly and sweetly, he laid lingering kisses upon her, and at the same time let his practised hands roam over her at his leisure.

She strove to keep hold of her senses; she felt as if she were being intoxicated against her will—made drunk by the potent nectar of his lips, and driven to frenzy by his long-drawn-out exploration of every sensitive area in her body. The man was an expert, who took a fiendish pleasure in playing upon a woman as a musician plays upon the strings of a violin . . . She must not give way to him —she *must* not—and yet for Gerard's sake she could not repel him either.

"You're still wearing too many clothes . . ." Jacques' voice made her tingle, as he pursued his advantage by nibbling the lobe of her ear.

"Yes—yes—" she gasped, trying to delay him. All she had to do was engage his full attention for a few more minutes, just long enough for Gerard to copy out the despatches and replace the originals where he had found them, in Jacques' pocket . . . It couldn't be much longer now surely? Striving to make every moment stretch as far as possible, she sat up, and added: "I'll take my dress off . . . Give me a moment—"

"No, no, Coral—you need do nothing—I will do it

286

all," Jacques assured her, and before she could stop him, he had taken control again.

She was helpless in his arms as he rolled her gently on to her back—and although she tried not to co-operate, it was awfully difficult to hold him off. He was so strong and powerful, and he seemed to know instinctively where and how to make every move.

She felt her dress being drawn up from her body—her arms coming free from the long sleeves—the skirts lifting higher and higher until the gown had been removed, and she lay beside him, dressed in nothing but her undergarments.

"Stop—please stop—that's enough—" she whispered, but he was deaf to her pleas.

His hands were ruthless, and she shook with a sudden *frisson* of desire, as he continued—as slowly and calmly as ever—to slide her petticoat down . . . Down . . . His fingers brushed against her breasts—her navel—and encountered the last barrier—the final wisps of material that prevented her from being totally nude . . . And then that last defense too was dragged away, and she knew with a surge of terror and excitement that she was totally open to his demands . . . Completely unprotected.

Oh, where was Gerard? Why didn't he hurry?

Still Jacques seemed to be taking his time. She lay and waited for his next assault and heard the rustle of linen, as he removed his shirt. She held her breath, expecting him to fling himself upon her.

And instead of that, she felt one fingertip sliding up very slowly and very lightly from her ankle to her shin tracing a very long path from her kneecap across her thigh and so up, higher yet.

The fingertip came to rest at last, as she knew it must, upon the fleece of curling hair between her legs. She clenched her fists, and longed to protest—or laugh—or cry—and tried with every ounce of her will-power to steel herself against the next move.

His next move—quite simply—was to tickle her.

With the utmost skill, and a sort of innocent playfulness, he began to tease her, making her squirm with helpless ripples of delight. She would not give way—she must not—oh, God—oh, *Gerard*—

"Please stop—please stop . . . Please—" she panted. "Oh, *please* . . ."

It was as if she had no strength left within her. She felt herself growing moist, and her lips parted—her legs began to open of their own accord, and she was lost—lost forever—

Jacques moved steadily forward, and she felt the thick, throbbing maleness of him, hard against her.

That was when the fireworks began.

With a noise like thunder, the first salvo of rockets leaped up into the sky, and exploded in fantastic flowers of white and gold, turning the night into day.

Jacques stopped short, and she saw him outstretched above her, silhouetted against the window which was momentarily a-dazzle with light.

At the same instant, she saw Gerard—leaning in to return the papers . . . At last: but perhaps too late.

Once again she pulled Jacques closer, trying to prevent him from turning away from her, and he took advantage of their position, urging his loins against her in a sudden thrust.

"Yes, yes," he gasped; and he too was breathless by this time. "Yes—I'll take you now."

"Oh, no, you won't, by God!" shouted Gerard; and another blaze of glory lit up the sky.

With a startled oath in his own language, Jacques reared up, and rolled away from Coral. For the rest of her life, she would never be quite sure whether the emotion that swept over her in that split second was relief—or regret.

"Who the devil are you?" Jacques cried. "That damned musician!"

Gerard was inside the room by now, and lighting the lantern. "Yes, sir—that damned musician, and this lady's husband."

And he had a pistol in his hand . . . (Borrowed from Lord Harry, and unloaded—but Jacques was not to know that.)

288

"Now take your clothes and get out of here before I put a bullet through you."

The plan went like clockwork.

Taken completely off guard, at this most vulnerable moment, the gentleman from Troyes was in no position to argue. He obeyed without a word—seconds later he plunged out of the window, and they heard him crashing through the undergrowth as he made his escape . . . Then a fusillade of firecrackers echoed around the pavilion, and the whole room danced in a glitter of green and gold.

"Merciful heavens—what took you so long?" demanded Coral, struggling to pull on her clothes.

"I was as quick as I could be!" Gerard was defensive. "There was one letter there from the Emperor himself!— it took time to copy that; I had a deuce of a job making out his handwriting . . . Still, it's all over now, and no harm done . . . You're all right, aren't you?"

"Oh, yes," she sighed. "I'm perfectly all right, thank you . . . But you'll never know what I had to suffer for your sake!"

"Poor love . . . Never mind—as soon as I've delivered the copies to Lord Harry, I'll take you home and then I'll make up to you for everything."

Some hours later, they lay side by side in bed at the hotel, naked in one another's arms, after a prolonged bout of love-making—more intensely passionate than ever before.

"My dearest love . . . it must have been a terrifying experience for you," Gerard comforted her at last, as they lay back—relaxed and contented. "I could tell how desperate you were—I've never known you so tense."

"Yes . . . it was—terrifying," said Coral, in a small voice. "I don't want to talk about it any more, Gerard . . . tell me about the letters—I hope Lord Harry was suitably grateful?"

"He was delighted. Particularly with the letter I told you about. It was a personal message from Napoleon to his lady—"

"You mean—the Empress Marie-Louise?"

"Of course . . . He said he was under great pressure

289

from the Allies, and he wanted his wife to leave Paris and move out to Rambouillet—I suppose they have a country house there, or some such. He told her he had decided to retire to the east, and operate against the Allied lines of communication as they closed in on Paris, in a last attempt to deflect their forces. That's what he said."

"And now you've passed that information to Lord Harry—the Allies will know what he plans to do?"

"Exactly—they'll be ready for him. You know, I really do believe, you and I have done our bit towards winning this war, tonight . . ."

He yawned, cradling her in his arms, as he went on: "I say—I know you had to pretend you were going to submit to that man from Troyes, to keep him occupied —but suppose the job had taken a few minutes longer . . . You wouldn't really have let him—would you?"

She snuggled closer, and said: "What do *you* think?"

"No . . . Of course not . . . I knew you wouldn't really."

And they settled down into a deep, contented sleep.

The next morning, they had a rude awakening.

They were still curled up together when the door burst open, and several uniformed men rushed into the room, led by M. Schindler, who was wringing his hands and protesting his ignorance of any misdemeanor.

He shook Gerard roughly, and explained: "Wake up— immediately—the police are here! They wish to question you . . ."

For Coral, it was like waking from a happy dream into a nightmare. She scrambled out of bed in her nightgown, pulling a *robe-de-chambre* about her shoulders, very much aware of the curious stares of the watching police officers.

She could not understand the rapid volley of French that they fired at Gerard, but she knew it had to mean serious trouble.

Gerard was arguing—shouting—protesting—but all in vain.

He turned to Coral in despair. "They want to see our papers. M. Schindler told them we are Americans, but they insist on seeing our passports."

"At this time of the morning? Why? Can't you persuade them to go away and come back later when we're dressed?"

"I'm afraid it's more serious than that . . . Someone has reported us—as spies."

They exchanged glances, and Coral's chin went up. Whatever happened, she would not let them see that she was afraid.

"They want us to get dressed immediately. We're to be interrogated by a senior officer . . ."

With that, the door opened, and a heavily built man, whose graying hair was tied back in a pigtail, walked in. He looked at Gerard—standing barelegged in his night shirt—and smiled slowly . . . A smile that emphasized the cast in his eye.

"So . . . My dear friend—we meet again," he said.

"Cock-eyed Alphonse!" exclaimed Gerard in dismay.

"Be more respectful when you speak to Commissioner Bertrand!" snapped one of the policemen, springing to attention.

"What—why—how did you find us?" Gerard stammered, reluctantly producing their Irish documents.

"Hand those to me at once, if you please . . ." Alphonse Bertrand scanned the papers quickly. "As I thought—these people are not Americans at all—they are British spies."

"That's not true—" began Gerard.

"We received a report on your activities at the Tivoli gardens last night, from a highly trustworthy source . . . It was not hard to trace you, thanks to the acclaim this young woman has received lately; we approached M. Schindler, and he told us where to find you . . . It was simplicity itself."

"I never knew they were enemy spies—I swear to you upon my knees—" the terrified Schindler began to babble. "They told me they were Americans—"

"Stop snivelling, you blockhead—and get out of my way." The police chief rapped out orders. "Bring the young man to my office for questioning—I shall deal with him—personally."

"And the girl?" asked one of the officers.

291

M. Bertrand shrugged indifferently. "For the time being, she can be held at the Temple . . . Desmarets will know how to deal with her—take her away."

When Coral realized what was happening, she began to shout and struggle—but it was hopeless. The last she saw of Gerard was one desperate look back over his shoulder before he was hustled off between two guards, with the Commissioner of Police following in triumph.

The day that followed was the very worst Coral ever endured in her entire life. She did not know at first where she was being taken; nobody seemed to speak English, and she could not understand what was said to her.

It was not until she had been kept waiting in a draughty corridor for several hours, with her hands tied behind her, that she was finally taken in for questioning—in English—by M. Desmarets, and he informed her that she was now an inmate of the women's quarters at the Temple Prison.

Remembering all that Harry Merton had said, she almost fainted with the shock of this revelation, but somehow managed to pull herself together, and said nothing.

She continued to say nothing, through a long afternoon of relentless questioning. This man would not tell her what had happened to Gerard, or where he was; very well—in that case she would refuse to answer his questions too.

She maintained her policy of silence despite every trick, every threat that Desmarets could think of. At the end, he said: "Very well . . . I have had trouble with incommunicative women before now—but I know how to deal with them. I do hope, my dear young lady, that after a spell of work in the prison laundry, you may change your mind . . . Put her in the cells."

A jailer came and tapped her on the shoulder, and she walked out under escort, her head held high.

When they reached the filthy cell, where half a dozen women stood or sat about, talking in whispers—wild-eyed and unkempt, staring at the newcomer—Coral was at the end of her tether.

She sank on to a heap of sacks in the corner, determined that she would not break down and cry. She would not give them that satisfaction.

She ignored the other prisoners—even the young girl who nursed a baby boy on her lap; and when the door was unlocked, and a newcomer joined them—a woman with matted, sodden hair, and sunken cheeks, with bowed shoulders, and her feet dragged down by the weight of an iron shackle—at first Coral ignored her too.

And the newcomer looked at her, and said in a cracked, lifeless voice: "Oh, mother of God—*Coral* . . ."

Even then, Coral didn't recognize Rosalie immediately.

(8)

Out of the Darkness

Never before, Gerard thought bitterly, had he experienced the sensation of being freezing cold and sweating at the same time.

Freezing cold, because he was in a draughty high-ceilinged room somewhere in the Headquarters of the police—and he was stark naked, stripped of every garment, with his hands behind his back.

Sweating with apprehension; for he was also handcuffed, standing in the middle of the floor, while Commissioner Alphonse Bertrand paced up and down, prowling round him on soundless feet—a fat cat, about to pounce.

They were alone for this "interrogation," and Gerard —knowing only too well what Bertrand's sexual tastes were—expected some assault at any moment.

So far, the Commissioner had contented himself with looking at Gerard's nude body; appraising his muscles, his broad shoulders and slim flanks—his sheen of golden body-hair, now glistening with silver rivulets of sweat . . .

So far, he had restricted himself to repeated questioning.

"You do not claim any longer to be an American citizen, I take it . . . ? No—you could hardly hope to keep up that pretense now."

Gerard shrugged slightly, feeling the cruel steel of the handcuffs clammy upon his wrists and cold against the base of his spine. He waited tensely for Bertrand's approach.

"And your documents purport to show that you are an Irish citizen . . . A rebel against the English rule, and a good friend of France—? Is that what you would have me believe?"

Gerard still said nothing.

"But between ourselves, my dear—" Bertrand took a step nearer, standing directly behind him, "I have a strange suspicion that those documents too are forgeries . . . I fancy that you are an Englishman—born and bred—and that you have been smuggled into this country as a spy . . . You know the punishment for spying, I presume?"

He moved closer still, and Gerard could feel the man's hot breath against the back of his neck. He had been chewing cachous to sweeten his breath, and the resulting combination of scent and garlic was disgusting.

"On the other hand," Alphonse Bertrand lowered his voice to a feline purr, "I might be able to intercede on your behalf—if you decide to behave like a reasonable young man—and conduct yourself in an obliging manner . . ."

Gerard's skin crawled as he felt the man's hand brush against his hips—stroking the curve of his buttocks—and continuing below, between his legs—probing—exploring—playing with him—trying to arouse some answering thrill of excitement—

He turned his head, and found Bertrand's fleshy, smiling countenance only a few inches from his own.

"I would rather die," he said, with all the hatred he could put into the words—and spat in the man's face.

Commissioner Bertrand did not flinch. Instead he stood quite still for a moment longer—then released his hold upon Gerard's sexual organs, and walked slowly the door.

295

He flung it open, and called to the guards who waited outside: "Take the prisoner away—do with him whatever you choose—I've no further use for him."

Then he took out a silk handkerchief and began to wipe his face, turning his back upon the scene.

In their cell at the Temple prison, Rosalie and Coral were clasped in each other's arms, half-laughing and half-crying—torn between their joy at this unexpected reunion, and grief at their hideous plight.

They hugged each other again and again, while the other women prisoners looked on with dull-eyed surprise, and Coral tried to explain both the lucky chances and the misfortunes that had finally brought her into captivity.

". . . And the last I saw of Gerard, he was being taken off by the police—I could not discover where he is now, nor what has happened to him."

"I have been hoping and praying that you were both safe," Rosalie said, her voice husky with emotion. "I guessed it must be Gerard who was with you in Paris—"

Coral stopped and stared at her sister.

"You *knew* we were in Paris—? But how?"

"Just the other day . . . Henri told me he had seen you."

"Henri—that villain—he tried to capture us when we went to your house—"

"Yes, he told me that too. You see—after you both escaped—the authorities decided to demote him for his blunders . . . They put him in here, as a prison guard; he lives in a cell along the passage, to keep watch on us . . . I see him every day." Rosalie hesitated, and added gently: "It was Henri who informed against Paul, you know. He was sent to spy upon him, in Ireland."

"And you still speak to the traitor? I would kill him with my bare hands—" Coral began indignantly.

"Oh, no . . . Don't you think there has been enough of killing already? Besides—in his own strange way— Henri has tried to make amends . . . He would help me if he could—I know that . . . When the baby was born— he was very good to me."

"The baby?" Coral repeated in stupefaction.

"Oh! How stupid of me—of course, you don't know! My darling—you have a little nephew—he was born on Christmas morning . . . Come—let me present him to you!"

Rosalie pulled Coral breathlessly across the room, where a young girl sat nursing the baby.

"Sophie—this is my sister—*ma soeur*—Coral—Sophie Duchatel . . . Poor Sophie's parents were both executed, because they were Royalists; she is my only friend here . . . And this—this is the only joy of my life . . . My little son."

The baby stretched out two starfish hands toward Coral, and gurgled with delight.

"Your baby . . . And I never even knew! May I?" Coral picked up the tiny child and held him to her bosom, kissing the soft fair hair upon his head, and smiling at him—forgetting all her own troubles in this moment of love. "Oh, but he's a little cherub . . . How could you care for him so well, in a place like this?"

"I can only do my best for him . . . And during the day—when I am at work in the laundry—Sophie looks after him, you see . . ."

"You work in the laundry? Of course. Now I begin to understand—we made some inquiries, and discovered that there was a Madame La Roche here in the Temple—but I said it could not be you, for she was a laundress, and she had a child, and—besides, they told us she was a deaf-mute."

Rosalie's smile faded. "Many people believe that . . . I try not to speak—except when I must . . . It is better so, I think. Work in the laundry is—not very pleasant . . ." The harsh, dead tone was back in her voice now.

"Well, at least you will have company from now on, for I'm told I am to be sent to serve in the laundry too —so we shall be together—" Coral began cheerfully.

Rosalie's face went white.

"What? *You?*—Oh, dear God—no, not that—I won't let you—"

"I don't understand—I'm not afraid of hard work, if that's what you mean."

"No, you *don't* understand . . . It's not only the work, my love. I will do anything to prevent you from being sent there . . ." Rosalie pressed her knuckles against her forehead, thinking fast. "Henri will be here soon; he brings our food in at mealtimes . . . He shall help us; he *must* help us!"

Shortly afterward, the door was unlocked again, and Coral recognized Henri, as he wheeled in a little wooden trolley, with a pot of vile-smelling stew, and hunks of black bread. But the prisoners crowded round eagerly, desperate to snatch pieces of the bread and dip them into the stewpot.

Coral hung back, saying: "I'm not hungry . . ."

"Nor am I—now . . . Henri—come here!" Rosalie called him across, and introduced her sister. "You already know Coral, I think . . . Now she has been arrested, and put in here with the rest of us."

Henri would not look Coral in the face, but kept his eyes on the floor, shuffling uncomfortably. Coral was shocked at the change in the man since she had seen him last; he had lost a great deal of weight, and his prison uniform hung loosely upon him.

"I'm sorry to hear that," he said at last. "If I could help—you know I would do so gladly, but—"

"You *can* help . . . Coral has been ordered to work in the laundry. Promise me you will find some way to prevent it, Henri . . . She must be spared that, at least."

"Yes . . . Yes, I understand . . . Leave it to me—I will see what I can do for you, my lady . . ."

With that slender hope, they had to be content. After he had gone, Coral asked again why Rosalie was so insistent; what was so very alarming about working in a laundry, after all? But Rosalie refused to talk about it.

The next morning, before dawn, the fat guard came to rouse all the women who were detailed for laundry-duty, as usual; but this time Coral's name was upon the list. He shook her rudely, and pulled her to her feet.

"Come on—don't keep us waiting—you too!" he wheezed.

"Oh, no—there's some mistake—not Coral—not my sister—" Rosalie began to plead with him.

The guard slapped her across the face with the back of his hand.

"Quiet, you! Look alive, all of you—do as you're told!"

Coral stiffened, ready to spring to Rosalie's defense, but her sister stopped her.

"Say nothing . . . And don't try to strike back—it will only make things worse for all of us . . . Better do as he says . . . But—oh, Coral—I'm so sorry . . . So very sorry . . ."

They were shepherded out, along the passage, and into another room where a number of cotton shifts lay in a tumbled pile—still damp from yesterday's labors. The guard clapped his hands, urging the women to undress, then sat down to enjoy the spectacle at his ease.

Coral gasped: "We must undress—while he watches?"

Rosalie said grimly: "Ignore him . . . He is the least of your worries"—and began to pull off her ragged gown.

Coral glanced around; the other women were all stripping without any sign of embarrassment, accustomed to this daily humiliation. She realized she had to follow their example, and started to unfasten her bodice.

Shivering, she stepped out of her dress and petticoat—feeling the guard's lecherous eyes upon her. She was a new-comer, and therefore doubly titillating. It was hard to do as Rosalie advised and ignore him, as he sat rocking to and fro on a wooden stool, licking his lips—but she forced herself to continue.

When she was naked, she asked: "Is there one of those shifts for me to wear?"

There was not; no one had thought to provide working clothes for the latest recruit. Rosalie indicated to the guard that Coral had nothing to put on, and he laughed, as if this were a great joke, pointing at Coral's breasts and winking lewdly.

She tried to cover her body as well as she could, crossing her arms in front of her; Rosalie picked up the petticoat she had just discarded, saying: "Put this on again. It will be ruined, of course, but it's better than nothing."

The guard got up and moved closer, watching avidly.

Now it was time to shackle the women to their leg-chains . . .

"Keep next to me, dearest—I'll try to protect you as much as I can," Rosalie said—but at that moment there was an unexpected interruption.

Henri Clavel walked in, and showed the guard a hand-written order which he had just managed to acquire from the chief warder's office. Coral Maguire was to be excused laundry duty today; Henri had applied for one woman to clean out his cell, and she had been transferred to this task instead.

With a sigh of relief, Rosalie allowed herself to be fastened to the chained line and marched out. For one day, at any rate, Coral had been reprieved.

When they reached Henri's cell, he closed the door and said: "Sit down for a moment. We can't talk for long—the other guards will become suspicious. I am afraid you will have to begin scrubbing the walls—and the floor . . . It is a filthy job, but it was the best I could do for you, my lady."

She perched upon the edge of the narrow cot where Henri slept at night, and he lowered his great frame to sit beside her. She was conscious that she was naked under her petticoat, and knew he must realize this . . . She trembled slightly, drawing away from him.

Her breasts stood out beneath the flimsy material; she noticed that her nipples were clearly outlined—and when she looked up, she saw that he was staring at them too, his mouth slightly open.

Then he swallowed hard, and said: "Do not fear—I shall not touch you . . . Oh—you are very beautiful—but . . . You are not Madame Rosalie . . ."

In that moment, she understood what he felt for Rosalie, and she knew also, without any doubt, why Rosalie had defended him when they argued last night.

"I will do what I can to keep you busy in this part of the prison," he said, "for as long as possible. I will try to keep you safe from the laundry."

"For *her* sake?" Coral asked quietly. "Yes—I see . . . Tell me though—what is it about the laundry which is so terrible?"

His eyes travelled down the length of her figure, from her bosom to her slim ankles, and he said at last: "Pray to God that you never find out . . . Now—if you please —you will start to scrub the floor."

So life continued for a few days in the Temple prison; each day Coral had to work hard—but the work was not unbearable, and Henri did his best to give her as much freedom as possible.

After a week, she was given a great privilege; along with some of the other female prisoners (though not, of course, those who worked below in the laundry cellar) Coral was permitted to take half an hour's exercise in the yard.

The prison was built around an inner courtyard, open to the sky, and by looking up—above three stories of honeycombed cell blocks—Coral could catch a precious glimpse of blue sky. It seemed like heaven itself, after the endless gloom to which she had become accustomed.

They were allowed to walk about freely, under the watchful eye of a guard; they were even permitted to exchange words with some of the male prisoners, who had been brought out of their own quarters for exercise at the same time. Coral saw several couples briefly reunited—kissing one another hungrily; there was an elderly man whose gray-haired, frail-looking wife seemed to glow with joy as they stumbled into each other's arms.

And there was Gerard . . .

She could not believe her eyes for a moment. Across the full width of the courtyard they stared at one another—then ran forward—meeting in a rapturous embrace, heedless of anything or anyone else around them.

"Oh—thank God—it *is* you—you're safe!" she exclaimed.

He put his left arm tightly around her waist and pulled her close to him, his mouth opening upon hers as if he had been starved of love for a lifetime.

"My darling, darling girl—" he breathed at last. "Are you well? How are they treating you?"

Then they both began to talk at once, desperately eager to make up for lost time. She told him about Rosalie— about the baby—about Henri, and Sophie Duchatel, and

301

everything else that had happened in the past few days.

"With any luck—perhaps we shan't have to endure this place for much longer," Gerard said. "I heard two of the guards talking outside my cell . . . They didn't know I understood them—apparently the Allied forces are closing in upon Paris . . . let us hope Napoleon's days as a tyrant are numbered, and we shall soon be released . . ."

"If they don't destroy us first," said Coral. "Oh, Gerard—I don't want to wait any longer—I want us to get out of here while we are safe—you and I and Rosalie, and the baby—surely we can make some plan to escape together?"

He looked at her and smiled sadly: "Dear Coral . . . as impulsive as ever! But you'd find me a pretty poor sort of champion if it came to a fight just now."

He indicated his right shoulder, and she realized with a sudden shock that his arm hung straight and stiff and remembered that he had only used his left arm when he embraced her.

"What is it? What's happened?"

"I was stupid enough to break my arm a few nights ago . . . Oh, it's setting well enough, but I can't use it yet . . . It will take time."

"Oh, Gerard—" She hugged and kissed him again "I'm so sorry—how did it happen? Does it hurt very badly?"

"It did then . . . Some of the guards were—playing a game with me . . . I didn't understand the rules, that's all . . ." He changed the subject—"So if you're thinking of organizing a prison riot, my love—I suggest you should wait until I have two fists to fight with!"

A whistle blew, and the guard began shouting out orders. Their exercise period was over, and they were to be marched back to their cells.

Later on, when Rosalie reappeared, exhausted and despairing after another day of degradation—Coral told her of her encounter with Gerard, and repeated what he had said, adding: "But surely—between us—we can think up some sort of plan?"

"I wish we could . . . For I fear Henri is not going to be able to keep you apart for special treatment very much longer. I wish with all my heart that we could find some way to escape before then . . ."

The following morning, Coral was sent as usual to Henri's cell, to receive her instructions for the day. To her surprise, she found him packing a battered old carpetbag with his few belongings; and he was in mufti.

"Quickly—shut the door, please," he said. "And I must ask you to say goodbye to Madame Rosalie for me —I shall not see her again."

"Are you leaving? Have they moved you to another post?" Coral asked.

"No . . . It's too late for that. It's too late for anything now. The enemy is entering Paris—God alone knows what will happen to us all . . . I am going to try and get away before I am caught by the invading armies."

"They would not attack civilians—" Coral began to argue.

"How do we know that? It is not the Prussians or the Austrians I fear—it is the Cossacks . . . I heard today that they are savages, who will stop at nothing—they say that they have already cut down the trees on the Champs Elysees, to burn as firewood!" He finished packing his bag, then said: "There—that's everything . . . All I am leaving behind is my prison uniform—I don't want anything that could connect me with this place."

Coral's thoughts were racing now: "If you're leaving— take us with you—please!"

"There is no time . . . And I don't know what will happen—the whole place is in chaos today. Many guards have left already, but those that remain are in a state of panic. If you were caught, they would shoot you on sight, without doubt . . . No, no—it is better for me to go alone."

Coral cudgelled her brains; Rosalie was in the laundry —Gerard was locked up in the men's quarters—heaven alone knew where. If anything were to be done now, she must do it on her own initiative.

"Before you go . . . Do me one last service," she said.

"Well?" He was halfway to the door.

"Leave me your keys . . . You are free to come and go as you please—but we are not. Give us that chance at least—for Rosalie's sake."

He looked at her for a long moment, then unbuckled the belt from his waist, and tossed it down upon the bed, with the heavy ring of keys still attached to it.

"Take it then . . . And may good luck go with you," he said.

Then he opened the door, and was gone.

It was certainly true that the prison was in an uproar. Gerard, released from his cell for another period of exercise, was surprised to find far more prisoners milling about aimlessly—and no sign of any guards. He was even more astonished, a few moments later, when Coral appeared from nowhere and dragged him into the doorway that led to the women's block.

"Don't argue—come with me," she said firmly, and took him up to Henri's empty room—empty, that is to say, except for the uniform that he had left hanging on a peg behind the door.

"Take off your jacket and your breeches," she commanded.

"My dearest, you know I am always very willing to play the game of love, but surely at this particular moment—"

"Don't be silly—and don't waste time talking! Get your clothes off!"

Slowly, he begin to understand what she was driving at, and obeyed; his injured arm hindered him considerably, and in the end she had to help him—pulling off his breeches, and easing him into the ill-fitting baggy trousers of Henri's uniform.

As she fastened the buttons of his fly, she felt his flesh stir into life under her fingers, and saw that he was smiling at her: despite herself, she found she was smiling too.

"Another time . . ." he said softly.

"Yes—another time!" she replied. "Now—I'll fasten that belt on you—and help you on with the jacket—and then you'll be ready to take Henri's place as a prison guard . . ."

"But what is the purpose of this fancy-dress performance?" he asked.

"You'll soon find out. You are going to escort two new

recruits down to the laundry—I don't know exactly where it is, but Rosalie told me it was in the cellars somewhere, so it shouldn't be too difficult."

When they returned to the courtyard, Gerard had Henri's peaked cap pulled well down over his face, and he was man-handling two frightened young females, who struggled and protested as he dragged them across to the cellar steps. Coral and Sophie Duchatel both carried armfuls of old clothes (including Gerard's own) and the other prisoners muttered to one another, and drew aside as they were hustled past.

Although none of them knew the way, there was no mistaking the laundry, for the stench of it came up the steps to meet them, and they all coughed and choked over the rank, greasy odor.

The door was open, and thick white steam billowed out, Coral took a deep breath and plunged in, not knowing what to expect.

The sight that met their eyes—when they became accusomed to the stinging fog, and the scene gradually revealed itself before them—was like an illustration from the *Inferno;* a glimpse into one of the lowest circles of hell.

The line of women—naked to all appearance in their soaking wet shifts, with their ankles chained together stood facing the battery of washtubs, endlessly pounding and sluicing like automatons, their bare arms red and sore in the scalding water.

There was only one guard in charge today, Coral noticed; that was fortunate . . . but where was Rosalie? The unhappy women all looked so defeated and hopeless, it was difficult at first to tell one from another. Then one of them glanced up and saw Coral watching her and her face changed. It was Rosalie.

Coral signalled her sister not to express surprise, and moved on; she gave Sophie the bundle of dirty laundry that she had been carrying and watch as the girl laid all the garments carefully into one of the wicker clothes-baskets. Then she and Gerard walked up to the guard, who stood frowning at them, more than a little puzzled.

"New workers?" he asked Gerard, as they approached. "Nobody told me about that—I don't know what's come over this place today—everything's at sixes and sevens—"

Gerard gunted, averting his face, and wandered across to the line of women, leaving Coral to the mercies of the prison officer.

He was an ape of a man; thickset and hairy, with matted black curls on his bare chest, and his shoulders gleaming with a combination of sweat and steam, as if he had been oiled. He looked her up and down, then asked: "Why aren't you wearing the laundry shift like the others? You'd better take off that dress—you don't want to get it spoiled, do you?"

To prove his point, he flicked a sopping wet towel at her; it saturated her bodice, and the sharp, cutting blow across her breasts made her gasp.

She forced herself to smile, and began as slowly as possible to unlace the ribbons of her corsage: the man's eyes widened, and he watched with interest as she proceeded to undress. At the same time, she was aware of Gerard working his way along the line of women with the bunch of keys—quietly unlocking their shackles. She heard a shrill whisper of excitement mounting, and redoubled her efforts to hold the guard's attention.

With maddening deliberation, she unfastened her bodice completely, and let her breasts tumble out before his astonished gaze. Then she tossed back her loose copper curls, and smiled provocatively, running her tongue over her shining lips. Inch by inch, she began to pull her dress down from her shoulders, loosening first one arm and then the other, and finally dropping the garment until she was naked to the waist.

The guard was breathing faster now, and he took a step toward her. This was an invitation such as he had never expected, and he was not going to waste his golden opportunity.

So intent was he upon Coral's shameless charms, he did not even notice that the other women had been released; he stretched out his hands greedily to take hold of her, and—

With one eldritch scream of revenge, the laundresses fell upon him. Before he could even touch Coral, the guard found himself being dragged to the ground, under a

306

furious onslaught of arms and legs. Now it was he, and not the washing, that took the full force of their pummelling and pounding. Like avenging harpies, the women made short work of him, tearing his stinking, sweaty trousers to ribbons, lacerating him with their fingernails until his skin was raw and bleeding—pulling and poking, kicking at his most vital parts, and at last, in a final access of rage, picking him up bodily and hurling him into a tub of scalding water.

Coral heard his screams echoing in her ears as she ran up the steps with the laundry-basket in her arms; behind her, Rosalie, Sophie and Gerard were hot upon her heels.

"Which is the quickest way out?" Coral asked.

"To escape? We can't—how can we?" gasped Rosalie. "I can't leave my baby—"

As they hurried through the crowded courtyard, Coral indicated the basket that she carried: "You don't suppose I'm taking this lot with me just for fun, do you?" she asked.

On a pile of crumpled linen, half hidden by a torn cotton chemise, the tiny boy lay curled up, sucking his thumb; he had been fast asleep through all the excitement, ever since Coral and Sophie brought him down from the cell.

Gerard was expecting trouble at the final barrier but when they reached the heavy oak door that guarded the side exit from the Temple Prison, there was no one on duty. He fumbled through the keys on the ring until he found the largest, and tried it in the lock. This was the way that the guards themselves went in and out, and he hoped desperately that Henri had had his own key.

It turned easily, and the little group of runaways stepped out of the darkness within the prison walls, and emerged, blinking and half-blinded into the full light of day.

It was plain to see why there was no one on duty; troops of cavalry, bearing the Allied flags, cantered past along the street, and the startled Parisians watched in alarm as the conquering army invaded their city.

Sophie Duchatel looked about her in wonder, with a dawning delight upon her little face; suddenly she seemed to be a child again.

"Can I go now?" she asked eagerly.

"Go? Go where?" said Gerard.

"I have aunts and uncles—a home—I will be with my family . . ." She leaned forward and kissed the sleeping baby, then kissed Rosalie too in farewell. *"Au revoir, bébé . . . 'Voir, Madame . . . Et bonne chance!"*

And she skipped off happily, disappearing into the crowds.

"She says she is going back to her family," Gerard explained. "But what about us? Where do we go from here?"

"Home—to Ireland," said Coral. "Our family will be together again, too."

"Ireland's an awfully long way off," said Rosalie. "How will we get there?"

Coral had an answer for that as well. A market-cart, pulled by an ancient horse, trundled by, and she hailed it with an imperious gesture, signalling to the rustic driver who held the reins.

"Ask him which way he's going, Gerard," she said. "And if it's in the right direction, tell him we're going with him. He'll never dare refuse you while you're wearing that official-looking uniform!"

By nightfall they were well on their way to the coast, along the familiar road that followed the River Seine. They had no money, and nowhere to stay, but that didn't matter. It was a balmy spring night, and they stretched out together in a sweet-smelling haystack; Gerard in the middle, with Coral to one side of him and Rosalie on the other. At her breasts, Rosalie's baby suckled serenely.

They huddled closer together for comfort, and looked up at the stars.

"I saw Prussians and Austrians and Russian flags in the city," Coral remarked drowsily. "But where were your English soldiery? Bringing up the rear, I suppose, as usual?"

"Slander!" murmured Gerard. "I'd have you know, our gallant army is moving in to France from the Peninsular, under the Duke of Wellington's command. It's odd to think that if I'd followed my father's wishes and joined the Third Dragoon Guards I'd probably be crossing the

Spanish frontier at this moment . . . somewhere like San Sebastian—St. Jean-de-Luz, perhaps . . ."

"I think you're better off here," said Coral. She kissed him lightly on the cheek, and snuggled comfortably up against him. "Don't you agree, Rosalie?"

"All that troubles me is how we are to get across the sea to Ireland," said Rosalie. "For we've no money and no papers—and I can't swim and nurse this young man at the same time!"

"Don't worry your head about that. When we reach Le Havre we'll find Captain Duffy—he'll see we get safely back to Ireland in his fishing boat . . ." Coral smothered a yawn, then added: "And as soon as we're home again —Gerard and I are getting married. Will you dance at our wedding, Rosalie?"

"With the greatest of pleasure . . . just as soon as I find Paul again, and introduce him to his son and heir."

Their voices faded in the soft night, and they drifted into slumber.

Gerard heaved a contented sigh; his arm wasn't hurting so much now—it would soon be completely mended. He felt the warmth of Rosalie's thigh pressed close against his own; at his other side, Coral lay in the curve of his good arm, while he cupped her gentle breasts within his hand. As he slipped into a peaceful dream, he reflected that he was a very lucky man . . .

Coral, too, closed her eyes and gave herself up to sleep with a smile upon her lips . . . she was very, very happy. The family was to be reunited at last. From this night on, she told herself, their troubles would be over.

Perhaps it was as well she could not guess how wrong she was.

PART THREE
UNITED STATES

(1)

A Wanted Man

It was amazing, Coral thought, how little Dublin had changed since she went away. It seemed as if she had been travelling in France for a lifetime, but here was the city—dear, dirty Dublin—just the same as when she left it.

Mrs. Riley's theatrical lodging house, in the little alley off Merchants Quay, hadn't changed either; and when that good lady opened the front door, she treated them to the same casual welcome as if they had merely been touring the West Country for a few weeks.

"Come you in now, Miss Coral—and Miss Rosalie, too. It's good to have you back; your uncle will be like a dog with two tails, so he will. Wait till I tell them you're here."

"Them—?" Coral queried, as she walked into the little front parlor, with Rosalie and Gerard following.

"Sure, they're upstairs rehearsing their parts for the play tonight—a rehearsal, *they* call it—I'd say they were after cracking a bottle and smoking a pipe, more like—but that's none of my business." Mrs. Riley peered closely at the baby in Rosalie's arms, and asked cheerfully: "Your own, would that be?"

"Yes, Mrs. Riley, I'm a married woman now, you know. This is my little son."

"He's a bright enough spark, by the looks of him but I dare say he's given you a hard time of it." Mrs. Riley frowned, and tilted Rosalie's face toward the light from the window. "You're none too grand at a guess—I don't like those shadows under your eyes, dotey . . . Still, that's nothing a good rest and a few square meals won't put right . . ." She moved on, without ceasing her flow of chatter, to Gerard: "And you, Mr. Whatever-your-name-is—I know the face, but I forgot how they call you —you weren't under this roof for very long, I'm thinking."

"No, Mrs. Riley—not very long . . . My name's Kean —Gerard Kean."

The landlady raised her eyebrows slightly.

"Ah . . . it seems to me I've heard them speak that name once or twice. Well, make yourselves comfortable now, while I go up and tell the old feller that you're home again."

"Don't say anything—I want it to be a surprise—" Coral began, but Mrs. Riley was out of the room and half-way up the narrow staircase already, and they heard her calling above: "Mr. Dermot dear, you'll never guess who's just arrived—wait now and you'll be over the moon when I tell you!"

Rosalie moved across to the mirror above the mantel-piece, and studied her reflection.

"It's true—I look a fright . . . Oh, Coral—what will Paul say when he sees me like this? He'll think he's married to an old hag."

"What nonsense!" Coral reassured her. "You're a little tired—no more than that."

But Rosalie turned to her, and continued unhappily: "Only of course he's not really married to me at all— so he could throw me aside if he wants to . . . I told you on the boat, about—his divorce."

"I'm sure that in the eyes of God, you're married," Coral argued. "When you went through the marriage ceremo ny, you believed in it, and that's what counts. Your intentions were right."

She broke off, hearing footsteps on the stairs, and a moment later old Dermot Maguire made a dramatic entrance, with his hands outstretched.

"The return of the prodigals!" he declaimed, and his booming voice set all the ornaments rattling upon the overmantel. "My dear, dear girls—and you too, Gerard, of course—I have no words . . . my heart is too full— my cup runneth over."

He pulled out a bandanna handkerchief with a flourish and mopped his eyes, which were already streaming with tears. (He was always, Gerard recalled, a very proficient weeper at emotional climaxes.)

It was a touching family reunion. He put his arms around Coral and kissed her; he put his arms around Rosalie—nearly squashing the baby—and kissed her— then he noticed the child for the first time and, on learning that he had become a great-uncle, he kissed his great-nephew, then began embracing his two nieces all over again.

"What a joyous moment, to be sure," he cried, and at last turned his attentions to Gerard, shaking him warmly by the hand. "You come most punctually upon your hour, my dear sir . . . We were only just thinking of reviving our plans to produce *Hamlet*, and here you are—ready to step into the role of Laertes, with Coral as Ophelia of course, just as we'd intended before you went away."

He looked at Rosalie, nursing her baby, and added: "Nothing in it for you, my dear, I'm afraid—but perhaps we could bring you on to recite some verses between the acts. A selection of poetry on the theme of motherhood— you could carry the infant on with you; it wouldn't require much rehearsal, and children are always a good draw."

"Uncle—don't get carried away!" Coral interrupted. "Give us a moment to get our breath back. Rosalie's a married lady; she will want to be with her husband."

"Do you ever hear anything of Paul nowadays?" Rosalie inquired. "Do you happen to know where he is?"

"Do I know?" Dermot stuffed his handkerchief away,

and laughed heartily. "What a question! We see him almost every day. He's been good enough to make himself responsible for mounting our present production at the Theatre Royal. *The Lily of Killarney*—not a masterpiece, perhaps, but it has some effective moments, and there's a fight in a burning barn in the last act with a burst of red fire from the wings—that goes down very well."

"*Paul* has been helping you to put on plays?" Rosalie asked.

"He has been the soul of generosity," said Dermot. "And of course it's an investment for him, remember. It's the takings from *The Lily* that have encouraged us to try our luck with *Hamlet* once again . . ."

"Excuse me, sir . . ." Gerard had been trying to break into the discussion for some time. "You talk of my playing Laertes—but in that case, who is to be your Prince of Denmark?"

"'Tis I—Hamlet the Dane!" replied a familiar voice; and Rory O'Malley walked in. "Welcome home, old son and Coral and Rosalie . . . it's good to see you all safe and well."

There were renewed rejoicings, of course, and still more hugging and kissing on every side. When they had stopped talking all at once, Gerard asked: "But tell me, Rory—you're the last person on earth I expected to see here, forgive my mentioning it, but surely when we last met, you were off to Galway on the run from the police?"

"I thought the Barneys were after me, sure enough," Rory agreed. "It seemed yours truly was a wanted man but luckily that's all blown over now."

"How? Why?" Gerard wanted to know. "As I remember there was a man killed accidentally in a struggle, in Bartholomew Lane."

"We won't go into the details of *that* little escapade, if you don't mind," said Coral firmly.

"I don't intend to, my love but the fact remains . . Rory was wanted for murder."

"Let's not go into all that now," said Rory uncomfortably. "I tell you, it's all over and done with—let's turn to more cheerful topics."

"Like the future of the Maguire Theatrical Company!"

Dermot pulled his chair up to the table. "Come now, let us draw up our plans for the next production; for I know Paul will back us, and we'll dazzle the Dublin audiences with our *Hamlet* . . . They are waiting with bated breath for a sight of my Claudius!"

"Yes, but—" Coral tried to interrupt, but she was swept away on the high tide of her uncle's enthusiasm.

"I tell you what—we don't want to waste our time on the locals—we'd be throwing our talents away, bringing caviar to the general—we're too good for Dublin!" maintained Rory. "Why don't we look further afield, and take the play on tour overseas?"

"To England? I don't know about that—" Dermot pursed his lips.

"No, no—forget Old England—I'm thinking of the New World!" Rory declared excitedly. "Couldn't we get Paul La Roche to back us in an American tour?—New York—Washington—"

"Now *that's* a notion worth thinking about!" Dermot's eyes began to shine. "Dermot Maguire—the toast of two Continents—it'll look very well on the bills."

"Do stop daydreaming, the pair of you!"

Coral thumped the table with a determined fist, and the two actors fell silent. Then she continued more quietly: "Here we are—just come home after a nightmare journey through France, and you're talking of sending us off again, halfway round the world! For pity's sake, come down to earth for a moment . . . we have plans of our own, you know!"

"Plans? What plans?" Dermot blinked.

"Gerard and I are going to be married at the first possible moment. We'll go and find a priest tomorrow and ask him to make all the arrangements—isn't that right, Gerard?"

Gerard put his arm around Coral and kissed her, to seal the agreement.

This was the signal for more jubilation and congratulations, and Gerard found himself shaking hands and being slapped on the back all over again. As soon as Coral could make herself heard, she continued: ". . . And you must give Rosalie time to be reunited with *her* husband as well . . . They have a lot to say to one another and he may not wish his wife to continue to travel with a theatrical company."

"Paul could come with us if he wants to," Rory suggested.

"He should be here at this moment to join in the festive occasion," Dermot exclaimed. "Rory, run along to his hotel and see if you can find him—bring him back here as soon as possible."

"No . . ." said Rosalie quietly. She had said very little until now, but something in her manner commanded their attention. "I'm sorry but I don't want to meet Paul here —like this. Give me time to bathe and change my clothes, and try to make myself presentable—then I shall go to his hotel this evening . . . Coral is quite right; we have a great deal to say to one another."

So it was arranged; and at half-past seven that night, when Paul La Roche was in his shirtsleeves, dressing for dinner, there was a timid knock upon the door of the set of rooms which he occupied at the Grand Hotel.

Interrupted in the act of fitting in his links, he frowned irritably.

"Who is it? Come in!"

The door opened, and Rosalie stepped into the room, with her child asleep in her arms. For a long moment, neither of them spoke. They stood and looked at one another, as if in a dream.

Then, very slowly, Paul walked across and took her by the hand, and shut the door behind her.

"Is it true?" he asked at last. "You are really here?"

"If you want me," she replied.

"Oh, *mon Dieu*—*Rosalie*—" he whispered: and for the first time he looked at the baby. "And—this—can it be?"

"Monsieur La Roche . . . allow me to present to you— your son."

His face slowly broke into a smile of incredulous joy.

"I had no idea—I never believed such a thing could happen—oh, *ma cherie*—you have made me the proudest man in the world . . . what is his name?"

"I have been waiting till I found you again, so that you could help me to decide."

"Time enough for that later. We must not disturb him now, when he is sleeping. He will need a cot—a cradle—"

"I'll make up a bed for him. Pull one of the drawers out from a cupboard; that will do very well. He is used to sleeping rough; it's something we have both learned, since he was born."

They made a crib for the child, as Rosalie suggested, from a wardrobe drawer in Paul's dressing closet and settled him comfortably in a little nest of clean linen.

Then, and only then, they were free to come together as lovers, and Paul took her in his arms.

"My own Rosalie . . . this is the happiest night of my life," he said, holding her close. "I want to know so much—I want to hear every detail of your story—but not now . . . later on . . . Afterward."

And with that he picked her up and carried her through into the bedroom, setting her tenderly upon the great four-poster bed.

"Oh, Paul, can you still love me when I am so old and ugly?"

He put his finger on her lips.

"You are the only woman for me . . . my beautiful Rosalie—you are the mother of my son—you are my wife, my mistress, my lover. And I want you—so very much."

Two hours later, they returned to the sofa in the drawing-room, and Paul opened a bottle of champagne that had just been brought up by a goggle-eyed chambermaid.

"I think the girl was a little put out to find us both dressed in nightgowns and little else!" Rosalie smiled.

"Why should she be shocked? We are a respectable married couple—" Paul popped the cork expertly, adding: "Give me your glass . . . let us drink a toast to our future happiness . . ."

As Rosalie sipped the champagne, she said quietly:

"Except . . . we are *not* married, are we, Paul?"

"What do you mean?" He stared at her.

"Henri Clavel told me the truth. I know you had another wife before me, and that you have been divorced . . So our marriage was a travesty—a mere pretense—"

"My dearest Rosalie . . ." Paul took her fingertips and kissed them lightly. "If that's all that troubles you—we

319

shall be married again, here in Ireland, if it will please you—we can get married twenty times over—"

"But we can't for your first marriage is the only one that can be acceptable to the Holy Church."

"Not even that," Paul smiled. "For my first marriage was a civil ceremony, under the law of the accursed Republic—the marriage itself was a legal formality, just like the divorce. We are free to be married in St. Peter's by the Pope of Rome, if that will make you feel better!"

Rosalie put down her glass and threw her arms around Paul's neck, in a sudden transport of happiness.

"Oh, Paul—do you mean it? I do love you—"

And then there was a knock at the door, and Gerard and Coral walked in. Coral began, blushing slightly at the sight of them in their nightgowns: "I'm sorry—I never thought—I mean—Gerard and I couldn't wait to see you both—we decided to call in and—and—"

"We can easily go away again," said Gerard. "Obviously we've picked an inopportune moment."

"Not at all!" said Rosalie, her eyes sparkling. "You must stay and help us to celebrate for Paul has just told me we can be married all over again. We must make it a double wedding!"

So the reunion turned into a party; Paul ordered more and more champagne to be sent up, and since none of them felt in the mood to go downstairs to the hotel dining room—a cold buffet supper was served in his suite.

There was so much to celebrate; apart from all personal matters, the news had just reached Ireland that Napoleon had surrendered to the Allies, and abdicated his throne. He was to be sent into exile, and the deposed King, Louis XVIII, would be restored to power in France immediately.

Paul La Roche looked forward to a happy return to his own country, free to take his place once more as a loyal monarchist, and set up house again at the Place des Vosges. Rosalie demurred; she had no wish to return to that house—it held too many unhappy memories for her.

"Very well, then—we will find somewhere else to live but there's no need to worry about that now, *cherie*—tonight is a night for rejoicing!"

The evening wore on, and the empty wine bottles mounted up; by midnight, the little party of four were sprawled drowsily across the sofa, in each other's arms, and Coral found herself hazily recalling an earlier night they had spent together, in Cork.

She saw that Rosalie was smiling at her, sharing the same memory.

"You put us to bed then!" Coral announced accusingly. "Gerard and me, together, with no clothes on—how could you do such a terrible thing?"

"It wasn't easy," Rosalie pointed out. "In fact it was very hard work—wasn't it, Paul? But you see we were right about you and Gerard—the way things turned out . . . I feel sure you're not nearly so shy of one another by now as you were then!"

Coral flushed, but she could not help smiling, too. She tried to struggle to her feet but, oh dear!—the room seemed to be revolving beneath her.

Gerard caught her as she lost her balance, and drew her down on to his lap again.

"If we're ever to get home tonight," he remarked, with the over-careful articulation of the inebriated, "I must call a cab . . . for it's certain we're in no state to walk back to Merchants Quay!"

"There's no need for you to go home at all," said Paul easily. "You must both stay here tonight—with us—isn't that right, Rosalie?"

"If that's what they wish," agreed Rosalie, comfortably.

"But you only have one bedroom—" Coral objected.

"One bedroom—and one bed . . . But it's a very large bed . . . Quite big enough to accommodate four, I assure you!" said Paul.

Coral shook her head uncertainly: "Four of us—in one bed? Oh, but—but—"

"Rosalie, my darling—help me to persuade your sister she is very welcome," said Paul. "Gerard, do you take the lead, and get undressed, so Coral may follow your example . . . why not?"

Coral was still disposed to argue but she knew that she could not walk home. And already Rosalie was leaning over her, helping her to unfasten her bodice and she saw Gerard, staggering a little as he tried to stand on one foot, stepping out of his breeches. Suddenly it all seemed light-hearted and intriguing and she found herself giggling.

"Why not?" she repeated. "After all—we are all part of the same family, really . . . one big happy family."

Then she shut her eyes and allowed Rosalie to remove her clothes. Half in a dream, she was aware of Gerard, his body naked against her own, trying to take her into his arms: but he kept stumbling, and Rosalie called out: "He'll let her fall—Paul, help him—"

So Coral felt another pair of arms heaving her up, and another naked, male body pressed against her upon the other side, as Paul lifted her gently but firmly. Between them, the two men carried her through to the bedroom, and she sighed with pleasure . . . So many men . . . So many strong hands, and arms, and legs . . . And all in the family, too.

The bed was blissfully soft, and she sank back upon it as if it were a fleecy cloud; she heard Rosalie's voice, in her ear, murmuring: "Are you all right, my darling? Are you happy?"

"Oh, yes . . ." she breathed . . . "very happy—and very sleepy—"

She wasn't sleepy for long.

First, she was roused by Gerard's lips upon hers; his mouth urging her on to new exploits. She put up her arms to embrace him and at once felt another man's hands upon her, Paul's skillful fingers, stroking and teasing her breasts, playing with her nipples. She shivered with a sudden stirring of desire and rolled on to her side finding herself face to face with Rosalie, who lay stretched out beside her, smiling secretly, and welcoming her into this magical circle of love.

There were no rules in this game; nothing was forbidden. She kissed Rosalie then watched as Rosalie turned to greet Paul with further kisses; Gerard found her mouth and kissed her again—and their four bodies met and melted together. Hands, breasts, lips, thighs, nipples and buttocks flowed into a kaleidoscope of physical delight. Their skins touched and caressed, now smooth and warm —now slippery as silk; their limbs entwined in unimagin-

322

able patterns of rapture, and Coral gave herself up totally to the joy of the moment, feeling the growing excitement in her loins like a flower bursting into blossom.

Then, at the instant when she knew she could wait no longer, Gerard turned her to face him, and she opened herself to his rigid urgency. Their bodies slid together and became one: his mouth descended upon hers, and simultaneously his tongue invaded her lips, possessing her completely.

At the same time, in the faint half-light, she was conscious of Paul and Rosalie coupling beside them; Paul's torso, olive-skinned and gleaming with sweat, his body-hair as black and lustrous as Gerard's was blond and fine. The two men strove side by side, as if they were rivals in a contest; their loins thrusting forward in partnership like well-oiled pistons. Coral heard the wordless notes of pleasure that Rosalie uttered, mingling with other cries of desire—and she realized that she was listening to the sounds of her own ecstasy.

Simultaneously, all four participants in the age-old ritual scaled the heights of sensual climax, then soared together, flying into infinite space. In one glorious fusion of body and spirit, they achieved the final mystery of passion, then fell back, shuddering and spent; sprawling contentedly together in a satisfaction too deep for words.

When Coral awoke with an aching head, which she attributed to over-indulgence in champagne, and a nagging conscience, which she attributed to over-indulgence in everything else—she felt embarrassed and guilty. She dressed as quickly as possible, and refused Paul's polite invitation to stay for breakfast.

"No—really—thank you—we must go," she said hastily. "Gerard—take me back to Merchants Quay, please. Uncle Dermot will wonder what has become of us."

"He'll be too busy plotting and planning his début as Claudius, if I know Uncle Dermot!" said Rosalie. "Don't worry about him, dearest . . . Don't worry—" she added, in all sincerity: "About *anything* . . ."

Coral looked at Paul and Rosalie lying side by side in the huge bed; they were uncovered to the waist, and Rosalie had the little boy—as naked as his mother and father

—at her breast. Coral softened enough to give a half-smile; they presented a very attractive family portrait.

"I'll try not to," she said.

"Be glad that we all know each other so much better," added Paul, slipping his arm about Rosalie's shoulders. "And that we all like each other so well."

Gerard put his arm around Coral, and brushed her cheek with his lips.

"That's the way to think of it," he said. "Cheer up my darling—after all, was last night really so very shocking?"

Coral struggled to answer.

"No—it was wonderful—but all the same—"

She broke off, unable to finish; she had enjoyed their strange, mutual love-making very much—too much, perhaps . . . And she knew in her heart that it must not happen again.

"Take me home, Gerard," she repeated, simply.

So Gerard obeyed, then left her with Mrs. Riley while he went out shopping. He would not tell Coral where he was going, but he knew what he must do.

What Coral needed after last night's adventure, he realized, was reassurance: and he had a very good idea of something to reassure her.

He made his way to the best jewelry shop in Dublin. Fortunately, on the previous evening, before they all had too much champagne, Paul insisted on reimbursing Gerard for the travelling expenses he had laid out during their quest through France. For the moment, therefore, Gerard was a comparatively wealthy young man.

Inside the shop, Gerard acknowledged the salesman who came to meet him—and noticed that the fellow was eyeing his travel-stained apparel critically.

"I want," he said firmly, "to buy a gold ring . . . A wedding ring—the best you have in the shop."

The man looked impressed.

"Certainly, sir—if you'll kindly take a seat, I will show you some samples."

It was while Gerard was examining the tray of rings that he heard a high-pitched feminine voice from another part of the shop. A young lady, with the lilting suggestion

of a Cork accent, was complaining: "Nothing at all?—
nothing but those tiresome cameos and those tedious
lockets? I declare you have a very poor selection, sir—I
shall take my custom elsewhere!"

Gerard looked up sharply; and at that instant, Miss
Bella Delaney came into view around a pillar.

Their eyes met—and she stared at him as if he were a
ghost.

"Gerard—as I live and breathe!" she gasped. "What on
earth are you doing here?"

She flew to him and kissed him eagerly; babbling on,
with such excitement that he could scarcely get a word in
edgeways.

"Oh, Gerard darling, what a wonderful surprise! For
haven't I been searching for you all this while, through
the length and breadth of Ireland? Ever since we had that
stupid quarrel, back in Cork, I've thought of you night
and day, and I wished again and again that we could
patch things up."

She sat down on a vacant chair beside him, and continued in a lower tone—

"After you'd gone, I felt so badly about writing that
letter to Uncle George—I really wished I'd never done
it—"

"You did *what?*" he interjected.

"Why, dearest cousin, I wrote to your papa—you remember, I threatened I would do it, to pay you out for
being so cruel and horrid to me—"

"You actually wrote and told him I'd run away from
the Army—?"

"And escaped to Ireland instead—yes, wasn't it wicked
of me? I'm afraid the poor old gentleman will have been
very upset; I was truly sorry later on when I thought
about it, but of course it was too late then. So I decided to
try and find you, to explain and apologize and put everything right between us . . . That's when I began hunting
all over the place for you and those theatricals . . . I even
asked the police if they could help me to trace you . . ."

She hesitated, and lowered her eyes, shyly.

"And of course—that's when I found out what had
happened . . . Oh, I realized at once that was why

325

you'd gone into hiding, when the police told me the dreadful truth—"

"What truth? What are you talking about?"

"You don't have to pretend with *me*, dearest—I know what you did; but it's all right—I don't hold it against you, it was in the heat of the moment and I dare say you felt badly about it afterwards—so we'll never speak of it again . . . But you can guess how I felt a moment ago, seeing you sitting here as bold as brass, as if you'd done nothing wrong!"

"Bella, for heaven's sake—I don't know what you're saying—"

"Don't trouble yourself, Gerard, for I won't let them catch you . . . I propose we leave Dublin right away and hire a coach to take us back to Cork. Once we're at Delaney Hall, you can lie low, and no one will be the wiser—I won't breathe a word to a living soul—so come along, dearest love, let's make a start this very minute—the sooner we get away, the safer you'll be—"

She took him by the hand, but he shook her off impatiently.

"I'm not going anywhere—I'm staying right here in Dublin. I don't know what crazy notion you've got in your head, Bella, but there's nothing more between us. For your information, I came in to this shop to choose a wedding ring. I'm getting married to Miss Coral Maguire in a few weeks' time."

She caught her breath and stared at him speechlessly. Slowly her face hardened into lines of anger and bitterness. Then she rose to her feet and said with biting venom: "That little gipsy with the red hair? How *dare* you—how dare you insult me so! I'll never forgive you for this, Gerard—never! But I won't let you ruin your life—do you hear?—I won't let you do it! I shall go straight to the police and tell them you're back in Dublin. They'll soon put a stop to your filthy tricks!"

With that, she turned on her heel and swept out, her nose high in the air.

When Gerard handed over the wedding ring to Coral that evening, she admired it enormously, hugging him and almost smothering him with kisses.

"Oh, it's perfect—quite perfect—what a darling you are . . . Of course I can't wear it till our wedding day, but I'll keep it safe until then, I promise you . . . it's the most gorgeous ring I ever saw—oh, I can hardly wait till we're married!"

Gerard tightened his hold around her trim waist, and pressed her closer to him as he whispered in her ear: "Neither can I!"

She broke from the embrace, aware that Dermot and Rory were looking on, and showed them the ring—which they duly admired.

"Very fine, my dear—very fine indeed," Dermot pronounced. "But now if you don't mind, let us continue with the business in hand. We were planning our *Hamlet* tour; I was just telling Rory that I think we should open in Cork—"

"No—not Cork—anywhere but that!" said Gerard, with feeling.

"And what's wrong with Cork, pray?"

"Well—" Gerard glanced warily at Coral. "You remember I have a Cousin Bella, who lives just outside of Cork?"

"How could I ever forget?" asked Coral flatly.

"The poor girl's got some sort of obsession about me, and I'd prefer to give her a wide berth. Only today she threatened that she—"

"Today?" Coral's eyes widened. "You saw that woman *today?*"

"For a moment only—we met by sheer chance—but I swear she's half-crazy . . . Do you know, she seemed to imagine I was some sort of criminal? She even threatened to go to the police and tell them I was back in Dublin . . ."

There was a tiny crash; Rory had been nursing a tot of whisky, and now the glass fell from his hands and splintered on the hearthstone.

"By Jesus!" he exclaimed. "D'ye think she meant it?"

"I don't know—she's mad enough for anything, if—" Gerard saw that Rory had suddenly grown pale; there was a greenish tinge under his tanned complexion. "Why —what's the matter?"

Rory and Dermot exchanged glances, then the old man mumbled: "We weren't going to say anything at first—

we didn't want to alarm you unnecessarily—but now . . ."

He paused, and Rory continued: "For your own sake —you must know the truth . . . That night in Bartholomew Lane—the night the man was killed—when I went on the run. We found out afterward that you'd left your coat behind, do you remember? And in the pocket there was a letter, addressed to you—a letter from Miss Delaney, as it happened . . ."

Gerard remembered the letter all too well: a vicious diatribe, penned in a jealous rage after Bella's last disappointment, and addressed to Mr. Gerard Kean.

"They came here to check up on you," Rory continued. "They weren't interested in me after that—they were sure you were the man they wanted."

"I told them you'd gone away, left the country, and we thought they'd called off the chase," added Dermot. "I hoped we'd heard the last of it."

"But now that bitch has put them on the scent again—" Rory stood up. "There's no time to be lost—we'll have to get you away from here before the Barneys come knocking at the door . . . I told you all along, Dermot— we've got to take ourselves off to the United States of America—he'll be safe there—"

"I don't understand!" Coral interrupted desperately: "Gerard's done nothing wrong—surely he can tell them the truth . . . We can't go away now—we're going to be married—"

"Your marriage can wait a bit," said Rory bluntly, "for if Gerard tells them the truth—and they believe him —then it's my neck that's put in the noose . . . And if not . . ." He hesitated, then concluded: "Don't you see? *One* of us is going to hang—for murder!"

(2)

Red Hair is Like That

It seemed that they had no alternative. As Rory said, Mrs. Riley's lodging-house was the last known address of Mr. Gerard Kean before his disappearance so obviously this would be the first place that the police would come looking for him.

Oh, he could keep on the move, from one lot of dingy rooms to the next, trying to remain one step ahead of the law, but sooner or later they would catch up with him.

America was the best hiding-place, after all.

Once this decision had been taken, they all set to work for there was no time to be lost. Dermot went out to round up the remainder of the company, and tell them of this unexpected change of plan; Rory set off to the harbor at Dun Laoghaire to make inquiries about the first available passage across the Atlantic—tonight, if possible—and Coral was despatched to the Grand Hotel, to break the news to Paul and Rosalie . . . and to ask for Paul's help.

"That will be no problem," Paul assured her, with a

smile, and unlocked a cashbox which he kept in his dressing table.

Coral stared, as he counted out several hundreds of bank notes.

"Are you sure you can spare so much?" she asked.

"*Cherie,* now that my property and estates in France are restored to me, I am a wealthy man again, have no fear. And you will need a great deal of money, to transport Mr. Maguire's entire company to America. It's not as simple as a quick jaunt across the Channel to Le Havre, you know!"

Rosalie, who had left them together while she went to attend to her son, now returned to the sitting room of the hotel suite, with the boy in her arms. He was wide awake, and crowing with delight as he recognized his pretty Aunt Coral.

"Let me hold him for a while," Coral pleaded. "It will be a long time before I see him again . . . I do wish you could all come to New York with us."

Paul slipped his hand round Rosalie's waist and said: "Alas . . . for me that is not possible. And I cannot let my wife out of my sight again—you understand. Now we are together—we stay together."

"If only you didn't have to go so quickly," Rosalie sighed, settling the baby on Coral's lap. "You'll not only miss our wedding—you're going to miss his christening as well!"

"Have you settled upon a name for him yet?" Coral asked.

"Yes indeed," replied Paul. "He is to be christened Blaise. It is an old family name—my grandfather's, and his father's before him, were both called Blaise La Roche."

"Blaise . . . yes—it is a good name." Coral tried it out, and liked the sound of it. "I think it suits you, Blaise dear! He's growing so fast, Rosalie. When I come home again, whenever that may be, I expect I shall not even recognize him."

The golden child gurgled with laughter, and dabbed at the silver chain around Coral's neck, with his pudgy fingers.

"It's strange—" commented Paul, frowning very slightly. "Sometimes I feel I scarcely recognize him myself. Certainly he does not take after either of his parents, for we are both dark—while he . . ."

He broke off, absently ruffling the boy's soft, blond hair.

"Perhaps he will take after Coral, and turn redhead later on," Rosalie suggested. "Red hair is like that—it crops up in the family when you least expect it."

"Perhaps . . ." Paul changed the subject. "What is to happen to your own plans for a wedding, my dear Coral? There will scarcely be time before you leave Ireland, I imagine."

"No, there will not." Coral hugged Blaise to her breasts, and kissed him. "That's another disappointment we must endure . . . but Gerard says we shall be married at the first possible moment, as soon as we arrive in the New World—it won't be much longer to wait."

"And you really hope to set sail *tonight?*" Rosalie asked. "At such short notice?"

"If there is a ship that will take us," Coral replied. "Rory is at the harbor now, trying to arrange it."

"Then we must take you home to your lodgings at once," said Paul. "Come, Rosalie—we shall go and see the travellers off on their journey, and wish them *bon voyage.*"

So the little party set out in a cab, back to Merchants Quay.

The alley-way where Mrs. Riley lived was too narrow to accommodate a coach-and-pair, so they left the vehicle at the corner and continued on foot. As they approached the house, Coral suddenly gasped, and clutched Paul's arm.

"We're too late—look!"

Two burly policemen—known in the Dublin slang as "Barneys"—were standing at the open doorway, questioning Mrs. Riley.

"Mr. Kean—Gerard Kean—" the senior officer repeated. "Is he here?"

"Mind your own business, will you!" Mrs. Riley responded with a flow of words that swept over the two policemen like a tidal wave. "What right have you to come poking and prying into a respectable widow-woman's house at all, with your impertinent questions and your big flat feet? Take yourself off, the pair of you, before I lift the rollingpin to you both—and don't think I'm making any idle threat, either—for wasn't it myself disposed of two drunken tinkers who came knocking on my door after the last Donnybrook fair?"

"This is a case of murder, ma'am," began the officer.

"Sure and it's no such thing—them two tinkers woke up the next day with nothing worse than a lump the size of a hen's egg on their foreheads and the print of me foot on their backsides—but I drew the line at killing them, so I did!"

"Hold your tongue, woman—I'm talking of Gerard Kean—wanted for murder. Stand back and let us in, for we have a warrant to search these premises."

They shoved the protesting landlady aside with no further ado, and were proceeding to enter the house, when Paul hailed them.

"Officer—one moment, please. We too have business at this address; what seems to be the trouble?"

"And who might you be, sir?" The policemen regarded Paul suspiciously, and cast an eye over the two young ladies and the child who accompanied him.

Paul drew a bulky document from his inner pocket, with a flourish.

"My credentials . . . you will find that I am Paul La Roche on a diplomatic mission from France, together with my family . . ."

He led the way in to the cramped parlor, which now seemed even more overcrowded than usual. Dermot was there, with Rory and Gerard. They looked tight-lipped and pale but determined to outface this latest alarm: the luggage was already packed, strapped up and ready to go.

"What's happening here?" asked the policeman, as he took in these details. "Gentlemen going on a journey, perhaps? Which one of you is Mr. Kean?"

There was a brief instant of silence, broken by Paul who said easily: "Allow me to introduce you, my dear sir . . . this is the celebrated actor-manager, Mr. Dermot

332

Maguire—and the leading man of his company, Mr. O'Malley . . . and *this* is their leading lady—Miss Coral Maguire."

He took a breath and continued in the same tone: "Miss Maguire is my sister-in-law and the rest of the group are my immediate family. My wife, Rosalie—my son Blaise —and my brother Jean-Pierre." (With a careless wave of the hand at Gerard.) "Unfortunately, my brother speaks no English—*c'est vrai, n'est-ce pas, Jean-Pierre? Vous ne parlez-pas l'anglais?*"

"*Mais non—pas du tout, m'sieur . . . Excusez-moi,*" said Gerard, in his best possible accent.

Dermot—who disliked any scene which did not enable him to take a leading role—now took charge of the situation, and said affably: "I'm afraid we must ask you to forgive us, my good man, but time presses, and we must make a move. As you see, we are setting off upon another theatrical tour tonight, and the show must go on!"

He hustled the two policemen out, saying: "As for this man Kean you're looking for—I suggest you try searching for him in England. I hear tell that there's an actor by the name of Kean playing in London now, at Drury Lane— no doubt *he's* the fellow you're after!"

And with that, the officers had to be content.

An hour later, the entire company assembled on board the sailing-ship *Amsterdam,* in the habor of Dun Laoghaire, and by the light of a swinging lantern Paul, Rosalie and Blaise stood on the jetty, waving them farewell.

The Dutch sea captain barked out orders as the last of the luggage came aboard, and the crew prepared to remove the gangplank.

"Are we all assembled?" Dermot asked, counting heads feverishly. "Mr. Wilkins—Mrs. Mountford—nobody's missing?"

"Wait!" Walter Wilkins spoke up urgently. "Where's Rory? He's not here!"

"Great heavens—what can have happened to him—I left him in charge of the skips—the last I saw, he was making sure that the costume baskets were all safely stowed in the hold."

"I think he went back on shore to say goodbye to some friends," Walter explained.

"But this is disastrous! Stop the Captain at once—tell him we can't sail without Rory—we can't take *Hamlet* to America without the Prince!"

A babble of voices broke out, as everyone argued at once; the Captain tried to make it clear in his broken English that he would miss the tide if he delayed any longer—and told the sailors to cast off, forward and aft.

Then, mercifully, at the very last moment, as the gangplank scraped across the cobbles, and they drew it in— Rory appeared.

He saw that the ship was already moving out; there was a slowly widening gap between the side of the vessel and the jetty. He judged the distance and took a flying leap across the oily blackness of the waters below and landed in a heap on the deck.

Gerard helped him to his feet, asking: "Are you all right?"

Dermot chimed in accusingly: "You nearly missed your entrance!"

"Of course I'm all right—right as rain," said Rory, brushing himself down. "I was detained by a—an old friend of mine, that's all . . ."

Then, as the little crowd moved off lining the ship's rail to wave a last farewell to Ireland, Rory added under his breath to Gerard: "An old friend of yours as well . . . your litle bitch of a cousin, the lovely Bella!"

Gerard glanced round to make sure Coral was not in earshot.

"Bella? Hasn't she caused enough trouble already?"

"That was the whole point . . . I think she's feeling sorry for what she did, now it's too late to put it right. Anyhow, she came looking for you, but she found me instead so she sent you this letter, and said I was to give it you."

"Thanks, Rory . . . I'll read it later. But I'd be grateful if you wouldn't mention this to Coral."

Rory winked: "What d'ye take me for? Mum's the word!"

334

The voyage to America was very long, and fairly disagreeable.

To begin with, although the sea remained comparatively calm, several members of the Maguire Company, who had never left dry land until now, found that the motion of the vessel distressed them considerably.

Mrs. Mountford was one of the principal sufferers, and unfortunately, as the only other woman in the troupe, Coral was forced to share a cabin with the good lady. It was particularly galling, when Coral herself was a good sailor, that she should have to spend so much time wiping Mrs. Mountford's fevered brow and trying to persuade her to cheer up and take a little exercise on deck.

"I don't want to go on deck, dear," moaned Mrs. Mountford, in the tragic tones of Cleopatra, about to embrace her asp. "I just want to lie here—and die . . ."

"Well, why not come to the dining-saloon and try to take a little nourishment?" Coral suggested. "You must be feeling so *empty* by now."

"Don't even mention food to me." Mrs. Mountford closed her eyes and shuddered. "Why did we have to travel upon a Dutch ship? The very air has an unpleasant aroma of cheese."

"We came on a Dutch ship because there are no British ships sailing to New York at present," Coral reminded her gently. "Great Britain and the United States are still at war, you know . . ."

"War? Oh, dear me!" Mrs. Mountford blanched, and wrung her hands. "So if I ever survive this odious voyage, I shall find myself in the midst of a bloody battlefield!"

"Don't worry," Coral tried to soothe her. "It's only a war on paper, I think. The British army has been far too busy fighting Napoleon to go and attack the Americans. Besides—we're all Irish, and Ireland's always been very popular in the USA, they'll welcome us with open arms!"

What Coral did not know was that, since the war in the Peninsular was now over, battalions of English troops were already on their way across to Bermuda, upon the first stage of their invasion of Maryland.

Dermot too suffered from slight attacks of *mal-de-mer*,

but nevertheless, he insisted upon remaining in command of his company. All those who felt strong enough to stagger out of their cabins were called at ten o'clock every morning, to assemble upon the afterdeck for a rehearsal of *Hamlet*.

Despite the fact that it was almost midsummer, there was a perpetual sea-fret in the air—a white mist that hung around damply; striking a chill into the actors as they struggled to learn their roles.

For Gerard and Coral it was doubly difficult; since they had taken a long break from acting, during their expedition to Paris, they found it very hard to get back into the routine of rehearsals, and they had some trouble in memorizing the words.

As Laertes and Ophelia, they had very few scenes together, and this meant that for long stretches of the day, they hardly even saw one another. Whenever they could snatch a few moments of freedom, they sat together in the dining-saloon, hearing each other's lines.

"Go back to *Rosemary—that's for remembrance*," Gerard said, trying to steer Coral through Ophelia's "mad" scene.

"Oh, those beastly flowers and herbs—I do hate them —I keep getting so muddled," she exclaimed crossly. "I still don't really know the speeches properly, that's the whole trouble . . . You'd better go back and practice your duel with Rory, and let me try to hammer the words into my head."

"I'd rather stay here with you," said Gerard quietly.

He stretched out and took the playbook from her hands, and shut it; then put his arms about her.

"Do you realize I hardy ever see you on your own nowadays?"

"There's so much to do—we're so busy all day—"

"And all night—you're sharing a cabin with Mrs. Mountford! Oh, Coral, why can't you slip out one evening and meet me on deck for an hour or so? I do want you so badly."

"I know . . . but if she woke up and I wasn't there, she'd be in a frenzy! When she isn't dying of seasickness,

336

she thinks the ship's about to sink to the ocean bed. I can't leave her."

She kissed him tenderly, and added in a whisper: "Be patient, my dearest. When we get to New York, we'll be married, and no one shall ever keep us apart, for the rest of our lives."

He kissed her again, hungrily.

"I'm counting the hours till then," he said. "The minute we set foot on shore, I'm going to the best hotel in the city, to book the bridal suite."

He was as good as his word. On the day that the *Amsterdam* arrived at last in the Hudson River, and sailed up to Battery Point, Gerard made it his first duty to inquire where the finest hotel might be.

With Rory as his companion—soon, they hoped, to be best man at the wedding—Gerard made his way to the Manhattan Hotel. There, he put down a deposit in advance on the bridal suite—a splendid set of rooms, overlooking the East River—and sent a pageboy with a message to Coral, asking her to join him in their new abode.

He also ordered a bottle of wine, and three glasses, and, as they awaited Coral's arrival, he said happily to Rory: "I don't want to be inhospitable but after you've had one glass, you will be a good chap and make yourself scarce, won't you? I—er—I'd be grateful if you'd leave us alone for a while, when she gets here."

Rory grinned, and protested: "Steady on, old son—you're not married to the girl yet, remember!"

"Well . . . we don't have to be too precise about the technicalities—we've endured that long sea-voyage, living like a nun and a monk. I fancy it's about time we put that situation to rights!"

"Then I'll wish you both the best of luck and I certainly envy you, my lad!" Rory sighed. "You should pity me alone in a foreign city, not knowing one single, solitary female."

"You could always try paying court to Mrs. Mountford." suggested Gerard wickedly, and dodged as Rory aimed a mock-blow at him.

Unfortunately, he tripped on the fur rug by the bed-

337

side, and stumbled back on to the silk counterpane. Rory followed up his advantage by launching himself upon Gerard, and when the door opened, both young men were rolling upon the bed, in a light-hearted wrestling-match.

"Well! I do hope I'm not intruding upon anything private?" asked Coral, as she swept into the room.

The two men sat up—looking and feeling more than a little foolish; the setting for their impromptu battle was bizarre indeed—the honeymoon bed was draped in flowing pink-and-white muslin, with a headboard in the form of a gigantic, snowy-white swan, that held up the canopy of bed curtains in its gilded beak.

"Oh—Coral—come in . . . make yourself at home,' Gerard said, a little breathlessly. "Let me open this bottle of wine—we must all drink a toast to our wedding day."

"I won't take any wine just now, thank you," said Coral politely. "For I'm not sure I could drink to that particular toast with any great conviction."

"What do you mean?" Gerard wrestled with a stubborn cork. "Rory, fetch the glasses. You won't drink a toast? Why not, pray?"

"Our wedding day may still be a long way off," Coral pointed out. "Nothing is definitely fixed yet, after all."

"Except the marriage-bed!" chuckled Rory, straightening the counterpane. "What do you think of it, Coral? Pretty ornamental, eh?"

"And when do you propose that we should move into this ornamental love-nest, Gerard dear?" Coral asked, in the same formal tone.

"Well—why not now?" asked Gerard. "Ah—*that's* go it!—glasses, Rory."

The cork came free at last, and he began to pour wine as he continued: "Rory's just leaving, aren't you, old boy? As soon as you've finished your wine—"

"That's right; you see, I've already found myself a single room here, on the floor above. Nothing as grand as this, of course, but I've got to go up and unpack my luggage, and get settled in."

"Please don't disturb yourself on my account, Rory, for I shan't be stopping very long. And Gerard—I *did* tell you I don't want a drink, didn't I?"

338

Gerard looked at her carefully, then said: "Coral, tell me, is there something wrong, by any chance?"

"Wrong? What makes you think that?"

"It's something to do with the way you keep smiling —only your eyes aren't smiling at all. Have I done something to annoy you, my love?"

"Don't call me that!" Coral's chin went up, and her back was as stiff as a ramrod. "Your *love* is a very casual thing, I'm afraid—a thing to be taken for granted; a trivial pleasure to be enjoyed before the wedding day. How could you shame me so? You expect me to move into that ostentatious bed with you—when all the world knows we're not man and wife—?"

"My darling, I had no intention of shaming you; I simply thought what difference does the odd day or two make when we're already—"

"Not another word! I won't listen to you!" Coral's Irish temper was fully roused now, and her cheeks were flaming.

"I think perhaps I'd better go upstairs and leave you both to talk things over—" began Rory tactfully, struggling to his feet.

"You stay where you are!" she flung at him in passing, and he sank back into his chair. "That's not the worst of it, either, I'd have you know. You tell me you love me, Gerard, and all the while I find you've been keeping up a correspondence with your darling cousin, behind my back. What have you got to say to *that?*"

She pulled a folded paper from her reticule, and flung it on to the bed. Both men recognized Bella's spiky handwriting immediately.

"Dear God—not *again!*" groaned Rory. "Don't tell me you left *that* letter in your coat pocket as well?"

"Certainly not. I put it away somewhere—now where the devil—" he broke off, and turned to Coral reproachfully: "Have you been going through my bits and pieces?"

"I have not!" Coral took a deep breath, her nostrils flaring. "It so happens that after the last rehearsal this morning, I must have picked up your copy of *Hamlet* in mistake for my own. And next time I came to look

339

through it, I found that hateful billet-doux in between the pages!"

Rory put his head in his hands. Gerard tried to take the offending letter, and tear it up, but Coral was too quick for him, and snatched it away, reading out some particularly choice phrases: "*So* sorry for what I have done to upset you but you must know I would never have done it if I didn't love you so *very* much, Gerard darling. When you told me about your sordid liaison with that dreadful gipsy girl with the carroty hair, I was so distracted, I didn't know what I was doing. But I feel sure you'll throw her aside one day which is no more than she deserves and then you will come back to me, and we will be like two lovebirds again, as we used to be in the good old days."

Coral screwed the letter up and threw it in Gerard's face.

"Carroty hair indeed! Take your beastly letter, and leave me alone!"

She made for the door, and flung it wide open.

"Where are you going?"

"I'm going to have Rory's luggage sent down here. I shall occupy the single room and you two can share this delightful suite. At least it's big enough for you to practice your swordfighting that should help you to pass the long, lonely nights together!"

And she stamped out, slamming the door behind her.

That night, as the two men glumly undressed before retiring to bed, Rory said sadly: "Just like the 'good old days' indeed. Little did I think I'd end up by sharing the bridal suite with you, old son."

Gerard looked him up and down, as he stood half in and half out of his breeches, and replied bitterly: "It was hardly what I had in mind for tonight either. Tell me one thing—do you still snore as loudly as ever?"

Half an hour later, as the gilded swan above the bed vibrated like a tuning-fork to the reverberations of Rory's guttural rasping, Gerard discovered that this was something else which had not changed.

The Maguire Company were to present their première

340

performance of *Hamlet* at the Park Theatre—a very magnificent building, situated between Ann Street and Beekman Street, on Park Row and it was here that rehearsals began, the following day.

Dermot had made himself busy from the moment he arrived in the city, drumming up support for the venture, plastering the front of the theatre with playbills, spreading word-of-mouth reports in all the saloons and billiard halls and, most important of all, endeavoring to draw upon the patronage of the upper classes.

"It's all going very well," he reported gleefully, when the curtain fell after the final dress rehearsal. "I've put word about to all the bankers and merchants—all the leading society ladies have promised to attend—I've even persuaded the Haskell family to take a box!"

"And who are the Haskell family, when they're at home?" Coral asked, wearily.

"You must have heard of them. Old Jedediah Haskell is one of the wealthiest men in America—a cattle baron from the middle-western states. He's brought the grandest mansion in Park Row, and transported his entire clan here to live in style. I tell you, he'd make the English Regent and his court look like paupers by comparison!"

"Delightful for them," remarked Coral. "Never mind the audience, Uncle, what about the play? You've hardly said a word about our performance."

"Oh—yes—capital, capital. You look lovely, my dear, quite lovely. Though I noticed your scenes with Gerard were rather flat—there's not a lot of feeling in the mad scene—it could do with a little more fire."

"Fire, is it?" muttered Coral under her breath, for Gerard's benefit, as he was standing beside her on stage. "For two pins I'd set fire to your breeches! It's no more than you deserve."

"Coral be reasonable! I can't help it if Bella chooses to write me a letter." Gerard tried to defend himself, for the hundredth time since their quarrel had broken out.

But it was no good. Coral would not listen to him. Tossing her head, she moved away, making for her dressing-room.

341

In the wings, she nearly collided with her uncle, deep in conversation with a young man in evening clothes, who wore a white gardenia in his buttonhole.

"Ah, Coral my dear, come and let me introduce you . . ." Dermot drew her forward. "This is our good friend and patron, Mr. Joshua Haskell—you remember my mentioning old Mr. Jedediah? Well, Mr. Joshua is his only son and heir . . . allow me to present my niece Coral, our leading lady."

"Glad to know you, ma'am," drawled the young man, crushing her hand in a powerful grip. "But heck, don't you go calling me Joshua. I can't abide it . . . all my friends call me Red, on account of my hair."

His hair was certainly very startling; a shock of bright orange, swept forward over his forehead in a rough cowlick. Now *there,* Coral thought, was someone who might in all fairness have been described as "carroty."

Still, he was certainly a good-looking boy; with massive shoulders and arms like young tree trunks which almost burst through the seams of his fine broadcloth jacket. His face was tanned dark by the sun, and in contrast his eyes were a very pale blue, and his teeth, when he flashed his engagingly boyish grin, were exceedingly white.

"Mr.—er—Red Haskell—" Dermot continued, "has kindly announced his intention of bringing a whole party of his friends to our opening night tomorrow."

"Just a handful of my real close buddies and their women-folk, you understand," Red explained to Coral, in his western drawl. "Nigh on sixty of them, I reckon."

"We shall endeavor not to disappoint you, sir," Dermot said.

"Are your companions interested in the works of William Shakespeare?"

"Well, sir—I wouldn't say that exactly. Most of the boys are interested in women, and liquor, and horse racing—and long-distance spitting. But I guess a change might be good for 'em—don't you think?"

He looked Coral up and down, and broke into another dazzling grin. "Mr. Maguire—if you've finished work for the evening, I'd sure like to take this young lady back

342

home to dinner, if you've no objection. Our place is only half a block away, and of course I'd see her safely back to her hotel afterwards."

Dermot shuffled uncomfortably, and glanced at Coral: "Well—that's very good of you, Mr.—er—Red—but you see, there are certain problems. My niece is not entirely free to accept engagements from other gentlemen now, since she—"

Coral had noticed Gerard following her into the wings, and although he was standing behind her, she could still sense him there, listening and watching. On impulse, she broke in: "Why, Uncle, that's perfectly all right. Thank you very much, Mr. Haskell. I'll be happy to accept your invitation."

"I was hoping you would." Red Haskell touched his hair and laughed. "Seems to me we ought to have something in common—we're both bricktops, for a start!"

He offered her his arm, and said: "Come on, Miss Coral—let's go!"

So Coral's night out on Park Row began: from her point of view, as a kind of challenge. What it was to be, on Red's side, she was soon to discover.

The Haskell residence was certainly palatial; the moment Red escorted her into the front hall, a little army of liveried servants sprang forward to take her coat, and a negro flunkey ushered them in to the dining-room.

"The rest of the family are out somewhere—they're off to some society ball or other. I don't go in for dancing myself—I always seem to finish up trampling all over my partner's feet," Red confided bashfully. "Anyway, that's why we've got the place to ourselves."

It felt faintly ridiculous: they sat at opposite sides of a long mahogany table that seemed to stretch away forever, to left and right. There were splendid candelabra, all aglitter with light, and an array of the finest silverware laid out before them.

"How did they know to lay two places?" Coral asked, as the first course was served. "You didn't even know I'd be coming back to dinner."

"I sure knew *someone* would be!" he grinned. "I can't

343

abide eating alone—I made sure I'd find me some company. Only I didn't know it would be someone as pretty as you."

The meal passed swiftly; Red had a voracious appetite, and he ate very fast, shovelling the food in eagerly, and washing it down with copious draughts of beer from a crystal goblet.

"I know they say wine is more fancy," he explained, refilling his glass yet again. "But I don't have the taste for that foreign stuff myself. I reckon beer's a good, clean drink—don't you?"

"Well—yes—I suppose so," Coral replied politely, taking a sip.

She would have preferred wine, but could hardly tell him so.

She would also have preferred him not to drink quite so much—or quite so quickly. By the time the meal was over, she noticed that his voice was a little slurred, and his bright red quiff of hair had fallen untidily forward across his eyes.

He brushed it aside roughly, then pushed back his chair.

"C'mon," he said ."Let's go to the parlor . . . through here."

He took her firmly by the hand, and they went in through a pair of folding doors into one of the most elegant drawing-rooms Coral had ever seen. The family must, she suspected, have hired someone else to decorate the house for them.

"Sit yourself down," he said, amost pushing her on to a sofa upholstered in lilac satin. He was, she realized, with dismay, really very drunk indeed. She decided that she would make an excuse to leave at the first possible moment.

"Aw, *shit!*" Red suddenly let out a bellow of rage, and Coral opened her eyes wide, hardly believing her own ears.

"What stupid asshole lit a fire in here? Don't those fool servants know this is the middle of summer?"

Red strode—weaving a little—to the huge marble fireplace, where a log fire was blazing merrily. It looked very fine, but it was certainly true that the room was overheated.

He unbuttoned his jacket and threw it on to the floor, then pulled off his silk cravat and unbuttoned his collar.

"Too darn hot . . . place is like a prairie fire," he grumbled, then he suddenly shouted with laughter, and fumbled with the buttons of his trousers. "Don't you worry, beautiful—leave it to me—I'll soon put a stop to it."

Coral couldn't see what he was doing, but the rippling sound of water, and the angry hiss of steam soon made it only too clear.

"That's better—a whole lot better," Red concluded triumphantly a moment later. "I pissed on the fire and put it out—how's that?"

And as he spoke he turned to face her, and she saw with alarm that he was still holding his member in his hands. But now it was stirring into life—its dimensions expanding—

"Get your clothes off," he said quickly, and began to laugh again. "You and me—we're going to have some fun . . ."

(3)

New York to Washington

"Behave yourself, sir—remember you are a gentleman
. . ." Coral sprang to her feet, and made for the double
doors.

"Horseshit, lady! I ain't no gentleman—come here."

He moved with a surprising turn of speed and caught
up with her as she fumbled for the door-handles.

"And I'm no lady but that doesn't mean you can conduct yourself like a pig wallowing in the mire. Let go of
me, or—"

"Or what?" He chuckled, grabbing her round the waist.

"Or you'll be sorry!" she threatened, and simultaneously made the threat good by stamping hard upon his toes,
punching him in the stomach with her left fist, and slap-
ping him across the face with her right hand, as hard as
she could.

He blinked, and recoiled instinctively, letting her go.

"Why, you little spitfire!" he grunted, clutching his belly. "Where'd you learn to fight like that?"

"I had an excellent upbringing in a convent for young

346

ladies!" retorted Coral, opening the doors at last. "Now will you kindly call your footman to bring my coat, so that I may go home."

"Aw, heck—there's no call for that. Sure I'll let you go, if that's what you want," he continued, pulling himself together and adjusting his clothing. "Since you ain't prepared to play . . . but I'll take you back as I promised I would. I'll whistle up the carriage and drive you home in style—how's that?"

Coral protested that there was no necessity—she could easily walk.

"At this time of night? There's some mighty rough characters around in this city, beautiful. No, I'll drive you: and no argument."

It seemed that he meant what he said, and Coral gave in with as good a grace as possible. In any case, she was feeling a little tired, and the sooner she got back to her bed at the Manhattan Hotel, the happier she would be.

The vehicle turned out to be an open carriage, pulled by a spanking pair of bays, and Red insisted on driving it himself. The night was warm, and the fresh air on Coral's face, ruffling her curls below her bonnet, was not at all disagreeable. Red cracked the whip and urged the horses on to a fair turn of speed.

"This is very pleasant," she admitted, pleased that he had come to his senses so swiftly, and doing her best to let bygones be bygones. "But, I know I'm only a stranger here—is this really the way to my hotel? Surely we're going in the wrong direction?"

"This way's only a few minutes longer—it's such a fine evening, I figured you might enjoy a turn around the Park."

And he directed the equipage into the Park gates, where a broad carriage-way led in a long ellipse among the trees and lawns; a handsome rural landscape in the heart of the city.

"It's very pleasing, I agree, but it *is* very late, and we have our first performance of the play tomorrow—" Coral began.

"Just one moment longer," Red persuaded her. "Hey—

347

I tell you what! Have you ever driven a team of horses before? Then now's your chance. Here—take the reins for a spell!"

Coral was rather surprised as he pushed the leathers into her hands, but she was prepared to humor him—if this would keep him happy, all well and good. And it seemed to be quite effortless; the two horses trotted along briskly, and required no special attention. They appeared to have the entire Park to themselves.

"Simple, isn't it?" said Red, and began to chuckle once again.

She wondered why; there was a mocking note in his voice that she did not trust.

With good reason, as she discovered a second later. Suddenly, without any warning, Red produced a pistol from an inside pocket, and flourished it in the air. Then, with an ear-splitting whoop, he fired it above the horses's heads, into the darkness.

The terrified creatures panicked instantly, and bolted; Coral pulled on the reins with all her might, desperately trying to restrain them, her arms almost pulled out of their sockets.

"You must be mad!" she gasped. "Why did you do that? I can't hold them."

The carriage was flying along at top speed now, lurching dangerously from side to side as Coral struggled to keep control.

"Take the reins—please—stop them—" she pleaded.

To her horror, Red did nothing but laugh.

"Hell, no—we both know you're a fighter—let's see how you hold your own against a runaway coach. And while you put your mind to *that* little problem—"

He broke off, and she was appalled to find that he had put his arms round her waist again. Now she felt sure he was insane: as they hurtled onward, seemingly bent on self-destruction, he began to grope for her breasts.

"Take your hands off me—" she cried furiously, still wrestling with the frenzied steeds that dragged her helplessly forward.

Then she realized that he had planned the incident

348

quite deliberately: she could not take her hands from the reins and meanwhile Red was taking advantage of her vulnerable sitation to pull aside her outer garments, and explore her body.

Shouting with laughter, he tore at the ribbons and lace of her corsage, ripping the silk apart, and pawing at her breasts, kneading her soft flesh with his coarse fingers, and pinching her nipples playfully.

She could do nothing to stop him—if she let the reins drop, the carriage might overturn and as she exerted every ounce of her strength she felt Red change the course of his attack. He tugged at her skirts and began to run his hands up between her legs.

"How'd you like a bit of excitement for once in a while?" he shouted in her ear, tearing at her flimsy undergarments.

With horror, she felt his prying fingers reaching into the most private areas of her body and there was nothing she could do about it. She had to submit to this vile indignity or risk death itself as the alternative.

"It's about time someone taught you a lesson, you little teaser!" he continued, thrusting brutally with a stubby middle finger.

A thrill of pain shot through her and then she cried aloud, but for a different reason.

They were not, after all, the only coach within the Park tonight. Ahead, approaching sedately round a curve in the road, was aother vehicle; a closed carriage, possibly containing a pair of young lovers on their way home from a ball.

A collision seemed imminent—the bay horses saw the carriage lanterns looming up, and swerved violently aside; the wheels left the roadway and sank into grass and the entire conveyance toppled over on to one side, as the desperate animals reared and whinnied.

By the greatest good fortune, there had been hay-making in the Park during the day, and piles of newly-cut grass were left to dry. Coral was flung from the coach, but landed in a soft mound of hay, totally unharmed. The horses, too, having come to a standstill at last, were suddenly quiet, their flanks heaving convulsively, and their muzzles white with foam. Red scrambled from the half-overturned vehicle, rubbing his head and swearing, as the approaching carriage pulled up.

The other driver called out: "Anyone hurt? Can we be of any assistance?"

"You certainly can," gasped Coral, getting to her feet, and fastening her top coat tightly over her torn dress. "I should be much obliged if you would take me back to the Manhattan Hotel—as soon as possible!"

When she reached the hotel entrance hall, she had recovered her breath, and some of her composure but inside, she was still trembling and very distressed. She asked the desk-clerk: "Is Mr. Kean in the hotel?"

The clerk checked the keys on the board.

"Kean? Ain't he one of them two Irish guys sharing the Bridal Suite? Kinda outlandish set-up to my way of thinking!"

Coral's cheeks flushed, and she pretended not to understand him.

"Mr. Kean—" she repeated. "Is he here?"

The clerk scratched his head. "Lemme see now—one of them is, and one ain't. I saw one go out with a party of friends, on the town—they had bottles sticking out of their pockets, and they wuz all set to raise a bit of hell. If you'll pardon the expression, ma'am."

That would have been Rory, of course. "And—the other gentleman?"

"He said as how he was going to have himself an early night—I guess he weren't feeling any too chipper."

Gerard, obviously suffering pangs of jealousy, since she had accepted Red's invitation to supper.

"Thank you—that's all I need to know."

She went up the stairs, and made her way straight to the Bridal Suite.

She knocked but there was no reply. He must be asleep.

But she had to see him; she needed comfort and consolation after her hideous experience tonight. She wanted to forget about Bella, and the letter, and their silly quarrel, and be reconciled again.

She tried the door cautiously, and found it was open.

Inside the room was in darkness, with a dim light filtering through from the window and she could just make out the sleeping figure huddled under the bedclothes. Rory would not be back till dawn, in all probability; once he was set on a carousal, it invariably lasted throughout the night.

Impulsively, Coral began to undress.

When she was quite naked, she lifted the covers and slipped into the bed beside the man she loved. It felt warm and safe and reassuring: he was turned upon his side, facing away from her, but she snuggled up closely to him, stroking his bare back and the curve of his hip.

She sniffed the familiar odor of masculinity, and wrinkled her nose . . . pah! He must have been drinking with Rory, earlier on; she detected a strong whiff of liquor about him. But she would forgive him that tonight; he must have tried to drown his sorrows. Tonight she would forgive him anything—and she would give him anything, too. Anything that he desired.

She let her hand stray across his leg and along his thigh, then began to tickle his rough body hair, stroking and stimulating.

Rory, who had been fast asleep, awoke from an erotic dream; he had believed he was in some strange Eastern harem—he was a slave, being tormented by a bewitching oriental princess with a cruel smile playing about her lips. When he was at a peak of sexual excitement, she would order him to be flogged or put to some nameless torture. It would not be much longer now; already he could feel the tension rising in his loins.

He shook off the dream and found himself in darkness. For an incredible moment, it seemed that the dream had come true—he was being gently but steadily caressed but by whom? And where was he?

Dimly, he remembered where he was. He was about to exclaim:

"Gerard, what the hell d'you think you're doing?"

But at the same instant, he realized that this was no man in bed with him; and simultaneously, as Coral felt

351

him stiffening under her hand, she knew with terrifying certainty that she had made a mistake.

She repressed a cry of dismay, as Rory rolled over to face her.

"Oh, dear God—I thought—" she began. *"Rory!"*

"Coral, by Jesus!" he exclaimed.

And as they stared at each other, transfixed and bewildered, the bedroom door opened, and Gerard walked in.

It was all explained eventually, of course.

Coral scrambled into her clothes as quickly as possible, hating herself for having been so foolish, hating Rory for having unwittingly aroused her to such an immodest display, and hating Gerard most of all because he had not been there when she needed him.

She told them how she had misunderstood the desk clerk; she had supposed it was Gerard who was asleep in bed and Rory explained that he had been feeling tired, and so elected to have an early night before the *première* of *Hamlet.* Gerard, who had indeed been trying to "drown his sorrows," said very little. He half believed their story and yet he didn't quite know what to believe. He could not throw off the sickening pang of jealousy that had swept through him when he first walked in, and saw them sitting up in bed together—naked. Had they been making a fool of him, all along?

Then, as Coral finished dressing, he noticed the state of her garments. Her bodice was torn wide open, exposing her breasts and her skirt was tattered and bedraggled.

"And when did *that* happen, I'd like to know?" he demanded.

"Oh—that had nothing to do with Rory," said Coral quickly. "It was Red—Mr. Haskell—he tried to assault me—I was so upset, that's why I wanted to be with *you,* Gerard."

"For a well-brought-up girl, you manage to lead an amazingly eventful life!" snapped Gerard. "How many more men do you intend to have before the night's over?"

Coral began to lose her temper.

"Don't you dare take that tone with me. You know

352

very well I've never looked at another man since—since you and I first—"

"And I've sworn off all other women and a fat lot of good that's done me!" retorted Gerard. "You do nothing but carp and criticize and throw tantrums for no reason at all."

"That's not true!" shouted Coral. "What about your cousin Bella?"

"For God's sake—" Rory tried to be the peacemaker. "It's very late—can't we postpone this slanging-match till some other time and get some sleep?"

But they ignored him.

"I've told you a thousand times, I'm not interested in Bella—I'm not interested in any other woman—"

"Oh, no? That's a black lie for a start. . . for I saw the way you looked at Rosalie that night in Dublin—you were excited by her, I could tell that—deny it if you dare."

"I don't deny it—your sister's a very fine figure of a woman, but—"

"There, you hear that? He actually admits it! He glories in his shame."

"Let me get to sleep, can't you?" demanded Rory. "Why don't you both go away and—"

"Oh, don't worry—I'm going—but not with *him!* I wouldn't stay with Gerard tonight if he went on his bended knee and begged me!" snorted Coral, snatching up her coat and scrambling into it. "Good night—and good riddance!"

And she swept out, slamming the door so violently that the noise seemed likely to wake the entire hotel.

Gerard cursed fluently for several minutes, and began to pull off his clothes. At last he crawled in beside Rory, and tried to settle down for what was left of the night.

The two men lay naked, side by side but rigidly apart, being careful that their bodies should not touch one another at any point.

At long last, Gerard said, into the darkness: "Just before I came in—what exactly were you and Coral doing?"

"I told you—she thought I was *you*—"

"Possibly. That still doesn't answer my question. What were you doing, Rory?"

"Well—she—she had her hand on—on me . . . and I was—well, you see—I couldn't help being—"

"And if I hadn't come in at that moment what do you suppose would have happened next?"

"Well, I suppose—if—if she'd gone on—going on—then we would—I mean—*I* would—well—"

His voice trailed off unhappily into silence. After a pause, Gerard said bitterly: "Yes—that's what I thought. Good night!"

And he rolled over angrily, trying to get to sleep.

This unfortunate, three-cornered feud continued throughout the following day; through final rehearsals at the theatre, and last-minute preparations before the curtain went up.

Outwardly, Rory, Gerard and Coral were behaving normally, and they went through their paces like old troupers, but it was noticeable that off-stage they avoided one another, and exchanged as few words as possible.

"Trouble ahead . . ." muttered Walter Wilkins, as he painted his face at the mirror in the men's dressing room.

"What's that?" Dermot paused, in the act of trying on Claudius's regal crown, and adjusting it over his flowing chestnut wig. "Trouble? What nonsense—we've got a house full tonight . . . every seat taken—even the boxes."

"I'm not talking about the receipts," Walter remarked. "I'm referring to our juveniles—Hamlet, Laertes, Ophelia. There's something wrong there: they're all working up some sort of quarrel, laddie."

"Surely not!" Dermot was concentrating so hard upon the success of tonight's venture, he had had no time to observe these details. "In fact, I thought they were all particularly quiet, not troublesome in the very least."

"There's nothing so quiet as a powder-keg just before it explodes," said Walter drily. "Well, let's hope I'm wrong. But I can see the danger signals."

Gerard and Rory also shared a dressing room, and they got into their costumes witout speaking. When Gerard caught Rory's eye in the long looking glass at one moment, Rory scowled and looked away uncomfortably.

Gerard took this as the expression of a guilty conscience, and raged inwardly, but still nothing was said.

In the ladies' dressing room, Mrs. Mountford, attired in Gertrude's voluminous velvet robes, cast an approving eye over Coral's appearance.

"Yes—very nice, dear—but a *little* pale, perhaps. Just a shade more rouge, to bring out your cheekbones? You do seem the least bit *piano* this evening, if I may say so."

"I don't feel very *piano*," said Coral, shaking back her curls and putting on the tight-fitting cap of pearls that did duty for Ophelia and Juliet and many other Shakespearean heroines. "I feel more like a trumpet, one of those that blew down the walls of Jericho!"

"Oh, you do say such quaint things—I don't know how you think of them, I really don't . . ." Mrs. Mountford's expression changed, and she added: "My dear— your gold ring—you've left it on the dressing table."

"Yes, I know . . . I meant to."

"But you always take it with you, wherever you go. It's to be your wedding-ring, isn't it?"

"That was the original intention," replied Coral evenly. "I don't choose to carry it with me tonight, that's all."

"Well, you certainly can't leave it lying about—it's not safe. Here—slip it into your bosom, my dear—it won't come to any harm there."

Reluctantly, Coral obeyed, and folded the wedding-ring inside the low corsage of her gown.

Someone knocked on the door, shouting: "Curtain going up! Everybody down for the first court scene."

The two ladies wished one another luck, and made their way to the stage.

At first the play seemed to go well enough, though it was noticeable that Hamlet appeared to be even sulkier and more out-of-sorts than usual. And Laertes rattled off his lines irritably, at top speed, as if he could hardly wait to get to the end of the play.

Alerted by Walter's warning, Dermot began to notice these disturbing details and he noticed a certain restlessness in the audience, too. This meant, inevitably, that he lost concentration upon his own role, and began to stumble over the lines, transposing speeches and generally betraying signs of insecurity.

When the first Laertes-Ophelia scene began, Gerard could scarcely bring himself to look at Coral, and they acted as if they were on two separate islands with a vast ocean between them. If Dermot had once considered this scene to be lacking in fire—tonight it was positively arctic.

To make matters worse, Coral could hear a lot of whispering and sniggering from the most expensive seats in the Grand Circle, and she guessed that this must be Red Haskell telling his sixty most intimate friends of the humiliation that he had inflicted upon her last night.

By the time the "graveyard" was reached, things had gone from bad to worse. Coral hoped that once her mad scenes were over, she could relax and stop worrying but of course she had to be carried in upon their bier for the funeral, lying in the stillness of death, and trying to breathe as inconspicuously as possible.

This was not helped by a voice—she felt certain it was Red himself which called out cheerfully: *"She* ain't no corpse—I can see her tits going up and down!"

Coral gritted her teeth and wished she were dead indeed.

There was an open grave, improvised from a few yards of green canvas spread over some old packing-cases, and into the uncomfortable hollow between them, Ophelia's remains were respectfully laid.

Mrs. Mountford sprinkled a handful of paper flowers upon her (*Sweets to the sweet—farewell!*) and one petal landed on her nose and made her want to sneeze, but she resisted the temptation heroically. She was aware all the time of Gerard standing by the grave, glaring furiously down at her, and professing brotherly love in tones that were highly unconvincing—with Rory, a few yards away, scowling at the pair of them.

As the gravediggers prepared to shovel the first spadeful of sawdust upon the corpse, Gerard cried crossly:
"Hold off the earth a while—
Till I have caught her once more in my arms . . ."
And, as rehearsed, he leaped down into the shallow grave, and embraced her. At the same moment, he hissed

356

in her ear: "You enjoyed making love to Rory last night —come on, confess—you know you did—"

Then he continued loudly, for the benefit of the audience: *"Now pile your dust upon the quick and dead—"*

"Take your hands off my breasts, you brute—" whispered Ophelia, struggling in Laertes' arms.

"To o'ertop old Pelion, or the skyish head of blue Olympus—" Laertes ranted on, and planted a firm kiss upon her lips.

"Don't you kiss me—don't you dare!" she protested, losing her head and beginning to fight him off.

Hamlet had to take up his next speech at this point, but he could hardly make himself heard, for the murmur of amusement that had arisen from the audience, and the sounds of Laertes and his late sister, engaged in a heated argument.

". . . This is I, Hamlet the Dane!" he shouted at last, and, in his turn, leaped into the grave to grapple with Laertes.

The makeshift sepulchre was hardly big enough to accomodate three bodies, and by now Laertes and Ophelia were engaged in hand-to-hand combat. Hamlet tried to drag them apart—Ophelia exclaimed: "Don't *you* start!"

—while Laertes carried on with his next line, which was: *"The devil take thy soul—"*

—at the same time kneeing Hamlet in the groin.

Hamlet thereupon gasped: *"I prithee—take they fingers from my throat—"* and gave him a swift clout across the jaw.

Ophelia shouted: "Get off me—the pair of you—you great lumps!"

And one of the packing-cases collapsed, as the three protagonists rolled across the stage, locked in battle.

Mrs. Mountford screamed, Dermot exploded with rage; the audience roared with delight, and from the wings, Walter Wilkins very sensibly rang the curtain down.

Oblivious of this, Gerard had got hold of Coral by the shoulders and was shaking her till her teeth rattled, shouting: "You damned infuriating, stubborn little baggage—for two pins I'd throw you over my knee and give you a good hiding—"

Walter commented laconically: "The poor soul's had a brain-storm—he thinks he's playing Petruchio now."

Then, with a little tinkle, Coral's wedding ring which had been shaken all the way down from its resting-place within her bosom—landed at her feet and rolled across the stage, while Mrs. Mountford moaned: "I think you dropped something, dear . . . Your wedding ring—"

"I don't want it!" yelled Coral. "I never want to see it again—and I never want to see you either, Gerard Kean. I wouldn't marry you if you were the last man on earth!"

And with that, she ran off into the wings.

Dermot went out before the curtain and tried to make an announcement, but the house was in an uproar. Red Haskell's best buddies in the Grand Circle had decided to improve the occasion by starting a few free fights of their own. It was clear that, as far as the Park Theatre, New York, was concerned—*Hamlet* would remain forever an unfinished masterpiece.

The company dispersed to their dressing-rooms, and someone extinguished all the lights, except for one working lamp which remained, casting long shadows across the empty stage.

But the stage wasn't quite empty. When everyone else had gone, Coral returned, stifling her tears, and dropping to her hands and knees. Patiently, she began to search every corner of the boards, looking for the lost wedding ring.

The next morning, the notices in the daily newspaper were universally bad—(except for one critic who had obviously abandoned his post before the end, and optimistically reported a "qualified triumph," with no mention of the last act disaster at all)—but what really wounded Dermot most deeply was a review that singled him out for special treatment, saying: "Last night Mr. Dermot Maguire played the King as if in momentary expectation that someone else was about to place the Ace."

It was a good line, and one that was destined to be used more than once as the years rolled on; so in his own small way, Dermot had contributed to theatrical history—but that was no consolation to him now.

He did not waste much time in reprimanding the three combatants whose quarrel had provoked the final disaster; one short sharp lecture upon their unprofessional and childish behavior was enough. He could see from their downcast expression that they had suffered already.

The important thing was to decide upon the next move.

"Obviously we can't stay here—we're a public laughing-stock by this time," he announced. "I have therefore decided to cut our losses and move on. Kindly pack your bags, ladies and gentlemen for we are going to open in Washington as soon as possible. Washington is a civilized city, a place of culture and refinement—they will appreciate us there."

"But won't our reputation travel ahead of us, after last night?" asked Walter Wilkins.

"I doubt that Washington ever takes much interest in events that occur in New York," said Dermot. "Besides, they're all politicians, and they've got quite enough to think about already, with these rumors of war . . ."

It was true that the newspapers were getting into a ferment about the war with Great Britain which had been dragging on for two years. In Europe, the politicians were trying to hammer out the terms of a peace treaty, but the British troops had landed in Maryland by now, and were intent upon a show of force.

So far, it had been a bloodless invasion, and the soldiers advanced up the course of the Patuxent river without any opposition until they arrived at Bladensburg. But there, the American troops were preparing to take a stand and suddenly it seemed that Bladensburg was, after all, only a stone's throw away from the capital city itself—a bare five miles from Washington.

When the Maguire Company arrived in Washington, they found the whole place in an uproar. Rumors were buzzing upon all sides, and yet, strangely enough, no one was prepared to admit the awful possibility that the British might actually dare to advance upon the very heart of the Republic, and storm Capitol Hill itself.

In consequence, everyone tried to pretend that life must go on as usual, and theatres, dinner parties, balls and routs still continued to flourish, in an atmosphere of feverish gaiety.

"I don't think they're in the mood for Shakespeare," Dermot pronounced, a few hours after they moved in to the Ford Theatre, and began to unpack their properties and costumes. "Let's postpone *Hamlet* until the times are more propitious. These people want something to take them out of themselves—I propose that we revive the dear old *Lily of Killarney*. Walter—do we have a plentiful supply of red fire?"

His judgement was sound; for once, Dermot appeared to have put his finger on the public pulse with complete accuracy.

The first night of the *Lily* was a huge success, and as soon as the curtain fell, several of the leading lights in Washington society made their way backstage, with congratulations, plaudits and invitations.

Most of the company had admirers of one kind or another, and were being kept busy accepting compliments and bouquets, or signing playbills but the unhappy trio of Gerard, Coral and Rory held back from the general throng, at the side of the stage.

They were still barely on speaking terms, even now; since Coral had so dramatically, and publicly, broken off her engagement, she had scarcely said a word to Gerard. And the two men were still avoiding each other as far as possible. When they acquired lodgings in this city, they went their separate ways; there was no question of their sharing a bedroom any more.

As they stood uneasily in the wings, an effusive lady with a plump but pleasing figure, and melting brown eyes —suddenly spied them there and descended upon them enthusiastically.

"Why hello!" she cried gaily. "My three special favorites and all together, too—now isn't that lucky? I simply *must* tell you how much I enjoyed watching you all in the play tonight. Miss Maguire, you were simply too delightful and Mr. O'Malley, so very dashing . . . and—" she hesitated, glancing a little shyly at Gerard . . . "It's Mr. Kean, isn't it?"

"How observant of you to notice me," said Gerard; with a polite smile. "For I have so little to do in this piece if you blink your eyes, you'd miss me."

"Oh, I noticed you all right," she said, with a touch of emphasis. "Yes, indeed, Mr. Kean . . . but you must allow me to introduce myself—my name's Vanderburg, Mrs. Esther Vanderburg. Of course my husband should really be here to perform the introductions, but he's so busy right now. Well, you see, Harry's got an important post in the Government—he's the President's right-hand man —so naturally, with all this trouble going on, he's away on business a great deal. And that's why I'm feeling quite lonesome, all by myself—and I hoped you three charming young people would be good enough to give me the pleasure of your company at dinner tomorrow night? Miss Maguire—Mr. O'Malley—and you too, Mr. Kean, of course."

They exchanged glances and looked away again. Coral reflected that the last thing she desired at this moment was a sociable evening with this amiable, but garrulous lady.

"I'm so sorry," she said with all the sincerity she could muster. "It's very kind of you, but we have to give another performance tomorrow night—we shan't be free—"

"Oh, I meant *after* the play, naturally . . . Come, you won't disappoint me, will you? I'd so much like to repay a little of the entertainment you've all provided for us this evening."

"Alas, ma'am," said Rory gallantly, taking his cue from Coral. "Nothing would give me greater happiness, but I fear I cannot spare the time."

Gerard looked swiftly at Coral; but she was determined not to meet his eye: her profile held high, she maintained an air of frozen courtesy, and he resented it. How dare she be so high-and-mighty after all they had been to one another?

Then he stole another glance at Mrs. Esther Vanderburg—she was certainly a very warm-hearted and genial lady and her curving shape held promise of an equally generous nature. She smiled at him hopefully, and some spark of understanding passed between them as she said: "That's too bad—but how about *you*, Mr. Kean? I'm sure you're not going to disappoint me, are you?"

Instantly, Gerard made up his mind.

"I hope not, Mrs. Vanderburg . . . Thank you for your kind invitation—I shall accept it, of course. With the greatest pleasure!"

(4)

Movement of Troops

When Gerard and Rory repaired to their dressing room, to get out of their costumes and remove their greasepaint, they were soon interrupted.

Coral tore in like an avenging fury, intent upon a confrontation with Gerard. It did not matter to her that both men were half-dressed—Gerard stripped to the waist, his face dripping wet as he bent over the wash-basin, and Rory in his drawers and undershirt, about to struggle into his streetclothes.

"Now just a moment!" Rory protested. "Are we to have no sort of privacy at all?"

Coral ignored him completely, and made for Gerard at once.

"How dare you make an assignation with that vulgar, overdressed female?" she demanded. "What on earth are you thinking of?"

"The same sort of thing *she's* thinking of, I should imagine," retorted Gerard, picking up a towel to dry his face.

"What d'you mean by that? She's fat—and forty if she's a day—old enough to be your mother—"

"My dearest girl, she's only invited me to dine with her. Aren't you reading a little too much into a harmless gesture of hospitality? You were both included in the invitation originally, after all," he reminded her.

"Oh, she didn't want *us*—it's you she had her eye on—I saw the way she was looking at you, the shameless hussy!" snapped Coral.

"Why shouldn't he dine with the woman if he wants to?" asked Rory, reasonably enough.

They both turned on him with one accord and told him to keep out of this—it was none of his business.

"You're planning to go to bed with the creature—come, admit it!" Coral accused Gerard, snatching the towel from his hands, and flinging it aside. "Look me in the eye and confess!"

"And why not?" Gerard was beginning to get really angry now. "Since you've told me plainly you want nothing more to do with me—"

"Oh, you brute—you profligate—you *fornicator!*" She seemed as if she would attack him physically, and he caught her wrists and held them as she panted: "Let go of me—you can't look at any woman without wanting to bed her—you even had lecherous thoughts about Rosalie —I could tell—"

The door opened, and old Dermot came in at this moment.

"What the devil is going on here? You're making enough noise to wake the whole city—what's got into you all?"

"It's your charming niece—accusing me of having lewd designs upon her sister."

Gerard flung Coral aside, and made for his shirt and jacket, continuing to dress himself.

"What? Saints preserve us all—what a notion—" Dermot was shocked.

"Oh, don't imagine I haven't been tempted, right enough," Gerard threw over his shoulder. "Rosalie and I have shared some moments of intimacy and affection before now and why not? For she's a generous, warm-hearted girl, strangely different from her nearest and dearest, her little shrew of a sister!"

Dermot began to protest against these shameless sentiments but Coral did not waste time on words. With her green eyes blazing and her copper curls tumbling about her shoulders, she began an assault on Gerard with every portable object that came to hand.

Pots of cream, boxes of powder, a jug, a kettle, a hairbrush—any and every item upon the dressing table was pressed into service, and Gerard put up both hands to ward off the shower of flying missiles.

At last, Rory and Dermot managed to control Coral's fiery outburst between them, and separated the two adversaries.

As they contrived to remove Coral from the room, she called out defiantly: "Keep out of my way from now on, Gerard Kean, for I've finished with you, for good and all ... I'll never speak to you again, as long as I live!"

Her furious temper sustained her at this pitch of indignation until she got back to her lodgings; but once she was undressed and in her bed, her mood changed completely, and she wept as if her heart would break, sobbing bitter tears until her pillow was wet, and at last crying herself into an exhausted sleep.

When she awoke, late the following day, she found Mrs. Mountford who slept in the adjoining room shaking her gently, and saying: "Get up, my dear—get up quickly. Your uncle has sent me to rouse you, for there's some terrible news."

She was awake instantly: "What is it? What's happened? Is it Gerard?"

"No ... whatever do you mean? Gerard's safe enough, as far as I know. Except of course, he isn't. We are none of us safe, not any more. That's the whole trouble!"

Coral rubbed her eyes and tried to make sense of the good lady's incoherent tidings.

"I'm sent to tell you to get dressed, and make yourself ready to leave as soon as possible ... The British are coming!"

"What? I don't understand—"

"Nor do I, my dear, but it seems there was a battle yesterday, and now the British army is marching upon Washington, to rape and pillage and murder us all in our beds. Everyone is preparing to flee from the city! Oh, woe is me!" she concluded, dramatically, wringing her hands.

"But what about the theatre—the scenery and costumes—"

"Your Uncle's over there now, with some of the gentlemen, trying to pack all he can take with him before the enemy arrives."

"But Mrs. Mountford, do stop and consider—we are British ourselves—how can we be in any danger? The English troops will never harm *us!*"

"It's best not to take any chances, Coral—if the soldiery catch us, they will not stop to ask questions—they will rob us and ravish us, poor helpless creatures that we are, without so much as a by-your-leave!"

Coral glanced at Mrs. Mountford's ample proportions, and reflected that it would be a very determined ravisher who would attempt any violation upon such an impregnable fortress but she held her tongue, and said nothing.

As soon as she was dressed, she went across to the theatre, half-expecting to find Gerard there, perhaps but Dermot was alone with Walter Wilkins, strapping up the costumes in their wicker baskets.

"Don't alarm yourself, my darling," her Uncle tried to calm her as best he could. "I've already made preparations for our safety. The theatre manager has relatives at Markwick, a farmstead some twenty miles outside the city —he has suggested we should all make our way there, while we consider what is best to be done."

"But where are the others? Rory—and—and Gerard—" Coral began.

"They're probably upstairs, clearing out the dressing rooms—now don't stop to argue, there's a good girl . . . I've arranged for a carriage to take a party of you off to Markwick Farm at the first possible moment—and the driver's waiting below, at the stage door . . . I will follow on as quickly as I can."

Coral was forced to obey; on her way down the echoing stone steps, she met Rory and Gerard on the half landing, carrying a heavy trunk between them. She caught her breath, and lifted her chin defiantly.

Ignoring Gerard altogether, she asked Rory: "I'm told there's a carriage waiting to take us out of town—are you coming with us, Rory?"

"Not yet—there's plenty to be done here—" began Rory.

"That's true . . . For I have an assignation with a certain lady this evening—or had you forgotten?" asked Gerard impudently.

She tossed her head and ran on down the stairs without another word or glance in his direction.

"Are you really planning to go through with that—even now?" Rory inquired curiously.

"Why shouldn't I? I'm not afraid of the British army . . . and it would be churlish to disappoint Mrs. Vanderburg!" Gerard winked.

"You're a cool customer and no mistake." Rory wiped his brow, before hoisting the trunk again. "Maybe I'll stay on in the city myself and follow your example—the stage-manager tells me all the saloons have been open since daybreak, and the liquor's flowing like water!"

So the carriage that was to take the first party away to safety finally departed with a lot of luggage tied up on the roof, and only two passengers inside—Coral herself, and Mrs. Mountford; both of them surrounded by every kind of bag and baggage.

Perhaps because the saloons were all doing a roaring trade, the coach-driver seemed a little unreliable. Coral smelled the reek of whisky on his breath, and noticed that his hands shook as he held the reins. He whipped up the elderly nag that struggled gamely between the shafts, and tried to effect their escape from the city as fast as possible.

After they had been rattling along for some twenty minutes, and had left the outskirts of Washington well behind them, he reined in the horse, crying: "Whoa back! Hold still, you pesky animal—just you stop right there!"

Inside the coach, Coral and Mrs. Mountford looked at one another. Then Coral opened the window and leaned out.

"What's the trouble, driver? Have you lost your way?"

"Not lost it, ma'am—but it strikes me we'd do better to take another route to Markwick after all."

"Why is that?"

By way of answer, he pointed the handle of the whip to a signpost at the crossroads just ahead. Directly in front was a dusty road which led—according to the sign—to Markwick . . . and Bladensburg.

"I ain't a-going no further in *that* direction—no, sirree . . . That's where the battle was, so I heard tell—and that's the way the British will be coming in directly . . . If we go on like this, we'll most likely drive straight into 'em! They'll be waiting for us with open arms."

Mrs. Mountford gave a little cry: "Oh, no—no," she moaned. "Anything but that—!"

"What are you proposing to do, then?" asked Coral.

"Why, I'll have to make a detour, I guess. Take one of the side roads and try to get to Markwick from another direction—cross country."

"Yes, yes—whatever you think best—only do let us make haste!" urged Mrs. Mountford.

"But what about Uncle Dermot, and the rest?" Coral asked. "If they follow us, as they intend to do—they will not know which way we are gone . . . and even worse—*they* might meet the troops advancing, too."

"We can't stay here arguing the toss," grumbled the driver, getting more and more agitated. "Let 'em take their chance—I'm getting out of here while the going's good!"

"Well, I'm *not!*"

Coral made up her mind, opened the door and jumped down by the roadside.

"Coral dear, where are you going?"

"I'm staying here until Uncle Dermot arrives; you two can go on and make your own way to the farm. I'll stop here and warn the others, and we'll join you as soon as we can."

368

"But my dear—the danger—the soldiers!" wailed Mrs. Mountford.

"I'll take care, don't worry. Drive on, coachman!"

He needed no second bidding; the carriage wheeled round and trundled off in another direction, setting up a fine cloud of dust as it disappeared.

Once the noise had died away, everything seemed amazingly still. Coral could hear a gnat singing, and the rustle of leaves in the little coppice that bordered the road. The air was heavy and close, and she sensed that there was thunder about. It was very hot.

Suddenly, she felt a pang of fear; she had no idea how long it would be before her uncle arrived. Had she behaved very foolishly—leaving herself stranded here, alone, and in the face of the advancing troops?

Well, it was too late to change her mind now.

She decided to take shelter among the trees. It would be cooler there, out of the sun, and if any unwelcome strangers appeared, she should be able to keep out of sight.

The little grove of trees was lush and green, and she threw herself down among the long grasses, to keep watch upon the road.

It was almost unbearably sultry, and she felt rather tired. Perhaps her night's repose had not been as restful as usual; after her last quarrel with Gerard, she—

But she must not think about Gerard. It would only upset her again. Better to put any thoughts of Gerard completely from her mind.

She would lie here and relax . . . and think of nothing at all. She let her eyelids close, and stretched out upon the soft carpet of grass and waited.

It seemed only a moment later that she heard the first sounds of the advancing army. The clip-clop of hoofs, and the jingle of harness; the heavy rumble of wagons and the blast of a bugle. Her muscles tensed as she remembered Mrs. Mountford's warnings. Suppose that the good lady were right after all, and the soldiers were intent upon attacking every unprotected female who came their way?

She heard the noise of the army's approach growing louder still, and the tramp of marching feet. As long as they stayed upon the road, she would be safe enough in her leafy hiding-place.

"Well, blow me down—what have we got here?"

A loud voice startled her almost out of her wits; she rolled over on one elbow, and looked up—to find a little group of soldiers in scarlet uniforms staring down at her.

They were sweating and dusty; they had been slogging along the hard highroad in the full blaze of the sun, and they had decided to turn off into the shadow of the trees, to escape from the heat.

"Go away—leave me alone—" she said, as firmly as she could; but her voice trembled a little.

"What? Leave a young lady all on her own? That wouldn't be very polite—would it now?" said the leader of the group.

With a sickening feeling of despair, Coral realized that they were moving slowly forward, surrounding her and they were all grinning broadly.

"I told you to go away!" she continued. "I—I'm waiting for some friends—they'll be here at any moment—"

"Lord love you, we're your friends, darling!" chuckled the ringleader, fumbling in the knapsack that hung over his hip.

"You're British soldiers, and I am—"

"You're our prisoner-of-war . . . ain't that so, mates?"

The men broke into a guffaw, and at the same moment, the leader pulled out a length of rope from his pack.

"Here—two of you—hold her fast, while I tie her up. That's how we treat prisoners, darling—we have to make sure you won't run away!"

She struggled violently, but she was hopelessly out-numbered, and she could see from their expression what their intentions were.

"If you do any harm to me—" she protested, her voice rising in fear.

"Quick, Joe, stuff a gag in her mouth—if there's one thing I can't stand, it's a female what's screaming in me ears . . . harm you, my little darling? Not a bit of it—

we're going to kill you with kindness—ain't that right?"

The men laughed again, as they tied her hands behind her, then passed the rope round both her ankles and pulled it tight so that she was forced back with knees bent, and her body straining in an arc. A grubby kerchief which had been round someone's neck was tied across her open mouth, and the smell of sweat and dirt was overpowering; she felt her gorge rising, and she fought for breath.

"Now then, my beauty . . ."

Suddenly the leader had a knife in his hand and her heart turned over. Was he, then, planning to kill her?

But no . . . the plan was more devilish than that.

Slowly and methodically, he put the point of the blade to her garments, unpicking a seam here, cutting away laces, ripping her clothes apart, piece by piece.

She lay helplessly on the grass, like a trussed fowl, unable to move or speak, while her attacker continued with his cruel preparations.

She felt her dress being slashed in two, and peeled away from her body, her bodice cut wide open and dragged down, until her breasts were exposed completely. The waistband of her half-petticoat was snipped in half, and the thin material tugged ruthlessly from her naked thighs. Finally, brutal fingers tore at her one remaining garment, and half a dozen hands tugged at her limbs, wrenching her knees apart, forcing her on to her back, her entire body open to their vile assault.

She could not speak, or scream, or struggle—she could do nothing to prevent the repeated attacks that must surely follow—

If only she could wake up!

And that is what she did.

She lay panting on the grass for a moment, her heart pounding, feeling trickles of cold sweat running down her spine.

How stupid! She must have dozed off, and dreamed the whole ghastly incident; it had been a nightmare, and nothing more.

Except—she caught her breath, and listened, hearing

the clip-clop of horses' hooves, and the jingle of harness, and the tramp of marching feet . . . was the nightmare about to become reality?

With infinite caution, she peeped out through the leafy undergrowth and long grass and with a thrill of recognition, she saw the English troops marching past; royal blue cavalry and scarlet foot-soldiers, heavy gun-carriages and wagons, all moving slowly forward, on the road to Washington.

Too frightened to move, hardly daring to breathe, she watched the military cavalcade passing by, from her hiding-place, praying she would not be discovered. And then—

The snap of a twig alerted her but it was too late. She heard a footfall upon the ground behind her, and a dry, cracked voice, with an unfamiliar twang to it, asked: "What are you doing there, lady?"

It wasn't an English accent, either; she felt sure of that. She rolled over than gasped in terror.

This was a nightmare of a different kind, for the man standing over her had a gray face, and his skin was disfigured by some hideous disease. Half his jaw was missing, and where his nose should have been, there were two holes for nostrils, raw and blood-red.

Seeing her recoil, he said: "Yeah—I'm a leper . . . so keep your distance, but what are *you,* lady?"

She could not reply; her throat was dry with fear—she shook her head dumbly, shrinking from the stranger.

He took a step toward her, continuing: "Tell the truth now—are you spying on the Britishers?"

They were interrupted by another newcomer.

"What is it? What have you found?"

And a second later, a young English officer stepped out between the trees, staring at Coral in surprise.

"I reckon this here woman's been sent to spy on us, Ensign—I came upon her watching the troops go by—hiding here, she was—" began the leper.

Coral interrupted desperately: "It's not true—I don't know what you're talking about—I fell asleep, and when I woke up . . . I saw them marching past. So I lay here out of sight till they were all gone. That's all."

She searched the young man's face; he was certainly very young—he had no hair on his smooth cheeks, and his voice was hardly broken. And, strangely, there was something about his manner—his tone—that reminded her of someone else.

"Very well—I believe you," the young officer said at last, then added to his companion: "Get along now . . . She's no spy . . . I'm sorry that you've been disturbed, ma'am."

Coral watched the leper go, trying to pull herself together.

"What is to happen to me now?" she asked, as calmly as she could. "Am I to be taken prisoner?"

The young Englishman smiled briefly and there it was again, that flash of resemblance!—then replied: "No, ma'am. We have no quarrel against the people of America—only against her government . . . I shall be very happy to leave you here—in peace."

He sketched a half-bow, and then walked on, to rejoin the remainder of his regiment.

Coral stayed where she was, and thought over this odd, inexplicable encounter. What was the Ensign doing, travelling in the company of that horrifying sick man? He was certainly a strange youngster. She felt sure she would remember him, whoever he was, for a long, long while.

The slow movement of troops continued for some time, but nobody else penetrated her hiding-place, or explored the little grove.

Eventually, as the daylight began to fade, and the shadows lay low across the trees and hedgerows, the last stragglers passed on and departed, and Coral was alone again, breathing a long sigh of relief.

She wondered what she should do; she wondered where her uncle was—had he taken another route after all? If so, how would she find her way safely to Markwick?

She knew which road the coach-driver had picked, and decided to follow that. Dusting the leaves and grasses from her skirt, she began to make herself ready for what promised to be a very difficult journey and then tensed, listening to the sound of yet another horse and cart approaching.

Undecided whether to hide once more, or ask for assistance, she recognized that it was proceeding from the general direction of the city, and took a chance.

She stepped out boldly into the road, and hailed the driver. Even before the horse drew to a standstill, she recognized the passengers in the carriage. Uncle Dermot popped his head out of one window, while Walter Wilkins gesticulated from the other.

"Coral—by all that's wonderful—what are you doing here in the middle of nowhere?" Dermot demanded. "Get in quickly, child, or we'll never reach the farm before dark—did you see the troops going by upon the road? We had to take shelter behind a haystack—I thought they'd never be done marching past . . ."

Coral climbed into the coach, and they continued upon their way to Markwick.

"In the words of the mighty bard—all's well that ends well," boomed Dermot.

Coral said nothing. She was not quite so optimistic as her uncle.

However, by nightfall, most of the Maguire Touring Company had taken up temporary accommodation at the farmstead.

"It's only a shakedown in a barn," Mrs. Mountford explained to Coral, when they were reunited, "but beggars you know, can hardly be choosers and at least we're all safe now, heaven be praised."

But were they?

Some time before midnight, Dermot said to his niece: "I feel like taking a stroll before I retire to rest . . . a little perambulation to stretch my limbs—would you care to accompany me?"

Coral agreed, and they set off upon a brief tour of the estate. Behind the farmhouse, the land rose steeply, and they made for the top of the little hill, walking side by side, without speaking.

When they reached the crest, they turned and looked back, the way they had come.

The sky was like black velvet above them but further off—some twenty miles away—the undersides of the clouds were glowing with a strange, unnatural light.

374

"That's Washington," said Dermot, quietly. "The city has fallen . . . they're burning it down."

They both watched, with a kind of sick fascination; the night sky changed color—red and orange—as the distant fires took hold. Everything here was still and peaceful, but over there, only a short distance away—hell itself was breaking loose.

In the silence, Coral said at last: "Not all the company managed to get away, after all . . ."

"No," said Dermot. "There are still two missing."

Coral wondered anxiously about Rory, in the midst of that infernal destruction. Did he escape in time? Was he safe? Where was he at this moment?

And then she faced the most agonizing thought of all; a thoght she had been trying to escape all day.

Gerard . . . what had happened to Gerard?

(5)

The Turning Point

For several days, time seemed to be at a standstill. The Maguire Company, with the exception of its two leading juveniles, established themselves comfortably enough in the farmstead at Markwick, and waited for news.

Soon, word came through that the British troops had departed from Washington, and fallen back upon their naval flotilla in the Patuxent River and Chesapeake Bay. It was said that the President, Mr. Madison, had returned to Capitol Hill with various members of his cabinet, with the intention of picking up the pieces that were left behind when the invaders moved out. Slowly, life was returning to the nation's headquarters—but of course it would be some while before the normal routine of social entertainment was resumed. While the theatres remained closed, there was little to be gained by returning to the city.

So, for the time being, Dermot Maguire's troupe stayed where they were and waited.

It was a hard time for Coral. Once or twice Dermot

asked her if she were still worrying about Gerard and
Rory, and she assured him that she was not. They were
both strong young men, well able to take care of themselves. No doubt they would turn up again one of these
fine days when they were least expected—as carefree and
irresponsible as ever.

But she wasn't sleeping well, and Mrs. Mountford grew
quite anxious over the heavy mauve rings beneath Coral's
eyes.

"You're pining, my dear—I can tell," she said, patting
Coral's hand as they sat outside the old barn one evening
at twilight.

"Pining? For Gerard? The very idea!" Coral tossed
her head. "I've forgotten him long since, didn't you
know?"

There was a little silence, broken by the sound of carriage wheels approaching, somewhere at the other side of
the farmhouse, and the sleepy, wordless music of some
hired hands coming in from the fields, singing to themselves.

Someone had lit a bonfire in the yard, and several members of the Maguire Company lay stretched out around it,
gazing into the flames.

Walter Wilkins was toasting lumps of cheese on the
end of a pointed stick, and he called across to Coral and
Mrs. Mountford: "D'ye want a snack before supper?"

They refused his offer, and Mrs. Mountford continued
after a time, in a low tone: "Well, that's what you tell
me, Coral dear, but I can't help having my own opinions.
You don't look at all well, child, and I confess I'm quite
concerned for you."

One of the farmhands stopped by the bonfire to exchange a few words with the assembled actors, and was
rewarded with a scrap of toasted cheese.

Idly, he remarked: "They say there's some more of you
folk that's just arrived by coach from the city. More
actors come to join you, as I heard tell."

Coral sat up quickly: "More actors—here? Who are
they?"

"I wouldn't know, ma'am. I saw a tall young feller

377

climbing out of a carriage when I was walking back from the meadow—that's all I can say for sure."

Coral clutched Mrs. Mountford's arm: "It will be Rory —and Gerard. Safe and sound, thank goodness. Not that I care, you understand but I'm glad to know they've not to come to any harm."

She stood up, straightening her dress and dabbing at her hair, as footsteps approached on the gravel path that led round the side of the barn.

The newcomer was Rory . . . and he was alone.

"Where's Gerard?" Coral asked as casually as possible, once the first exchange of greetings had been concluded, and Rory had joined the circle around the fire.

"Ah—yes—I was coming to that . . ."

Rory's face darkened, and he scratched his head uncomfortably.

"I rather lost touch with Gerard, the day the British marched in . . . I went on a drinking-bout with our stage-manager, and—well—the next couple of days and nights were a bit confused."

He cleared his throat, then resumed: "The next thing I knew—the British were gone, and the Yankees were back. And that's when I began making inquiries about young Gerard. Nobody seemed to know what had become of him, but finally I ran across a character called Harry Vanderburg—it seems he's the husband of that society hostess who invited us all to dine with her—do you remember, Coral?"

"I remember very well," said Coral evenly.

"And for some reason he'd made it his business to trace Gerard's movements over the last week or two . . . he told me that he's been taken prisoner by the British troops—"

"What?"

"It's all right—don't look so alarmed—he's still alive and well . . . Only—mind you, I don't understand all this, but seemingly they claimed that our Gerard is really an English military officer who'd got separated from his regiment . . . Ensign Gerard Mallory, his real name is."

"I don't understand—what are you saying?" Coral put

her hand to her bosom, as if she would subdue the furious beating of her heart. *"Where is Gerard?"*

"Gone off to the war, in an Ensign's uniform, to fight with his comrades-in-arms . . . they do say the British are now preparing a fresh attack—upon the city of Baltimore."

There was a moment of silence, and then Coral turned and walked away without another word. As the evening shadows lengthened, she left the cosy farmyard and climbed the little hill behind the house. She had to be alone—she had to think.

Rory glanced across at Mrs. Mountford, uncertainly.

"Will she be all right? I realize it must be a shock to her but I had no way of breaking the news gently. Besides, after the way she and Gerard parted the last time, I wasn't sure how much she'd care, anyway."

Mrs. Mountford said: "She cares, Mr. O'Malley—Oh, yes, she cares. Go after her and try to cheer her if you can. She's a very unhappy young lady."

So Rory set off in pursuit of Coral.

He found her at last, seated under a thorn tree at the top of the hill. It was almost dark by now, but she was gazing out at the night sky, as if she could see for a very long way.

She heard him coming, but did not turn her head.

"Coral?" he began, a little breathless after the climb. "It's me . . . we wondered where you'd hidden yourself."

Gazing straight ahead, she remarked: "Washington's over there . . . we came up here and saw the sky ablaze, the night they set fire to the city. And somewhere beyond that—there's Baltimore."

"Don't trouble yourself too much. I'm sure Gerard will be safe—he'll struggle through somehow, you'll see—"

Now she turned to look at him, and her eyes were shining like stars.

"How can you say that? How can you know what will happen to him? At any hour of the day or night, he might be in danger—he's a soldier now—a soldier in battle. And if he were to die a soldier's death tomorrow, I would never see him again."

"Coral, don't think such things—"

She rose to her feet, her fine, determined profile pale against the velvet night.

"What a fool I have been . . . I let him go, God help me, I turned him away—"

"You had a quarrel, that's only natural—"

"But a quarrel over such futile, petty things. Pride—and jealousy . . . as if any of that mattered! Because I know now, without any doubt I love him, Rory. I love him with all my heart . . . and I am going to him."

"What? That's impossible—"

"Oh, no—I shall find him, sooner or later. I don't care where he is, or how long it takes me—I've been so selfish and stupid, and I said such dreadful things to him. But now I know for certain that he's the one man in this whole world for me and it's not too late to put things right."

"But—how?"

"You said the British forces plan to attack Baltimore. Very well—then I shall go to Baltimore and find him."

"Just think for a moment—consider the danger you will be in."

"A fortune-teller once told me I was in danger of death. Well, so is he—so we may challenge death together! Besides, I ran risks every bit as great when I was in France."

"In France you had Gerard with you—you were not alone."

Rory hesitated for a split second, then took a deep breath, and continued: "And you won't be alone this time, either . . . for I shall come with you."

"No—Rory, that's not necessary."

"It is what I wish to do. Don't you see? I feel responsible for what happens to Gerard. If it were not for me, and a man that died one time in Dublin, Gerard would not have had to flee from Ireland. Probably none of this would ever have happened. The least I can do now is to help you to find him again."

It wasn't as straightforward as that, of course; nothing ever is. They had to explain the situation to Dermot, and for the second time the old man had to face the prospect of losing his leading players. But he could tell

380

from the expression in Coral's eyes that her mind was made up, and he could not stand in her way.

This was the turning-point. From this moment, Coral never again wavered in her commitment to Gerard, or her undying love for him. Come what may, he was her man; and she would never rest until they were reunited once more.

There were some maddening delays before they could set out upon their journey to Baltimore. No one could be sure how long they might have to travel, so Coral had to take all her luggage with her—and it took Rory several days to find a horse and buggy with a driver bold enough to escort them to the scene of another battle.

But Baltimore was in a very different situation from careless, unprepared Washington. From the first possible moment, the city had made its preparations to withstand an enemy attack; earthworks were dug, artillery mounted along the shoreline, and army reinforcements sent in from all quarters. When the British finally launched their assault, Baltimore was ready for them, the American flag was flying from the city fort at nightfall, and the next morning when the sun arose, it was flying still.

By the time Coral and Rory arrived in the city, the battle was over, and the British had retired once again to lick their wounds in the streets; broadsheets were already on sale to celebrate the American victory.

Rory bought one and scanned it quickly for news.

"Why—it seems that there's a poet among us somewhere," he reported. "Some young American lawyer who sat out the night of the bombardment—he's celebrated his country's flag by writing some verses . . . *'Oh, say can you see—by the dawn's early—'*"

Coral interrupted him impatiently. "Never mind the verses—where are the English troops now, Rory? Which way must we go to follow them?"

This was a problem indeed; according to the latest intelligence, the majority of the British forces had retreated to the fleet which still remained at anchor, safely out of range in Chesapeake Bay . . . and there was no way to communicate with them there.

"Where will they go next, do you suppose?" Coral

asked, as they sat over a scratch meal of bread and boiled bacon at a waterfront inn.

The landlord, pouring a tankard of ale for Rory, overheard the question and answered it.

"The Britishers? If they've any sense at all, they'll head for the South. They've had a sound thrashing up here, and they won't risk another, I'll take my oath on that. But if they were to move down to the southern states, they'd be assured of a much warmer welcome."

"What? Why?" Coral wrinkled her brow. "Why should the Southerners love the English any better than their northern cousins?"

By way of reply, the landlord jerked his thumb, indicating a huge bale of cotton that stood immediately outside the window of the inn, awaiting shipment from the quayside.

"Cotton . . ."

"Cotton?" Rory and Coral looked at him blankly.

"The cotton-growers down south don't want this war. The British are some of their best customers—they'd be very glad to make peace again, and unload all their stocks of cotton on to the English market as soon as possible. If that there British Admiral has any sense at all, he'll head southwards and try to do a deal."

The man moved off, and Coral nodded slowly.

"I think he's right . . . so that means—we should make for the South as well." She shivered a little, and drew her cloak about her more closely. "Will you make arrangements for us to travel on tomorrow, Rory?"

"It's going to be a horribly long, slow journey," Rory warned her. "This is a huge continent—we'll have to cover many hundreds of miles—thousands, even . . . and you're not looking well."

"Nonsense. I'll be as right as rain after a night's sleep. But if you're not anxious to accompany me, then I'll travel on alone."

Rory sighed.

"Very well . . . I'll go and make inquiries. It'll mean travelling by stagecoach."

So the expedition began. Day after day, they journeyed onward, by roads that followed the Atlantic coastline

382

for the most part, and day after day the weather became more and more sultry and oppressive as they headed south.

The stage coach was not a comfortable mode of conveyance, and they were forced to share cramped accommodation with a motley crew of fellow passengers—a fat cleric, who dozed and snored and refreshed himself from a pocket flask and snored again; a brassy blonde lady with a feathered hat who announced that she was travelling to Charleston to find her husband (Rory whispered in Coral's ear: "I'll wager the poor unsuspecting gentleman doesn't even know of her existence yet!") and an assortment of salesmen and bagmen who carried bulky samples of their wares, and grumbled over the high prices.

It was slow—it was hot—it was extremely tedious. And for Coral, it soon became a good deal worse than that; for on one point she had been totally in error.

She was *not* "as right as rain" when she set out upon the journey to the deep south. Whether she had eaten something that disagreed with her—could it have been the boiled bacon?—or whether she had picked up some infection along the way, she never knew. But she was certainly feeling very ill indeed.

By the time the stagecoach rattled to a halt at their first overnight stop where they were to be accommodated at a posting-inn by the side of the road, every bone in Coral's body was aching. Her head throbbed unbearably, and her skin seemed to be on fire.

Rory asked her if she would like him to bring supper up to her bedroom, since she was clearly not strong enough to join the rest of the party in the dining-room below, but she said she could not eat anything at all.

She managed somehow to throw off her outer garments and lay upon the lumpy mattress in her petticoat and bodice, gasping for breath, and fearing she would suffocate. She did not dare to tell Rory how ill she felt; she was afraid that he might refuse to let her travel any further . . . and she had to find Gerard.

She closed her eyes and fell into a restless sleep, dreaming of Gerard.

She tossed and turned, thinking of his dear, handsome

face, of his strong arms round her, of his hands, so powerful and yet so gentle, travelling down her body, easing her out of her remaining garments. That was better—oh, yes, so much better—she felt more rested now—Gerard's cool fingertips touched her skin with loving care. She felt him stroking her breasts—her waist—her thighs.

And a refreshing dampness, water-drops trickled over her, tickling her as they rolled down in the most secret places of her body. He was washing her with a sponge of cool, sweet water, and she loved him all the more for his thoughtfulness.

"Gerard—" she breathed softly. "Oh, Gerard, my darling—"

And she opened her eyes. For this was no dream.

She was lying upon the narrow hotel bed, quite naked; and certainly a gentle pair of hands was ministering to her with soap and sponge and towel . . . but the hands were not Gerard's hands, and the face—

"*Rory,*" she gasped with dismay. "What—no—how dare you—"

She struggled to sit up, but he restrained her.

"Lie still, my dear girl—don't try to talk—for you are running a fever, and you'll only make yourself feel worse still if you attempt to argue. Trust me, Coral—I'll look after you."

"But—it's not right—it's not proper—"

"Sure, I've seen you half-dressed often enough before now, when we've been on tour in some of those tumbledown fleapits they call theatres! What difference does the extra stitch or two make, I'd like to know? We've all got bodies . . . and we're all as God made us. Close your eyes and let me get on with this . . . I'm hoping to bring down your fever, or you'll not be fit to travel tomorrow. So be a sensible girl now, and don't make things more difficult."

Reluctantly, she obeyed . . . his hands were very soothing, and she was not strong enough to protest.

"All the same—" she murmured, allowing him to continue the soft, relaxing movements. "What will other people say—if they know you're nursing me like this, in my bedroom?"

"That's no problem at all," he replied calmly. "Roll over now, like a good child, and let me wash your back ... for you're wringing wet with perspiration."

She did as she was told, and closed her eyes; his hands stroked and caressed her hips, and the slippery, soapy sponge proceeded to bathe every inch of her skin, while she snuggled down more comfortably under the pleasure of his touch. All the same ...

"What do you mean, it's no problem?" she asked drowsily.

"I seem to remember Gerard saying that when you were travelling in France, it was simpler to let people imagine that you were husband and wife ... so I took a leaf out of his book, and followed that good example—I told the innkeeper that you're Mrs. Rory O'Malley!"

Her eyes opened at once, and her body tensed.

"You're proposing to share this bedroom with me? No, Rory—I won't let you—that's out of the question."

"Not at all," he said soothingly. "I'll sleep on the couch, and leave you in peace, never fear. Besides, it will save us paying out good money for two rooms when we can manage with one. And you need someone to look after you—isn't that true?"

"Well—I suppose . . ." she broke off doubtfully. "But are you sure you won't try to—I mean—you wouldn't— "

"My dear girl, you'll be as safe with me, as if you were our Blessed Lady herself, I swear it! Now stop worrying and settle down again, and try to take some rest—for you require all the sleep you can get."

It was true that she needed help, for she was very far from well.

The following week passed in a kind of blur for Coral. Sometimes she felt a little stronger, and sat up to take notice of the strange landscapes they travelled through; at other times she dozed, and rested against Rory's firm shoulder, hardly aware of their continuing journey. Virginia, North Carolina, South Carolina—one State after another received them, then sped them upon their way—one inn after another provided beds of a sort, and tasteless food and drink. A red curtained window here—a cracked ceiling there—a garden with vines growing in it—a road

385

that circled an inland lagoon. The succession of images swam together in her mind, while she fought her own inner battle against the fever that consumed her.

The summer had long since gone, replaced by the golden glow of the fall—and now September and October drifted away like autumn leaves; beneath the humid climate of the Southern coast Coral detected a new chill in the air.

"Where are we now?" she asked one morning, as Rory helped to dress her for the next stage of the journey.

"This is Charleston," he told her, and looked at her more closely. "Do you know, it's the first time you've bothered to ask me that, since we left Baltimore. You must be feeling better."

"I really believe I am." She looked at her reflection in the brown-flaked mirror over the dressing table. "My pulse isn't racing anymore—and my head has stopped aching."

"Glory be—you're on the road to recovery at last!"

Rory put his arm round her shoulders, and kissed her on the cheek—a companionable, brotherly kiss that conveyed nothing but sincere affection.

"Oh, Rory, whatever would I have done without you to nurse me?" she asked, and impulsively returned his kiss.

"It's part of an actor's job to be able to turn to and portray any character that may be required," he shrugged it off with a laugh. "This time I was cast in the role of a ministering angel—that's all!"

"And what news is there of the British—of Gerard? Have you gathered any more information?" she asked.

"They say the British have moved their ships down to these waters, sure enough," he told her. "They made an attempt on Mobile recently—and they're reported to be planning to try again for another landing."

"Then we must move on and be there, ready to meet them," said Coral, putting on her bonnet and tying the strings beneath her chin. "To Mobile—wherever that may be!"

The road now ran south-westerly, and they travelled on through Georgia and Alabama. Sometimes Coral wondered if their quest was hopeless; would the journey stretch on forever, until they had travelled the entire length and breadth of the United States? For all they knew to the contrary, Gerard might have been shipped off home to England long ago. She might never succeed in finding him at all.

But she must not think like that. She *would* find him. Of course she would—she had to!

When they reached Mobile at last, the chill in the air was even more marked, and when the sun had set, a thick white mist rose from the waters of Mobile Bay.

Coral ate a light supper, in the parlor of the small commercial hotel where they were to spend the night; afterward, Rory asked her if she wanted to accompany him on a tour of the waterfront. He was hoping to pick up more immediate news of the British forces in the vicinity.

Coral looked at the weather outside—wet, cold, and uninviting—and refused the invitation. She would go to bed early, and try to keep warm: she had no wish to run the risk of catching any more ailments!

So she was already snugly tucked up in bed and fast asleep when Rory returned, some time after midnight. She woke at the sound of the door, and sat up quickly:

"Well? Did you find out anything new?"

"Yes and no. You were right not to venture out; this damp cold strikes right through to your bones."

Rory lit a candle and began to undress quickly, with his back turned to Coral.

"What do you mean—yes and no?"

"In the last saloon I went into, I got into conversation with an old man—a fisherman of French descent. I think he came from New Orleans, originally. I explained what I wanted, and I said I would pay well for any information that might lead me to a certain young officer in the British forces."

"And what did he say?" she asked eagerly.

"He said he would have to make inquiries. It seems he has friends at an island called Grande Terre, off Lake Barataria."

"All these strange names—how far is it from here?"

"I don't know exactly—from the way he spoke, it's in

the direction of New Orleans. But he knows some gentlemen—he wouldn't even tell me their names—who are in touch with the British fleet. That's all I can tell you at this stage: but he has promised to come back tomorrow with more definite information."

"Oh, let's hope he does not disappoint us . . . I feel somehow that we are so close to Gerard now—pray God nothing will go wrong!"

"Amen to that." Rory pulled off his breeches and threw them over a chair, then, naked except for his shirt, he picked up a blanket, and blew out the candle.

"What are you doing?" Coral asked, in the darkness.

"Making up my bed for the night, of course—on the settle below the window," came the reply.

"Oh . . . Yes . . . Rory, you have been so very good to me. I can't tell you how grateful I am for all your help."

"Think nothing of it, my dear girl . . . go to sleep."

"Yes, but . . . it's such a bitter cold night—you'll be half-frozen on that horrid settle, with nothing but a single blanket to cover you!"

A pause: then Rory asked: "What are you saying?"

"I'm saying . . . since we have travelled together so long as man and wife—don't you think perhaps—just for this one night—we might share this comfortable double bed?" asked Coral in a small voice.

"But—surely—you don't mean—"

"I mean that you have never behaved with any sign of disrespect toward me: we have shared the same rooms night after night, as chastely as if we were brother and sister . . . so—just to keep you from catching a chill—wouldn't you like to come and share this bed with me now—brother Rory?"

He crossed the room in three strides, and climbed into the bed beside her.

"If that's *all* you mean, sister Coral—" he began, and she could hear that he was smiling.

"Oh, Rory—yes, that's all I mean," she replied, and she put her arm around him. "For you know that although I love you very much—as a brother—I am *in* love with

Gerard, and I always will be . . . and that's the difference . . ."

"I understand that." He held her close, and he sounded curiously contented. "Am I allowed one goodnight kiss —a brotherly kiss?"

She put her lips to his: his mouth was full and generous, and she could taste the sweetness of his kiss—but she knew instinctively that her body did not cry out to be possessed by this kind-hearted, unpredictable man. There was love between them, of a sort, but no passion. His body, hard and warm against her own, was undemanding . . . his loins touched hers, but no spark of fire was struck between them.

"We don't need one another in that way," she said quietly.

There was a long silence, and he let her face rest against his cheek—bristling with a day's growth of beard. When he spoke at last, his voice buzzed in her head, and she felt his breath tickling her ear.

"Perhaps I will never need any woman—in that way," he replied softly.

"I don't understand . . . you were always a great one for chasing the girls, in the old days, back in Ireland—"

"A certain kind of girl . . . who would give me a certain kind of satisfaction," he said, awkwardly.

"What do you mean?"

"My tastes in love-making are not like other people's . . ." he confessed. "Tell me this . . . have you ever heard of men who enjoy being hurt? Men who take pleasure in pain? Who thrill to the sting of a whip, or any other physical punishment?"

"Yes—I think—I've heard people hint . . ." She broke off, a little embarrassed. "Are you telling me—*you*—are like that?"

He nodded, and continued to hold her close to him, running his hands up and down her slim smooth back, as if he were searching for the answer to a question that eluded him.

"That is how I am . . . oh, it wasn't always so—it began slowly; at first it was only a sort of game for me—

389

an extra amusement to give spice to the feast of love. But as time went by, the game became the only thing that mattered. Love-making alone was nothing to me—I could not even play my role in the activity unless my partner were to do certain things . . ."

His voice trailed away hesitantly, and Coral suddenly felt a deep pang of pity for this lonely man.

"Rory, I'm sure that's not so—when the right girl comes along—"

"No. It's like a drug to me now; I cannot do without it . . . and I can do nothing—without it."

He took her hand in his, and drew it down to the base of his stomach, to the place where his manhood lay—flaccid and lifeless, in a tangle of pubic hair.

"You see? There's nothing there. I have a beautiful creature like you in my arms and I might as well be dead, for all the good it does me."

He hesitated, then added—so quietly she could scarcely distinguish the words: "But if you were only to punish me now . . . to take a strap to me—or—or a sharp blade—"

She clung to him desperately:

"I can't do that, Rory—I'm sorry, but I *can't*—"

"No . . . I knew you couldn't . . . and I'm sorry too —but in a way I'm glad of it."

"Glad?"

"Because this way we can go on being good friends . . . and that's the right thing for both of us. And for Gerard, too."

They said no more, but curled up in each other's arms, and so fell asleep at last . . . like brother and sister.

When dawn came, a knocking at the bedroom door roused them both, and Rory sat up—on the alert at once.

"What is it?" he demanded. "Who's there?"

"Dominic," replied a guttural voice that was half-French and half-American, and wholly foreign to Coral's ears. "I must talk with you!"

"You'd better come in, then . . ."

Rory grinned at Coral, as she pulled the bedclothes up to her chin, and prepared to receive their visitor.

The door opened to admit one of the strangest little

390

men she had ever seen; brown as a nut, with a gnarled face, and one gold ring in his left ear. He was not much taller than a child, and looked like a gnome from a fairy story. He blinked a shrewd eye at Coral, and bobbed his head rapidly.

"*Je suis* Dominic—at your service, madame," he croaked. "I met with your husband last night . . ."

"Yes—so he told me," said Coral. "What news have you for us?"

"It is well arranged," said Dominic, showing a flash of gold teeth as he cracked a smile. "I have my boat below at the harbor, ready to take you to Grande Terre. There you will meet a very important man—a man who knows the leaders of the British Army and Navy . . . one of the most powerful men in this part of the world."

"An American who deals with the British? You mean a traitor?" asked Rory.

The little gnome drew himself up to his full height, eye to eye with Rory, who was still lying in bed.

"By no means!" he exclaimed, exceedingly shocked. "He is a great leader of his people, and no traitor. He owes no loyalty to the British or the Americans either— he is his own man."

"And what is the name of this independent hero?" Rory wanted to know.

"Have you never heard tell of Jean Lafitte—Lafitte the corsair? Lafitte the king of the high seas? Lafitte—" he closed one eye, and concluded triumphantly: "*Jean Lafitte, the pirate!*"

(6)

Grande Terre

The vessel that Dominic commanded was small, like its
master; a shrimpboat, that plied the waters of the Louisiana coast, trawling for a catch—and possibly, Coral suspected, engaging in a little smuggling on the side. She
remembered the contraband aboard Captain Duffy's fish-
ing-boat, and held her tongue.

Dominic's boat was named *Voiles Blanches*—"White
Sails"—and with its sails outspread, it skimmed over the
rolling waves beyond Mobile like a great sea-bird.

Dominic himself stayed at the wheel, peering ahead into
the mists—for although he knew every shoal and every
current in these waters, the light was treacherous, and it
would not do to take chances. Occasionally they heard
him mutter to himself—sometimes he sang a snatch of an
old folksong, in his hoarse, French-Creole accent but for
the most part he was silent and withdrawn, wrapped up in
his own thoughts.

Coral sat in the stern, with Rory close beside her, and
they huddled together for warmth.

"Who is this man we are going to see—this Jean Lafitte?" she asked quietly. "Is he really a pirate?"

"From what I could make out he's not only a pirate, he's the leader of a whole family of pirates: he has two brothers and an uncle, all in the same line of business!"

"But why should he be able to help us get to Gerard?"

"Because, as Dominic pointed out, these pirates are a law unto themselves. They are just as likely to enter into a private treaty with the English commanders as with their own countrymen. Being outlaws, they owe allegiance to no government."

"I see . . ." Coral shuddered a little, and Rory glanced at her with concern.

"Are you catching a chill, my dear? Let me wrap a blanket around you."

"No, no—I wasn't shivering with cold . . . just a sudden feeling—as if . . . you know what they say—someone walked over my grave."

"We'll have no talk of graves or death, if you please!" Rory tried to lighten her mood. "Cheer up—just think— you may be seeing your beloved Gerard again, very soon."

"I wonder . . ." Coral laced her hands together, and squeezed them hard, until her knuckles showed as white as ivory. "I can't help remembering . . ."

"What?"

"The last time I talked to Gerard at the theatre, after that awful quarrel, the very last words I said to him . . ."

"What were they?"

"I'll never speak to you again as long as I live!" She bit her lip, choking back the tears that welled up in her throat. "Oh, Rory, do you suppose that could turn out to be true?"

"Don't think of such things. Take heart, and look forward to the future, as I do! It won't be long now until we reach the island."

"Tell me about the island. What is it that we shall find there?"

"According to the stories I've heard, our Mr. Jean Lafitte has taken possession of the island of Grande Terre,

393

at the entrance to the Bay of Barataria. It's an area some thirty or forty miles south-west of New Orleans far enough from law and order for him to do as he pleased, and rule his own little kingdom and with a commanding position that allowed the pirates to control all the waterways thereabouts. It's on this island that Mr. Lafitte set up his headquarters, living in high style with all his followers and hangers-on. And it's there, at the center of his spider's web, that we are to meet him."

"Lafitte . . . it sounds like a French name—is he another Creole, like Dominic?"

"They say he hails originally from Haiti and he was schooled in Martinique. They also say he has the reputation of being quite a ladies' man, so I shall keep a strict eye upon you all the while we are there!"

Coral smiled, despite herself, and put her hand gently upon Rory's arm.

"Dear Rory . . . it's odd, isn't it? When I first knew you, when we first acted together, in Uncle's company, I used to think you were the most boorish, insufferable, conceited young man who ever lived. And now I think of you as my dearest friend in all the world . . . except for Gerard, of course, and—that's not exactly friendship."

"Have I changed so much?" Rory's eyes twinkled. "They say wisdom comes with maturity—perhaps it's old age creeping up on me."

"Never that!" she laughed. "You'll never be old, that's one thing I feel sure of."

"Land ahead!" Dominic's sharp cry broke in upon their conversation, and he pointed forward across the bows of the little ship.

The mist had grown even thicker now; a chilly white cloud that rolled across the waters—as white as the sails of the *Voiles Blanches* and seemed as if it would draw them in to its treacherous embrace. But just ahead, emerging from the swirling vapours like a ghost, they saw the silhouette of gaunt trees upon a shore, and the shadowy outline of a house.

"Grande Terre," muttered Dominic, with satisfaction. "I leave you here."

394

There was a little landing-stage, and he made fast alongside. Once Rory had paid him for his trouble, they climbed ashore, and watched as the boat turned about and disappeared again, swallowed up by the white mist at last.

"There's no one in sight to welcome us," said Rory, looking around. "We'd best make our way up to the house and announce ourselves."

"I can't *see* anyone—" Coral agreed, adding: "And yet I have an eerie feeling that we are being watched."

"That's hardly surprising. If the island is really populated with pirates and smugglers, they'd keep a sharp lookout for any newcomers."

"I suppose so."

They wandered up the narrow path that led to the house; a path bordered by tall trees, each one shrouded with rags and tatters of Spanish moss. Coral felt that she had never seen such a mournful, desolate place.

When they reached the front door, they stared in surprise—for the door was wide open. They peered into the gloomy hall, and saw that there was a scattering of dry leaves upon the floor. It seemed that the door must have been standing open for some time.

"Hello—is there anyone at home?" Rory called boldly and his voice echoed and faded on the still air.

"It appears to be deserted. Wherever can they all be hiding?" Coral asked.

Cautiously, they moved inside to investigate.

The hall was empty. There were marks upon the walls where a picture had once been or a mirror. Another open door led into a reception room; and again this room was completely empty. There was no furniture—no carpet on the wooden boards—nothing but a hook which showed where a chandelier had originally hung from the ceiling. The long windows were grimy, and the whole place smelled of dust and dampness and decay.

"I'm afraid our bird has flown," said Rory quietly. "Damn that crafty devil of a boatman for bringing us to the back of beyond, and ditching us . . . how the deuce will we ever get back to dry land?"

"Perhaps there are people somewhere else on the island," suggested Coral. "This may not be the only house, after all."

"Possibly . . . I'll go and reconnoiter—you stay here till I get back."

"Let me come with you—"

"No, my dear—I'll make a circuit of the whole place, and I can travel more quickly by myself. You wait for me; I will be as fast as possible."

Rory turned and strode out.

She listened to his footsteps in the hall and the fainter sounds of his tread upon the path outside and then the house settled down into silence again.

A silence that was almost unbroken . . . almost, but not quite.

She listened hard, and thought she could detect a very small noise somewhere above her head, somewhere on the upper floor. She held her breath—could there be rats in the house? There it was again—a soft, scraping noise. Someone, or something, was moving up there.

Then she heard a more welcome sound; somebody was whistling a little tune. It was the same Creole melody, she realized, that Dominic had been singing to himself on the ship, and she thought for a startled second that perhaps the little fisherman had somehow made his way into the house.

But of course that was impossible.

She went out into the hall in investigate and stopped dead.

Whistling cheerfully, a tall, elegant young man was walking down the broad staircase to meet her.

"Good day, mam'selle," he said, appraising her with a smile. "This is a pleasant surprise."

He could scarcely be more than thirty years old; he was dressed in the height of fashion, and when he smiled, he showed dazzlingly white teeth—perhaps especially so, in contrast with the color of his skin, which was so dark as to be almost black . . . Though whether he really had a half-caste strain in him, or whether he was merely tanned like mahogany by wind and weather, Coral could not tell.

Summoning all her courage, she began: "Good day,

sir—do I have the pleasure of addressing Mr. Jean Lafitte?"

He paused, and raised one eyebrow.

"What makes you think so?" he inquired.

"Because I believe this is Mr. Lafitte's house and you appear to be quite at home here."

"So—if I may say so—do you," replied the stranger. His glance travelled down her slim figure; he was inspecting her quite frankly, letting his eye roam over her breasts, her waist, her hips. Clearly he liked what he saw.

"They also say that Mr. Lafitte is the king of the high seas," she continued recklessly. "And you, sir, seem to me to be—"

She broke off, and he completed the sentence for her.

"A king? I am flattered, mam'selle. You pay a pretty compliment."

He came closer; the scent of expensive toilet-water stung her nostrils, and she found herself gazing up into his face, only a few inches away from her own.

"Very well—I confess—you have guessed correctly. Jean Lafitte—*à votre service* . . . and now, perhaps you will be good enough to tell me in return who you are, and what in heaven's name you are doing here?"

There was something amazingly penetrating about the man's steady, unwavering gaze; she felt as if she were being drawn into a spell—as if he were hypnotizing her.

Slowly at first, and then with more confidence as she continued, she found herself telling her story; how the man she loved had been pressed into military service, how she had to find him and be reunited with him and how she and Rory had travelled all the way from Baltimore, to finish up in this lonely island and this deserted house.

"Dominic the fisherman, you say?" Lafitte's expression was touched by ironic amusement. "The old man is behind the times—where has he been, that he does not know the latest news, I wonder?"

"I'm sorry—I don't understand—"

"A few months ago, everything he told you would have been true . . . you would have found me taking my ease here in this house—the master of my own domain. But times have changed."

"You mean you cannot help me?" she exclaimed, despairingly.

"I did not say that . . . come, mam'selle—let us go into the salon; or what used to be the salon. I fancy there are still one or two pieces of furniture in there."

He offered her his arm courteously, and led her through an archway into yet another room, where there was a broken chair perched upon three legs and a battered sofa with the stuffing tumbling out through gaping holes in the fabric.

"You must forgive this squalor . . . it is all that the raiding party left behind when they called to find me."

"Why, what happened?"

"I suggest we seat ourselves upon the sofa. At least it has the customary number of legs!" They sat side by side, and he continued: "We had a surprise visit from Commodore Patterson, of the United States Navy. Luckily, I was not at home—but my friends and relations were put in chains and taken to New Orleans—and our visitors loaded twenty-six ships with all they could remove in the way of merchandise. The result is—as you see it now. I can live here no longer, I only make an occasional tour of inspection, as I do today, to keep the island under my *surveillance* . . . and to remember it as it used to be."

"I'm sorry," Coral said at last. "And of course you must feel very bitterly toward the United States authorities now—I suppose that is why you are prepared to throw in your lot with the British?"

"You might suppose so—and the British supposed the very same thing . . ." Jean Lafitte let his arm fall along the back of the sofa as he talked, and edged slightly closer to Coral. "In fact, Captain Nicholas Lockyer, of the British fleet, actually came to parley with me. He has offered me thirty thousand dollars and a commission in the Royal Navy if I will co-operate with the British forces."

"Oh, but that's wonderful—" Coral exclaimed eagerly.

"Co-operation can indeed be a very wonderful thing . . ." Lafitte remarked, and without any hesitation, encircled her within his arms, and brought his mouth down upon her lips.

She struggled instinctively, taken completely off guard but thinking at the same time that she needed this man's assistance, and that she must do nothing that might antagonize him.

He ran his hands down her body, taking advantage of her momentary surprise to explore her warm, enticing curves: she felt his practiced and playful fingers that seemed to be everywhere at once . . . and at the same time, his tongue penetrated her lips, and she began to respond instinctively to his skillful assault.

As the kiss ended, and she gasped for breath, he moved on to a fresh attack, bending his head, and covering her bosom with soft, feathery touches—lips, tongue, fingertips all combining to thrill her with tremors of ecstasy.

"No—no—you must not—*we* must not—" she tried to protest . . . but it was so hard to stop him when he was making such a determined onslaught upon her person.

Already, he had unfastened her corsage, and now she felt his lips upon her breasts; his tongue darting like quicksilver as it teased and tickled her nipples, making her squirm with helpless desire.

"Mam'selle—" he whispered, giving her a breathing-space before renewing his maneuvers, "I have never seen you before and perhaps I will never meet you again, but I swear by all that's holy, you are the most ravishing young lady I ever knew. *Mille tonnerres*—I declare, for your sake, I would almost break my word and accept the British offer."

She stared at him, as the meaning of his words sank in to her brain.

"You mean—you've decided *not* to?"

"That is correct." He looked at her horrified face, and laughed aloud. "But how *triste* you look! Did you really imagine I was going to give you a safe-conduct to the British commanders, and help you find your lover?"

"I thought—oh, you brute—you misled me completely—" she cried indignantly. "No, no—take your hands from me, sir—I'll have nothing more to do with you!"

She began to readjust her dress, covering her bosom modestly, while Jean Lafitte chuckled at her discomfiture.

399

"Does that surprise you so much? I sent the documents I had from the British to the American authorities. I said I was prepared to be a loyal patriot and put myself at the service of the United States—myself and my men also— in return for the freedom of my relatives, and a public proclamation that will grant pardon to us all."

"Then we have been talking at cross-purposes, and I have wasted your time," said Coral, with icy politeness. "Now I will go and find my companion, and we will make our way back to—"

She broke off, realizing too late that this was easier said than done.

"And how will you leave this island—without my 'co-operation'?" Lafitte teased her. "I told you—cooperation is a very wonderful—and a very necessary thing!"

He stood up, and clapped his hands sharply.

Almost instantly, the room was crowded with people —swarthy, sinister individuals, who stared at Coral suspiciously, and seemed as if they had materialized from the shadows. These, she realized, must be the remnants of Jean Lafitte's band of followers, and she noticed with a sudden shock that two of them had brought Rory into the room with them, as a prisoner under escort.

"We found this one wandering around outside," his captor grunted.

"Very well, let him go . . . he is our guest—they are *both* our guests," said Jean Lafitte, with a charming bow in Coral's direction. "And now we must speed them upon their way. I want the pirogue brought around to the landing-stage at once."

"Where are you taking us?" Rory asked angrily.

"I'm sorry, m'sieur—I cannot tell you that exactly. I will only say that for this delightful young lady's sake, I am prepared to risk a certain amount of trouble. I will set you on the course which you wish to follow."

He snapped his fingers, and signalled to another of his aides.

"Blindfolds—quickly."

Two strips of black cloth were produced, and Lafitte apologized to Coral: "I am afraid I must ask you to submit to this indignity. The routes that lead in and out of my kingdom are very secret indeed, and must always remain so. You may not see where you are being taken—you must simply trust me."

"Why should we trust you?" Rory was beginning to grow argumentative.

"Why indeed? But I think you have no alternative. Do *you* trust me, mam'selle?" Lafitte asked Coral, abruptly.

To her surprise, she found herself replying before she even had time to consider the question: "Yes—I trust you . . ."

"That is good. Let us go—I will fasten your blindfold myself, as soon as we cast off."

They set sail from the little jetty, in the pirogue, a flat-bottomed boat with two masts, that had been carved from the hollow trunk of a tree. Having no keel, the little vessel was able to slip through the shallows of the creeks and bayous that criscrossed the whole territory, taking them through channels that would have been impassible to any other type of boat.

Coral sat rigidly between Rory, blindfolded like herself, and Lafitte, feeling the young pirate's thigh pressed tightly against her own. She could not tell where they were going, for they seemed to change course time and again, until she had lost all sense of direction.

She was, however, very much aware of Jean Lafitte's body beside her, and his supple fingers—surprisingly deft for such a powerful man—softly massaging her knee, then proceeding slowly but surely along her thigh. She gritted her teeth, and silently reviled him—how could he be so base, turning every occasion to his own selfish advantage? He knew that Rory could not see what he was doing, and he took care to make no sound as he caressed her—and he also knew that she would not risk any further trouble by voicing her objections, or alerting Rory to what was happening.

When Lafitte's hand reached her lap, she gave an involuntary gasp, and Rory asked immediately: "Are you all right? What's wrong?"

With her heart beating wildly and with spasms of sensual excitement quivering through her body—she answered breathlessly: "I'm perfectly—all right—thank you . . ."

She felt Lafitte's body shaking, and knew that he was laughing soundlessly.

At last he remarked, his voice rich with secret amusement: "Alas!—all good things must come to an end, and this is where we have to part company. I can take you no further . . . just ahead, you will find the gates of a plantation, the Villette plantation. That is where the British Commanders have made their headquarters. You must address yourself to them and I must wish you good fortune in your quest."

Coral and Rory found themselves being put ashore, and felt soft mud squelching under their feet. There was a tiny ripple of water, lapping against the boat's hull and then silence.

They put their hands to their heads, and tugged at the knots of the blindfolds—the moment they could see again, they spun round. To find that the flat-bottomed pirogue had already vanished, disappearing among the winter mists as though it had never existed.

The landscape that met their eyes was bleak indeed.

Upon one side, the little stream that had carried them through the Barataria swamps now emptied into a wide, sluggish river—gray and yellow and unfriendly.

"That must be the Mississippi," said Rory. "As I recall from the map, it links New Orleans with the ocean."

Bordering the water's edge, as far as they could see, were the sugar cane plantations, an endless jungle of green mud and spiky foliage, broken at long intervals by paling fences. Behind the plantations, looming up from the fog and dripping with moisture, were the mysterious, ominous shapes of cypress trees, in a dense and impenetrable mass.

"What a God-forsaken place," said Rory. "It feels as if we have come to the end of the earth. Which way should we go now, do you think?"

"Mr. Lafitte told us to look for the gates of a plantation just ahead. We'd better keep on going in the same direction, I suppose."

Walking on this amphibian territory was far from easy;

402

up to their ankles in mud and water at one moment then striding over tussocks of sharp-edged grasses at the next. The humid air hung clammily upon them, and their clothes felt heavy and damp.

"I was wondering," Coral began, negotiating a wide puddle of green mud and slime with some difficulty, "how it happens that the British are established here in a private house, as their headquarters. Surely if they have made a landing that must mean they are renewing their attack?"

"No doubt of it. Perhaps the British chiefs-of-staff have made up their minds to bring this tiresome war to an end, once and for all, with one last attempt on the mainland."

"But in that case if war has broken out again, we must be very near to the center of the fighting?"

As if in reply to her question, there was a sudden crack of rifle fire from the opposite bank of the river. Half a dozen shots rang out in quick succession, and they could see the flash of the guns. Bullets seemed to sing through the air, and exploded in the mud and water around them.

"Down! Get down, for God's sake!" gasped Rory, flinging himself forward.

Coral was quick to follow his lead, throwing herself on to her face in two inches of water and slime. She lay still, feeling the cold seeping through her dress, and waiting for another volley of bullets but nothing more happened.

With difficulty, Rory pulled himself up from the sea of mud, and rested against the stump of a tree.

"Damn sharpshooters—" he said breathlessly. "Sentries, I dare say, among the American lines. They must have seen us walking along and decided to take a pot shot at us."

"Quickly—let's find the Villette plantation," Coral urged him. "Don't waste time—they might be reloading to fire at us again!"

She scrambled to her feet, trying to keep under cover of the sugar cane as well as she could. "Look—" she added eagerly. "There are the gates—only about a hundred yards away. We're nearly there now!"

Sure enough, the mist and fog seemed to lift for a moment, and they could both see a wooden levee at the water's edge, and a pair of wrought iron gates, holding up a sign that proclaimed the name: *"Villette."*

"Come on, Rory, hurry up!" Coral urged him. "Once we get through, we'll be safe!"

"I'm safe enough right here," said Rory, and smiled lazily, propped up on one elbow, with his back to the tree stump. "There's no special hurry for me to stir myself— you go on ahead if you want to. I'll wait here for a bit."

"What's the matter?" Coral stared at him. "You can't stay there sprawled out on the mud."

"Let's say, I don't feel presentable enough to meet a pack of English officers," he grinned. "You go and fascinate 'em, Coral—I'll follow you presently."

"Are you afraid of being shot at again, on the way?" she asked bluntly.

"Ah—you guessed my guilty secret. I'm absolutely scared stiff!" he admitted. "But I'll get my bravery back in a moment, don't worry. Just you get along and tell 'em I'm on my way—tell them to roll out the red carpet for the arrival of Rory O'Malley!"

"Oh, you!" Coral couldn't help smiling. "You're always the same, you actors—building up your grand entrance!"

She glanced round once more; everything seemed quiet on the opposite bank of the river, and she decided to take a chance.

"Well, then, I'll go without you, but don't stay out here all night, mind! I'll be waiting for you!" she said. "Wish me luck."

"That I do, my dear girl . . . I wish you all the luck in the world," said Rory.

She ducked down as low as possible, and made a dash for it—covering the hundred yards as fast as she could, in the swirling mists. Not much further to go now—fifty yards, perhaps—twenty—ten . . .

Another fusillade of shots crackled around her, and she redoubled her speed, though her lungs seemed to be bursting. Then she threw herself in between the wrought-iron gates: she was safe at last.

404

At once, two sentries in scarlet uniform appeared from nowhere, and challenged her: "Who goes there?"

"A friend," she panted, out of breath, covered in mud and filth, with her wet hair hanging down her back, and her face plastered with dirt. Then she drew herself up, and said with all the dignity she could muster: "Take me to your commanding officer."

A hundred yards away, Rory lay quite still, his fractured shoulder-blade supported upon the tree stump, and every muscle of his body contorted grotesquely in a final agony. It was the second shot which had done for him: shattering the back of his skull and killing him instantly.

In that last moment of anguish, his lips had twisted into a smile. It was not, after all, a very grand entrance. But it wasn't a bad exit.

(7)

Journey's End

The house that stood upon the Villette plantation was a mansion, by any standards, and until it had been commandeered by the British officers, it had undoubtedly been the scene of many an elegant *soirée*.

Now it stood a little defiantly, as if it refused to accept the turn of events that had overtaken it; Coral looked around as she was taken in through the imposing front door and the high entrance hall, remembering Jean Lafitte's ghostly residence. Here, life was very much in evidence—not just in the shape of the red-coated orderlies, who escorted her from room to room, passing her from one interrogator to another up a chain of command; the rooms themselves bore witness to a whole world of gaiety and luxury—handsome oil paintings on the walls, reflected in gilt mirrors—crystal chandeliers that winked and blinked in the candlelight—and rich velvet hangings at the tall windows. The Villettes, like so many of the Louisiana plantation-owners, must have enjoyed life to the full.

At last she was ushered into the largest salon of all—

at the back of the building, with wide french windows giving on to a terrace. Dusk was gathering outside, but she saw the outline of a trim, formal garden that led to another cypress grove beyond.

There were flames flickering in the marble fireplace, and a man with his back to the door stooped to throw on another log for even indoors, the air was clammy and chill.

Then he straightened up as the orderly who accompanied Coral saluted and announced: "Miss Coral Maguire, sir . . . a British citizen—requesting an interview with the Commanding Officer."

The man turned and looked at her for a moment. Then he said, in a deep, vibrant tone: "Very well, Hatchard. I'll call when I require you . . . you may leave us."

The soldier saluted again, and retired, closing the door behind him.

Much later, Coral looked back upon this moment, and decided that she had met three extraordinary men within the space of twenty-four hours; first Dominic, the gnome-like Creole fisherman—then the glamorous and magnetic Jean Lafitte. But she knew without any doubt that this third and last encounter was the most important, and that the man she now faced was far and away the most vital and impressive of them all.

It wasn't simply his physical presence—though that was striking enough, in all conscience: for he was tall and broad-shouldered, built like an oak tree. He was in early middle-age, and there were traces of silver in his leonine mane of hair—and his bronzed face was marked with a scar that ran from his left eye up to his temple. But his eyes . . . his eyes were palest blue—eyes that seemed to pierce her soul; she felt that he could look through her and see every thought and emotion she possessed—nothing could be hidden from that penetrating regard, which combined both ice and fire.

And yet it was his personality that was the most striking thing of all; the feeling of immense power waiting to be unleashed—the feeling of authority—of decision—of justice. Here Coral knew instantly, was a true leader of men.

"Good day, Miss Maguire," he said at last, and his face

creased briefly into a smile. "What brings you so far from home?"

He offered her a chair, with a courtly gesture, and as she sat, she felt like a visiting head of state. This man, with the bearing of a king, had the power to make her feel like a queen.

She began once more to tell her story; how she had come to America with the Maguire company, and how, in the sacking of Washington, she had become separated from the man she loved. She told him how she had discovered that her love had been pressed into service with the British Army, as an Ensign; and how she and Rory had set out on their long journey to find him again.

She even heard herself adding: "I have to put things right between us, sir, because I have been very stupid. We were engaged to be married, and I was foolish enough to quarrel with him. I must find him, and tell him that I love him—and ask his forgiveness."

The commanding officer smiled again, and said: "Then he is a fortunate young man indeed . . . and if I can help you, I will—but first you must tell me his name."

"His name as an actor is Gerard Kean—but I suppose now he will have reverted to his family name, which is Mallory."

There was a long pause, during which the log on the fire shifted and fell with a shower of sparks, and then he rose to his feet.

"In that case I may be able to help you—for Gerard Mallory is my brother-in-law. I am married to Garnet, his sister," said Major-General Brock Savage, holding out his hand.

Coral clasped it in her own, and said impulsively: "I have never been happier to learn anything in my whole life. Tell me—quickly—where is Gerard now? In this house?"

"No, he is out on maneuvers. The enemy made an impudent sortie earlier today, and we sent a platoon out to dispose of their sharp-shooters. But you shall see him soon enough—tonight, or perhaps tomorrow. Meanwhile, let me call for some refreshments—this unexpected family

408

reunion deserves some sort of celebration, I think. And at the same time, I'll send two of my men to find your travelling-companion who is waiting bashfully outside . . . what did you say his name was? O'Malley?"

Ten minutes later, after these orders had been given, Coral sipped a glass of wine and listened to Brock's own story.

He explained why he had a great personal sympathy for her, since his own wife had set out on a quest that was not altogether dissimilar.

"I won't trouble you now, Miss Maguire, with all the details—but the strangest part of the tale is that when your Gerard went off to Ireland and became a strolling player, my Garnet took his place, and his uniform, and enlisted as the youngest Ensign in my regiment . . . We went through the Peninsular together, and were then posted to Maryland, where we took part in the Washington campaign. After that, we were married and sent home and there Garnet lives now, waiting for my safe return; for I was not allowed much respite, but despatched to this new theatre of war quite recently, along with your young man."

"Did you say your wife, Garnet, actually took part in the march upon Washington, sir?" A memory stirred in Coral's brain; the slim young Ensign with the beardless cheek and the tantalizing similarity to someone else. Of course, she realized now the reason for that resemblance. "Then I believe I may have seen her once—for a few moments . . ."

"It's quite possible . . . very soon after that, Gerard was taken prisoner—and he and Garnet managed to exchange identities, so he took her place in the regiment, and she resumed her true role as a girl . . . And I married her."

Brock poured a little more wine into their glasses, and added: "As I trust—when this damned, muddle-headed battle is over—you and Gerard may be joined in matrimony also."

"And how long do you suppose that may be?" Coral asked quietly. "For I have not patience enough to wait very much longer . . ."

The door opened again, and Brock glanced up: "Ah—this will be your friend Mr. O'Malley at last—"

But the orderly came in alone, saying:

"Beg pardon, sir . . . we found the gentleman you sent us to fetch—and between us we managed to carry him back to the house."

"Carry him?" Coral repeated anxiously. "Is he hurt?"

"Not hurt, ma'am . . . he's done for . . . shot through the shoulder, and through the head. The adjutant's making a report now and going through his papers . . . for the gentleman's dead."

Brock frowned.

"My dear Miss Maguire—I am so very sorry."

She sprang to her feet, almost distracted.

"I can't believe it—we heard shooting—but I never guessed—I never dreamed—Rory *can't* be dead!"

"I'm afraid there's no question about it, ma'am." The orderly stood to attention, gazing straight ahead like a wooden image.

"This complicates matters, I fear," said Brock. "The man was a civilian—a British subject, on foreign soil—there will have to be reports and inquiries—an inquest. You will be called to give evidence, no doubt—it may take some time."

Coral scarcely heard him; her mind was in a turmoil.

Rory—dear, faithful, unhappy Rory—lying in the mud with two bullets in him; her thoughts recoiled from the mental picture. He, who had done so much to help her —she had wished she could repay his kindness, but now there was nothing at all she could do for him. Nothing that anyone could do, and the Major-General talked of inquiries and inquests—and *time*.

The room seemed suddenly to have become a prison; in her fear and distress, she could think of nothing but Gerard. She had to find him—to be with him—now, today, at once! Nothing must keep them apart for one moment longer.

While Brock walked up to the orderly and began discussing the formal procedure for notifying the death of Rory O'Malley, Coral slipped quietly away behind their backs.

"It will need a memorandum in writing, countersigned by the Chief-of-Staff—do you know if Sir Edward Pakenham is in the building?"

Brock turned to explain to Coral: "Ned Pakenham's a good fellow—he won't make any unnecessary—"

He broke off sharply: "Why, where the devil is she?"

The french windows stood ajar, and a coil of white mist snaked into the salon. Outside, the light was fading fast.

"Quick, man—send out a search party—go after her! She must be stopped!"

The orderly set off at a run: but they both knew it was already too late.

It was almost dark, but Coral welcomed the darkness as a friend: she could hide among those cypress trees, and they would never discover her . . . and somewhere beyond, Gerard waited. One last effort, and she would be with him again.

Lifting her skirts to avoid the clinging weeds, and the treacherous swamp that sucked at her shoes, she ran with all the speed she could muster—into the unknown. She didn't know where she was going, or how far away Gerard might be—but that didn't matter. She would find him, somehow . . . she *had* to find him.

Suddenly, she heard the terrifying rattle of rifle fire and ahead, in the black distance, the trees were briefly silhouetted in the flash of the guns.

But she was no longer afraid; instead of running away, she ran toward the sound of gunfire—these must be the sharp-shooters that Brock Savage had spoken of; this must be where Gerard had been sent on maneuvers.

She ran on blindly, her clothes torn and slashed by the sharp branches of the cypresses that clawed at her in her flight. Then there was another explosion—nearer, this time, and much louder.

A brilliant flash illuminated the scene for a moment, and a shell burst only a dozen yards ahead, sending up a fountain of mud and debris.

In the same instant, she saw a clearing among the trees, and a tumbledown shanty—a cabin of stakes and wattle, which served as a refuge for the slaves on the plantation in time of peace. Now it was almost deserted.

411

But not quite. In that single lightning flash, she was aware of a man at the entrance to the shanty—a young man who saw her coming towards him and shouted: "Get back, by God—do you want to kill yourself?"

She stopped then, not on account of his words, but because she knew the voice that uttered them.

"Gerard . . . !" she gasped. It was all she could say, but there was no need for anything more.

There would be time enough for explanations later.

As if in a dream, he moved toward her. There was one more burst of light, as another shell exploded—further off, this time—and they found themselves face to face in its ghastly glare.

He, in a mudstained scarlet tunic, and she, tattered and filthy, holding out her arms to him.

Then darkness enclosed them once again, as they clung together.

At that moment, the fog that covered the swamps began to turn to rain—a violent tropical rain, that lashed down from the low clouds as if preparing for the coming of a second deluge.

They did not care. The downpour soaked them to the skin within seconds, and washed the dirt from their bodies, and still they pressed together, their wet faces cleansed at last, exchanging the first of many kisses.

Then Gerard led her into the shack, which afforded some sort of shelter, and they lay together upon a heap of straw, and listened to the rain battering upon the flimsy roof; and found sanctuary and solace in each other's arms.

At long last, they lay still—totally contented, and totally at peace: and it was time to talk.

She told him all she could of her story; of her meeting with Brock Savage—and Rory's death. In return, he told her something of his own situation, and the preparations afoot for one final assault on the enemy.

"They're planning to attack the American defenses but *I* know it's hopeless, and I fancy old Brock knows it too. We're stuck here in the middle of nowhere, miles from the supply-lines, like sitting ducks. And there's nowhere near enough preparations made—not enough brushwood fascines to ford the swamps, nor enough scaling-ladders to breast their ramparts. If Pakenham gives the command to push ahead now, our men will be slaughtered—I swear it."

"Oh, Gerard—no—do not say such things—"

He smiled at her.

"Until now, I didn't really care. There did not seem to be much point in living in any case. It was all one to me. But now the circumstances are very different," he concluded, and he sat up, stripping off his scarlet jacket.

"What are you doing?" she asked.

"Throwing away my uniform. My soldiering days are over—I am going to become a deserter," he replied crisply.

"What? But, if they catch you—"

"They won't catch me, never fear . . . I understand now that there's only one kind of loyalty that matters. You remember how we battled our way through France together: we weren't concerned with the English or the French, or the rights and wrongs of their quarrel. All that concerned us was Rosalie—and one another. And I tell you, my darling, that I'd give all the patriotism and glory in the wide world in return for your safety. And I'm determined to see you safe—even if I have to become coward, renegade and traitor to achieve it. For I found you again, my dearest love—and I will never let you go."

One of the slaves had left a patched pair of trousers and an old cloak hanging in the shack, and Gerard now donned these quickly: his military uniform was rolled into a bundle, and flung into a deep creek among the bayous.

"Perhaps it will serve as a nest for a clutch of alligators!" he smiled.

"Come, my love—give me your hand, and let us be on our way."

But the alligators did not discover Gerard's cast-off clothes after all; they were found, the following morning, by a party of soldiers out on reconnaissance, and brought back to the Villette mansion.

Brock Savage examined the tunic, and scanned the faded documents that were within the breast pocket, his face expressionless.

Eventually he said: "Hatchard—take a memorandum,

413

and have it posted in despatches . . . Ensign Gerard Mallory—missing, believed killed in action . . . that is all."

The orderly saluted and left the room. Brock began to fold the bedraggled uniform automatically, adding under his breath: "God will be with them, wherever they are."

All through the night, Gerard and Coral had travelled on—it was slow going, through the cypress swamps, and across the plantations of sugar-cane—and at every step they were alert for the sound of gunfire, or the challenge of a sharp-eyed sentry.

But there was no more shooting, and the long night passed uneventfully. After many hours of struggle, they made their way across a wide expanse of bog and finally struck a road . . . a highroad, bordering the slowly-gliding Mississippi river.

"This must be the main thoroughfare into the city," Gerard decided. "Somehow we've made a complete detour around the enemy lines, and now we're inside their territory."

"But we haven't seen or heard any troops during the night," Coral said. "Why are they so quiet? Are they all in hiding?"

Even the road was quite empty. In the cold gray light, as the first yellow wash of dawn slipped over the wintry sky, they could see the road stretching away, without a single traveller in sight. And there were no craft upon the river; everything was dead, and still.

"It's like Jean Lafitte's house, on Grande Terre," Coral shivered slightly. "Did I tell you about that? There seemed to be no one there at first—it was uncanny."

Ahead, they could just make out the rooftops of New Orleans, and they set off with new heart, now that their journey's end was in sight.

"Heaven alone knows what will become of us when we get there," said Gerard, but he did not sound particularly worried. "Well—we've got our health and strength—I'll find a job somehow, and earn a little money . . . Enough to get us back to Washington, and your uncle—"

"Perhaps we could find Mr. Lafitte again—for I'm sure he would help us—"

They broke off, listening. Somewhere on the horizon,

414

there were bells ringing in a steeple; they could hear a distant peal echoing across the river.

"Is it Sunday?" Coral asked. "I've lost all track of time . . ."

"It's not Sunday, I'm sure of that," said Gerard, and then he gave a shout of laughter. "No wonder we've seen no one abroad this morning—today's a holiday! I'd forgotten until this moment—last night was Christmas Eve!"

They heard the bells chiming, giving voice to the joyful tidings, and then Coral hugged Gerard and kissed him.

"A happy Christmas, my dear love . . ."

He kissed her in return, saying ruefully: "A happy Christmas but not a prosperous one, I fear, for I have no gift for you."

She smiled: "Oh, but you have—you've given me the best Christmas gift of all, and I have it here with me . . ." She put her hand into the bosom of her dress, and pulled out the silver chain and crucifix she always wore around her neck . . . and upon the chain was the gold wedding ring.

"I found it on the stage, where it had fallen after that performance of *Hamlet* . . . do you remember?—and I've kept it safe ever since."

It was the work of a moment to slip the ring from the chain; and then Gerard placed it gently upon her finger, saying quietly: "With this ring, I thee wed. I have no worldly goods to give you, my darling, but with my body, I thee worship."

They embraced once more; a long embrace, and the most important they had ever shared—for it marked the ending of their old lives, and the start of a new life for them both—Together.

Suddenly they heard the sound of wheels approaching, and a horse's hooves; a little gig was coming along the road, with a young negro in a wideawake hat holding the reins: the new day was stirring at last, in New Orleans.

Gerard hailed the driver, and called out: "Merry Christmas to you!—and can you direct us to the nearest parish priest?"

The negro stared, then grinned: "Sure thing . . . are you folks going to hear a Mass—for Christmas?"

"No, sir," replied Gerard. "We are going to be married," and he looked down fondly and proudly at his bride-to-be.

Coral placed both her hands in his.

"At last—" she murmured. "And forever."

And so it was.